Last Orders

"From our perspective seventy years later, we're accustomed to thinking of WWII's outcome as being inevitable. Not so, says [Harry] Turtledove. . . . Disdaining broad brush strokes, Turtledove's focus on the characters serves to fill out the big picture with patient, nitty-gritty detail. It's all quite plausible. . . . Armchair warriors will have much to ponder." —*Kirkus Reviews*

Two Fronts

"[Harry] Turtledove has another major twist in store for the readers and his alternative world." —*SF Site*

"Turtledove's new variation on the theme of WWII is departing more and more from the original, sometimes in subtle ways and sometimes in less subtle ones. . . . What's next is anybody's guess, except that it will almost certainly be more surprises." —*Booklist*

"This is what alte   Novel Society

The Big Switch

"The Hugo Award winner continues to delight in exploring the world of 'what if?'" —*Library Journal*

West and East

"There's plenty to satisfy fans of military strategy, tactics, and armaments." —*Publishers Weekly*

Hitler's War

"Turtledove is always good, but this return to World War II . . . is genuinely brilliant. . . . The characterizations in particular bring the book to extraordinary life." —*Booklist*

By Harry Turtledove

The Guns of the South

THE WORLDWAR SAGA
Worldwar: In the Balance
Worldwar: Tilting the Balance
Worldwar: Upsetting the Balance
Worldwar: Striking the Balance

Homeward Bound

THE VIDESSOS CYCLE

VOLUME ONE:
The Misplaced Legion
An Emperor for the Legion

VOLUME TWO:
The Legion of Videssos
Swords of the Legion

THE TALE OF KRISPOS
Krispos Rising
Krispos of Videssos
Krispos the Emperor

THE TIME OF TROUBLES SERIES
The Stolen Throne
Hammer and Anvil
The Thousand Cities
Videssos Besieged

A World of Difference
Departures
How Few Remain

THE GREAT WAR
The Great War: American Front
The Great War: Walk in Hell
The Great War: Breakthroughs

AMERICAN EMPIRE
American Empire: Blood and Iron
American Empire:
The Center Cannot Hold
American Empire:
The Victorious Opposition

SETTLING ACCOUNTS
Settling Accounts:
Return Engagement
Settling Accounts: Drive to the East
Settling Accounts: The Grapple
Settling Accounts: In at the Death

Every Inch a King

The Man with the Iron Heart

THE WAR THAT CAME EARLY
The War That Came Early:
Hitler's War
The War That Came Early:
West and East
The War That Came Early:
The Big Switch
The War That Came Early:
Coup d'Etat
The War That Came Early:
Two Fronts
The War That Came Early:
Last Orders

THE HOT WAR
Bombs Away

Last Orders

THE WAR THAT CAME EARLY

Last Orders

HARRY TURTLEDOVE

DEL REY | NEW YORK

2015 Del Rey Trade Paperback Edition

LIBRARY OF CONGRESS CATALOGING-IN-PUBLICATION DATA
Turtledove, Harry.
Last orders / Harry Turtledove.
pages cm—(The war that came early)
ISBN 978-0-345-52472-0—ISBN 978-0-345-52471-3 (hardcover)—
ISBN 978-0-345-52473-7 (ebook)
1. World War, 1939–1945—Fiction.   I. Title.
PS3570.U76L37 2014
813'.54—dc23   2014016645

Printed in the United States of America on acid-free paper

randomhousebooks.com

9 8 7 6 5 4 3 2 1

Last Orders

Chapter 1

A French second lieutenant wore one gold bar just above each cuff on his tunic and one gold ring on his kepi. A French full lieutenant was exalted with two gold bars above each cuff and two gold rings on his tunic. A French colonel—who reveled in five gold bars on his sleeves and five gold rings on his kepi—presented Aristide Demange with the tokens of his new rank. "Congratulations on your promotion, Lieutenant!" he said.

Demange saluted with mechanical precision. "Thank you very much, sir!" he replied woodenly, in lieu of the *Big fucking deal* that shouted inside his head. He'd been in the Army since the last war: his whole adult life. He wished like hell he were still a noncom.

You couldn't show those things, though. Oh, you could, but it wouldn't do you any good. Demange kept his ferrety face as expressionless as his voice. *Never let the bastards guess what you're thinking* made a good rule. They'd screw you if they did. They'd screw you anyhow, come to that—screwing you was their job—but they'd screw you harder if they did.

The colonel stepped forward for the ritual embrace. He brushed cheeks with Demange, first on one side, then on the other. Demange shifted his smoldering Gitane from one corner of the mouth to the other in turn, so he didn't singe his superior. He smoked whenever he wasn't sleeping or getting his ashes hauled, and he'd been known to make exceptions for the second. Hardly anybody on the front line didn't smoke. On the other hand, hardly anybody smoked like Demange.

"Well, Lieutenant, with your experience, do you feel capable of commanding a company?" the colonel asked.

"Whatever you want, sir." Demange wasn't going to volunteer. He'd been in too long for that. But he wasn't going to say no, either. With his experience, he thought he could run a brigade and do a bang-up job. He might need a captain with eyeglasses—a smart Jew, say—to give his orders the proper upper-crust tone. He sure as hell knew what needed doing, though.

"We'll give it a try, then," the colonel said, with the air of a man who thought he was doing Demange a favor. "We've had more casualties than I care for since we started pushing the *Boches* out of Belgium."

"Yes, sir," Demange said, more woodenly yet. The fighting in Belgium was just as ugly, just as brutal, and just as murderous as trench warfare in the last war had been. Both sides had tanks now. Those were supposed to smash through enemy defenses, to get the snail out of his shell so you could eat him, or at least kill him.

For a while, it had worked. At the end of 1938, German panzers smashed through the Low Countries and northeastern France, and almost—almost!—got around behind Paris. The Nazis would've won the war if they'd managed to bring that off. But they didn't . . . quite.

Over on the far side of Europe, German and Russian tanks still had plenty of room to maneuver. Demange had been over there while France and Germany were on the same side for a while. He'd never dreamt of country so vast till he saw it himself. You couldn't fortify all of it.

You could fortify damn near all of Belgium and Luxembourg, though, and Hitler's chums damn well had. New tanks—especially the German Tiger—were a lot tougher to brush aside than the old ones had been, too. You didn't, you couldn't, storm forward here. You slogged.

You especially slogged if your Army and your government still weren't a hundred percent sure they really wanted to be fighting the *Boches*. It had taken what amounted to a military coup to kick England out of the Nazis' bed. France stayed palsy-walsy with Hitler even longer. Plenty of rich people thought he made a safer bet than Stalin.

Demange hated Germans worse than Russians. If you pointed him at Russians, though, he'd kill them, too. He knew they'd do the same to him. He also hated his own superiors, and the poor *cons* those superiors' dumb orders got killed. He despised the whole human race, in fact, himself included.

While Demange brooded, the colonel, after donning a pair of bifocals, studied a map. In due course, he said, "I know of a company in front of Rance that lost its captain. What say you go there?"

"Whatever you please, sir." Demange had only a vague notion of where Rance was: a little farther north than he had been before he stopped this promotion (and that was how he thought of it—much like stopping a bullet). Wherever it was, the Germans would do their best to kill him there. Their best hadn't been good enough through half the last war and all of this one. Maybe he'd last a while longer.

"*Bon*," the colonel said. "We'll do that, then. Captain Alexandre, the officer you'll replace, was a man of uncommon quality. His father is a major general—an expert in artillery, I believe."

"I'll do my best, sir," Demange said. Of course he would—that was his best chance to stay alive. He didn't much fear death. But dying in combat commonly hurt like hell. That, he feared. He lit a fresh Gitane from the stub of the old one to keep his narrow features from showing too nasty a grin. So an aristo had been running this company, had he? Well, now they'd have to deal with a gutter rat from a long line of gutter rats. And if they didn't like it, too damn bad!

He rode toward Rance in an American truck. The beast was enormous, and tough and powerful as a tank. He thought it might even stand up to horrible, roadless Russia. French trucks went to pieces in short order when they tried to cope with Russia's ruts and rocks and bottomless bogs (to Demange's somber satisfaction, so did German machines). But this hulking beast might have what it took.

The countryside was the cratered moonscape he remembered too well from the last war. Here and there, he saw a shattered tree, one wall of a stone farmhouse, or a tank's burnt-out carcass. The air stank of smoke and shit and death.

Some of the craters scarred the road. The driver went around them when he could and across them when he had to. The truck jounced and bounced, but showed no signs of falling apart no matter how roughly it was used.

"A formidable machine," Demange said after a while.

"Sir, it sure is!" the driver agreed enthusiastically. "How come we can't make 'em like this?" Since Demange didn't know why that was so, he went back to keeping quiet.

When artillery started coming in only a few hundred meters in front of them, the driver hit the brakes. Demange hopped out of the cabin and went ahead on shank's mare. Before long, a sentry challenged him without coming up out of the foxhole where he hid from fragments.

"I'm looking for what used to be Captain Alexandre's company," Demange answered. "For their sins, I'm their new commander."

"For their sins, is it?" Now the sentry stuck up his head, like a rabbit wiggling halfway out of its burrow at a noise that surprised it. He pointed. "Take that communications trench up to the front and then bear left."

"*D'accord.*" Demange zigzagged up the communications trench. A German machine gun started hammering as he got to the forward trenches. Keeping his head down, he made his way along them till he found the outfit he was looking for. A couple of *poilus* took him to a rather prissy-looking second lieutenant who was running the company for the time being.

That worthy sent him a fishy stare. "*You're* in charge now?" he said. "Pardon me, but you don't seem much like Captain Alexandre." He crossed himself, as if the late captain were a saint.

"I'm not much like him," Demange said, nodding. "He's deader than dog shit, and I'm here to give you grief."

Now the junior officer's stare was of unabashed horror. Demange laughed and lit a fresh Gitane. He'd just made another friend.

Russian winter was colder than anything Arno Baatz had ever dreamt of when he was back in Germany. Russian summer didn't last as long, but it got hotter than the *Reich* ever did. It got muggier, too; like the men in his squad, the *Unteroffizier* always had sweat stains under the arms of his wool *Feldgrau* tunic. Being sweaty all the time made him itch.

All kinds of things in Russia could make you itch. Corporal Baatz had fleas. He had lice. Whenever his outfit got pulled out of the line, the first thing they did was go to a delousing station. That helped till their uniforms cooled off from being baked, and till the men dried off after bathing in hot, medicated water.

The *Wehrmacht* issued powders and pump sprays that were supposed to kill off pests while you were in the field. Arno Baatz was as patriotic as the next guy. Most of the time, he made a point of being more patriotic than the next guy. But even he had to admit that all the promises on the labels to the powders and sprays were a crock of *Quatsch*.

And, of course, along with the fleas and the lice came swarms of mosquitoes, plus flies ranging in size from next to invisible to just smaller than a Bf-109. When they bit you—and they would, and they did—all you could do was smear grease on it if you had any grease and try not to scratch. And pretty soon your face and your neck and your hands turned into sausage meat.

One of the senior privates in Baatz's squad dolefully surveyed himself in a polished steel shaving mirror. "Don't see much point to getting out a razor," Adam Pfaff said. "I'd cut me more than I'd cut my whiskers, all bitten up the way I am."

"You'll shave like everybody else," Baatz growled. "It's in the regulations."

"A lot of things that are in the regulations sound great in Germany, but they turn out to be really stupid here in Russia." Insubordination was Pfaff's middle name.

Baatz glared at him and ran a hand over his own bitten-up but reasonably well-shaven face. "If I can do it, you can do it. And if I've got to do it, you've fucking well got to do it, too."

He never could gauge ahead of time what would work on the *Obergefreiter*. "All right, Corporal. I guess that's fair," Pfaff said now, and started scraping away.

No sooner had he rinsed off his razor and stuck it back in his kit than the Ivans started shelling the German positions in the area. All the *Landsers* jumped for the closest foxhole, and most of them got into cover while the Russian shells were still screaming down. The ground shook from one burst after another. The Russians weren't the most efficient soldiers God ever made, but they always seemed to have artillery falling out of their assholes.

If a 105 came down right on top of you, cowering in a foxhole wouldn't do you a pfennig's worth of good. Baatz knew that all too well. If a shell came down on top of you, they'd bury you in a jam tin . . . if they could scrape enough of you from the mud to bother with a burial at all. He knew one fellow who'd taken a direct hit and vanished from the face of the earth, teeth, belt buckle, boot-sole hobnails and all. Gone. Off the map.

You tried not to think about things like that. Sometimes, though, your mind kept coming back to them, the way your tongue kept coming back to a bit of gristle stuck between two teeth. Because there were plenty of worse things than dying from a direct hit. Then, at least, you never knew what happened. Baatz had listened to men shriek for hours, sometimes for more than a day, begging their friends and even their enemies to kill them and end their agony. He'd never had to do that himself, but he knew men who had.

Anything that can happen can happen to you. One more truth that wartime brought out, and one more Baatz did his best not to remember. He already had one wound badge, and an amazing scar on his arm. He wasn't anxious for fate to do any more carving on him.

His anxiety or lack of same, of course, might have nothing to do with anything. "They're coming!" someone bawled through the roar of bursting shells.

The Ivans had come up with a hideously sneaky trick. They would stop shelling a narrow corridor—sometimes only fifty meters across—and send in their infantry there while they kept plastering the rest of the front. Any defender who wasn't in the corridor and stuck up his head to shoot at the advancing Reds was asking for a fragment to blow it off.

If you didn't stick up your head and shoot, the Russians would get in behind you. They were like rats—they squeezed through any little hole. Then you could kiss your sorry ass good-bye. They'd shoot you or bayonet you or smash in your skull with an entrenching tool. Or they'd take you alive and see what kind of fun they could have with you. The USSR never signed the Geneva Convention. Neither side in the East played by any rules this side of the jungle's.

Swearing and praying at the same time, Baatz popped halfway out of his hole and started shooting. The Mauser slammed against his shoulder again and again: a good, familiar ache. An Ivan in a dun-colored uniform tumbled and fell. Baatz wasn't sure his bullet got the bastard, but he'd been firing in that direction. He'd take credit for the kill in his own mind.

A couple of foxholes farther south, Adam Pfaff was also banging away at the Russians. He'd painted his rifle's woodwork a gray not far from *Feldgrau*. He claimed it improved the camouflage. Baatz thought that was a bunch of crap, but the company CO let Pfaff get by with it. What could you do?

Right this minute, trying to stay alive mattered more than the weird paint job on an *Obergefreiter*'s rifle. Baatz slapped a fresh five-round clip into the magazine of his own Mauser and went on firing. A tiny, half-spent shell fragment clanged off his helmet. It didn't get through. When the last war started, they'd gone into battle with head-gear made of felt or leather. Baatz remembered his old man talking about it, and about how in the days before the *Stahlhelm* any little head wound was likely to kill you. You couldn't make a helmet strong enough to keep out a rifle bullet but light enough to wear. Just block-ing fragments, though, saved a hell of a lot of casualties. Baatz knew that, without his helmet, he'd be lying dead now, with no more than a trickle of blood in his hair—maybe not even that.

No matter how sneaky the Russians were, they weren't going to

ram through the German lines this time. Along with the stubborn riflemen, an MG-34 and one of the new, quick-firing MG-42s hosed the
Ivans' corridor down with bullets. Russians could be recklessly, even
maniacally, bold. Or they could skedaddle like so many savages. This
time, they skedaddled, dragging their wounded behind them as they
pulled back.

Some of their wounded: a soldier in a khaki greatcoat thrashed and
screamed just a couple of hundred meters in front of Baatz's foxhole.
He took aim to finish off the sorry son of a bitch—and to shut him up.
But then another Russian ran back, waving his arms to show he wasn't
carrying any weapons.

Baatz was about to pot him anyhow. Yes, he was a brave man. To
Baatz, that meant he needed killing all the more. One of these days,
he'd show up again, this time toting a machine pistol. But a couple of
Germans yelled, "Let him live!" Reluctantly, Baatz didn't pull the trigger.

The Russian waved toward the German foxholes—he knew he
could have got his ticket punched right there. He hauled his countryman onto his back and, bent almost double, lumbered away toward
the east.

Squeezing liver paste from a tinfoil tube onto a zwieback cracker
later that day, Baatz was still discontented. "I should have nailed that
turd," he grumbled, and stuffed the food into his face.

"World won't end," Adam Pfaff said as he lit a cigarette. "Sometimes they let us pick up our guys, too. The war's hard enough the way
it is. We don't need to make it even worse."

"They're Russians. Do 'em a favor and all you get for it is a kick in
the balls," Baatz said. Since he outranked Pfaff, he got the last word. He
wished like hell he'd got that Ivan, too.

Vaclav Jezek hadn't known what summer heat was like till he came to
Spain. The Czech had thought he did, but now he owned he'd been just
a beginner. The sun northwest of Madrid beat down on his head as if
out of a blue enamel bowl that focused all its heat right there.

He lay in a shell hole in the no-man's-land between the Republicans' barbed wire and the stuff the Fascists strung. He had branches and bits of greenery on his helmet and here and there on his uniform. They didn't block the heat. They weren't supposed to. They did help break up his outline, to make it harder for Marshal Sanjurjo's men to spot him out here.

His antitank rifle also had its long, straight barrel bedecked with leaves and twigs. The damn thing wasn't much shorter than he was. It weighed a tonne. The French had made it to fire a slug as wide as a man's thumb through a tank's armor. It could do that . . . to any tank made in the 1930s. It was as powerful a rifle as one man could carry and fire. Even with a muzzle brake and a padded stock, it kicked harder than any mule ever born.

No matter how powerful it was, it couldn't kill the bigger, heavier modern tanks the war had spawned. To the logical French, if it couldn't do the job for which it was made, it was useless.

French logic, though, reached only so far. The antitank rifle fired a very heavy bullet with a very high muzzle velocity. The round flew fast and far and flat. It might not be able to cope with a Panzer IV, but it could knock over a man at a couple of kilometers. It was, in other words, a perfect sniper's rifle.

In France, Vaclav had killed German officers who made the fatal mistake of thinking they were too far behind the line to worry about keeping their heads down. When France hopped into Hitler's arms for a while, she generously allowed the Czechs who fought for their government-in-exile to cross the border into Spain and take service with the Republic. Vaclav brought the antitank rifle with him. By then, he would have killed anybody who tried to take it away from him.

After a couple of years here, he knew enough Spanish to get fed. He knew enough to get drunk. He knew enough to get laid. He could cuss some, too. He had the essentials, in other words. Anything past the essentials, no. He spoke pretty good German—a lot of Czechs did— which helped him with the men of the International Brigades but not with the Republicans. Most of the Spaniards who could *Deutsch spre-chen* fought on Sanjurjo's side.

Like the rest of the Czechs, he'd made himself useful here. He'd actually used the rifle on enemy tanks. Sanjurjo's men tried sending some old Italian tankettes against the Internationals. They had enough armor to laugh at ordinary small-arms fire. Not at what his overmuscled elephant gun could do, though.

And he'd killed General Franco with the antitank rifle. Not as good as blowing off Sanjurjo's jowly head, but the next best thing. He'd got a medal for that, and a wad of pesetas to go with it that gave him one hell of a spree in Madrid.

Marshal Sanjurjo had an even bigger price on his head than his late general had. If the marshal ever decided to inspect these lines and came within 2,000 meters of wherever the Czech happened to be hiding, Vaclav vowed that he was one dead bigwig.

Meanwhile . . . Meanwhile, he waited. He spied on the Nationalists' lines with a pair of binoculars wrapped in burlap. He'd stuck cardboard above their objective lenses so no untimely reflections would give him away. And he'd taken the same precaution with the objective on the rifle's telescopic sight.

Careless snipers had short careers. He wanted to go back to Czechoslovakia after the war ended . . . if the war ever ended, and if there was any Czechoslovakia to go back to once it did. Dying in France fighting against the Nazis, he would at least have been playing against the first team. Making a mistake that let some Spaniard in a diarrhea-yellow uniform plug him would just be embarrassing.

No, not just embarrassing. Painful, too.

Not much was going on now on either side of the line. Here and there, a rifleman would take a shot at somebody in the wrong uniform who was rash enough to put himself on display. Most of the time, the would-be assassin was a crappy shot and missed. His attempted victim would dive for cover.

Vaclav was anything but a crappy shot. He'd been good when the Czechoslovakian Army drafted him. Plenty of practice in the years since left him a hell of a lot better than good. He could have killed plenty of careless Nationalists at the front line.

But that would have been like spending a hundred English pounds for a glass of beer. Ordinary privates and noncoms weren't worth killing with an antitank rifle. If he yielded to temptation and let the air out of one of those bastards, he'd have to find a new hiding place. Shooting twice in a row from the same spot was more dangerous than lighting three on a match. You were telling the enemy right where you were. You were telling him you were stupid enough to stay there, too.

So he ignored the jerks who stuck their brainless heads up over the parapet for a look around. He scanned farther back, to the places where most of the time you wouldn't need to worry about getting shot. Nationalist officers wore much fancier uniforms and headgear than the men they led. Killing a colonel might do more for the Republican cause than exterminating a company's worth of ordinary soldiers.

For the moment, though, nobody worth shooting was showing himself. So Vaclav brought down the glasses and surveyed the shattered ground ahead of where he lay. Every once in a while, Sanjurjo's men sneaked out to hunt snipers. He'd blown big holes in a couple of those guys. He was ruthless about keeping himself in one piece.

And the Spanish Fascists sent snipers of their own out into no-man's-land. They didn't have anybody with a monster gun like his. But a good shot with a good rifle could kill a man a kilometer away—not every time, maybe, but often enough to be dangerous. Vaclav knew what the ground was supposed to look like from here. He knew what it was supposed to look like from almost every centimeter in front of the stretch of trench the Czechs held. Knowing such things was like a life-insurance policy. Any little change might—probably would—mark trouble.

He didn't see any little changes, though. The heat made everybody move at half speed. Let the sun kill the bastards on the other side, the thought seemed to be. Shooting them was too much trouble for soldiers.

After a while, it got to be too much trouble for Jezek. He ate brown bread and crumbly Spanish sausage full of fennel. It could give you the runs, but it tasted good. To kill some germs, he washed it down with sharp white wine from the canteen on his belt. He would rather have drunk beer—he was a Czech, all right. But most Spanish beer tasted like piss, and smelled like it, too. Wine was also easier to come by here.

He wanted a cigarette. He didn't light one. Smoke could give you away. He wouldn't get too jittery before he went back inside the barbed wire among his friends and countrymen. He'd puff away once he did.

Some days went by without his firing a shot. If he didn't see any-thing worth firing at, he just stayed where he was till it got dark. Let the Nationalists think they'd finally killed him while they were shell-ing no-man's-land. It might make them careless. Then they'd give him better targets.

What was this? A truck coming up toward the Fascists' lines. Can-vas tied down over hoops covered the rear compartment. When the truck stopped, soldiers got out. A man hopped down from the pas-senger side of the front seat, too. That and his uniform told Jezek he was an officer.

Nothing much had happened yet today. So . . . why not? The officer gestured, getting his men ready to do whatever they were going to do. Vaclav took careful aim. Not much wind. Range about 1,100 meters. You might even do this with a Mauser, though you'd need a little luck as well as skill. Luck never hurt, of course. But with this much gun, skill alone could turn the trick.

Breathe. Let it out. Bring back the trigger, gently, gently . . . The antitank rifle thundered. It kicked, not even a little bit gently. The Na-tionalist officer grabbed his midriff and fell over.

"Earned my pay today," Vaclav said. He took out a cigarette to cel-ebrate. He could smoke it now. He wouldn't be staying here more than another few minutes anyhow.

To say Lieutenant Commander Julius Lemp didn't enjoy summer pa-trol in the North Sea was to beggar the power of language. He wasn't quite up at the latitudes where the sun never set, but he was plenty far north to keep it in the sky through most of the hours.

He and several ratings stayed up on the conning tower, scanning sky and horizon for enemy ships and airplanes. You had to do it all the time. The Royal Navy was looking for the U-30, too, and for all the other boats the *Kriegsmarine* sent to sea.

The Royal Navy was looking hard. It had ways to look no one had dreamt of when the war broke out, almost five years ago now. Radar could spot a surfaced U-boat no matter how cunningly its paint job mimicked sea and sky. And, when it dove, English warships hounded it with their pinging hydrophones. Unlike the ones both sides had used in the last war, these really could help a surface ship track—and sink—a submarine.

Gerhart Beilharz popped out of the hatch like an elongated jack-in-the-box. The engineering officer grinned like a jack-in-the-box, too. He was two meters tall: not the ideal size for a man in a U-boat's crew. This was the only place on the boat where he didn't have to worry about gashing his scalp or knocking himself cold if he forgot to duck.

"You've done your two hours, skipper," he said. "I relieve you."

Lemp lowered his Zeiss field glasses and rubbed his eyes. They felt sandy under his knuckles. "I feel like a bug on a plate," he said. "A black bug on a white plate."

Beilharz pointed back to the *Schnorkel*. The breathing tube—for the diesels, not the men who served them—stuck up like an enormous stovepipe. "Don't worry about it," he said. "As long as we've got that baby, we can slip under the glazing."

He could say *Don't worry about it*. The U-boat's survival wasn't his responsibility. Lemp had to worry about everything; that was what command entailed. And worry he did: "They can see us under the glazing, too, dammit, or rather hear us with those stinking hydro-phones."

"We've slithered away before," the tall man said. "We can do it again."

"I hope so." Sighing, Lemp went below—out of the sunshine, out of the fresh air, into a steel cigar dimly lit with orange bulbs and stinking of everything from shit and puke and piss to diesel oil to the reeks of rotting food and dirty socks. However nasty, the odor was also infi-nitely familiar to him. And well it might have been, since his own fug made up a part of it.

Only a green curtain shielded his tiny cabin—cot, desk, chair, safe—from the corridor. Still, command's privilege gave him more pri-vacy and space than anyone else on the boat enjoyed. He logged the events on his latest watch: course, position, observations (none sig-nificant), the fact that a radio tube had burnt out and been replaced. His handwriting was tiny and as precise as if an automaton had pro-duced it.

But as he wrote, he was conscious of all the things he wasn't saying, all the things he couldn't say—not unless he wanted some serious attention from the *Gestapo* and the *Sicherheitsdienst* and the *Abwehr* and, no doubt, other organizations of State and Party about which he knew nothing . . . yet.

He couldn't write, for instance, that the U-30 wasn't such a happy boat as it had been. He didn't like the way the sailors eyed one another. He didn't like the way they didn't come out with what was on their minds. The U-boat service tossed surface-Navy formality over the side. Living in one another's pockets, the men had no time to waste on such foolishness. They were brothers, brothers in arms.

Or they should have been. But there was at least one informer on board. And Lemp didn't know who the polecat was. That worried him worse than anything. Anything this side of the Royal Navy, anyhow.

The thought had hardly crossed his mind before a rating spoke from the other side of the curtain: "Skipper, they've spotted smoke up on the conning tower."

"Oh, they have, have they?" Lemp said. "All right. I'll come." He stuck his cap back on his head. Like every other U-boat officer in the *Kriegsmarine,* he'd taken out the stiffening wire so the crown didn't stick up above his head but flopped onto the patent-leather bill. That crown was white, not navy blue: the sole mark of command he wore.

His shoes clanked dully on the patterned steel of the ladder rungs leading up out of the submarine. The first whiff of fresh air made him involuntarily breathe deeper. You forgot how foul the inside of a U-boat really was till you escaped the steel tube.

As he emerged, Gerhart Beilharz pointed north. "Over there, skipper," he said. "Not a lot of smoke, but some." He offered his binoculars.

Lemp scanned with them. "You're right," he said as he gave them back. He called down the hatch to the helmsman, who stood near the bottom of the ladder. "Change course to 020. All ahead full."

"Course 020. All ahead full. Aye, aye."

They swung toward the smudge of smoke in the northern sky. Lemp wanted to get the U-boat out ahead of it if he could. That would let him submerge and give it a closer inspection through the periscope without the other ship's being likely to spot them in return.

Meanwhile, he kept his eye on the smudge. Things often happened slowly on the ocean. Ships weren't airplanes. They needed time to cross the kilometers that separated one from another.

Actually, he hoped he would spy the unknown ship before he had to submerge. It put out a lot more smoke than the U-30's diesels did. It rode higher in the water than the U-boat did, too. And he got what he hoped for. Through the powerful, column-mounted binoculars on the conning tower, he got a glimpse of a small, chunky steamboat—not a warship at all.

Not an obvious warship, anyhow. In the last war, English Q-ships—freighters with hidden heavy guns and gun crews—had surprised and sunk a couple of the Kaiser's submarines. Their captains made the fatal mistake of thinking anything that looked harmless was bound to be harmless. They'd come close to use a deck gun instead of launching an eel from a distance—and they'd paid for their folly.

Lemp took no such chances. Maybe the steamer was as harmless as it looked. But if it was, what was it doing out here in the middle of the North Sea? Its course would take it from Scotland to Norway. It might be bringing help for the Norwegian bandits who still did their best to make trouble for the German forces occupying the country.

He ordered the boat down to *Schnorkel* depth. It was faster underwater on diesels than with battery power. As the unknown ship approached, he had plenty of time to work up a firing solution. He launched two torpedoes from less than a kilometer away.

The explosive in one of the eels would have been plenty to blow up the steamer. But the blast that followed a midships hit from one of the eels was far bigger than a torpedo warhead alone could have caused. The U-30 staggered in the water; it felt and sounded as if someone were pounding on the boat with iron rods the size of telegraph poles.

"Der Herr Gott im Himmel!" Lieutenant Beilharz exclaimed. "What the devil was that?"

"I don't exactly know," Lemp answered. "No, not exactly. But whatever it was, I think the *Reich* is lucky it never got to Norway." He peered through the periscope. Nothing was left of the steamship but small bits of flotsam and a hell of a lot of smoke. Somebody in England and Norway would be disappointed, but he wasn't.

Chapter 2

Shibe Park was a pretty good place to see a ballgame no matter where you sat. With the Philadelphia A's duking it out with the St. Louis Browns to see who'd have bragging rights to seventh place and who'd mope in the basement, Peggy Druce felt as if she had the grandstand to herself.

She didn't quite. A couple of thousand other optimists raised a cheer for Connie Mack's men. But, though she'd bought a ticket well back in the lower deck, the ushers didn't fuss when she moved down closer to the action. When you had a small crowd in a big ballpark, nobody worried about such details.

From right behind the third-base dugout, she could hear the players chattering among themselves. They cheerfully swore at one another and at the umpires. As far as they were concerned, they were by themselves out there. A delicately raised woman might have been shocked—they talked as foully as soldiers. Peggy found herself more amused than anything else. The filthy language held no malice she could find.

"Hot dogs! Get your hot dogs!" a vendor shouted. Peggy got herself two. At her request, the man slathered them with mustard and onions. She liked onions. And she was here by herself. If her breath smelled strong, she wouldn't offend anyone she cared about.

She got herself a couple of sacks of roasted peanuts, too, and a bottle of beer, and then another bottle of beer. She was good for the long haul, in other words. The game would have been more fun with Herb sitting next to her and complaining about how lousy the Athletics were.

But Herb wasn't there. Herb wouldn't be there. She glanced down at her left hand. Yes, she could still see the pale line on her fourth finger, the line where her wedding ring had shielded the skin from the sun for so long. She didn't wear a ring on that finger any more, though. Why should she, when she wasn't married any more? Herb had gone on a trip to Nevada for the government, and he'd Reno-vated her while he was there.

Now that he was back in Philadelphia, they were both doing their best to be civilized about it. He'd been more than generous in the settlement. She had the house and the Packard. He was living in a flat near his law office and driving a ratty old Hupmobile.

The war and the long separation it forced on them had killed their marriage as surely as a U-boat's torpedo killed the luckless sailors aboard a destroyer. Peggy didn't want to be divorced. But being married hadn't been a whole lot of fun lately, either.

The A's went ahead, 3–2, in the bottom of the fourth. There were a lot of short fly balls. The horsehide didn't go *smack!* off the bat, the way Peggy was used to. It made kind of a dull thud instead. The cork that livened up the center of the ball was a strategic national resource these days. She didn't know what they were using instead. By the way the ball didn't move, she suspected it was a cheap grade of cement.

But the Philadelphia cleanup hitter somehow caught one square. He put it over the head of the Brownies' center fielder. It rolled all the way to the base of the center-field fence. In Shibe Park, that was 468 feet from the plate. The batter wasn't a gazelle on the bases, but he didn't need to be. He didn't even have to slide to score on his inside-the-park homer.

She whooped and hollered and raised a beer bottle high in salute.

A gray-haired man sitting a few seats down from her was cheering, too. They grinned at each other, the way people will when they're both rooting for the same team. Then he said, "Now let's see if we can hold on to it."

"It's only the Browns," Peggy answered. "They're as rotten as we are, or just about. Half their guys are in the Army." Half the Athletics were, too, but she didn't dwell on that. She was a fan, not a sportswriter.

In the top of the fifth, the first St. Louis batter took four in a row high and wide and trotted down to first base. The second Brownie up swung at the first pitch and missed. Over in the St. Louis dugout on the first-base side, the manager screamed "Shit!" at the top of his lungs. Everybody in the park must have heard him. In his shoes, Peggy would have said the same thing. If the pitcher was wild, you wanted to make him throw a strike before you started flailing away.

He eyed the runner, went into his stretch, and delivered again. And the Brownie batter swung again. This time, he lofted a lazy pop foul. The third baseman ran toward the stands to see if he could get it. But he ran out of room—it came down in the seats.

It came down, in fact, in the hands of the guy sitting a few seats away from Peggy. He made a smooth two-handed catch, a catch that said he'd played the game a time or three.

"Sign him up!" yelled a leather-lunged fan a bit farther back. Any nice catch in the stands meant you'd hear that. With the goons the A's had in the outfield, it might not even have been a terrible idea.

The gray-haired man looked as pleased with himself as if he were seven years old. Peggy didn't blame him. "I'm so jealous," she said. "I've been coming to games since before the turn of the century, and I never once got a foul ball even before they started letting you keep them. This is about as close as I ever came, as a matter of fact."

He tossed the baseball up and down a couple of times. Then, to her amazement, he tossed it to her. She managed to catch it—not so neatly as he had, but at least it didn't land on the concrete and roll away. "Enjoy it," he said. "Give it to your son so he can play with it."

He could have said *grandson;* she'd admitted she was no spring chicken. But he was too nice. "I don't have kids," she said. She'd miscarried with Herb till her doctor told her she'd be putting herself in danger by trying again. After that, it was French letters and perversions. She wondered what kind of mother she would have made. She'd never get the chance to find out now.

"No?" He raised a busy eyebrow. "Too bad." He touched the brim of his fedora. "I'm Dave—Dave Hartman."

Peggy gave her own name. Meanwhile, the Browns' batter struck out. Their manager gave him more hell when he glumly slammed his bat into the rack in the dugout.

She and Dave kept talking while the game moved forward. She found out he was a master machinist currently between jobs because he had a bad back and the shop he'd been working for didn't want to give him a chair while everybody else had to stand in front of a lathe.

"Well, to heck with 'em, then," Peggy said, full of irate sympathy.

"That's what I told 'em," he answered. "'Course, I might've put it a little stronger—yeah, just a little."

"I sure hope you did." Peggy nodded emphatically.

By then, he'd slid over till he was only a couple of seats from her so they could talk more readily. When the fellow with the tray of beer bottles came by, Dave held up his hand with two fingers raised. He handed Peggy one of the bottles. "Well, thank you," she said, and reached over with it. They clinked. They drank. They smiled.

They talked through the rest of the game. She found out he was a widower with two grown sons and a granddaughter. She told him of her own status. He thoughtfully scratched his chin. "A guy who'd toss out a gal like you, he's gotta be kind of a jerk, you want to know what I think," he said at last.

Peggy wasn't used to thinking of Herb as a jerk. He'd always struck her as plenty smart. "I don't know," she answered after some thought of her own. "We weren't in love any more—heaven knows that's true. We still liked each other okay, but we were just going through the motions."

"That's a darn shame," Dave said.

The A's won the game, 5–3. When they walked out of the park together, Peggy found herself giving him her phone number. He touched the brim of his hat again and walked toward a bus.

As she walked toward the trolley that would take her home, Peggy was surprised at herself. No, she was astonished at herself. She'd met somebody. She didn't know what would come of it. She didn't know if anything would. She didn't much care, either. The thing was done. She hadn't even imagined that much. Why should she have? She hadn't needed to worry about it for more than thirty years. But it could. That was pretty astonishing all by itself.

An air-raid siren howled in the middle of the night. Hans-Ulrich Rudel leaped from his cot, threw on a helmet—he'd been sleeping in his *Luftwaffe* tunic and trousers—grabbed his boots, and ran for the nearest slit trench in his stocking feet.

He jumped down into the trench a few seconds before bombs started falling on this stretch of western Belgium. While the ground shuddered under him, he pulled on first one boot and then the other.

Nights were short at this season of the year. But this airstrip wasn't far from the front. French bombers could easily come here under cover of darkness. So could the RAF, whether taking off from bases inside France or from across the Channel. He didn't know whether the enemy flyers were specifically after this Stuka squadron or whether they were doling out presents all over German-occupied territory.

He also didn't know whether that mattered. Night bombing was the next thing to dropping blind. Sometimes it wasn't the next thing, but rather the same thing. You flew by dead reckoning, maybe by your navigator's star sights that might or might not be worth anything. You looked down through the bombsight, and you probably couldn't see much of anything. You dropped anyhow, hoping for the best, and you got the devil out of there.

One bomb burst was followed a split second later by a much bigger explosion. Cowering in the trench a few meters away from Hans-Ulrich, Sergeant Albert Dieselhorst said, "Somebody got lucky there."

"If that's how you want to put it," Rudel replied.

His radioman and rear gunner chuckled, then abruptly cut it off. "I don't much care about the bombs or shells or whatever the hell that was. But I'm afraid some good guys got blown to the devil along with them."

"I'm afraid of the same thing," Hans-Ulrich said. "I'm worried about the munitions, too, though. The enemy throws them at us as though he hasn't got a care in the world. We need to be careful with what we use."

"That's—" A far closer bomb interrupted Dieselhorst. For a split second, Rudel feared it would collapse the trench wall on them, even though boards and sticks shored up the dirt. When it became clear that wouldn't happen, Dieselhorst laughed shakily. "Where was I before I pissed myself?"

He might have been joking. Or he might not. Hans-Ulrich never had fouled his drawers, but he'd come close several times. When you thought you were going to die in the next few seconds, the animal in you could take over. People who'd been through the mill laughed at such things because they knew it could happen to them, too.

As for the other part of the question . . . "I don't know where you were going with that. You'd just started whatever it was."

"*Ach, ja.*" Dieselhorst paused for a moment, perhaps to nod. Then the older man went on, "Now I remember. I was starting to say that I'd noticed we needed to watch what we threw at the other side, but I didn't know you had, too."

"Well, I have," Hans-Ulrich replied with a touch of pique. He knew the sergeant thought he was painfully naive. "No matter how it looks to you, I'm not a hundred percent blind."

"Whatever you say, sir," Dieselhorst said: agreement that felt like anything but.

The bombers rumbled on to the east. Hans-Ulrich and the other *Luftwaffe* men booted out of sleep tracked them by their engines' drone, by the thumps from the bombs they kept dropping, and by the Germans' searchlights and flak barrages. One burning bomber fell out of the sky and split the night with a thunderous blast when it hit the ground.

Twenty minutes later, the enemy bombers came back overhead, now homeward bound. "I hope you all crash when you land, you bastards," Dieselhorst said. "That's what you deserve for waking me up in the middle of the night."

Hans-Ulrich stared in surprise toward the spot in the dark his voice was coming from. He'd felt that way about the Russians—he didn't know any German who didn't. But the English or French flyers were just doing their jobs, the same as he was. In war, your job involved hurting the people on the other side. Hans-Ulrich felt no personal malice when he flew here. He rather hoped the enemy planes would get back safe. He just wanted the bombs they dropped to miss.

Most of them would. In night bombing, you had to lay down a carpet of explosives to do any good at all. Flying the Stuka was a very different business. The dive-bomber was like an artillery piece with wings. He could put a 500-kilo bomb on top of a fifty-pfennig piece—or within a few meters of one, anyhow, which was commonly better than good enough.

He could if enemy fighters didn't give him grief, anyhow. Even the biplane fighters of the newly hatched war outclassed the Ju-87 in air-to-air combat. Today's English, French, and Russian machines treated them as snacks—there was no other word for it. If Bf-109s and FW-190s couldn't protect Stukas from enemy planes, the dive-bombers were doomed.

Logically, that meant scrapping the Stuka and replacing it with something that had a better chance of surviving. Indeed, some FW-190s carried bomb racks these days, so they could do some of the same job as the Ju-87. But the ugly old dive-bombers with the inverted gull wings soldiered on. With the *Reich* under pressure from both east and west, *Reichsmarschall* Göring didn't want to lay aside any weapon that could hurt the foe.

After a few hours of fitful sleep, Hans-Ulrich gulped ersatz coffee and oatmeal enlivened with bits of ham in the squadron's field kitchen. A gourmet forced to down such fare would have slit his wrists. Rudel wasn't so fussy. As long as they fed him enough to fill his belly, he wouldn't complain.

He also didn't complain to discover that the bomb which had almost buried him hadn't cratered any of the airstrip's runways or planes. It came down near the joining of the north-south and east-west runways. It made an enormous hole in the ground there, but a work crew with snow shovels cleared the dirt it threw on the runways in an hour or so.

While the *Luftwaffe* troops in undyed cotton drill worksuits got the airstrip ready to operate, groundcrew men hauled the Stukas out of their revetments, fueled them, and bombed them up. Colonel Steinbrenner, the squadron commander, briefed his flyers: "We're going after two railroad bridges just inside French territory." He whacked a map with a pointer to show where the bridges were. "Taking them out will help keep the froggies from moving men and matériel into Belgium."

He didn't say it would stop the French from doing that. Even Hans-Ulrich, who worked hard not to think about politics, noticed as much. The war wasn't going the way Germany'd wished it would when it started. She kept on all the same. What else could she do? Admitting defeat was worse. The *Volk* had seen that after the last fight.

Up in the sky, sucking in rubber-tasting oxygenated air, Rudel didn't have to worry about any of that. He followed the Stukas ahead of him; more followed his plane. As Steinbrenner had promised, Messerschmitts escorted the Ju-87s toward the railway bridges.

French fighters jumped the German planes before they reached their targets. The French aircraft industry started behind the *Reich*'s. After so much war, though, it had almost caught up. As the two sides' fighters spun through the air in wild fury, the Stukas dove toward the deck and sneaked southwest, in the direction of the bridges.

Hans-Ulrich dropped his bombs from not far above treetop height. As he hauled his pig of a plane around, Sergeant Dieselhorst whooped in the rear-facing back seat: "Frenchies won't be using that bridge for a while!"

"Good," Rudel said. An antiaircraft shell burst behind the Stuka. It bucked in the air, but didn't seem hurt. He gunned it back to Belgium and what should be safety as fast as it would go.

Ivan Kuchkov wasn't in a penal battalion. The Russian sergeant didn't care about anything else. The Germans could still kill him, of course.

They'd come too close too many times. The Ukrainian bandits who called themselves nationalists could still do him in, too. Those were the chances you took when you served the Soviet Union.

But his own side wouldn't just throw him away like a shitty asswipe. Penal battalions got officers and men who'd screwed up badly enough to piss off the guys set over them in a big way. Stavka shuffled them around the long front and threw them in where things were hottest. Clearing a path for the troops behind them was what they were for.

Minefield in front of an entrenched Nazi position? No problem, Comrade Colonel! The boys in the penal battalion will find those mines! They'll find them with their feet while the German machine gunners shoot down the ones who don't blow up. Then you won't waste so many soldiers who might actually be good for something.

German tanks in the neighborhood? No Red Army tanks to drive them off? Don't worry, Comrade Major General! We'll hand the lads in the penal battalion magnetic limpet mines. They can run forward and stick them on the Fascists' side armor! The tanks will be firing at them while they run? So will German foot soldiers? That's hard luck, all right. But the dumb cunts should have known better than to wind up in a penal battalion to begin with.

If you lived through whatever suicidal mission they sent you on, they gave you back your old rank and put you in an ordinary unit again. You'd wiped away your sin, the way you could in an Orthodox monastery by penance. They did if they felt like it, anyhow. Otherwise, they stuck you in another penal battalion and gave you a new chance to expend yourself. That was how they talked, as if you were a shell casing or a worn-out boot.

One of the sentries in Ivan's section had shot—had not just shot but killed—the regimental political officer when the stupid *politruk* wouldn't give him the password. The company CO didn't dare cover it up, any more than Ivan had when he found out about it. Somebody would blab, and then all their dicks would go on the chopping block.

So the NKVD came down on poor Vitya Ryakhovsky, and on Ivan, and on Lieutenant Obolensky, too. And in the end, the *Chekists* decided sending them to a battalion like that would be more trouble than it was worth—too fucking many forms to fill out if they did.

Ivan neither read nor wrote. If scribbling stuff on a bunch of papers was that big a pain in the ass, he was goddamn glad to be illiterate. (He'd also heard that the Nazis shot Russians they captured who could read and write. He didn't know for sure that that was true, but it sounded like something the Hitlerites would do. It was one of the few things having to do with Germans that he didn't need to worry about.)

So here he was, still down in the Ukraine with his old unit. So was Lieutenant Obolensky. So was poor Vitya. Ivan didn't make the mistake of thinking all was forgiven or forgotten. He knew better. They were watching. They were waiting. As soon as they saw the chance, they'd give him one in the nuts if the Germans hadn't taken care of the job for them by then.

Maybe, just maybe, the Germans wouldn't be able to do it. He'd developed a healthy respect for Hitler's pricks. He'd been fighting them since the war broke out. He'd been a Red Air Force bombardier then. After he bailed out of his burning SB-2, he'd kept fighting on the ground. Nobody could ever say that the Fritzes didn't know what they were doing. Nobody could ever say the bastards weren't brave, either. They wouldn't have been anywhere near so much trouble if they weren't brave.

But they were stretched too thin these days, when they had to fight the Red Army here in the East and the English and French on the other side of their country. Like a hungry peasant padding out wheat flour with ground peas, the Nazis here in the Ukraine padded their lines with Romanians and Hungarians.

Both sets of Fascist jackals wore khaki darker than the Red Army's. Figuring out which was which could be confusing. The Hungarians used German-style helmets. The Romanians had a different model, domed on top but long fore and aft.

The other interesting thing was that Hitler's little chums couldn't stand each other. The Nazis didn't dare stick a Romanian unit next to one full of Magyars. They had to keep Germans between their allies. Otherwise, the Hungarians and Romanians would go at each other and forget all about the Russians they were supposed to be fighting.

More and more Red Army soldiers and tanks and planes swarmed into the Ukraine. The Germans kept hitting back as hard as they could.

The Hungarians and especially the Romanians began to realize they weren't bound for glory. They threw down their rifles and threw up their hands whenever they saw the chance. They figured their odds were better in the gulag than in fighting it out. Ivan thought that showed they were morons, but it wasn't his worry.

Stavka understood the enemy's woes. The big pushes went against soldiers in khaki, not against the pricks who wore *Feldgrau*. When the Hungarians and Romanians didn't give up, they fell back. That meant the Germans on their flanks had to fall back, too, or else risk getting cut off.

Most of the time, that was what it meant, anyhow. Ivan had just finished robbing a Romanian who was sobbingly glad not to get killed out of hand. The swarthy jerk in the brownish uniform had hardly anything worth taking. But he did carry a folding German entrenching tool. Ivan had wanted one for a while. It took up less room than the ordinary Soviet short-handled spade. And you could use it as a pick if you locked the blade at right angles to the handle. It was a nifty piece of work.

He'd just stuck it on his own belt when German 105s to the south opened up on the fields through which the Red Army was advancing. A moment later, German shells started screaming down from the north, too. If that didn't mean a counterattack to slice off the head of the oncoming Russian column, Ivan was even dumber than he gave himself credit for.

He forgot about the Romanians. The enemy's good players were coming. "Hit the dirt, fuckers!" he yelled to his own men.

The Red Army men did, all except for a couple of raw replacements who stood around twiddling their foreskins because they'd never been shelled before. The Romanian who'd been about to shuffle back into captivity flattened out among the growing stalks of wheat, too. Marshal Antonescu's boys might not be the fiercest soldiers ever hatched, but they weren't virgins at this business, either.

Ivan used his new toy to dig himself a little scrape in the rich, bread-smelling black earth. Even a shallow hole with the dirt thrown up to either side might keep you from getting gutted like a barnyard goose at a wedding feast. You could also fight with an entrenching tool if you had to.

When Ivan heard a Soviet tank's cannon fire, he knew for sure the Germans were coming. When he heard the tank's machine guns go off, he knew they were just about here. He carried a PPD submachine gun: an ugly little piece of stamped steel that could slaughter anything out to a couple of hundred meters.

A Russian T-34 blew up. The Red Army had more tanks, many more, but the Germans had just about caught up in quality. When there were Tigers in the neighborhood, they'd gone ahead. Ivan didn't see any of the slab-sided monsters, which made him feel a little better, anyhow.

He did see the wheat stalks rippling as Fritzes crawled through them. He hosed down the area in front of him with the machine pistol. Shrieks and thrashing among the battered crops said he'd done somebody a bad turn.

But the Germans didn't want to be driven away here. When mortar bombs started whispering down, Ivan decided he'd had enough. "Back!" he shouted. "Come on, you bitches! Back! We'll get the cock-suckers the next time."

He wanted to make sure there'd be a next time. If they hung around here much longer, there was liable not to be. And so he retreated. If his superiors didn't like it . . . they'd stick around and get killed.

A new Panzer IV. Theo Hossbach almost smiled as he eyed the factory-fresh machine. Inside the fighting compartment, it smelled of leather and paint. They hadn't swabbed it down with gasoline. That was what they used to mask the odor of rotting flesh, the stench that said the last crew hadn't made it even if they'd salvaged the panzer.

With Theo's crew, it was just the opposite. They'd bailed out after a hit from a T-34 knocked a track off their last Panzer IV. As far as the radioman and bow gunner knew, that panzer was a write-off. But none of the five men in black coveralls got so much as a scratch. For a crew that had to abandon ship, so to speak, that was amazing luck.

Theo opened and closed his left hand. One finger there was only a stub: a souvenir of the last time he'd fled a crippled panzer, back in France. He'd got out of the Panzer II all right. Trouble was, they didn't stop shooting at you after you made your escape. He'd been hit running for cover. It hardly seemed fair.

Adalbert Stoss, the driver, smacked his new mount's armored flank with rough affection. "Another horse to put through the paces," he said.

"I thought you'd talk about scoring goals in it," Sergeant Hermann Witt said. The panzer commander grinned. Theo found himself nodding. Adi Stoss was the best footballer he'd ever seen.

But Adi didn't rise to the gibe. All he said was, "My main goal is coming out of this mess in one piece." He ran a hand through his dark, wavy hair. "What else can we hope for?"

A National Socialist Loyalty Officer would have thundered forth bromides about victory and conquest and smashing the Jews in the Kremlin and the hordes of Slavic *Untermenschen* those Jews led. Nobody in the panzer crew thought that way, though. They'd all seen and been through a lot. Theo knew too well that they weren't going to be part of a triumphal parade through Red Square. Hell, they'd never made it into Smolensk, much less Moscow. Once you came to grips with that, what could possibly matter more than getting home with two arms and two legs and two eyes and two balls?

Adi, if course, had more things to worry about even than the rest of the panzer men. He had to worry about Soviet panzer cannon the same way they did. But the country whose uniform he wore—and wore well—could be more dangerous to him than the Ivans were.

Theo said nothing about that. His crewmates would have been surprised if he had. He surprised them every time he opened his mouth, because he did it as little as he possibly could. He lived almost all his life inside the bony box bounded by his eyes, his ears, and the back of his head.

He would have said even less than he actually did if the *Wehrmacht*, in its infinite wisdom, hadn't made him a radioman. He couldn't believe that the aptitude tests he took when he got conscripted said he was ideal for the slot. Maybe they'd been short of men for the school and just grabbed the first five file folders that happened to be lying on the table. Or maybe some personnel sergeant back in Breslau owned a truly evil sense of humor.

Years too late to wonder about that now. When the *Wehrmacht* told you to do this, this was what you did. Oh, you could tell them no. But that was how you found out about what places like Dachau and Bergen-Belsen were like on the inside. Sensible Germans knew such bits of knowledge came at too high a cost.

Sergeant Witt clambered up onto the new panzer's turret. The panzer commander opened a hatch and slid inside. His voice came from the bowels of the machine: "All the comforts of home!"

"Oh, yeah?" That was Lothar Eckhardt, the gunner. "Where's the bed? Where's the broad with the big tits in the bed?"

Witt's head popped out of the hatch. "Don't worry about that, Lothar. You've got a bigger gun here than you do in the bedroom." All the panzer crewmen laughed, some more goatishly than others. Theo didn't count laughter against his starvation ration of speech.

"Right, Sergeant," Eckhardt said with exaggerated patience. "But I have more fun with the one I've got on me. And I don't need Poske here to help me shoot it off, either." He nudged the loader, who was standing next to him.

Kurt Poske pushed back. "You'd better not. You'd be some kind of fairy if you did."

Witt flipped a limp wrist. "Come on, girls," he said in a lisping falsetto that would have won him a pink triangle in a camp. "Why don't you see how you like it in here?"

Theo found his spot in the right front of the panzer hull only a little different from the same seat in the last Panzer IV. But no rungs were welded to the inside of the machine to hold his Schmeisser. He stowed the personal-defense weapon between his feet. Sooner or later, somebody in the company repair crew could take care of it for him.

Adi didn't have a place to hang his machine pistol, either. He couldn't stash it the way Theo had, not when his feet needed to work the brake and clutch and accelerator. He set it behind Theo's radio set. "Just for the time being," he said apologetically. Theo nodded. That didn't count against his speech ration, either.

"Fire it up, Adi," Hermann Witt said, and Stoss' finger stabbed the starter button on the instrument panel in front of him. The motor roared to life at once. That was what a fresh battery would do for you. The engine noise was higher and smoother than it had been in the old machine. This power plant hadn't been worked to death shoving twenty tonnes of panzer across the rutted, unforgiving Russian landscape.

Yet.

As the panzer rumbled and rattled up toward the platoon's assembly area, Theo hooked himself back into the regimental radio network. Shifting frequencies, he heard different voices in his earphones. He had to do some talking of his own, to let the owners of those voices know this panzer and its crew were attached to them. Since those words were strictly line-of-duty, he didn't feel obliged to count them.

They didn't stay assembled in the area for very long. Half an hour after the Panzer IV joined its mates, they moved out to try to blunt a Russian westward thrust. The *Reich* didn't have the bit between its teeth in Russia any more. Now hanging on to some of what it had gained in happier times was as much as it could hope for.

The new panzer clanked past the burnt-out hulk of a German armored car. Fifty meters farther on sat the chassis of a Russian T-34, with the turret blown off and upside-down beside it. Theo did use a word: "Tiger."

"You bet it was," Adi agreed. The German heavy tank's fearsome 88 could devastate a T-34 like that. A Panzer IV's long-barreled 75 could kill one, but couldn't smash it that way. And a T-34 could kill a Panzer IV just as readily, while a Tiger's thick frontal armor laughed at anything the Russian machine threw at it.

And then Witt shouted, "Panzer halt!"

"Halting." As Adi spoke, he trod hard on the brake.

At Witt's orders, the turret traversed to somewhere between two and three o'clock. The gun rose slightly. Theo could just see it move. A shell clanged into the breech. "Fire!" Witt yelled.

"On the way!" Lothar Eckhardt answered. As he spoke, the big gun roared. Flame leaped from the end of the muzzle, and out to either side of the recoil-reducing muzzle brake.

Then Theo used another word: "Hit!"

Flame and smoke burst from a Russian panzer he hadn't even seen till the big gun spoke. It was more than a kilometer away. When he peered out through the armor glass in his narrow vision slit, he couldn't tell whether the crew escaped. Part of him hoped so—they were members of his guild, in a manner of speaking. But they'd try again to kill him if they did. Maybe hoping they died fast and without much pain was better.

Chapter 3

Summer days over Germany were long, summer nights short. In winter, when things reversed, the RAF and French bombers struck deep inside the country. At this time of year, they couldn't hope to do that and fly back out of danger before the new dawn showed them to the *Luftwaffe*.

In summer, then, the raiders concentrated on the western part of the *Reich*. They could drop their bombs on towns like Münster and be landing at their distant bases before the sun came up again.

As it sank in the northwestern sky this evening, Sarah Bruck apprehensively eyed the stretching shadows and the red-gold lights streaming in through the dining-room window. "Do you think they'll come tonight?" she asked.

Her father paused with a forkful of boiled potatoes and turnip greens halfway to his mouth. Samuel Goldman considered the question as gravely as if it touched on the death of Socrates or the assassination of Julius Caesar. He had been a professor of ancient history and classics at the university. Since he was a Jew, that didn't matter once the Nazis took over. Because he was also a wounded veteran from the last war, he still found employment: he was a laborer in a work gang that cleared streets of rubble and tore down shattered houses and made repairs after the enemy struck.

Having considered, he nodded. "*Ja,* I think so. There will be plenty of moonlight to help show them the way."

"Samuel!" Hanna Goldman said, as if he'd come out with something filthy. Well, in a way he had.

"I'm sorry, sweetheart," he told his wife. "She asked me what I thought. Should I have lied to her? Then, when the air-raid sirens start screaming, she'll think *My father is a stupid old fool!,* and she'll hate me."

"What happens if the raiders don't come tonight, though, and everything stays quiet?" Sarah's mother sounded sure she'd won that one.

But she hadn't. Father answered, "She'll think *My father is a stupid old fool!*—and she'll love me."

They all laughed. The Nazis did everything they could to make life in the *Reich* as miserable for Jews as possible. They might have done a better job of it than any other gang of persecutors in the history of the world. Try as they would, though, they couldn't wipe out every single happy moment. Some sneaked past in spite of them.

"If they come," Sarah said, "maybe they'll drop some on the *Rathaus* and on the square in front of the cathedral. That would be terrible, wouldn't it?"

"Dreadful. Frightful," Samuel Goldman agreed, his voice full of plummy, pious hypocrisy. When you couldn't be sure the house wasn't bugged, you didn't want to give the authorities any excuse to cause you trouble. They could do it without an excuse, of course, but why make things easy for them?

A bomb hit on the *Rathaus* in daylight would blow the *Burgomeister* and the Nazi functionaries who ran Münster straight to heaven—or, more likely, to some warmer clime instead. A bomb hit on the *Rathaus* at any old time might destroy all the city records, including the ones of who was and wasn't a Jew. Plenty of people in town knew, of course, but Sarah suspected few would squeal on her parents and her if they somehow found an excuse to take the yellow Stars of David off their clothes. The National Socialist regime was less popular than it had been before it led the *Reich* into an endless, unvictorious war.

Which was why a bomb hit on the square in front of the cathedral would bring few tears to anyone in town. Bishop von Galen had dared to protest against the Nazis' policy of euthanizing mental defectives (though he'd said not a word about how they treated the Jews). The *Gestapo* had seized him, and the Catholics in town, backed by some Protestants, rioted to try to gain his release. They rose not once but twice. Sarah had almost got shot from accidentally being on the fringes of their second eruption.

These days, armed SS men held the cathedral and the square. If the RAF sent them some presents, wouldn't that be a shame? Sarah was sure lots of Münsterites were just as worried about it as she was.

She really did worry about bombs coming down close to the house here. In their infinite generosity, the Nazis had decreed that Jews weren't allowed in public air-raid shelters. They had to take their chances wherever they happened to be.

Her mouth tightened. She'd been married to Isidor Bruck for only a few months when he and his mother and father had to take their chances in the family bakery and the flat above it. She would have taken her chances with them if she hadn't been out. A direct hit leveled the building and killed them all. Now she was a widow, living with her parents again.

This house had been lucky. Most of the windows still boasted glass panes, not cardboard taped up in their place. But the Brucks had thought the bakery was lucky, too. And so it was . . . till it wasn't any more.

The radio blared out saccharine music and Dr. Goebbels' latest lies about how wonderfully things were going and how happy the German people were under the *Führer*'s divinely inspired leadership. Neither Sarah nor her mother and father felt like staying up late to listen to more of that. They slept as much as they possibly could, Samuel Goldman because he worked so hard in the labor gang and all of them because they didn't get enough to eat to have much energy.

Sarah didn't think she'd been in bed more than a few minutes before the warning sirens began to howl. All the dogs began to howl with them. The sirens scared the dogs, and the animals had learned what happened after those sirens shrieked. They had plenty of reason to be scared.

So did Sarah. Along with her parents, she stumbled down the stairs in the inky darkness and huddled under the sturdy dining-room table: the best protection they could get. Just because it was best didn't mean it was good.

"*Heil* Hitler!" Samuel Goldman said dryly. That was the punch line to a bitter joke the Germans made about air raids. If you'd grabbed some sleep in spite of the bombers, the next day you greeted people with *Good morning!* If the raid had kept you from getting any sleep and you desperately needed some, you said *Good night!* And if you'd always been asleep, you said *Heil Hitler!*

How many thousand meters up there did the bombers fly? Not far enough to keep the drone of their engines from reaching the ground. Searchlights would be probing for them, trying to spear them and pin them down in the sky so the flak guns could get at them. The cannons' quick-firing snarls punctuated that steady industrial drone.

Here came the bombs, whistling down. The first bursts were a long way off, but they kept getting closer and closer and . . . . *Make them stop! Please, God, make them stop!* Sarah wanted to scream it. She swallowed it instead, all but a tiny whimper. God would hear anyway. Or, by all the signs she'd been able to glean, more likely He wouldn't.

Boom! Boom! Boomety-boom! The ground shook. The windows rattled. But the house didn't fall down on top of them. The windows didn't blow in and slash them. Their neighborhood had missed the worst of it again.

After twenty minutes or half an hour (or a year or two, depending on how you looked at things), the droning faded off into the west. The flak guns kept banging away, probably at nothing. Every so often, a falling fragment from their shells would smash a roof and start a fire or land on some luckless man's head. A couple of guns went on even after the warbling all-clear sounded.

By then, Sarah was already back in bed. So were her folks. As soon as they decided nothing was coming down on their heads, they slowly and carefully climbed the stairs again. If you were tired enough, you could sleep after almost anything. They were. They could. They did.

Next morning, Father rolled a cigarette of tobacco scavenged from other people's discarded dog-ends. A certain predatory gleam lit his eyes as he walked out the front door. "I wonder what we'll be cleaning up today," he said.

In smashed houses, the laborers stole whatever they could: real cigarettes, food, clothes. Once, *Herr Doktor Professor* Samuel Goldman would have been ashamed to do such a thing. Not Samuel Goldman the work-gang man. Sarah understood the change only too well. What Jew in Nazi Germany had any room left for shame?

Anastas Mouradian went through the preflight checklist in the cockpit of his Pe-2 with meticulous care. His copilot and bomb-aimer, Isa Mogamedov, sat in the other chair there. He helped Mouradian run down the list.

They spoke to each other in Russian, the only language they had in common. Each flavored it with a different accent. Their home towns lay only a hundred kilometers or so apart, but neither knew or wanted to know a word of the other's native tongue. Mouradian was an Armenian, Mogamedov an Azeri. Their peoples had been rivals and enemies for a thousand years, ever since the Turkic Azeris invaded the Caucasus. Mouradian had been born a Christian, Mogamedov a Muslim. Now they both had to do their best to be New Soviet Men.

"Comrade Pilot, everything seems normal," Mogamedov said formally when they got to the end of the checklist.

"Thank you, Comrade Copilot. I agree," Mouradian replied with equal formality. New Soviet Men had no business quarreling with one another, especially when the Fascist enemy remained on Soviet soil.

Part of Stas Mouradian wanted to believe all the Soviet propaganda that had bombarded him since he was very small. Part of him simply thought some personnel officer had played a practical joke on him by sticking an Azeri in his cockpit. But Mogamedov was plenty capable. With that being true, Mouradian could ignore the rest.

He could, and he had to. Russians didn't officially dominate the Soviet Union the way they had in the Tsar's empire. The leader of the USSR, after all, came out of the Caucasus himself—Stalin was a Georgian. But, even though he spoke the country's chief language with an accent thick enough to slice, Stalin often acted more Russian than the Tsars. Any of the blackasses—Russian slang for the mostly swarthy folk of the southern mountains—who wanted to get ahead needed to do the same.

Mouradian not only wanted to get ahead, he wanted to get airborne. He shouted into the speaking tube that led back to the bomb bay: "Everything good for you, Fetya?"

"Everything's fucking wonderful, Comrade Pilot," Sergeant Fyodor Mechnikov replied. The bombardier was a Russian, all right: a foulmouthed thug dragged off a collective farm and into the Red Air Force. He was as strong as an ox—another reason his station was back there with the heavy packages of explosives—and not a great deal brighter.

But if everything looked good to him, too . . . Stas waved through the bulletproof glass of the windscreen to the waiting groundcrew men. They waved back and spun first one prop, then the other. Smoke and flames burst from the exhausts as the engines bellowed to life. Mouradian eyed the jumping needles on the instrument panel. Fuel, oil pressure, hydraulics . . . Again, everything seemed inside the normal range.

He waved to the groundcrew men once more. They pulled the chocks away from the Pe-2's wheels. Mouradian eased up on the brake and gave the plane more throttle. It bounced down the dirt runway west of Smolensk. The runway was barely long enough to let a fully loaded bomber take off. Stas pulled back hard on the yoke. The Pe-2's nose came up. If anything went wrong now, he'd be dead, and the bombs would make sure there was nothing left of him to bury.

But nothing went wrong. The Pe-2 climbed into the air. The ground fell away below it. The SB-2, the plane this machine replaced, had been a typical piece of Soviet engineering: homely but functional, at least till it went obsolete. Comrade Petlyakov's bomber, by contrast, was slim and elegant. It had started life as a two-engined fighter, and still wasn't helpless against Nazi 109s.

Mouradian took his place in the V of planes winging west to pound the Hitlerites' positions somewhere east of Minsk. The Germans had fallen back a good deal since England and France started up the war in the West again. They didn't have enough men or machines to do everything the *Führer* wanted.

A man's reach should exceed his grasp, or what's a heaven for? Some foreign poet had said that. Stas couldn't remember who. Hitler's reach had exceeded his grasp, and a lot of Germans were going to hell on account of it.

Now I have to make sure they don't send me to the Devil to keep them company, Mouradian thought. If you flew long enough, your number was bound to come up. He hadn't flown long enough yet, the proof of which was that he was still flying. *If I make it through the war, I won't go any higher than the top floor of a three-story building.*

He felt faintly embarrassed thinking about the Devil or making a wheedling bargain with God. There wasn't supposed to be room for either in a New Soviet Man's philosophy. But plenty of others acted the same way. When things went wrong, you'd hear Russians screaming about the Devil's uncle over the radio. Their fathers would have let out the same curses in the last war, and their great-great-great-grandfathers while fighting Napoleon.

Antiaircraft fire came up at the Pe-2s. Stas did some cussing of his own: they hadn't crossed the front yet, so that was their own side shooting at them. It happened about every other mission. Maybe the Pe-2 looked *too* slick—the dumb bastards down on the ground figured it had to be German. Or maybe that had nothing to do with anything. Red Army men had fired on Stas in an SB-2, too. Too many soldiers thought any airplanes flying over them had to be dangerous.

"Approaching the target!" The squadron commander's voice blared in Stas' earphones, and in Mogamedov's as well. "Prepare for the bomb run."

"Acknowledged," Mouradian answered. Mogamedov slid down to the glassed-in bottom of the nose to man the bombsight.

There it was, all right: a big supply dump by a railroad spur, with trucks and wagons hauling munitions up to the troops who banged heads with their Soviet counterparts. Mouradian pushed the yoke forward, and the bomber's nose went down. He used the dive brakes to control and steepen his descent. The Pe-2 couldn't stand on its nose like a Stuka, but it was a far better all-around aircraft.

"Bombs away, Fetya!" Mogamedov yelled.

"Bombs away!" Mechnikov echoed. "The whores are fucking gone!" And they were. Mouradian heard them tumble out of their racks and felt the plane, suddenly a tonne lighter, get friskier under his hands.

He needed all the friskiness he could find, too. Bf-109s tore into the squadron, pouncing from on high and pounding the bombers with heavy machine guns and cannon shells. A pair of Pe-2s tumbled out of the sky, both burning, one with half a wing shot away. Stas didn't see any parachutes open. He hoped the flyers died fast and without too much pain.

He hoped he *didn't* die in the next few minutes. The machine gun in the dorsal turret spat out a long burst, and then another one. Mechnikov was on the job. He probably wouldn't shoot down a 109 attacking from above and behind. He might make the pilot pull up and spoil the bastard's aim.

He must have, because the Pe-2 didn't crash. Half the needles on the gauges were at the edge of the red, but that was because Stas had mashed the throttle hard against the panel wall. The needles didn't leap crazily into the danger zone, the way they would have if the Nazi had shot the engines full of holes.

Most of the time, Stas would have tried to gain altitude. Now he stayed down on the deck, hoping the German fighters would have a hard time spotting his brown and green plane against the ground below. It must have worked—no Messerschmitt shot him down.

Isa Mogamedov climbed back into the copilot's seat. "Well, we got through another one—I think."

"I do, too, now." Stas allowed himself the luxury of a nod. "Only five thousand to go till peace breaks out." He laughed, pretending to be joking. So did Mogamedov, pretending to think he was.

A nurse cut off the latest set of bandages that swaddled Chaim Weinberg's left hand. Dr. Diego Alvarez leaned forward to get a better look.

Chaim didn't, but then the hand was attached to him. He tried to remember how many times Alvarez had carved him up, working to repair the damage a mortar round did. He tried, but he couldn't be sure if it was seven or eight.

When the bandages came off, the hand stopped looking like one from Boris Karloff in *The Mummy* and started looking like one from Karloff in *Frankenstein*. It had more scars and sutures and what-have-you than a merely human hand had any business possessing.

But when Chaim said, "It looks good, Doc," he wasn't being sarcastic. He counted himself lucky not to be auditioning for Captain Hook in a road company of *Peter Pan*. That mortar bomb had smashed his hand to hell and gone—and had killed his longtime buddy, Mike Carroll. When the other Internationals from the Abe Lincoln Brigade brought Chaim back to the aid station, the surgeon there almost decided to amputate on the spot. Then he remembered Dr. Alvarez, back in Madrid. Alvarez specialized in repairing such wounds.

"How does it feel?" the doctor asked now. His English, though flavored by Castilian Spanish, was more elegant than Chaim's. A street kid from New York City, Chaim quit school after the tenth grade to go to work. Dr. Alvarez, by contrast, had studied medicine in England. Except for his lisp and the occasional rolled *r*, he sounded like a BBC newsreader.

"Not . . . too bad," Chaim answered after a pause to consider. He'd found out more about pain the past few months than he'd ever wanted to know. He'd also found out more about morphine than he'd ever dreamt he'd learn. He was off it now, and hoped he wouldn't need to go back on.

"Can you move your thumb so the tip touches the tip of your index finger?" Dr. Alvarez asked. He'd concentrated his work on Chaim's thumb and first two fingers. The other two would never be good for much, no matter what he did. But those—especially the thumb and index finger—were the ones that mattered most.

"Let's see," Chaim said. He hadn't been able to do it yet. That hand was one hell of a mess before the surgeon got to work on it. Christ, it was still a hell of a mess. But it wasn't—quite—a disaster any more.

Moving his thumb hurt. So did moving his first finger. Too much in there had been repaired too many times for any of it to work smoothly now. But he *could* move both digits. A good Marxist-Leninist, he didn't believe in miracles. If he had, he would have believed in that one.

Not only did they move, but, after effort that made sweat pop out on his forehead, the tip of his thumb met the tip of his forefinger. "Kiss me, Doc!" he exclaimed. "I did it! Look! I did it!" Those seven or eight operations had finally led to this: a hand that might work half as well as it had before it got smashed.

And damned if Dr. Alvarez didn't kiss him on both cheeks. Chaim hardly even resented it, though he would have liked it better from the nurse. She wasn't gorgeous, but she was definitely cuter than the surgeon.

"Now you need to gain strength," Alvarez said.

"No kidding," Chaim agreed. He thought he might be able to pick up a dime with his reconstructed thumb and first finger, but a half-dollar would be too much for him.

"You are not my first case of this sort, though I think your injuries are among the most extensive I have succeeded in repairing," the doctor said. "I have developed a series of exercises that will help your digits approach the power they had before you were wounded."

"Approach it, huh?" Chaim said. Dr. Alvarez nodded. After a moment, so did Chaim. "Okay, Doc. You level with a guy. I give you credit for that. You never promised anything you didn't deliver. How long do I have to do these exercises, and how bad will they hurt?" He assumed they would hurt. It was a pretty safe bet. Everything that had happened to his left hand since the mortar bomb whispered down had hurt like hell.

"You will have to do them for several weeks. Your muscles need strengthening. Your tendons need to work more freely. I have done everything I could to assist that process, but time and practice are also necessary."

"And after that, I go back to the Internationals?" Chaim asked.

Dr. Alvarez looked unhappy. "After we have spent so much time and effort getting you to this point, it seems a shame to send you back to where you are liable to be wounded again."

"Doc," Chaim said, as patiently as he could, "if I hadn't wanted to take those kind of chances, I never would've come to Spain to begin with."

"I suppose not." Alvarez sounded unhappy, too. He didn't want all his hard work gurgling down the drain if Chaim stopped a slug with his face.

"You can take it to the bank I wouldn't have," Chaim said. "And you can take it to the bank that there's a bunch of Sanjurjo's *putos* who wish I would've stayed in the States. You with me so far?"

"Oh, yes," Alvarez said dryly. What were his politics? He'd never said much about them. He was here in Madrid, on the Republican side of the fence. If he preferred the Nationalists, the only way he could hope to stay alive was to keep his big mouth shut.

Chaim wasn't about to push him, not when he'd been gifted with an almost-working hand instead of a hook. "When I get as strong as I'm gonna get, will I be able to handle a rifle, or at least a Tommy gun?" he asked.

"I think it is possible," the surgeon said carefully. "I also think it is on the very edge of what you will be able to do. For your thumb and those two fingers, the exercises will get you back most of your fine motor skills. The hand has had too much damage to be as strong as it was. I'm very sorry, but that seems to be the situation."

"Well, it gives me something to shoot for." Chaim grinned crookedly. He was short and squat and not too handsome. That kind of grin suited him, in other words. "Shoot for! Get it, Doc? It's a joke."

Dr. Alvarez, by contrast, was slim and elegant. "Amusing," he said. A slight twitch of one eyebrow delivered his editorial verdict. With a verdict like that, Chaim was lucky Alvarez wasn't a judge.

The exercises hurt, all right. As far as Chaim could tell, everything that had anything to do with getting wounded hurt. *Funny how that works, isn't it?* he gibed to himself. At first, he couldn't do everything with the hand that the surgeon wanted him to. Everything? He could barely do anything, and the effort left him more worn down than hauling a sack of concrete should have.

"Patience. Patience and persistence," Alvarez told him. "You must have both."

To Chaim, they sounded like a couple of round-heeled Puritan girls. Patience and Persistence Mather: something like that. He imagined himself in bed with both of them at once, because he had an imagination like that—especially after he'd been stuck in the hospital for so long without any friendly female company.

A few days later, as he healed more, he started being able to do things he couldn't at first. That made him feel better. It also made him think—again—that the doctor might know what he was talking about after all. And, a couple of days after that, La Martellita paid him a rare visit.

The Little Hammer—that was what his ex-wife's *nom de guerre* meant. Communist activist, drop-dead gorgeous woman with a mane of blue-black hair, mother of his son . . . Even a glimpse of her made his dreams of wicked Puritan maids pop like pricked soap bubbles.

"I heard you might be able to take up arms again for the cause after all," she said gravely. "That's good news—better than I expected when they brought you here."

"Better than I expected, too, *querida*." Chaim's Spanish wasn't smooth or grammatical, but it got the job done. "Wish I could take *you* in my arms."

"No." Her voice went hard and flat. "It's over. Don't you see that?"

"I see it. Doesn't mean I have to like it." Chaim sighed. "How's Carlos Federico?" He'd never expected to have a son named for Marx *and* Engels, especially not in Spanish.

"He's well. Maybe I will bring him here again. It is good to see you are doing better, too. Now I must go." And La Martellita did. Five chilly minutes—that was all he'd got. He could count himself lucky . . . or he could go back to daydreaming about Patience and Persistence.

German 105s pounded the trench line in which Staff Sergeant Alistair Walsh crouched—well, cowered, if you wanted to get right down to it. In the last war, the Germans would have—had—shot 77s at him. Those were a lot less dangerous; they didn't fly as far, and, because they came from flat-shooting guns rather than higher-trajectory howitzers, they had a smaller chance of coming down into the trench with you and going off.

He hadn't thought in the last war that he'd still be soldiering in this one. But the other choice was going back into the Welsh coal mine from which the Army had plucked him. A soldier's life, especially in peacetime, seemed better than that. So did anything else, hell very possibly included.

So he'd stayed in. He'd risen in the ranks, as far as a lad plucked from a Welsh coal mine could hope to rise. Staff sergeants saluted subalterns and first lieutenants. They called them *sir*. But, with their years of experience, they mattered more than the junior officers nominally set over them. A smart regimental colonel would sooner trust a senior sergeant than any lieutenant ever hatched, and would back him against quite a few captains, too.

All of which was fine when there were choices to be made and courses to be plotted. When Fritz was throwing hate around, all you could do was hunker down and hope it missed you. No, you could do one more thing besides. Walsh fumbled in the breast pocket of his battledress tunic, pulled out a packet of Navy Cuts, and stuck one in his mouth. The shelling hadn't made his hands shake too much to keep him from striking a match.

He sucked in smoke. Logic said that couldn't make anything better. Logic be damned, though. A cigarette relaxed him to some small but perceptible degree. He wasn't the only one, either. Nobody in the front-line trenches ever quit smoking. Plenty of people who'd never had the habit before picked it up when the Germans started trying to kill them, though.

Sure as hell, the Cockney who'd pushed up against the muddy front wall of the trench next to him nudged him and said, "'Ere, Sarge, can I bum a fag orf yer?"

"Here you go, Jack." Walsh handed him the packet.

"Fanks." Jack Scholes took one and gave it back. He was young enough to be the staff sergeant's son. He had close-cropped blond hair, a tough, narrow face with pointed features, and snaggle teeth. He looked like a mean terrier. He fought like one, too. He was the stubborn sort of soldier who took a deal of killing.

Walsh leaned close so Scholes could get a light from his cigarette. Most of the German fire was a couple of hundred yards long. That was about the only good news Walsh could find.

He'd just ground the tiny butt of his latest smoke under the heel of his boot when the barrage stopped. Beside him, Scholes flipped off the safety on his Lee-Enfield. "Now we see if the buggers mean it or not," he said.

That was also how things looked to Walsh. If the Germans did mean it, they'd throw men and tanks into the attack and try to push the British forces back toward the border between Belgium and France. Otherwise, they'd sit and wait and make the Tommies come to them.

They'd done a lot of sitting and waiting lately. With positions hardened by reinforced concrete, with MG-42s waiting to turn any enemy attack into a charnel house, with tanks that had bigger guns and thicker armor than anything the Allies boasted, why shouldn't the Nazis wait? The Western Front was narrow. Their foes had to come at them head-on. They could bleed them white without paying too high a butcher's bill of their own.

But trusting the Germans to do the same thing every time didn't pay. Several English Bren guns started shooting all at nearly the same time. A mournful shout spelled out what that meant: "Here they come!"

Scholes popped up onto the firing step, squeezed off a couple of rounds, and quickly ducked down again. Alistair Walsh stuck his head up for a look, but only for a look. In place of a rifle, he carried a Sten submachine gun, one of the ugliest weapons ever invented. The stamped metal pieces were more botched together than properly assembled. Some of them looked as if they'd been cut from sheet metal with tin snips; for all Walsh knew, they had. If you dropped a Sten, chances were it would either fall apart or go off and shoot you in the leg.

At close quarters, though, it spat out a lot of slugs in a hurry. A Lee-

Enfield could kill out past half a mile. Inside a couple of hundred yards, the Sten was the horse to back.

The Germans weren't inside a couple of hundred yards yet. They had to work through the gaps in their own wire, cross the space between their stuff and the stuff the English had put up, and get through *that* before they could start jumping down into the trenches.

Their machine guns made it dangerous for any Tommy to stick his head up over the parapet and shoot at them. Twenty feet down the trench from Walsh, an Englishman bonelessly toppled over backwards. A bullet had punched a neat hole in his forehead. It had probably blown half his brains back into his tin hat, but Walsh couldn't see that—a small mercy.

Possibly a bigger mercy was that he hadn't seen any German tanks moving up with the foot soldiers. He especially dreaded the fearsome Tigers, which smashed British armor as if it were made to the same shoddy standards as the Sten gun.

He popped up again and squeezed a short burst at the oncoming Germans, more to encourage his own men than to put the fear of God in the Fritzes. "Keep your peckers up!" he called to the soldiers in dirty khaki. "Stand firm and they'll turn tail. Wait and see!"

They did, too. Some of them lurked in no-man's-land for a while. A few machine-gun teams set up in shell holes so they could rake the English line from shorter range. You could do that with an MG-42. No other gun—certainly not the Bren, fine weapon though it was—combined mobility and firepower so well.

But MG-42s that came out of their concrete machine-gun nests were MG-42s that trench mortars could reach. The mortar bombs weren't noisy leaving their tubes, and flew almost silently. They went bang only when they burst. One by one, the Fritzes' gun crews either died or pulled back toward their own line.

As things quieted down, Jack Scholes turned to Walsh and asked, "'Ow'd you know they was bluffin', loik?"

"No armor," Walsh answered.

"Ah. Roight." Scholes nodded. What trade would he ply if he weren't a soldier? Sneak-thief was Walsh's first guess. "They'd've been roight up our arse'ole wiv a few tanks along, eh?"

"Too right, they would," Walsh said. "But without 'em they were just yanking our chain. They killed a few of us, we killed a few of them, and none of it will change the way the war turns out even a ha'penny's worth."

"Wot would?" Scholes sounded interested and intrigued, as if he weren't used to thinking this way but found he liked it. "Droppin' a bomb on 'Itler's 'ead?"

"That ought to do something," Walsh agreed.

"Too many back in Bloighty like the bastard, though," Scholes said. "We never would've gone in wiv 'em if Winston 'adn't bought 'imself that plot."

"No. We wouldn't," Walsh said tightly. The Cockney kid couldn't know he'd met Winston Churchill. He remained convinced Churchill's death hadn't been an accident. Afterwards, it had taken what amounted to a military coup to oust the let's-pal-with-the-Nazis appeasers. And, if the war didn't start going better, another coup might put them right back in.

Chapter 4

Sergeant Hideki Fujita didn't mind days on Midway—not too much, anyhow. There wasn't a lot to do on the small, low island at the northwestern tip of the chain that led down to Hawaii. But the weather was mild even if it was often muggy. You could fish from the beach. You'd eat whatever you caught, too. It was more interesting and tastier than the rations that came from the Home Islands. Midway was at the very end of the Japanese supply lines, and sometimes a line frayed. Fishing helped people from going hungry, too.

Japanese G4M bombers could reach the main Hawaiian islands from Midway. They could, and they did. Sometimes they dropped explosives. Sometimes they found other presents for the Americans. Fujita was there as part of the bacteriological-warfare detachment. He'd had experience with such things in Manchukuo and Burma. To the people here, that made him an expert, even if he was just a sergeant.

And so he'd made the long flight to Oahu in the belly of a G4M, doing bombardier duty. He'd launched pottery bomb casings full of plague-infected rats and anthrax powder and cholera germs on Honolulu. In spite of an amazing fireworks display of antiaircraft fire, he'd made it back here, too.

But, while Japanese bombers could fly southeast down to the main Hawaiian islands, American bombers could also come northwest up to Midway. Like most Japanese soldiers, Fujita scorned America's fighting spirit. When U.S. soldiers found themselves in a bad position, they surrendered. Dozens of Marines became experimental animals for the Japanese bombers in the compound outside of Harbin. Men who hadn't fought to the death deserved no better.

Whatever you could say about the Americans, though, they were rich. They knew what to do with machines, too. That was why Fujita hated and feared Midway nights. Japanese G4Ms flew occasional missions against Hawaii. When they flew, they went one or two at a time. Here at the end of the supply lines, the Japanese Empire could afford no more. It could barely afford so much.

When the Americans flew against Midway, they sent bombers in great swarms, a hundred at a time—two hundred, for all Fujita knew. Bombs rained down on the island by the thousands. He knew that entirely too well. The only shelter was in shallow trenches scraped in the sand. Midway had hardly any real dirt. It was sand or rock.

Every bombing pounded the Japanese living quarters worse. The Americans weren't all that accurate, but they didn't need to be. They dropped so many bombs, some were bound to hit. Those barracks halls weren't in great shape to begin with, either. Japan had captured them from the Yankees when the Empire seized Midway. After each air raid, engineers worked to repair the damage. It grew faster than they could keep up with it.

The only thing on Midway that the Japanese engineers went out of their way to fortify were the desalinization plant and the fuel dump that kept it going. Those got covered over with steel-reinforced concrete. Freighters brought in the stuff along with rice and munitions. They had to. Without the desalinization plant—captured from the Americans—Midway was uninhabitable by more than a handful of men. It simply didn't have the fresh water to support more.

When the sun came up after yet another U.S. air raid, Fujita stood up in the trench where he'd been trying to grab a little sleep. The landscape reminded him of nothing so much as one of the shabbier suburbs of hell. Most of Midway was nothing but dunes with scraggly bits of grass here and there. The bombs tore the sorry vegetation to bits.

They did worse to man's works on the island. The runways were cratered. Some of the American bombs had hard, thick noses. They penetrated before their delay fuses went off. That made for more damage to things like runways. Fujita wondered if those bombs could also pierce the reinforced concrete protecting the desalinization plant.

If they could, they hadn't done it yet. The plant's motors kept chugging away. It pulled salt water out of the Pacific and turned the stuff into something people could drink. The water still tasted metallic, but the doctors swore it wouldn't hurt you. They drank it, too, so they evidently believed what they said.

All the Japanese planes on the island hid in sandbagged revetments covered with camouflage netting. The only way a bomb could find them was by luck. Drop enough bombs and one or two were bound to get lucky. Two pyres of black, greasy smoke climbed high into the blue, blue sky. The netting burned, too, adding its smoke to that from the planes.

The barracks . . . Well, the less said about the barracks, the better. They'd been pounded hard before. They were even more knocked around now. A couple of small fires burned in them, too, but those were as nothing next to the blazing airplanes.

Another sergeant stood up a few meters from Fujita and also surveyed the damage. *"Eee!"* Ichiro Yanai said mournfully. He gave Fujita a sour grin. "Aren't you glad you volunteered to come way the demon out here and give the round-eyed barbarians a kick in the slats?"

"Well, I was," Fujita answered. "But now they're kicking *our* slats, and that isn't half so much fun."

"Hai! You've sure got that right!" Yanai looked southeast, in the direction from which an American fleet would surely come. "What do we do if they send soldiers here instead of just bombing us?"

Fujita's glance went toward the smoldering barracks. He knew where his rifle was, but he wouldn't want to try to get it right now. He shrugged broad shoulders. He was a peasant from a long line of peasants; he'd been working on his father's farm when conscription got him.

"What can we do?" he said. "Fight till we can't fight any more. Maybe we'll throw them back into the sea." His wave encompassed the whole broad, blue Pacific. "Or if we don't . . . Well, our spirits will meet at the Yasukuni Shrine, *neh*?"

"That's right. That's just right!" Yanai nodded vigorously. The spirits of all Japanese war dead gathered at the shrine in Tokyo. Fujita was as sure of that as he was of any religious matter.

His eye searched for the little separate tent compound not far from the desalinization plant. Captain Ikejiri's bacteriological-warfare unit kept tight security, even on an island like Midway, from which no rumor could easily escape.

No bombs seemed to have hit it. He let out a silent sigh of relief. If the infected animals got loose, or if the bombs splashed germs all over the island, that wouldn't be so good. Yes, the garrison here had been immunized against everything this side of housemaid's knee. It wouldn't be good even so. Chances were people would come down sick anyway—not even Japanese science knew how to immunize against everything.

And the island would become uninhabitable to anybody who hadn't been immunized like that. Anthrax spores could sit in the soil—well, in the sand here—for years, maybe for centuries, till a suitable host came along. Then they would stop being spores and start being germs again. If you weren't immunized, they would kill you in short order.

"At least they don't seem to have wrecked any of the supply depots," Yanai said. Those weren't far from the desalinization plant, either. Yanai must have thought Fujita was looking at them. He knew in a general way which unit Fujita was attached to. Even in a place like this, where everyone was in everyone else's pockets, he didn't know any details. Yes, the bacteriological-warfare people knew how to keep their lips buttoned.

"Wouldn't be so good if they broke our rice bowls, would it?" Fujita said. Some of his training involved ways to make sure outsiders didn't learn anything they shouldn't know. In a garrison on the Empire's fringes, food was always a good way to change the subject.

Sure enough, Yanai shuddered and said, "I don't want to go hungry!"

"Who does?" Fujita agreed. Inside himself, he smiled. Damned if the training didn't work.

As a veteran U.S. Marine, Sergeant Pete McGill had done almost everything a fighting man could do by land or sea. He hadn't done much in the air, though. At any rate, he hadn't till now.

The C-47 droned along over central Oahu. He'd already fitted the long strap that connected his parachute to the static line that ran along the starboard side of the transport's fuselage. They didn't trust you to pull your own rip cord. This did the job for you, and made sure you wouldn't end up as a big splatter on the ground several too many thousand feet below.

A gunnery sergeant with a drill instructor's lemon-squeezer hat firmly strapped to his head stood by the portside door. "In about a minute, the light'll start going green," the gunny yelled over the noise of engines and wind. All the twenty-odd paratroopers were supposed to know that, but he was a good instructor, and took nothing for granted. "Every time it flashes, one of youse goes out. One! Youse guys got that?" He thrust out his chin and looked very fierce.

"Yes, Sergeant!" the men chorused. Pete hid a grin as he shouted out his answer. He said *youse* and *youse guys,* too—he came from the Bronx. The gunny's accent wasn't the same as his—he would have guessed Philly—but there was another big-city man among the hicks and Rebs who filled out the Corps.

"Okay," the instructor went on. "Slide forward one place every time a guy goes out of the plane. You get to the door, hang on to the sides, one with each hand. Put your left foot on the sill. Swing your right foot forward and step out. Don't jump. That'll take you too goddamn close to the tailplane, which you don't want. Just step. You'll fall. Oh, yeah. Bet your ass you will." He looked at the guy closest to the door and barked, "Take your place!"

The leatherneck obeyed. Everybody else slid down one. Pete moved from sixth to fifth. The jump light went green. The first Marine half stepped, half jumped from the C-47. No matter what the gunny said, the urge to leap if you were going to go at all was strong.

"Number two, take your place!" the instructor shouted. The next Marine did. The light turned green. Out he went. "Number three, take your place!"

Number four didn't go out as soon as he saw the green light. The gunny put a strong hand on the small of his back and shoved. That took care of that, and wasted less than a second. McGill had heard they had somebody like that stationed by the door on every combat run. No paratrooper with a sudden case of cold feet would be able to gum up the works.

Number five stepped out into space according to plan. Then it was Pete's turn. The wind tore at him and stripped tears from his eyes. He grabbed at cold aluminum with both hands and planted his left boot on the metal sill. When the light turned green, he brought his right foot forward and fell away from the plane.

You were supposed to yell *Geronimo!* when you jumped. What came out of his mouth that first time was a long, heartfelt "*Shiiiit!*"

It cut off abruptly as the strap attached to the static line yanked the chute out of its canvas pack and opened. His world went gray for a second at the jolt. Then the blood came back to his brain. Here he was, floating in the air under the world's biggest umbrella canopy.

In battle, he'd go in a lot lower. The Japs would be shooting at him while he descended on them. The less chance to do that they had, the better. But this wasn't battle. It was training. He could look around and gawk and admire a view only soaring birds had enjoyed till a few years before.

Down he came. Much of northwestern Oahu didn't have much on it and wasn't soaking wet. The combination made good landing country. You needed to bend your knees and tuck your chin against your chest. When you hit, you took the impact as best you could. They told you to roll with it.

The ground swelled—not anywhere near so fast as it would have if he were falling free, but it did. He'd thought about soaring birds in general a moment before. Now he thought about albatrosses in particular. Some other Marine had told him about watching them glide in at Midway and crash-land every goddamn time. The way he made it sound, it was hilarious.

Well, if any albatrosses were landing on Midway these days, the goddamn Japs were watching them. And watching a crash landing might be funny. If anybody was watching Pete right now, the bastard might laugh his ass off. Going through a crash landing was a whole different ballgame.

An albatross who didn't like the way things were going could flap and gain height and try it again somewhere else. A guy under a parachute didn't have that luxury. You were supposed to be able to spill wind from the canopy by shifting your weight. So the instructors claimed. Maybe you could, too, after a few more practice jumps. This first time, Pete wasn't inclined to experiment.

Here came the ground. He bent and tucked as he'd been told to do. *Wham!* He might have controlled his crash a little better than an albatross did, but not a whole lot. And he hit *hard*. Not long before he joined the Marines, his girlfriend's musclebound brother unexpectedly walked into the apartment they shared with their folks. He'd gone out a second-story window then, and landed like a ton of bricks. He thought he hit harder now.

Now, though, he had boots, knee and elbow pads, and a helmet on his head. He rolled a couple of times, realizing he hadn't sprained or broken anything. Then he used the lines that attached him to the chute to get the air out of it. He didn't have to cut himself free to keep from being blown all over the place. The bookkeepers would be happy—here was another parachute they could use again.

More and more men came down from the sky. They landed to the west of him, in the direction the C-47 was flying. One of them let out a yell he could hear from a couple of hundred yards away. The luckless guy didn't get up. He lay there clutching an ankle and howling like a wolf.

A jeep chugged up to Pete. "Hop in," the driver said, so he did. The little utility vehicles could go damn near anywhere. The only trouble with them was, after they'd jounced over rough terrain for a while, you thought your kidneys would fall out.

McGill pointed toward the hurt Marine. "Pick him up next," he said. "He landed bad."

"Okey-doke." The driver put the jeep in gear and went over to the man. "Give you a hand, pal?"

"You better," the other leatherneck answered. "I sure as shit busted somethin' in there. I heard it crack when I hit, an' it hurts like a mad son of a bitch." He did some fancier cussing as the driver and Pete hauled him up and got him into the back of the jeep.

"Got your morphine syrette in your wound kit?" Pete asked him. "If you want, I'll stick you."

"Yeah, that'd be good," the other Marine said. His face was gray and drawn; he had to be hurting bad. Pete knew what that pain was like. He'd broken bones before. He fumbled in the pouches on the guy's belt till he found the one with the wound dressing and the sulfa powder and the syrette. Pulling off the cap, he drove the needle home and pushed the plunger.

"I'll take you both back to Schofield Barracks," the driver said. "They got a hospital there."

Even on the road, the jeep didn't have the smoothest ride in the world. The injured Marine groaned at every bump till the morphine took hold. Then he let out a soft sigh of relief.

Schofield Barracks, west of the central town of Wahiawa, had taken damage from Japanese air raids. It was an Army base. The hospital accepted the injured man without any trouble. The driver had to talk to a light colonel, though, before he got permission to return Pete to his fellow leathernecks.

Since the Army was doing him a favor, even if with no great enthusiasm, McGill kept his opinion of it to himself. But he remained damn glad he was a Marine. And now he was a Marine who could fly!

When Julius Lemp brought the U-30 into Namsos, he wondered whether the U-boat base in the far north of Norway would be ready for him and his rowdy crew. Namsos had been a nothing town before Germany occupied it. But its position made it important in wartime. German U-boats staging from Namsos could easily get out into the North Atlantic. Or they could go up into the Barents Sea and harry the English convoys bringing supplies to the Russian ports of Murmansk and Archangelsk.

Proper U-boat bases had bars and brothels where sailors who'd been cooped up inside a smelly steel tube for weeks could blow off steam. The last couple of times the U-30 put in there, Namsos had been badly deficient in such amenities. His men sparked disorders that came within centimeters of turning into open mutiny.

When the U-boat tied up at a pier this time, Lemp discovered it had a welcoming committee, all right. A couple of dozen stalwart shore-patrol men stood waiting in the planking in naval-infantry uniforms that looked a lot like what the *Wehrmacht* wore. Each of them had a *Stahlhelm* on his head, a truncheon on his belt, and a Schmeisser in his arms.

"What the devil is this?" Lemp called from the conning tower as his soldiers tossed lines to ordinary *Kriegsmarine* personnel on the pier, who made the U-30 fast.

"Sir, we don't want any trouble when your men come ashore," answered the young lieutenant, junior grade, who seemed to be in charge of the shore-patrol detachment.

"I don't want any trouble, either. And my men don't," Lemp said irately. "They just want to be able to have a good time."

"What you mean by having a good time is tearing the place to pieces . . . sir," the junior officer said.

"*Leck mich am Arsch!* That's a bunch of *Scheisse*!" Lemp yelped. "They never would have got out of line if there were anything to do here. But I guess when you've got to stay *am Arsch der Welt*, you don't notice things like that."

"Sir," the puppy said one more time, his voice so stiff it would have snapped if you tried to bend it, "accommodations have improved since the last time the U-30 made port here, *sir*." He plainly used the title of respect twice in one sentence to convey the exact opposite: insubordination by supersubordination, you might say. After a long, angry breath, he went on, "Your men will be allowed out from the barracks in small groups, with armed escorts. They may drink. They may enjoy female companionship. If they put one foot out of place, I promise we will jug them . . . sir."

"Christ on His cross! I think you'd treat an English U-boat crew better than you're treating us," Lemp said.

"They'd probably behave better, too, sir," the junior officer retorted. "Your other choice is remaining confined to the boat during refitting."

That was no choice at all, as he and Lemp both understood. The first thing you wanted to do when you came into port was get the hell off the cramped, stinking boat. Lemp was tempted to swing the deck gun around and start lobbing 88mm shells at the base commandant's headquarters. The scary thing was, he knew his sea wolves would not only do it if he gave the order, they'd cheer while they were doing it.

But no, you had to act like a grownup, even—often especially— when you didn't want to. "All right," Lemp said with a sigh. "We'll do it your way. We'll come out peacefully, and we'll play nice. Wait here. I'll go below and give the lads the good news."

They took it as hard as he'd expected. Their objections were loud and profane. "You should have told that *Schokostecher* where to put it, skipper!" one of them shouted. He was a petty officer with several years' service, too, which really alarmed Lemp.

"No, dammit. We've got to play nice," he said, as he had to the punk on the pier. "This isn't a joke."

"You bet it isn't!" another sailor yelled.

"This is for the boat," Lemp said—if that didn't hit them where they lived, nothing would. If nothing would, Lord help them all. "We've got into trouble twice here. Third time and they really would scuttle us. Drink some beer. It sounds like they do finally have a brothel, so screw the girls. But don't brawl and don't break things. You hear me?"

They heard him. They didn't like it, but they did. They came up the ladder, down the conning tower, along the deck, and onto the pier in their filthy clothes, with long, greasy hair and badly groomed beards. They hardly looked like members of the same species as the spick-and-span shore patrolmen, much less members of the same armed force.

But they had their own pride. As they passed the neat men with helmets and machine pistols, they asked them things like "Ever been seasick, pal?" and "Ever done any fighting?" and "Know what fuel oil smells like?" and "Did you tell your mommy you were coming way up here?" The shore patrolmen didn't answer. They gave a good, game try at not changing expression. Try as they would, though, they couldn't keep the backs of their necks and their ears from going red as hot coals.

Julius Lemp waited in front of the junior lieutenant until that worthy, his own ears on fire, saluted. With a certain irony, Lemp returned the gesture. Escorted by the shore patrolmen, the U-30's men went off to the ratings' barracks. The lieutenant, junior grade, took the U-boat's tiny contingent of officers to the slightly better quarters their rank entitled them to.

"Is there an officers' brothel, too, sonny?" Lemp inquired. "Or wouldn't you know about that?"

"Sir, there is one," the puppy answered stiffly, and his ears went red all over again.

"Well, isn't that nice?" Lemp scaled his unstiffened, white-crowned officer's cap onto a cot. "Might as well freshen up a bit before I go find it. Somebody ever tell you where it was at?"

Biting the words off between his teeth, the junior officer gave precise directions. Then he spun on his heel and hurried away, as if to escape before he said something that might not be in the line of duty. Lemp's quiet chuckle behind his back only made him go faster.

Lemp had a duty call to the base commandant to make before he could visit the brothel or the officers' club. Cleaning himself up before he saw Captain Böhme also seemed a good idea. He couldn't give his superior the same kind of hard time he'd inflicted on the very young lieutenant. After a bald report about the latest patrol, he did say, "I think singling out my crew the way you have is unfair, sir."

The commandant fixed him with a cold gray stare. "That, Commander, is too damned bad," he growled. "I did not single out your hooligans. They did it to themselves when they tried to turn this base inside out and upside down two leaves running."

"If they would have had a better chance to relax—" Lemp began.

Waldemar Böhme cut him off: "It's a rough old war for everyone, Commander. You are dismissed. Try to keep *your* nose clean, too."

"Zu Befehl, mein Herr!" Lemp put as much spite as he could into his salute. He feared the commandant was immune to such childish gestures, but it was all he could do.

Having been dismissed, he drank bad schnapps at the officers' club and had a skinny blonde in the brothel perform an unnatural but enjoyable act on him. Afterwards, they talked a little, a luxury his men wouldn't enjoy. She spoke fair German, with a singsong Scandinavian intonation. "What will you do after the war?" he asked her.

"Change my name and move away," she said matter-of-factly. "What will *you* do?"

He started to answer, then realized he hadn't the faintest idea. He'd made no postwar plans. It was as if he didn't expect to be around to worry about it. And maybe he didn't. When you were a U-boat skipper, the odds weren't on your side.

Now Aristide Demange had a name for the prissy second lieutenant who'd been running this company after the late Captain Alexandre stopped a machine-gun burst with his belly and chest. The *con* was called Louis Mirouze. He practically exuded spit and polish.

Past making sure his men kept their weapons in good working order, Demange didn't care about spit and polish. He would have got rid of Mirouze in a heartbeat except for one thing: the youngster was recklessly brave. He took chances Demange thought suicidal, and hardly seemed to notice he was doing it. An officer like that had no trouble getting his men to follow him.

Things in southern Belgium being what they were, too often officers had to try to get men to follow them straight into the blast furnace. It wasn't as if the Germans didn't know they were there and didn't know they were coming. It wasn't as if the *Boches* hadn't had plenty of time to get ready for them, either.

One attack on a farm village that—surprise!—turned out to be much more strongly fortified than it looked thinned the company of men whose names Demange hadn't even learned. The doctors would learn some of those names as they tried to put the poor bastards back together. Others would be for the graves detail to find out.

After they drew back to their start line, Demange took Mirouze aside and said, "We would've been better off if you hadn't tried to push so hard there."

"I thought we could take the place," Mirouze answered. "We were ordered to, so we had to do our best."

Demange rolled his eyes. "Spare me! The jerks who give those orders don't know their assholes from their sisters. All that happened was, we took more casualties than we needed to 'cause you wouldn't see it was hopeless."

"If we could've got into that lane—" Mirouze started.

"*Merde!*" Demange cut him off. "That was no good, either. What do you want to bet they had a couple of MG-42s around the corner waiting to chop us into ground round? You get into trouble when you start sending the *poilus* out to die and they see they haven't got a chance in hell to carry out their mission."

He knew the hard way how true that was. In 1917, several French divisions had mutinied instead of making the big attack the clowns in the fancy kepis told them to put in. The government and the Army eventually got things under control again by mixing executions and concessions, but it was close. More importantly, they managed to keep the *Boches* from finding out about the mutiny. The Kaiser's bastards could have torn a hole in the line kilometers wide, but they never moved.

Louis Mirouze wasn't around yet in 1917. He might have learned about the mutinies in his training, but they were just school lessons to him. And who ever gave a damn about school lessons? Nobody, not since Cain sneaked away from Adam to play hooky. Abel stuck around for all the classes. No wonder Cain went and murdered him!

"We have to keep the pressure on the enemy," Mirouze insisted. "It keeps him from sending reinforcements against the Russians."

"Fuck the Russians. Let them take care of themselves. I'm worrying about us," Demange said. "Only reason Stalin's better than Hitler is, he's farther away."

"You are of course an expert on this, sir?" Mirouze asked with frigid politesse.

"Hell of a lot more than you are, kid," Demange said. "I was fucking *in* Russia with our expeditionary force. I've seen the place. The only reason more Russians don't go over to Hitler is, he jumps on 'em even harder'n Stalin does. Proves he's a damn fool in the end, you ask me. But plenty'd sooner see him than Uncle Joe any which way. Russia! Pah!" He spat out his cigarette butt with the disgusted exclamation and lit a new one.

"I . . . did not know you had served in the Soviet Union," Mirouze said slowly.

"All kinds of things you don't know, aren't there, buddy?" Demange growled. "And, like I said a little while ago, we do what we've got to do, sure, but you won't win the goddamn war all by your lonesome. This stinking company won't win the war all by its lonesome, either. So try to keep the guys alive, all right? They'll like you for it, and you won't need to worry about getting shot in the back 'by accident,' know what I mean?"

Louis Mirouze's expression said he knew only too well. Such things did happen—usually when you couldn't pin them on anybody. Then the youngster's eyes narrowed as he studied Demange. He had to know Demange had won a field promotion. Nobody his age who hadn't would be just a lieutenant. The French Army's tolerance for fuckups was enormous, but not limitless—not unless you were a general, anyway.

No doubt Mirouze was wondering whether Demange had shot an officer in the back "by accident" while he was a common soldier or a noncom. Demange hadn't, not personally, even if there were a good many officers whose untimely demises he'd mourned not a bit. But if the kid wanted to think he had, he didn't mind.

They got the order to go forward again a week later. This time, they had a couple of Somua S-42s with them. The latest French *char* was almost as good as a long-gunned Panzer IV. It had thicker, better-sloped armor than the German machine, but its cannon wasn't as powerful. Still, it did stand a decent chance against most of Fritz's panzers, and it was hell on infantry.

"On les aura!" Mirouze shouted as he trotted up with the *poilus.*
We'll get 'em! It had been Pétain's slogan at Verdun. You saw it on posters in the last war. Demange wondered how the puppy had heard of it.

The S-42s sprayed machine-gun fire at the German positions
ahead. One thing that made them pretty fair *chars* was that they'd stolen a leaf from the German book. They'd stopped asking the commander to make like a one-armed paperhanger with hives. Now the
turret held a gunner and a loader, too, so the commander didn't have
to try to do everything at once.

Then, quite suddenly, there was a noise like a bad accident in a
steel mill. One of the S-42s stopped running and started burning.
None of the crew got out. As Demange loped past, he saw a hole in the
glacis plate you could throw a dog through. A Panzer IV could kill an
S-42. He hadn't thought a Panzer IV could murder an S-42 like that.

A moment later, somebody yelled "Tiger!" and pointed behind
what was left of a barn. At a distance, you could mistake a Tiger for a
Panzer IV. More often, it worked the other way round—*poilus* thought
the medium was the heavy, and panicked because they did. There was
a family resemblance. But the big brother was a much rougher cus-
tomer than his smaller sibling.

And this *was* a Tiger. The surviving S-42 fired at it. The 75mm AP
round hit, too. Demange could see sparks fly where hardened steel
slammed into hardened steel. But the French *char's* shot didn't pene-
trate the Tiger's thick armor. The German machine's long, fearsome
gun swung to bear on its new target. It didn't traverse very fast—that
turret was heavy indeed—but the Tiger's 88 spoke before the S-42
could fire again.

One shot was all it took. With a Tiger, one shot was commonly all
it took. Flame blasted out of every hatch in the French *char*. An enormous smoke ring blew from the commander's cupola, as if the Devil
were in there smoking a fat Havana. Ammunition started cooking off
inside the steel carapace, with roars from the cannon shells and cheerful popping noises from the machine-gun cartridges. Again, no one
came out. The most Demange could hope for was that the poor *cons* in
there died before they hurt too much. He feared even that was a for-
lorn hope.

Then the Tiger started lobbing HE at the French foot soldiers. An 88mm shell was big enough to have a good-sized bursting charge and to throw plenty of knife-edged fragments.

"Down!" Demange yelled. "Dig in!" He yanked the entrenching tool off his belt and followed his own order. Yes, if they couldn't advance, they could at least try to survive.

Chapter 5

Getting pulled out of the line for a while felt wonderful to Theo Hossbach. As soon as you got beyond range of the Red Army's guns, the food improved. You didn't need to worry about waking up dead in the morning. Well, you didn't need to worry so much, anyhow. You wanted to keep a Schmeisser handy, in case of partisans.

Mechanics who weren't hampered by front-line tool shortages and frantic rush went over the Panzer IV from muzzle brake to exhaust pipe. Any time in the field was hard time for a panzer. This one would run a lot better for a while after it went back into combat. When you could count on your machine to do what you needed, you fought more boldly.

Some of the crew visited an army whorehouse. Theo stayed away. Shy among men, he was even more so with women. Adi Stoss didn't go, either. "I don't mind buying it, as long as the girl's there for the money," he said. "But when they use bayonets to drag 'em out of the village . . ." He shook his head. "That's not my idea of a good time."

"Nope. Not mine, either." Theo gave forth with a few words.

Instead of fornication, they had football. Some Polish troops were getting in a little rest and recuperation not far from the German en-campment. Among their supplies, they had goals and nets—they used football to keep fit. When they challenged the panzer crews to a match, national pride forbade turning them down.

Theo was a goalkeeper—fittingly, the loner on the pitch. And Adi was a center-forward: a striker. A pretty decent player himself, Theo knew Adi outclassed him . . . and almost everyone else. The Poles didn't know it yet. Well, they'd find out.

The pitch was the flattest stretch of nearby field they could find. German and Polish soldiers gathered by the touchlines to watch and to bet. A lot of the Poles spoke German (some of the Polish soldiers spoke Yiddish, one of the more interesting complications in a war full of them). To most of the *Wehrmacht* men, Polish was just as much mooing and barking as Russian was. Not to Theo, who came from Breslau, not far from the border. Lots of Poles lived and worked in Breslau. He would never be fluent in their language, but he under-stood bits and pieces of it.

He said no more about that than he did about anything else. What the Poles didn't know wouldn't help them.

The referee was a German. Both linesmen were Poles. With a little luck, their biases would offset each other. Without that luck, they might turn the spectators and gamblers into brawlers.

No one on either side or in the crowd expected the referee to call the match closely. Army football was a different beast from the game the professionals played on close-cropped grass. You bumped, you shoved, you elbowed, you got away with whatever you could. It wasn't quite rugby, but you could see rugby from there.

As soon as the match started, the Poles discovered that Adi was faster and more nimble than any of them. They started roughing him up to slow him down. That was how army football worked. Then one of the Poles staggered away from him with blood streaming from his nose.

"Sorry, buddy," Adi said. "Didn't mean to do that." If they elbowed him, he'd elbow them right back. If he claimed he didn't do it on pur-pose, well, that was how army football worked, too.

He scored a lovely goal a couple of minutes later—or he thought he did. But the linesman's flag was up, signaling offside. The goal didn't count. He thought he'd been onside when the ball was kicked. So did Theo, though he had to admit the linesman was closer and had a better viewing angle than he did.

Even without any one player who could match Adi, the Poles were good. They seemed to have played together more than their German foes. They ran plays: one guy knew where the other guy was going, and did his best to put the ball there. Their greenish khaki uniforms were always down close to the German goal.

A slick pass put the ball at the feet of a Pole in the penalty box. Theo ran toward him, spreading his arms. *Make yourself big* was a 'keeper's first commandment. It made the shot harder for the attacker.

"Far post!" another Pole yelled.

Guessing the guy with the ball would follow the advice, Theo flung himself to his left. The ball took a deflection off his hand and bounced wide of the post. The Poles got a corner kick, but not a goal.

"Gowno!" the shooter said loudly, the way a German would have said *Scheisse!* He sent Theo a suspicious stare. "Did you understand him?" he asked in Polish, as if that would have been cheating. Theo gave him a high-grade idiot stare. The man asked the same thing *auf Deutsch*. Theo looked just as blank. Shaking his head, the Pole jostled for position for the corner.

When Theo punched the ball away, another German booted it farther down the pitch. The Poles had brought up their backs in hopes of converting the corner; their defense was in momentary disarray. Adi Stoss got to the ball a split second ahead of a Pole. He faked right, went left, and squirted past him. The Pole tried to knock him down, but he jumped over the fellow's upraised leg.

The Polish 'keeper ran out to close down the angle. Adi softly chipped the ball over the luckless man's head. It bounced once in front of the goal, then rolled into the net.

Not even the Polish linesman down there could find any way to disallow the score. He looked as impressed as everybody else, in fact. The German soldiers watching the match whooped and cheered like maniacs. Even some of the Poles applauded. The goal was that pretty.

Two Polish forwards stood catching their breath in the German penalty area. "Not bad," one of them said to the other, "but let's see the fucker do it again." His friend nodded.

It was 2–2 at the half. One of the Poles' scores was an own goal—a cross bounced off a German defender's behind. It was past Theo and into the net before he could do anything about it.

After the break, they switched ends and went at it again. The Poles scored—that one went right through Theo's spraddled legs. He was mad, because he thought he should have stopped it. A few minutes later, the Germans leveled. Adi made a sweet pass into the area, and another German headed it home.

There things stuck. Theo made a good save. So did the Poles' goal-keeper, who jumped as if on springs to tip a rifle shot of Adi's just over the crossbar. Adi waved to him, paying his respects. The 'keeper sketched a salute in return. He'd seen what he was up against.

As they neared the final whistle, Theo grew just about sure the match would end in a draw. He wanted a win, but a draw wasn't so bad. Nobody's national pride would be damaged that way. He did wish he hadn't let in the last goal.

The Polish 'keeper must also have decided it was safe to relax a little. He took a couple of steps forward, away from the frame of the net. Why not? Safe as houses. The ball was out near the halfway line.

Theo could have told him nowhere on the pitch was safe when Adi was around. He could have, but he didn't need to. Adi showed the Pole instead. He launched a howitzer shot with his right foot, high and looping and dropping down straight toward the goal. The 'keeper staggered back, desperately throwing up his arms. He got the finger-tips of his right hand on the ball. Theo hadn't thought he could even do that. It wasn't enough. He couldn't flip the ball over the bar this time. It went in. Adi'd done it again, all right—in spades.

When the referee blew the whistle a couple of minutes later, the triumphant Germans carried him off the field on their shoulders. He was grinning like a fool and laughing like a lunatic. Part of that might have been triumph, too.

Part of it, Theo judged, was something else altogether. Had the *Wehrmacht* men knew more, they likely would have celebrated less.

Adi had more in common with some of the soldiers in Polish uniform than he did with them. Most of the Poles wouldn't have been happy about that, either. Theo cracked a smile. Not only had his side won, he shared a joke with only one other man out of the whole crowd.

Dr. Alvarez clucked like a laying hen. "You really should not leave hospital so soon," he insisted.

He'd been trained in England, all right; any American would have said *leave the hospital*. Chaim Weinberg noticed, but he didn't care. "Doc, you've said you're not gonna do any more carving on me, right?" he said.

"Yes," the hand surgeon answered with a reluctant nod. "But you have not done enough exercises to give you the full strength and dexterity possible in your hand."

"So I'll keep doing 'em once I get to the front," Chaim answered. "And I'll do other stuff with it, too. You gotta understand, Doc—I'm just sick to death of laying around here on my butt."

"Lying," Alvarez said.

"No, honest to God, it's the truth." Then Chaim realized what the doctor meant. He started to laugh. Wasn't it a hell of a note when a foreigner knew more about your language's grammar than you did? He went on, "I'll be okay—I really will. You can't tell me the Republic doesn't need another soldier who doesn't halfway know what he's doing, either. *¡Viva la República!*"

"*¡Viva!*" Dr. Alvarez echoed. He had to do that much. If he didn't, somebody was liable to report him as a Sanjurjo sympathizer. If his actual politics lay on the Nationalist side, Chaim no more wanted to know about it than Alvarez wanted him to find out.

One way the surgeon could have kept him in Madrid would have been not to give him any clothes. The filthy, bloody uniform in which he'd come here had long since been thrown away—or, more likely, burned to prevent contagion. But they fitted him with a pair of dungarees and a peasant's collarless cotton shirt. That would do to get him to the front. They'd issue him a new uniform there . . . or maybe they wouldn't, if they didn't happen to have one. If they didn't, he could wear this in the trenches till it got too ragged to stand. It wasn't as if he'd never been ragged before.

When he stuck his good hand in the pocket of the dungarees, he found a small roll of pesetas in there. He started to thank the surgeon, then clamped down on it. By the look in his eye, Alvarez wanted no thanks and would have denied putting the money in there. Some people were like that: they didn't care to admit, maybe even to themselves, that they could be nice.

A couple of the nurses kissed Chaim before he left. One of them was halfway cute, or more than halfway. Why couldn't they have been a little more friendly when all he could do was lay there—no, lie there—in bed like a sack of peas, dammit?

He was sweating before he'd walked even a block. Part of that was Madrid's fierce summer heat and the blazing sun overhead. And part of it was that he'd spent too goddamn long lying there like a sack of peas. He hadn't realized how far out of shape he'd got.

Madrid itself kept the hectic gaiety he'd always found here. Buildings without damage were scarce, glassed windows scarcer. Nationalist, Italian, and German bombers had pounded the Republican stronghold since the civil war started in 1936. Madrileños repaired, rebuilt, and carried on.

Chaim needed a little while to orient himself. He hadn't been at his best when they brought him to the hospital, which was putting things mildly. And the building, like most here, had boarded-up windows. So he hadn't known where he was. Now that he did . . .

Luckily, Party headquarters was only a few blocks away. The first person he saw when he walked in there was La Martellita. She was hurrying across the lobby with a fat folder of papers squeezed between her arm and her sweetly curved side. She saw him, too—with no great delight. "What?" she said. "They turned you loose?"

"Afraid so," he answered.

"And so you came over here to bother me?" She jumped to a natural conclusion.

But he shook his head with more dignity than he could usually muster. "Sorry, *querida,* but no. I came over here to ask where I could get a ride up to the Abraham Lincoln Brigade."

"Oh," La Martellita said in a different tone of voice. That was business. She told him what he needed to know. The bus depot wasn't far, either, for which he was glad. Then she asked, "And your hand—it's better?"

"It's good enough." He showed her he could bring thumb and forefinger together. He tried not to show her it still hurt. His pride was of a different sort from the Spaniards' flashy variety, which didn't mean he had none.

"It's still not pretty," she said.

He shrugged. "It'll never be pretty. *Así es la vida.* You, now, you're pretty."

Flattery got him nowhere. He hadn't expected it would. Hoped, sure, but not expected. "Go find your bus," she told him. "If you stay here very long, you won't find anything but trouble."

He blew her a kiss as he turned to go. "*Hasta la vista.* Say hello to my son for me."

She headed for the stairway without answering. He suspected Carlos Federico Weinberg wouldn't get the hello. Sighing, he walked out and trudged over to the depot.

Every last bus in the Republic would have been junked for spare parts in the States—except the ones old and strange enough to go straight into a museum. The ancient French ruin he boarded might have rushed troops from Paris to the Marne in the darkest days of 1914. It wouldn't have been fresh from the factory then, either.

It rattled. It farted. It stank of gasoline—something was leaking somewhere. At least half of what should have been teeth on the gears in its transmission were only memories. Its shocks weren't even memories, because Chaim didn't think it had ever had any.

But it still ran. The maniac behind the wheel drove with a cheerful disregard for life and limb: his own, his handful of passengers', and those of anyone else unfortunate enough to come anywhere near him.

Heading north and west was getting a picture of how the war had gone. The Nationalists came within a whisker of taking Madrid. They pushed into the northwestern suburbs, and onto the campus of the university. Little by little, the Republican forces had driven them back, till now the front lay well out of artillery range. As the bus clattered along, craters in the ground—sometimes craters in the road—got fresher and deeper. Less grass grew in them. The rusting hulks of burnt-out armored vehicles from both sides grew more modern and dangerous-looking.

After a while, brakes screeching, the bus shuddered to a stop. "The sector of the Internationals!" the driver shouted. He undid the wire around the handle that held the door closed. Chaim got out.

A lot of so-called Internationals nowadays were Spaniards. Casualties and time had thinned the foreign Marxists' ranks, and the bigger European war meant few new volunteers came here. But the ones who were left, Europeans and Americans, were uncommonly hard to kill.

"What do you need?" asked a man who spoke Spanish with some kind of guttural Central European accent.

Chaim held up his much-scarred, much-repaired left hand. "I'm just over a wound," he answered. If the other fellow had trouble with his crappy Spanish, he figured Yiddish would be the next thing to try. If you knew German, you could cope with it. "Where do I find the Abe Lincolns these days?"

The Central European followed him. The guy pointed up and to the left. "They're over there. So you're back for more fun, are you?"

"Fun? Oh, of course." Chaim flexed the fingers that still worked. "Any more fun and I'd be dead. Round that got me killed one of my friends."

"I'm sorry," the other man said. "We all have stories like that by now. Well, go on. *Buena suerte.*" Chaim nodded as he headed up toward the line. Good luck was as much as you could hope for, and more than you usually got.

A groundcrew sergeant regretfully spread his hands. Anastas Mouradian eyed the callused palms with the dirt ground into the ridges of leathery flesh. "I'm very sorry, Comrade Lieutenant, but the hydraulics on your bomber are totally shot to shit," the noncom said.

"How long will you need to fix things?" Mouradian demanded. "We'll be flying again tomorrow as long as the weather stays good."

Before answering, the groundcrew man used a strip torn from

Pravda and some *makhorka* he took out of a pouch on his belt to roll himself a cigarette. After he scraped a match on the sole of his boot and lit the smoke, he courteously offered Mouradian the makings. When the pilot shook his head, the mechanic blew out a stream of smoke and said, "We'll do the best we can. I don't know what else to tell you right now."

"*Khorosho,*" Stas replied, although it wasn't good or even close to good. The longer he served in the Red Air Force, the more time he spent among Russians, the better he understood why they'd raised profanity to an art form practiced by virtuosos. The reason was simple: they had to deal with other Russians practically all the time. And if dealing with Russians all the time didn't make you want to swear, nothing ever would.

He went back to the officers' tent and gave Isa Mogamedov the news. Armenians and Azeris had been rivals, usually enemies, since time out of mind. All the same, Stas understood his copilot in ways he would never understand a Russian. The two peoples had lived in—and picked—each other's pockets for so long, they'd rubbed off on each other.

Mogamedov's tiny shrug meant *Well, what can you hope for when Russians are working on something?* Aloud, the Azeri said, "Maybe someone will come down sick and we'll fly even if the plane can't go."

"You never can tell," Stas said. "We serve the Soviet Union."

"We serve the Soviet Union!" Mogamedov agreed loudly. You could never go far wrong saying that where plenty of other people heard you. He went on, "If we fly, we fly. If we don't, it's . . . that we don't, is all."

"Sure," Mouradian said. What had his crewmate almost come out with before changing course? *If we don't, it's God's will,* maybe? Something like that, Stas guessed. Something that sounded not only religious but Muslim. Something you *didn't* want to say where plenty of other people heard you, in other words.

Stas let his eyes very casually flick around the tent. He didn't think any of the Russians in here had noticed Mogamedov's tiny hesitation. Even if they had noticed it, chances were they would be too dim to understand what it likely meant. They were only Russians, after all. A lot of things men from the Caucasus took for granted sailed right over their heads.

When Stas' eyes came back to Mogamedov, he noticed that the Azeri was watching him. An instant later, Mogamedov wasn't any more, at least not in any noticeable way. But the copilot would know that he knew; Mouradian knew that much himself. And he knew Mogamedov would worry, knowing that he knew. You could drown in all the permutations of knowing and knowing-about-knowing and worrying-about-knowing-about-knowing and . . .

"*Nichevo,* Isa. *Nichevo,*" Stas said. There was a useful Russian word, a *Russian* Russian word. It meant *What can you do?* or *You can't do anything* or *It can't be helped.* Russians had put up with a lot over the years. Their language showed it.

He hoped Mogamedov also understood he didn't intend to do anything with what he thought he knew. A word whispered where it would find its way to an NKVD man's ear could land the Azeri in water hot enough to boil him. Stas didn't love Azeris. He didn't suppose he ever would. But Azeris were wonderful fellows when measured against informers.

Late that afternoon, the groundcrew sergeant hunted down Mouradian and said, "Comrade Lieutenant, the work crew has overhauled the hydraulics. Everything is good as new."

Which might mean they'd really done it. Or which might mean somebody'd told the sergeant that Pe-2 was going to fly no matter what. His broad, stubbly face betrayed nothing of what went on behind it. He was a Russian, all right.

"For sure, Comrade Sergeant?" Stas said. "*Yob tvoyu mat'?*" The all-purpose obscenity literally meant *Fuck your mother,* but, like any good curse, it stretched and twisted like a rubber band. Here, Mouradian had in mind something like *You're not shitting me?*

"*Yob tvoyu mat',* Comrade Lieutenant," the groundcrew man said firmly. *No shitting around. I really mean it.* Stas had to be content with that. He wouldn't get any stronger assurance if he dragged the noncom into court. Considering how strongly the Party put its thumb on the scales of justice, this was probably better than any testimony on oath.

When they did fly out at sunrise the next morning, the hydraulics retracted the landing gear. He didn't have to crank it up by hand. He had Fyodor Mechnikov check the bomb-bay doors. "Fuckers work like they're supposed to," the bombardier reported.

"He wasn't kidding," Stas said to Mogamedov, impressed in spite of himself. "They really did fix things."

"You hope. Don't jinx it," the copilot said. Stas nodded. That was good advice.

They flew on. Getting to the front took a while. Pretty soon, they'd have to move up to an airstrip farther west. The Nazis were falling back. They devastated the country from which they retreated. Not even Red Army men, notorious for foraging like wild animals, would find much to eat in this burnt-out terrain.

Somewhere not far ahead lay the border between the RSFSR and Byelorussia. Maybe the Germans and Poles would try to hold on to White Russia. Maybe they'd move back all the way to the Polish border. If they didn't do that of their own accord, the Soviet Union would have to kick them out.

German flak guns fired at the Pe-2s. Most of the shells burst behind them. The Russian bombers were faster than the men on the ground gave them credit for. Somewhere up ahead lay the target: a Hitlerite artillery concentration that had held up a Red Army advance in this sector for days.

We're artillery ourselves—flying artillery, Stas thought. The *Luftwaffe*'s Stukas had pioneered the idea. They dropped more explosives farther away than guns could reach, and softened up the opposition so the men on the ground could slice through it. Stavka had grabbed the notion with both hands. Now the Red Air Force and Red Army were using it against its inventors.

More German antiaircraft guns protected the 105s and 155s in their pits. The flak seemed thick enough to walk on now. Near misses buffeted Mouradian's Pe-2. He clung to the yoke as he tipped the plane nose-down for his attack run.

"Let 'em go!" Mogadmedov shouted to Mechnikov, and the bombs fell free. Stas zoomed back toward Soviet-held territory at just above barn-roof height. He watched one startled German soldier start to dive for a foxhole, but was gone before the Fritz made it in.

"You know," Mogamedov said after they got back to their own side of the front, "I think we are starting to gain on it."

Stas was beginning to think the same thing. Even so, he answered, "Weren't you the one who was talking about not jinxing it?" Mogamedov's oxygen mask didn't show much of his face, but the Azeri wagged a wry finger.

Now, Stas thought, *let's see if the landing gear works going down, too.* And damned if it didn't. He'd have to find that groundcrew sergeant a bottle of vodka or some good tobacco—not that crappy *makhorka,* which wasn't worth smoking if you had anything better.

They bounced once when they hit the airstrip. Riding the brakes, Mouradian brought the Pe-2 to a stop. He pulled off his flying helmet. Beside him, Isa Mogamedov followed suit. "Another one down," the Azeri said.

"We'll probably go out again tomorrow," Stas answered. He'd read Shakespeare only in Russian, which he figured put him level with the poet: it wasn't his language, and it wasn't the Englishman's, either. Even in translation, though, he remembered some tolling lines:

> *Tomorrow, and tomorrow, and tomorrow,*
> *Creeps in this petty pace from day to day,*
> *To the last syllable of recorded time;*
> *And all our yesterdays have lighted fools*
> *The way to dusty death.*

He remembered them, yes. He only wished he could forget them.

Ropes and sawhorses with boards across them kept civilians out of the square in front of Münster's cathedral. In a way, that annoyed Sarah Bruck. Now she had to take a long detour to get from the shops back to her house. Life was hard enough for Jews without any more added *tsuris.*

In another way . . . She'd called things when she hoped out loud that RAF bombs would land there. They'd damaged the cathedral. That was a shame because it was a handsome building that had stood for centuries. But they'd done worse to the SS men garrisoned in the square to hold the cathedral against Münster's Catholic community.

Those barricades weren't there just to keep people from falling and hurting themselves in bomb craters. They were there so civilians wouldn't see what had happened to the Nazis' *Übermenschen* and their tools of war.

The bodies were gone now. Sarah's father hadn't taken them away, but he'd been cleaning rubble in the square when the people who were in charge of such things came to do their jobs. His comment was, "I've seen bad things in bombed-out houses. I saw worse things in the trenches during the Kaiser's war. But I never saw anything that bad before."

Here and there, glancing in as she hurried past, Sarah could still make out bloodstains on stones and bricks. Once the blood soaked in, you had a devil of a time washing it out. You had to paint over it, and even then you could sometimes see it, like the ghost of death.

You could smell it, too. Sarah's nostrils twitched at that faint odor, like a pork roast that hadn't gone into the icebox. She didn't think she'd ever smelled death till the war started. She knew that stench much too well now.

Speaking of paint . . . Someone had daubed a graffito on a wall. *God's vengeance for Bishop von Galen,* it said. The letters ran into one another, and paint dripped down from them. The commentator must have sneaked out in the dead of night and written while he couldn't see what he was doing. He managed to get his message across even so.

If anyone had caught him doing it . . . Sarah didn't like to think what would have happened after that. The *Gestapo* had all kinds of ingenious tools for making people unhappy.

That people were already unhappy with the regime, she knew. That they were unhappy enough to keep showing their unhappiness was new. The authorities' response seemed to be that, if they killed enough unhappy people, and killed them publicly enough, the rest would either stop being unhappy or stop daring to show they were unhappy. The first struck Sarah as unlikely. The second? Maybe not.

She hurried away from the graffito. If a policeman or a blackshirt saw she was near it, he'd also see the yellow Stars of David on her clothes. He'd put two and two together and get five. But would he care? Not even a little bit, not when he'd nabbed a Jew.

She'd done better shopping than she often managed these days. She had a pretty good head of cabbage in her stringbag, along with some parsnips and rhubarb that cattle wouldn't have turned up their noses at. Considering what was usually in the shops, especially in the late-afternoon hours when the Nazis let Jews get what the Aryans hadn't bought, it was something of a triumph.

A tram rattled past. It was as sorry as everything else in civilian Münster these days. Its iron wheels were rusty. Rust streaked the fading paint on the side of the car, too. No one had touched it up since the fighting started, and that was a long time ago now. The whining electric motor sounded as if it would turn up its toes and die any day now. Of course, it had sounded that way for the past year and a half, so maybe it wouldn't.

She watched it go without trying to flag it down: one more thing that would land a Jew in hot water. Public transport was for Aryans only. Jews had to hoof it.

She wouldn't have got far with this one, anyhow. So she told herself, and not all in the attitude of the fox convinced the grapes had to be sour. The Aryans would be getting out three or four blocks ahead. A labor gang had filled in a big bomb crater in the middle of the street, but no one had laid replacement tracks yet.

Sarah wondered whether the new tracks would ever come. They were made of steel, after all, and steel went into panzers and U-boats and big guns and helmets and a host of other things soldiers and sailors and flyers needed. What soldiers and sailors and flyers needed, the *Reich* gave them.

Civilians in Münster? They were a different story. They would eat whatever the soldiers didn't want. If they needed to get off the tram, walk past the damaged stretch in the line, wait for another car, and board again, Party *Bonzen* didn't care. It was all part of the war effort, wasn't it? After Germany won, civilians wouldn't need to do things like that any more.

After Germany won. If Germany won.

Quietly, people were starting to wonder what would happen if

Germany lost. People a generation ahead of Sarah remembered what things had been like after the last war: the shortages, the humiliation, the crazy inflation that turned years of savings into pocket change. Everybody seemed convinced it would be worse this time around.

Sarah's mother seemed pleased at the vegetables she'd brought home. "They'll go fine with the barley cakes in the oven," she said.

"Yes, they will." Sarah worked hard to hide her lack of enthusiasm. Barley cakes were uninspiring. And even what claimed to be barley flour probably had peas and beans ground up in it. They were easier to disguise there than they would have been with wheat, since barley rose less on its own than the more costly grain did.

Samuel Goldman came home with a tin can whose label had come off. "I found it in the gutter," he said matter-of-factly. "It's not rusty. It's not dented. It's not bulging. Open it up and see what's in it. If it smells all right, we can try it." His mouth twisted. "Isn't life grand, when we get to be guinea pigs?"

"With our luck, it'll be beets, or maybe sauerkraut," Hanna Goldman said.

"Just the same, it'll be food we wouldn't have had otherwise," her husband replied. He smiled that lopsided smile again. "Always assuming we live through it, of course." Even talking about scavenged canned goods, he sounded like a professor.

"I'll get the can opener," Sarah said. Before she used it, she washed the can and inspected it herself. Father was right—it looked fine. She let out a little yip even before she got the lid all the way off. "Chicken!" she exclaimed, as overjoyed as Lancelot might have been when he first beheld the Holy Grail.

Father picked up the can and sniffed it. He smiled and nodded. "Smells great," he said. Sarah nodded, too—it did. Father handed Mother the can. "Why don't you cook it on the stove?" he told her. "That will help kill anything bad that may be in there."

"I'll do it," Mother answered, and reached for a frying pan.

"In America, I hear, they even put meat for dogs and cats in cans," Father said. That was something to think about in a country where people were starting to eat dogs and cats. He went on, "If this were dog food, I think I'd eat it anyway. If I barked afterwards, I'd bark on a full stomach."

"If you think I'll argue with you, you're barking up the wrong tree," Sarah said. Her father looked suitably pained.

The canned chicken tasted as good as it looked. Sarah went to bed happy. The RAF didn't come over Münster. She didn't wake up puking. It was a fine day.

Chapter 6

Alistair Walsh eyed the new piece of military hardware with a veteran's suspicion. "What in God's name is that?" he asked.

"Somefin' from the Yanks." Jack Scholes brandished what looked more like a stovepipe than anything else Walsh could think of offhand. It was made of cheap sheet metal and painted the dark green the Americans called olive drab—they painted the trucks they sent across the Atlantic the same color. Scholes went on, "They call it a bazooka. Suppose to beat the PIAT all 'ollow."

"Huh," Walsh said thoughtfully. That would be good—that would be wonderful, in fact—if it turned out to be true. The PIAT (short for Projector, Infantry, Anti-Tank) was the Tommy's personal antitank weapon. A powerful spring sent a shaped-charge bomb flying at enemy armor.

You could kill a tank with a PIAT. You could if you were brave and lucky and very close to the damn thing, at any rate. Otherwise, your chances of killing yourself were much better. People had done the job with it. But you could also rupture yourself cocking the miserable beast—that was a *powerful* spring. And the PIAT was almost impossible to cock lying down. You looked like a monkey humping a football when you tried. It was easiest (not easy, never easy, but easier) standing up. Of course, standing up gave Fritz a clear shot at you most of the time.

No wonder the PIAT wasn't popular.

"What do you shoot through this bloody thing?" Walsh inquired. "Spit wads?"

"Gordo's comin' up wiv a sack o' the bombs," Scholes answered.

"Why am I not surprised?" Walsh said. Gordon McAllister was a hulking Scotsman. He wasn't long on brains, but by God he was strong. People called him the Donkey, but not where he could hear them— not more than once, anyhow. When he spoke, which was seldom, he had a thick burr. It was hard to believe his accent, Walsh's buzzing Welsh consonants and odd vowels (at least to an Englishman's ears), and Scholes' glottal Cockney all belonged to the same language.

McAllister came up a couple of minutes later, with a large canvas sack, also olive drab, slung over his shoulder. It clanked when he set it down. Scholes reached inside and displayed the round that went through a bazooka. "'Ere you go, Staff."

Walsh whistled softly. A PIAT bomb looked like the makeshift it was. This thing . . . "Like something out of a Flash Gordon movie, isn't it? Except for the paint job, I mean." Like seemingly everything else that had anything to do with the American military, the round was painted olive drab.

"You're a smart one, you are. It does at that, don't it?" Scholes sent him an admiring glance. He went on, "You load it into the tube 'ere. There's a battery, like, connected to the trigger, an' it fires orf the rocket motor." He chuckled. "They say you don't want to be be'ind it when it goes—not 'arf you don't."

"I daresay. If there's a rocket in that thing, it'll fry your bacon for fair," Walsh said. "How far will it shoot?"

"Couple 'underd yards for tanks, they tol' us," Scholes replied. "Farther'n that for 'ousebreakin'."

"Right." Walsh nodded. You could hit a house or a bunker out past three hundred yards with a PIAT, and you'd hurt it when you did. A tank? You might nail one at a hundred yards. Twenty-five or thirty made your odds better—if you didn't buy your plot trying to sneak in so close.

"I want to go 'untin', I do," Scholes said. "Bag me a Tiger. Bleedin' shyme I can't take the 'ide 'ome an' 'ang it on me wall."

"Mind the claws," Gordon McAllister rumbled. Like a lot of what he did say, that seemed very much to the point.

"Will it get through a Tiger's armor?" Walsh asked with interest. A PIAT wouldn't pierce the monster German tank from the front. Neither would anything else in the English or French armory. Too many brave tank crews and antitank gunners had found that out the hard way.

"It's supposed to." Jack Scholes didn't sound entirely convinced, either. Walsh couldn't blame him. No one who'd seen a Tiger in action had an easy time believing anything could stop it.

"So you and Gordo are trained up on this beast, are you?" the staff sergeant asked.

McAllister's long-jawed head bobbed up and down. "It's dead easy," Scholes said. "Gordo shoves the round in till it clicks, like. 'E stands so I don't singe 'is whiskers when I shoot. I fire it off. Then I duck, on account of the Fritzes'll shoot at where I was."

"Think so, do you?" Walsh's tone was dry. If that thing with fins was a rocket, it would leave the tube trailing fire. Yes, something like that might draw a German's interest. But something that let a foot soldier take out a tank from a couple of hundred yards away would draw any Tommy's interest, and never mind the chances he took using it.

Walsh wondered whether the Germans already knew about the new tank-buster from America. Maybe some other English or French units had used them. Or maybe some of the Belgians had blabbed. This part of Belgium was full of French-speaking Walloons. Some of them liked the Nazis even if they did speak French, dammit.

Two mornings later, they were ordered forward for a reconnaissance in force against the German positions. Scholes carried the bazooka. McAllister lugged the sack of rounds. Walsh wondered what would happen if a rifle bullet hit one of those rockets. He didn't wonder long. They'd bury Gordo in the proverbial jam tin, that was what.

An MG-42 started buzzing away ahead of them. The Tommies hit the dirt. That horrible thing spat out so many bullets, one of them was bound to punch your ticket if you stayed on your feet. Walsh peered through bushes. There it was, muzzle flashes winking malevolently. Sure as hell, it sat in a concrete emplacement, safe against anything but a direct hit from an artillery shell. Or . . . a bazooka round?

"See the bugger, Jack?" Walsh called, not lifting his head far from the dirt. "Can you hit it from where you're at?"

"I'll give it a go," Scholes answered. Then he said something Walsh couldn't make out, probably to Gordo.

There was a roaring *whoosh!* and, yes, a blast of fire. The forward end of the tube had a screen of wire mesh sticking out around it to keep the rocket motor from roasting the man who launched it. A moment later, the round slammed into the machine-gun nest. There was another blast then, a bigger one. The MG-42 abruptly fell silent.

"Cor!" Scholes said. "Bastard really works, don't it?"

"It'll give Fritz something to think about, all right," Walsh agreed.

What the Germans thought soon became plain enough. They thought they needed to eliminate anybody who carried something that could smash up a hardened machine-gun position. In their jackboots, Walsh would have thought the same thing. They didn't seem to have any more machine guns close by, but they raked the ground with fire from rifles and Schmeissers.

Then another machine gun did speak up: one mounted in the turret of a Panzer IV. A moment later, the tank's bow gun started shooting, too. This time, Walsh didn't shout for Scholes. If the kid from the East End of London couldn't figure out what needed doing . . . he had to be hurt or dead. In which case, Gordon McAllister would take hold of the bazooka . . . unless he was hurt or dead, too.

Before Walsh could worry about what he'd do in that case, the bazooka belched fire and went *whoosh!* again. The rocket flew from it and slammed into the Panzer IV's turret. A fraction of a second later, the German tank brewed up as spectacularly as any Walsh had ever seen. He would have shot the tankmen in their black coveralls had any of them made it out through a hatch, but none did.

The burning tank set the bushes by it on fire, too. The blaze flushed a few more Fritzes out of their holes. Walsh cheerfully banged away at them with his Sten gun. It was long range for a machine pistol, but he didn't care. Hitler's lads had something brand new to give them night-mares when they curled up under their blankets. And wasn't *that* nice?

Arno Baatz paused at the western edge of a field of growing grain. He thought the grain was barley, not wheat, but he wasn't sure—he was a city man. He was sure it was a damn sorry field of whatever the hell it was. It had been badly tended ever since it was planted, and not long before this panzers and halftracks had run through it and knocked half of it flat. Crows pecked at the unripe heads of grain the armored fighting vehicles had threshed.

He cared about that no more than he cared about whether it was wheat or barley. He stuck his thumb in his mouth and thrust it up over his head to gauge the wind. Adam Pfaff laughed at him. "Since when did you turn Red Indian?" Pfaff asked.

"Oh, shut up," Baatz said. "Shut up unless you know a better way to tell which direction it's from, I mean." He waited. Pfaff kept quiet, so Arno assumed he didn't know any better way. As a matter of fact, he'd already assumed that. He nodded importantly. "It's coming out of the west. That's what we need."

"*Jawohl,*" Pfaff muttered, perhaps sarcastically, perhaps not.

Baatz didn't gig him the way he would have most of the time; the *Unteroffizier* had other things on his mind. Puffing out his chest, he called to the troops of his squad, who stood with him, lined up along the edge of the grainfield: "Get your torches ready, men!"

"It's not motherfucking close-order drill," Pfaff said. Baatz ignored him again; he was treating it as if it were. And the *Obergefreiter* had his torch—a stick with a lump of tallow and straw at one end—ready along with everybody else.

"Light your torches!" Arno Baatz commanded. He loved giving or-ders. He started his torch with a flint-and-steel lighter. Some of the *Landsers* had ones like it. Others used matches to get theirs burning. Baatz bellowed again: "Swing your torches over your heads!"

They did, all of them counterclockwise. The flames in the tallow swelled; black smoke trailed the circling torches. It would have been pretty on a practice field. But this wasn't practice. This was war.

"Throw your torches!" Baatz yelled. The soldiers obeyed, as if they were flinging potato-masher grenades. They didn't get that kind of distance with the torches, but they didn't need to.

Down fell the flaming lumps of tallow and straw, in amongst the growing grain—and, better yet, in amongst the dying, yellowing strips of grain the armored vehicles' tracks had crushed. Each torch started a little fire. The fires grew and spread through the field, pushed on by the wind Baatz had successfully identified. Smoke climbed into the sky. The crows flew away, screeching with fear.

"Well, all right! The Reds won't march through that any time soon," Baatz said, inflating his chest again. "And when they do try it, we can put a machine gun in those woods over there and shoot them down like the mad hounds they are." He pointed to the trees that overlooked the burning field.

Then he scowled at *Obergefreiter* Pfaff, waiting for him to come out with some crack along the lines of *When are you getting your field marshal's baton?* He would have jumped all over Pfaff for that. Talk of a field marshal's baton was all the more galling to a man who couldn't even get promoted to *Feldwebel*. But the senior private just said, "The Ivans won't be able to eat that grain, either."

The grain wasn't that close to ripeness. Baatz grunted and nodded even so. The Russians would eat it anyway if they happened to be hungry. They ate bugs and slugs and newts and mushrooms and ferns and anything else they could get their hands on. The Red Army didn't give its men any more in the way of rations than it could help. Munitions, yes. Food? The Ivans were on their own for that. They foraged like wild animals. The resemblance didn't always end there, either.

So, scorched earth. If the *Wehrmacht* had to fall back, the Russians wouldn't be able to do much with the land they advanced through. It made perfect military sense to Baatz. It might not have if the Red Army were retreating through Germany and burning and wrecking as it did, but that never once crossed his mind. The Red Army in the *Vaterland*? Unimaginable!

"Come on, boys," he said, his sense of self-importance restored. "We've got another ten kilometers to go before we make it to our rest line."

Predictably, the men groaned. They didn't like wearing out their boots marching. Baatz didn't like it himself; he was a heavyset fellow. But he had his orders. Give him orders and he'd carry them out. He'd make sure everybody to whom he gave orders carried them out, too.

Slyly, Adam Pfaff said, "If we fall back ten kilometers every day, how many days till we're retreating through Berlin? It's like a problem in a math book, isn't it?"

"It's no such thing!" Baatz sounded furious, and he was. "We're just shortening our front and getting into more defensible positions. That's the only thing we're doing—the *only* thing, you hear me?"

He hoped Pfaff would argue with him. *Miserable barracks lawyer,* Baatz thought. But arguing here would come within millimeters of defeatism, and defeatism was a capital crime.

Instead of arguing, Pfaff just kept marching along. He left Baatz's words hanging in the air, all by themselves. Somehow, that worked better than any fancy hairsplitting might have.

When they got back to the rest line, they found themselves only a couple of hundred meters from a field kitchen. "Goulash cannon!" Pfaff said happily. There, Baatz wasn't inclined to quarrel. Seeing the pipe sticking up from the wheeled cart with the stove and boiler made him happy, too. He wouldn't have to fill his belly with hard crackers smeared with butter from a tinfoil tube or dried fruit or any of the other delicacies he carried on his person.

He brought his mess tin over to the field kitchen. The boiler was full of stew, with turnips and carrots and onions and chicken and duck and whatever else the cooks could scrounge, all done together . . . done and done and done, till the chicken tasted like onions and the carrots tasted like duck and everything tasted like everything else. It wasn't anything he would have made for himself or ordered in an eatery. It was wonderful all the same. When you'd been marching all day, anything that plugged up the hole in your belly was wonderful.

Adam Pfaff cleaned out his mess kit after making what was in it disappear. When he came back from the nearby creek, he stretched out on the ground at full length and lit a cigarette. Blowing a long stream of smoke up into the sky, he said, "I got a pretty decent supper in me. Nobody's trying to kill me right this minute. Life's not so bad, you know?"

"No, not so bad," Baatz said. "Now if they'd set up a brothel anywhere around here . . ."

"That'd be nice," Pfaff agreed. "But I'll tell you—if they let me sleep till noon tomorrow, I'd like that just about as much. I've got to be a year and a half behind on shuteye since they conscripted me." He yawned till something in his jaw cracked like a knuckle.

When you watched someone else yawn, you wanted to yawn yourself. Baatz yielded to temptation before he even thought he might fight it. Then he wagged a finger at Pfaff. "You rotten pigdog, you! Now you've gone and reminded me how tired I am, too. Noon? I could curl up in a cave somewhere and sleep till spring like a bear."

"Wouldn't that be great?" Pfaff said.

They both woke before sunup. The Russians were shelling the snot out of the German line somewhere not far enough north of where they were. Ivan hadn't tried a summer advance before this year, but he had his tail up now. Baatz and Pfaff and the rest of the *Landsers* filled their mess tins from the goulash cannon one more time and emptied them as fast as they could. Then they started tramping west again. Pfaff said nothing more of math problems. Arno Baatz thought about them anyhow.

The Japanese Navy had flown more G4Ms in to Midway. They replaced the bombers destroyed by American air raids. Revetments protected a plane against blast and fragments. Nothing protected it when a bomb burst right on top of it. All you could do was get rid of the wreckage so you could use the revetment again.

Hideki Fujita didn't like seeing what a bomb could do to an airplane. It made him think about what an antiaircraft shell could do, or a burst of heavy machine-gun bullets from an American fighter.

He didn't want to think about such things, but he didn't have much choice. If more G4Ms had come here, they'd come to be used. Before long, the Japanese would likely be dropping more germ weapons over

Oahu. That meant he would have to climb into one of those bombers and do some of the dropping. He'd chosen such things when he volunteered to come to Midway.

G4Ms had enormous range. They could fly from here to Oahu and back. As far as bombers went, they were fast. That was the good news. The bad news was, they were nowhere near so fast as the latest fighters. And, to get that great range, they were as light as possible, which meant they were flimsy. They caught fire easily, too. If you got intercepted, if you got hit, you would die. It was about that simple.

Fujita marveled that no bomb had smashed the bacteriological-warfare unit's little tent compound. That was luck, nothing else but. Some *kami* watched over rats and fleas and test tubes and the men who tended them.

Whether it was a good *kami* or one of the other kind, he wasn't so sure any more. A few days later, sweating like a pig in his flying togs' fur and leather, he climbed into a G4M's bomb bay and hooked himself to the oxygen line. The engines thundered to life. The plane bounced down the poorly repaired runway and lumbered up into the air.

Off to the west, in the direction of the Home Islands, the sun sank toward the Pacific. It soon set. The G4M droned on through the darkness. America and Japan raided each other's bases at night. The quarter moon spread sparkles of light across the blue-black water.

Tonight, the pilot flew south of the usual course. American carriers sometimes lurked partway up the chain of islets that led from Midway to the main Hawaiian islands. Their fighters would come up at night, hunting for bombers. Every once in a while, they'd catch one. But what they couldn't find, they couldn't catch.

Fujita shivered. Now that he was at altitude, he was glad for the gear in which he'd sweltered on the ground. Even in these subtropical latitudes, it was frigid up here at six or seven thousand meters. He wished he had more clothes, thicker clothes, to put on.

The pilot's and copilot's voices came faintly back to him through the speaking tube. They had nothing to say to him yet; they chatted with each other about how the plane was doing. As far as he could tell, it was doing fine. Listening to them gave him something to do while he sat there shivering in the dark. He hoped they had their navigating in good order.

They must have been about halfway to Oahu when the two men in the cockpit suddenly exclaimed together. The moon had shown them a string of bombers flying north and west. As they were going to hit Honolulu, so the Americans were taking a fresh whack at Midway.

"*Zakennayo!*" Fujita muttered. If the Yankees cratered the runways again, landing would be an adventure. He couldn't do anything about that but worry. Worry he did.

He also hoped the American pilots hadn't noticed the G4Ms, the way the Japanese pilots had seen their planes. If this raid was like the others, the Americans would have far more bombers in the sky *to* notice.

If the Americans had seen them, they would radio the news back to Honolulu. Then the night sky would light up with even more fireworks than usual when the Japanese flyers came overhead. Fujita hoped the moon was down by the time they arrived. They'd be harder to see then. It would be close. Moonset should be somewhere near midnight, which was also about when they were supposed to reach Oahu.

Nothing to do but wait and brood. Every so often, Fujita would check the luminous dial on his watch. He kept thinking forty-five minutes or an hour had gone by since the last time he'd looked at its radium-painted hands. He kept finding out it was only ten or fifteen minutes.

At last, when he was sure he'd spent a week in the air and the plane would either fly on forever or run out of gas and crash into the Pacific, the pilot's voice came metallically through the speaking tube: "Be ready, Bombardier! We are nearing the target."

"*Hai!*" Fujita couldn't help adding, "Good to hear it, sir."

No response to that. A few minutes later, though, the pilot said, "Open the bomb-bay doors."

"*Hai!*" Fujita repeated. He cranked them open. The moon wasn't quite down. He could see ocean far below, and then dark land. Freezing wind tore at him. The American blackout got better every time he flew over Honolulu. If he wasn't wrong, they were coming up from the south. Raiding from that unexpected direction might keep the Americans from realizing they were there till they'd dropped their bombs and headed back toward Midway.

Or, of course, it might not. In fact, the thought had hardly passed through Fujita's mind before lights winked on, all those thousands of meters down below. Some of those were the muzzle flashes of antiaircraft guns. Others were searchlight beams stabbing up to pin the Japanese planes on their bilious blue beams so the gunners could see what they were shooting at.

The G4M started jinking violently, going faster and slower, higher and lower, left and right to confuse the gunners. Gulping, Fujita feared his stomach was a few jinks behind the plane. Then he gulped again, for a different reason. Not far enough away, the antiaircraft shells began to burst. Fire and smoke lay at the heart of each explosion. Fragments flew much farther. And the blast from the bursts threw the bomber around, too.

"Bombs away!" the pilot shouted. "Let them fall!"

"Bombs away!" Fujita echoed. He yanked hard on the levers that released the pottery bomb casings full of fever and death. At least one of the G4Ms flying with his had ordinary explosives aboard. He saw the bombs burst down there as he closed the bomb-bay doors to make the plane more aerodynamic. The faster they got out of there, the better their chance of making it back to Midway.

By the way the pilot gunned the bomber's motors, he didn't want to hang around here, either. All the Japanese in the Midway garrison said the flat little island was a hellhole. Fujita had said so himself. When the other choice was getting shot down, though, the hellhole seemed heavenly by comparison.

Near misses shook the G4M for another long couple of minutes. One fragment tore a hole in the plane's thin aluminum skin a meter behind Fujita. Had it hit him, it would have gutted him like a salmon. The wind screamed through the hole. No fluid leaked out of it, though, and no torn cables writhed in that wind. The bomber kept flying.

Fujita stayed nervous till the cockpit crew's chatter told him the plane had got past Kauai on the way back to Midway. That meant American fighters were unlikely to come after them. They would probably make it back . . . and find out what the U.S. bombers had done to their base.

Or they would unless they met the returning American bombers head-on. The Yankee planes bristled with machine guns. The G4M might be able to outrun them, but it would never win an air-to-air gunfight.

The sun was just rising when the bomber jounced to a stop on the runway. The pilot came in slow, just above stalling speed, and braked so hard Fujita could smell burning rubber from the tires. He stopped as short as he could, so the plane had the smallest chance of going into a crater and flipping over. Fujita scrambled out onto the tarmac. He was at sea level again, and sweating hard again, too. He didn't care. He'd made it one more time.

Benjamin Halévy stuck a cigarette in his mouth and lit it. He offered Vaclav Jezek the pack. Vaclav took one. "Thanks, Lieutenant," he said.

"Up yours, Sergeant," Halévy replied. They grinned at each other.

Before the war, Vaclav hadn't had much use for Jews. But the Jewish conscripts in the Czechoslovakian army had hung in and fought the Nazis along with the Czechs, while Poles and Ruthenians and especially Slovaks either just gave up or went over to the enemy. Jews had even better reasons than Czechs for hating Hitler and his minions, and that wasn't easy.

Halévy wasn't, or wasn't exactly, a Czech Jew. His parents had gone from Prague to Paris after the last war. He'd been a French sergeant and, because he spoke both French and Czech, a liaison between his own armed forces and those of the Czechoslovakian government-in-exile. When France made its temporary truce with Hitler, he'd accompanied the Czech soldiers into exile in Republican Spain. He couldn't stomach fighting on the German side.

He was a lieutenant here for the same reason Jezek was a sergeant. The Spaniards had an inferiority complex about their own fighting skills. They automatically promoted foreigners one grade. A lot of Vaclav's pay still came in promises, but they were bigger promises than they would have been otherwise.

After blowing out smoke, Vaclav asked, "Do Sanjurjo's bastards promote the Germans and Italians on their side, too?"

"I know they do with the Germans," Halévy said. "I'm not so sure they bother with Mussolini's boys. I mean, would *you* promote an Italian?"

"Not unless I wanted him to cook noodles for me," Vaclav answered, and they both laughed. The German *Legion Kondor* had good men, picked men, in it. There were more Italians in Spain, but they were mostly conscripts who didn't want to be here, and fought like it.

Vaclav's canteen was full of harsh red wine. He swigged from it. He had a better chance of steering clear of the trots with wine than with water. And the trots were something nobody in the trenches needed, much less someone who spent a lot of his time quietly waiting in no-man's-land. Hard to wait quietly when you had to yank down your trousers and squat.

He hadn't gone out this morning. He couldn't have said why. He hadn't felt lucky when he woke up before sunrise—that was as close as he could come. No one in the little Czech force gave him any trouble about it. They'd all served together for a long, long time. They knew he wasn't malingering. He'd done plenty to Sanjurjo's Nationalists, and chances were he would again. Only not today.

Not today. Tomorrow. *Mañana.* That was one of the Spanish words Vaclav did know. You couldn't be in Spain long without learning it. When he said it, he commonly meant *tomorrow.* A Spaniard who said it might mean *tomorrow,* too. Or he might mean *in a few days—I don't quite know when.* Or he might mean *go away and quit bothering me.* It all depended on how he said it.

Czechs had spent a lot of centuries living next door to Germans. Attitudes rubbed off, even if no one intended that they should. When a Czech said *in an hour,* that was what he meant. When he said *tomorrow,* he meant that, too. Discovering how abstract and theoretical time could be in Spain came as a painful surprise.

It cost lives, too. If an artillery barrage came in two hours late—and such things happened all the time here—foot soldiers who should have attacked a softened-up position advanced against one with the defenders ready and waiting. They usually paid the price for it, too.

In the Czech army, as in the *Wehrmacht*, an artillery officer whose guns didn't fire when they were supposed to would get it in the neck. He'd wind up a corporal, one posted where the fighting was hottest. Among the Spaniards, Republicans and Nationalists alike, people just shrugged. Such things were sad, absolutely, but what could you do?

Maybe the weather had something to do with it. Jezek drank more wine. "Christ, it's hot!" he said. You never saw weather like this in Central Europe. This would kill you if you gave it half a chance. Here in Spain, sunstroke wasn't just a word.

"It is," Halévy agreed. He'd turned brown as an Arab, brown as old leather, under the harsh Spanish sun. Like most Czechs, Vaclav was much fairer than the Jew. He'd burned and peeled, burned and peeled, over and over again, till he finally started to tan. He knew he wouldn't tan like Halévy if he stayed here another fifty years.

Before he could say anything else, the Nationalists' artillery woke up. That didn't happen every day any more—nowhere close. Marshal Sanjurjo got most of his tubes from Germany and Italy. Since France backed away from her deal with Hitler, the marshal hadn't been able to get many any more. The ones he had were old and worn. They'd lost a lot of accuracy. Spanish-made shells (on both sides of the line) were much too likely to be duds.

Artillery could still kill you, though. Jezek grabbed his antitank rifle and folded himself up into a ball in the bottom of the trench. Any pillbug that happened to see him would have been impressed. But his bet was that any pillbugs down here were folding themselves into balls, too.

He opened his eyes for a second. Beside him, Benjamin Halévy was also doing his best to occupy as little space as he could. Not all the Nationalists' shells were duds, dammit. Some of them burst with thunderous roars near the Czechs' trench line. Dirt fountained up into the air. Clods fell down and thumped Vaclav. He flinched every time one did, afraid it would be a speeding, whining fragment and not a harmless lump of earth.

While he lay there, his hands were busy under him. He stuck a five-round box into the slot on his elephant gun and worked the bolt to chamber the first cartridge. He'd left the monster rifle unloaded. He hadn't thought he would need to do any shooting from the trench. But if Sanjurjo's men were shelling like this, what was it but the prelude to an infantry attack?

Halévy had to be thinking the same thing. As soon as the artillery barrage eased off, he bounced to his feet, yelling, "Up! Up, dammit! They'll be coming after us any second now!"

Vaclav scrambled onto the firing step. Grunting, he heaved up the heavy antitank rifle and rested the bipod on the dirt of the parapet. Sure as hell, soldiers in German-looking helmets and pale yellowish khaki were swarming out of the Nationalists' trenches and foxholes like angry ants.

He didn't worry about picking off officers now. He pulled the trigger as soon as he got one of Sanjurjo's men in his crosshairs. When you hit some poor bastard dead center with a round intended to pierce two or three centimeters of hardened steel, you almost tore him in half. The luckless Spaniard's midsection exploded into red mist. He didn't crumple; he toppled.

The thumb-sized cartridge case clinked off the top of Vaclav's boot after he worked the bolt again. He killed another Nationalist a few seconds later. This one did a graceful pirouette into a shell hole. He wouldn't come out again, either, not with most of his head blown off.

Ordinary rifles were banging away from the Czech line, too, along with a couple of machine guns. When Republican artillery woke up and started giving no-man's-land a once-over, the Nationalists decided they wouldn't be breaking through to Madrid today after all. Some hunkered down in whatever cover they could find while others scurried back to their start line. Even Fascist Spaniards were recklessly brave, but war was a Darwinian business. The longer it went on, the more pragmatists survived.

Somebody not far away was wailing for his mother in Czech. Vaclav and Halévy shared pained looks. That sounded bad, and the poor guy wouldn't be the only Czech hurt or killed, either. The government-in-exile's army had been a regiment when it got to Spain. It was a lot smaller than that now, and kept shrinking all the time.

Chapter 7

Bend your knees. Roll when you hit. Don't let the canopy blow you all over the place. The first time Pete McGill jumped out of a C-47, he had to think about all that stuff. No more.

This was his seventh jump now. He knew what it was like to step out of a plane and come to earth under a king-sized umbrella. Somebody'd told him that was just what the Germans called them, that their word for *paratrooper* literally meant *umbrella rifleman*.

He'd discovered he enjoyed floating down out of the sky. It was as close to flying as you could come without strapping on an airplane. And you were out in the air yourself with a parachute, not inside a machine that smelled of gasoline and lubricating oil.

He was only a couple of hundred feet off the ground and bracing himself for the landing when a little bird fluttered past him. Maybe he was imagining things, but he thought he saw surprise in its beady black eyes. What was a human doing up here in bird country?

"Oof!" he said when he landed. He bent his knees. He rolled. He wrestled the canopy into submission and detached himself from it.

Then he lit a cigarette while he waited for a jeep to come by and pick him up.

The C-47 from which he'd parachuted was droning off toward the horizon. When he went in for real, the transport would fly in lower, so the men inside wouldn't have so far to drop . . . and so the Japs on the ground wouldn't have long to shoot at them while they hung in the air like ripe fruit dangling from a tree.

Here came the jeep, with a couple of leathernecks already in it. Pete stuck out his thumb, as if he were hitching a ride. When the jeep stopped so he could get in, the driver asked, "Where to, Mac?"

"Take me to the nearest saloon," McGill answered. "If it's next door to a cathouse, that's better."

Everybody laughed. One of the other guys who'd gone out of the C-47 said, "That sounds good to me, too. Let's go do it."

"Fuckin' comedians, that's what you are," the driver said.

"I want to be a fuckin' comedian. That's how come I asked for a bar with a cathouse next to it," Pete said.

"Funny. Funny like a truss," the driver said, shaking his head. "Yeah, you'll be on the radio next week, tellin' dumb jokes for fuckin' Palmolive soap."

He took them back to Schofield Barracks, as Pete had known he would. No fleshpots there. The Marines climbed aboard a bus that hauled them back to Ewa, the base west of Pearl Harbor. Before they got there, though, a roadblock manned by MPs stopped them.

"The fuck is going on?" the bus driver, a Marine himself, bawled out of the window. "What are you guys doing here?"

"Ewa's under quarantine," one of the MPs answered. In case the driver didn't know what that meant, he amplified it: "Nobody in, nobody out."

"You nuts? What for?" the driver said.

"On account of a couple of guys down there are down sick with cholera, that's what for," the MP said. "I hear one of 'em's dead, but I don't know that for sure. They don't want it getting loose all over the place."

"Fuck me," Pete said to the leatherneck sitting across the aisle from him. "Didn't we get shots for that shit?"

"I think so," the other Marine answered. "We got so many shots, both my arms swole up like poisoned pups and my ass was too sore to sit down on it for two days. I ain't had an ass like that since my old man used to lick me before I joined the Corps. They say the training is rough, but, man, it was a walk in the park after my pa, I tell you."

"I know what you mean," Pete said. His father hadn't walloped him that hard, but he hadn't had an easy time growing up, either. He didn't know many Marines who had. Most guys who joined the Corps were tough to begin with, and boot camp only made them tougher.

Meanwhile, the bus driver was saying, "Well, what am I supposed to do with these guys now?"

"Take 'em to Pearl," the MP told him. "They'll find somewhere to stash 'em till things at Ewa get straightened away."

"Goddamn pain in the ass," the driver grumbled.

"Don't blame me, buddy," the MP said. "Blame the stinkin' slanties. They're the ones keep dropping that poison shit on Hawaii."

"It's a crock of crap, is what it is," the driver said. "How many bombers fly outa here two, three times a week to pound the crap outa Midway? But the Japs still keep sending planes back here."

"Write your Congressman if you don't like it—I can't do nothin' about it any which way." The MP jerked his thumb eastward, toward Pearl. "Write your Congressman after you take these apes where they gotta go."

Since they were coming from the direction of Ewa, the sentries on the road into the Pearl Harbor naval base didn't want to let them in. The driver threw a tantrum a four-year-old would have been proud of. The sentries had a field telephone. They spent twenty minutes going back and forth with their superiors. Finally, shaking their heads as if they were dealing with a busload of plague-carrying rats, they let the leathernecks proceed.

Pete counted himself lucky that the mess hall hadn't closed by the time he finally walked in. The fried chicken was rubbery and the mashed potatoes were tired, but he didn't care. By the time he finished, he had enough bones on his plate to build himself another bird.

He also didn't care where they put him for the night. It was Hawaii, for crying out loud. He would have curled up on some grass some-where and slept like a log till the sun woke him up come morning. No, on second thought he wouldn't. Some damn Shore Patrol clown would have rousted him in the middle of the night.

At last, the paratroopers were given a hall in a barracks that, by the musty smell, hadn't been used for anything for a long time. Except for the risk of prowling SPs, Pete would rather have slept outside on the grass. He didn't get to make such choices, though. People told him what to do, and he did it. That was what being a Marine was all about.

He didn't get to the mess hall late the next morning. Eggs, bacon, fried potatoes, toast, coffee ... He filled himself very full again. It wasn't fancy food, but it was the kind of stuff even Navy cooks had trouble ruining.

Then he and the rest of the paratroopers had to get the brass to notice that things were screwed up for them. As far as the people at the airstrip where the C-47s took off and landed knew, they'd gone back to Ewa the way they were supposed to. As far as the brass at Ewa knew, they were AWOL. Yes, Ewa was under quarantine, but what did that have to do with anything?

They spent most of the day getting all that straightened out. By the time it was fixed, or Pete thought it was, he'd got good and disgusted. "We should've gone straight into Honolulu yesterday, had ourselves a spree on Hotel Street," he said. "They still woulda figured us for AWOL today, and we coulda got smashed and laid."

"What about the bus driver?" one of the other paratroopers asked.

"Hell, he coulda come, too," Pete said magnanimously. "I mean, he was a Marine himself, so why shouldn't he have a good time along with us?"

"You got all the answers," the other leatherneck said, nothing but admiration in his voice.

"I wish," Pete said. "If I'm so goddamn smart, how come I ain't rich?" He stuck a hand in his pocket. A few coins clinked inside there, but only a few. Unless he got lucky rolling poker dice or something, he wouldn't have had much of a spree in Honolulu's red-light district.

In spite of the snafu, he and his buddies jumped from another

C-47 the next day. This time, nobody tried to take them back to Ewa. As far as Pete was concerned, that was progress.

Peggy Druce lit her first cigarette of the morning as she poured herself her first cup of coffee. She put in cream and a teaspoon and a half of sugar. She would rather have put in two, but they were more serious about rationing sugar than they were about most things. She smiled as she drank. It might not be exactly the way she would have wanted it, but it was better than anything they were drinking in Europe. For starters, the coffee was real coffee. The tobacco was miles better than the harsh, adulterated stuff they had over there, too.

She popped two slices of bread in the toaster and fried a couple of eggs in lard. As she sat down to breakfast, she opened the *Philadelphia Inquirer* to see what had gone wrong in the world since she fell asleep the night before.

MORE JAPS GERM BOMBS HIT HAWAII! was the front-page headline. Peggy shook her head as she buttered her toast and slathered it with strawberry jam. "Filthy bastards," she muttered to herself—who else was going to hear her?

She read the story below the headline. The War Department and the Navy Department admitted to a few small, isolated outbreaks of disease among military personnel on Oahu. Peggy smiled a tight, cynical smile as she worked her way through the story and her breakfast. If they admitted to a few small, isolated outbreaks, the real outbreaks were bound to be not so small and not so isolated. Dr. Goebbels didn't oversee news here in the USA, but people who thought like him sure did.

A War Department spokesman was quoted as quoting the Bible on sowing the wind and reaping the whirlwind. That sounded good: no two ways about it. How the United States was going to make it come true . . . The *Inquirer* didn't quote the War Department spokesman on that. Which, Peggy supposed, meant the illustrious spokesman had no idea, either.

She almost said as much out loud, just so Herb could make some pungent comment of his own in return. Little by little, though, she was getting used to the idea that Herb wasn't sitting across the table from her, wasn't and wouldn't be. Herb was either reading the *Inquirer* after making his own breakfast in the little apartment near his law office or, more likely, sitting at the counter of some greasy spoon and reading the paper there.

Peggy had thought about selling the house. It was really too big for one person. She rattled around in it like a solitary pea in a pod. An apartment would be more sensible.

But she'd lived here most of her adult life. And moving was a colossal pain. Packing up all the books and dishes and knickknacks and clothes and furniture . . . Even thinking about it was enough to tire her out.

So she rattled around. When she didn't feel like being by herself any more, she would go into town. Some of her former friends and acquaintances, though, raised their eyebrows when she came around. Being a divorcée was nowhere near so shocking as it would have been before the start of the last war. Then women who remained married didn't raise eyebrows; they cut you dead. Divorce did still bring a breath of scandal, but only a breath.

Outside of Philadelphia, her marital status or lack thereof wasn't whispered about behind her back. That meant she looked forward to her trips out of town to flog war bonds and to raise money for the Democratic Party more than she ever had while she was still married to Herb. They gave her something to do, and there was no room to rattle around in a hotel room in Easton or York or Shamokin or any of the other towns she'd seen on such trips.

She washed the breakfast dishes. Then she did some sweeping and dusting. If she took care of part of the house every day, she wouldn't get too far behind with any of it. She sorted dirty clothes into two piles: the ones that had to go to the cleaners and the ones she could put through the washing machine and the wringer. She did those, and hung them up on the clotheslines behind the house to dry.

She hoped they would dry. It was hot, but it was muggy. Things always took longer in weather like this. Something in the sticky air, though—she couldn't have said what, but she could feel it—said summer wouldn't last much longer.

When she went back inside, she turned on a fan in the front room.

It didn't do enough to cool her down, so she went into the bathroom and splashed cold water on her face. That felt wonderful, but she had to repair her powder and her eye makeup. Lots of mascara claimed it was waterproof, but she'd never found any that lived up to the claims.

She had a half-gallon milk bottle in the refrigerator full of ice water. Drinking a glass from that also helped beat the heat. She looked at the clock over the stove. It was lunchtime. She didn't know how that had happened, but it had. Housework kept you hopping, all right.

Two slices of bread. Ham and cheese and mustard and pickles. A little mayo—only a little, because she didn't like gloopy sandwiches. A couple of softly purple plums. Another cup of coffee to wash everything down. Not a fancy lunch, but not a bad one, either.

Peggy was washing the knife she'd used to spread the mustard and mayonnaise when the telephone rang. She quickly dried her hands on a dish towel and hustled into the living room.

"Hey, good-lookin'!"

"I'm sorry. You must have the wrong number," Peggy said, smiling.

On the other end of the line, Dave Hartman laughed. "I don't think so," he said. "How you doing?"

"I'm okay," Peggy said. "How are *you*?"

"At my lunch break," he answered. He'd found a factory that would let a machinist who knew what he was doing perch on a stool so he could do it. "Long as I'm not on my pins from morning till night, I'm happy as a cow in clover. Only they pay me better, and I don't think I'll end up roast beef."

"You're crazy," she said.

"Yeah, but I have fun," Dave said. "Want to watch the new Bogart movie tonight? It got a pretty good writeup in the paper this morning—did you see?"

"I just glanced at it, but that sounds fine. Shall we meet downtown?"

"Why don't I pick you up? I've got gas—and I haven't even eaten yet." Dave laughed at his own joke.

"Har-de-har-har," Peggy said, which only made him laugh some more. He knew he came out with some cornball stuff. He would have been much less fun to hang around with if he hadn't.

He came by just past six. He drove an old Ford, but he kept it clean and shiny, and it ran quiet as a watch. He did almost all the work on it himself. He wasn't an auto mechanic, but he understood machinery the way a pianist understood Beethoven. If it wasn't working the way it was supposed to, he could fix it.

He pecked her on the cheek when she got into the car with him. He didn't paw her as if he thought he might never get another chance. If he had pawed her like that, he wouldn't have. Unlike some men, he had sense enough to understand as much.

The movie was . . . a movie. Bogie had done better. No doubt he'd also done worse. It was a way to kill a couple of hours without paying as much attention as you needed to reading a book. It was also a way to keep company with someone else for a couple of hours.

After the movie ended, they went to a cocktail lounge down the street and had a drink. Then he drove her home. Peggy kissed him good-bye at the door. They hadn't gone any further than that. If they kept seeing each other, she expected they would, but they hadn't yet.

"Thanks," he said as he turned to go. "I had a good time. Always have a good time with you, seems like. I better head on back—got to be at the plant at eight o'clock sharp."

"I had a good time, too, Dave." Peggy let herself in and closed the door behind her. She smiled to herself. She really meant it. Who would have imagined that?

When Ivan Kuchkov peeked out of his foxhole, he saw something you didn't see very often: a German waving a white flag. In this part of the front, the Nazis and the Red Army were pretty mixed up. They'd been going back and forth at each other for a couple of weeks now. The Germans had given up more ground than they'd taken, but some villages had gone back and forth two or three times. There wasn't much left of those places.

The Hitlerite with the white flag shouted something in his own language. It was just noise to Kuchkov. "Hey, Sasha," he called, "what the fuck is the dumb cunt going on about?"

Sasha Davidov knew Yiddish, not German, but they were closer to each other than Russian and the Ukrainian grunting they used down here. The Jew could follow what the *Feldgrau* bastard was saying, anyhow. "He wants a truce to pick up the wounded," Davidov reported.

Firing on both sides eased off as men saw the white flag and waited to find out what would come of it. Ivan waited to discover whether any Soviet officers were in earshot. They'd speak German, odds were. And they could decide about the truce, too, so he wouldn't have to take out his dick and lay it on the block.

Only there didn't seem to be any around. He wondered what had happened to Lieutenant Obolensky. Maybe the company commander'd caught one in this latest firefight. Wounded men moaned. A couple of wounded men wailed. Russian and German agony sounded pretty much the same. Some of those sorry buggers might live if they got picked up. Of course, the NKVD pricks had their eye on him because of the mess with the *politruk,* and they were liable to say he was plotting with the enemy if he accepted the ceasefire.

Fuck them, too, in the neck, he thought. To Davidov, he said, "Tell him he can have an hour."

When the point man yelled to the Fritz, it didn't sound as if they were speaking quite the same language. The German shouted back. "He agrees," the skinny little point man said. "He says thank you, too."

"Tell him to screw himself," Kuchkov said. When the Jew hesitated, Ivan snapped, "Tell him, dammit!"

Davidov yelled again. The German shouted back, in accented but understandable Russian: *"Yob tvoyu mat'!"*

Ivan laughed. He came out of his hole and stood up. Most Germans didn't seem like human beings to him at all. But if you cussed one and he cussed you back, you couldn't very well *not* see a man there.

Cautiously, Red Army men and Hitlerites emerged from cover. Nobody put down his rifle or machine pistol, but nobody fired, either. A couple of Germans swigged vodka from Russian canteens. A couple of Russians drank German schnapps. The Fritzes swapped some of their tubed meats for Russian tobacco. Ivan thought his side won that deal, but everybody knew Germans were dopes when they weren't killing things.

Stretcher-bearers from both sides lugged away the wounded men they could find. Kuchkov noticed a Russian dragging a dead German off by his boots. They were good boots; he suspected the Red Army man would wear them if they fit and sell them if they didn't. He also suspected the Germans would try to stop the Russian if they noticed him stealing their *Kamerad*'s corpse. But they didn't, so he didn't need to worry about that.

"*Fünf Minuten!*" shouted the Fritz who'd asked for the truce. He held up his hand with the fingers spread.

"Five minutes," Sasha Davidov translated.

"Thanks a fuck of a lot, bitch," Ivan said sarcastically. Sasha looked wounded. "Yeah, yeah," Kuchkov soothed him. "Some of our guys are stupid pricks. I know." He needed to keep Davidov happy, or as happy as Davidov could get. The Jew started at his own shadow, but he didn't run from a fight. And when they were moving forward, he made the best point man Ivan had ever seen. Because he was so skinny and nervous, he never led the rest of the guys into a trap.

That German waved to Ivan, then turned and walked toward the hole from which he'd come. Ivan's right index finger twitched—he wanted to fire a burst from his PPD into the Hitlerite's back. The son of a bitch would never know what hit him. But Kuchkov couldn't see enough advantage in it to make it worth his while.

A German ceremoniously fired a Mauser into the air to signal that the ceasefire was over. Kuchkov squeezed off a three-round burst with his machine pistol, also aiming at nothing and nobody. A minute later, one of Hitler's saws opened up. Both sides got back to the serious business of trying to slaughter each other.

"Hey, Sasha!" Ivan called.

"What do you need, Comrade Sergeant?" the Jew asked. He was only a senior private, but he had more sense than anybody else in the section. Kuchkov thought his judgment worth having.

So he asked, "You think we can get around behind that little swell of ground off to the right? I saw the Nazi dickheads didn't hardly post anybody over there."

"Can the guys who don't move lay down enough fire so they don't know we're sliding around till we take 'em from the flank?" Davidov asked in return.

Ivan considered. After a few seconds, he said, "Fuckin' right, they can. Take half a dozen men and do it. We won't let the Hitlerite cocksuckers have a clue they're gonna get it up the ass."

Davidov and the soldiers he'd chosen crawled away through the weeds and bushes, their bellies as flat against the ground as if they were so many slugs. The rest of the Red Army men sprayed bullets around so the Germans wouldn't suspect the flanking move. About half of them carried PPDs or captured Schmeissers, so they had no trouble making a big racket.

As soon as the firing from the right started, Kuchkov yelled, "Come on, you sorry fuckers! Let's get 'em!" He scrambled out of his hole and scurried toward the German positions. Other khaki-clad men came with him. If they'd sat there playing with their dicks, they could have got rid of him for good.

One of the Fritzes fired at him from no more than ten meters away. The rattled German missed. Ivan cut him down with a long PPD burst while the Nazi was still working the bolt on his rifle. He smashed in another Hitlerite's face with his German-made entrenching tool when the man popped up in front of him like a rabbit coming up out of its burrow. The German screamed like a rabbit, too, and fell over on his back.

Then all the Nazis were running away. They liked flank attacks no better than Russians or anybody else.

Somewhere back there, the Germans had a couple of more MG-42s. Their pitiless snarl warned the Red Army men with Kuchkov not to get too bold in the pursuit. Instead, the Russians fell to plundering the corpses of the Fritzes they'd killed. Food, leather goods, grenades, trench knives, folding entrenching tools, water bottles—none of that stuff would go to waste.

Ivan kicked a dead German's helmet as if it were a football. It spun through the bushes. He wished he could paint it khaki and stick it on his own head. It was of better steel and protected more of a man's dome than its Soviet equivalent. But that wouldn't work. The instantly recognizable shape would get him shot by his own side.

Here came Sasha Davidov with German black bread and tubes of meat paste or butter. "Good job, motherfucker!" Ivan said, and slapped him on the back hard enough to stagger him.

"Thanks, Comrade Sergeant." The Jew squeezed something pale and yellow onto a chunk of bread and offered it to Kuchkov. "Here. I know which side it's buttered on." They both laughed and laughed. Why not? They'd both stayed alive to do it.

The men in Hans-Ulrich Rudel's squadron sprawled on the grass by their airstrip. Rudel had his visored officer's cap pulled down low on his forehead, and he wasn't the only one. It had started drizzling a little while earlier. The sky was the color of pewter. Summer might not be over, but it wouldn't last much longer.

Colonel Steinbrenner stood in front of the assembled flyers and groundcrew men. "Boys, I know you'll be glad to listen to a talk from the National Socialist Loyalty Officer, Major Keller. so pay attention to what he's got to say to you, right? *Heil* Hitler!"

"*Heil* Hitler!" the men echoed. Beside Hans-Ulrich, Sergeant Dieselhorst spoke up as loudly as anyone else. You couldn't just be loyal these days. You had to be seen and heard to be loyal. Hans-Ulrich didn't care for that, but he didn't know what he could do about it, either.

As the squadron commander stepped back, Major Keller stepped forward. He wore the ribbon for an Iron Cross Second Class thrust through the third buttonhole on his tunic. The Iron Cross Second Class wasn't quite like a vaccination scar; not *everybody* had one. But even Sergeant Dieselhorst sported an Iron Cross First Class. The rest of the loyalty officer's decorations were Party awards, not ones earned in the field.

"We must be ruthless in our devotion to duty! Ruthless!" Keller declared. "The Jews and Bolsheviks who hate the *Reich* and plot to destroy the German *Volk,* we must root out and eradicate without mercy. They would give us none, and so they deserve none themselves. We must prosecute the war as if there were no tomorrow. If our enemies triumph, there will be none for us!"

Beside Hans-Ulrich, Dieselhorst reached into a tunic pocket. He pulled out a pack of Gauloises. Rudel wondered where he'd got them. From a Belgian farmer who'd got them from a Frenchman, seemed the best bet. The rear gunner and radioman stuck one in his mouth and lit it. He made a horrible face, but kept puffing away. Even Hans-Ulrich, who didn't use tobacco, could smell how harsh the smoke was.

"We must fight. We must keep on fighting till Germany has the final victory and the *Lebensraum* our *Volk* require," the loyalty officer went on. "We must back the *Führer* of the *Grossdeutsches Reich*, Adolf Hitler, and the National Socialist German Workers Party with all our heart, and with all our soul, and with all our might. *Heil* Hitler!"

"*Heil* Hitler!" the *Luftwaffe* men chorused again. *Thou shalt love the Lord thy God with all thine heart, and with all thy soul, and with all thy might.* How often had Hans-Ulrich heard that verse from his minister father? Did Major Keller even know he was quoting Scripture—and the Old Testament, at that? Or was he just pulling a phrase that sounded good out of thin air? Even Hans-Ulrich could see that asking him wasn't the smartest thing he could do.

"The *Führer* is always right!" Keller thundered. "That is why we must back him with blind courage and blind obedience. He and he alone knows what is best for us and best for Germany. *Sieg heil!*"

"*Sieg heil!*" his audience responded. Albert Dieselhorst sent smoke signals up into the damp, drippy sky from his stinking French cigarette. No Red Indian stood on a hilltop to read what those smoke signals meant. Hans-Ulrich thought that might be just as well.

He joined in the polite applause as the National Socialist Loyalty Officer clicked his heels and took two steps back. Colonel Steinbrenner strode forward again. "Thank you, Major," he said. "Thank you very much."

Then Keller stepped up to stand beside him again. "One more thing, sir, if I may, which I unfortunately forgot to mention," he said. The squadron commander waved for him to continue, so he did: "You must ignore—ignore absolutely—any reports of unrest coming from the homeland. Either they are lies spread by the enemy to weaken your spirit or the unrest was fomented by Jews and other traitors to the *Reich*." He clicked his heels and withdrew once more.

"Thanks for making that plain," Colonel Steinbrenner said. "*Aber natürlich,* reports of unrest at home can only be lies or treason."

Keller nodded vigorously. Sergeant Dieselhorst coughed. It might have been the Gauloise's fault—if that wasn't poison gas he was breathing, what was it? Or the sergeant's irony detector might have gone off. Hans-Ulrich's had, and he was sure it was less sensitive than Dieselhorst's.

By all appearances, the Party hadn't issued Major Keller a working irony detector. After all, he still plainly believed everything he said himself. Well, Hans-Ulrich believed most of it, too, though he wasn't so sure all the unrest in Germany was lies and provocations. Albert Dieselhorst, being more ironical, believed rather less.

"Now that you men have listened to Major Keller, listened to him carefully and with the great attention a National Socialist Loyalty Officer deserves, you may return to your regular duties," Steinbrenner said. The loyalty officer looked pleased with himself. He was sure he deserved to be heard with great attention, all right.

Hans-Ulrich wasn't so very sure Colonel Steinbrenner was so very sure of that. He didn't think the squadron commander was a defeatist, or anything of the kind. Steinbrenner had replaced an officer who wasn't loyal enough to satisfy the security forces. But the colonel didn't care to have anyone tell him how to think.

Neither did Sergeant Dieselhorst. He stuck another Gauloise in his mouth. "Those things are filthy," Hans-Ulrich said.

"So's your granny . . . sir," Dieselhorst replied. He scraped a match against the sole of his boot. After he lit the cigarette, he coughed some more. He took it out of his mouth and eyed it with mingled caution and respect. "Does kind of feel like I'm smoking sandpaper," he allowed. That didn't stop him from taking another drag—or from coughing afterwards.

Hans-Ulrich took a few steps to get upwind of him. The Gauloise was so harsh, he didn't want anything to do with it. In a low voice, he asked, "And what did you think of Major Keller today?"

For a few seconds, he thought he'd been too quiet and Dieselhorst hadn't heard him. Then, without seeming to, the sergeant looked around to make sure no one else stood close by. As quietly, he answered, "In the time I needed to listen to that, I could've taken a good shit. *Quatsch mit Sosse,* nothing else but."

Rubbish with sauce. That was further than Rudel wanted to go—further than he might dare to go. "We do have to win the war, you know," he said mildly.

"*Aber natürlich.*" Dieselhorst did a good job of echoing Colonel Steinbrenner's dry tones. "But you know, sir, I could figure that out all by myself. I don't need some would-be Party *Bonz* to shove it up my asshole."

"He does try," Hans-Ulrich said.

"He's trying, all right," Dieselhorst answered, which sounded like agreement but wasn't. "If the Party wants to tend to politics, fine. It can tend to politics. I'm a *Luftwaffe* sergeant, for God's sake. What do I know about that crap, or care? But if the Party wants to run the goddamn war, it should do a better job." He breathed out more smoke, either from the Gauloise or from his own ire. Then he paused and added one more word: "Sir."

"Oh, yes." Hans-Ulrich nodded. "As long as you tack that on the end, it makes everything that came before it *wunderbar.*"

They both laughed. They'd been flying together since before the war started. Not many crews from those days were still alive, much less still flying together. They'd saved each other's bacon too many times. They didn't always agree, but neither one would ever report the other.

You followed your superiors' orders. You hoped the people set over you were there for a good reason and knew what they were doing when they gave them. Most of the time, they put their lives on the line along with you. You couldn't ask for more than that. In the end, you had to hope it would prove enough.

Chapter 8

Chaim Weinberg felt like a stranger in the one place in Spain where he should have been most at home. He'd been away from the Abe Lincolns for months while the fancy surgeon in Madrid put his left hand halfway back together again. The same mortar round that wounded him killed his best buddy. Too many faces in the trenches were Spanish-speaking strangers, not American idealists who'd come over here understanding that *somebody* had to stand first in line to give Fascism a good kick in the teeth.

Only one thing made coming back to the front worthwhile: the distant faces on the far side of the barbed wire and the hammered ground between the trench lines sill belonged to the bastards who fought for Marshal Sanjurjo. As far as Chaim was concerned, anybody stupid enough to fight for a dictator who was a fat, homely pig besides deserved to get his ticket punched.

The dumb *putos* over there probably thought that, if by some mischance their God was too busy watching a sparrow fall to keep them from catching a bullet in the ear, they'd head straight for a ghastly

Catholic heaven. Robes. Harps. Halos. Wings. No screwing. No drinking. Forever.

That vision of what lay beyond the Pearly Gates struck Chaim as more hellish than heavenly. He expected to die dead when he died, as if he went under ether without coming to again on the other side. He'd found out more about ether and going under these past few months than he'd ever wanted to know, too. But dying that way at least meant you were out of your pain, once and for all.

Nationalist loudspeakers still bragged about how good the food was on the other side of the line. Whenever a Nationalist soldier came over or got captured, he was always as scrawny as his Republican counterparts. So Chaim knew that was a load of crap.

Once, when the Nationalist with the microphone was wetting his pants about how good the mutton stew was, Chaim had mocked him so well, he'd touched off a big firefight. He'd learned his lesson. Mutton stew wasn't worth dying for.

When he got a little money, he bought a bottle of Spanish rotgut brandy and took it down the line to the stretch the Czech army-in-exile held. The French Jew whose folks came from Prague told him Vaclav Jezek was out between the lines, lying in wait to murder some Fascist big shot more than a mile away.

"Good luck to him," Chaim said. He held out a pack of cigarettes. "Want one?"

"Sure. Thanks," Benjamin Halévy answered. He and Chaim grinned at each other. Most of the Czechs spoke German—that was how Vaclav talked to Chaim. Halévy knew German, too. But, like Chaim, he spoke real Yiddish. Using the *mamaloshen* and knowing he'd be understood was a treat for the American.

Halévy seemed to enjoy it, too. "What language would you talk if you had your druthers?" Chaim asked him.

"My folks used Yiddish and Czech at home—sometimes one, sometimes the other, sometimes both mixed together," Halévy answered. "They knew French, too, of course, but they spoke it with an accent. Me, I learned from the other kids when I was a kid myself, so I lost my accent pretty quick if I ever had one. When I took regular

German in school, though, the guy who taught me said I sounded like a newspaper reporter from Prague. I used Czech vowels, see. Of course, my teacher was from Alsace. He had a hell of a funny accent himself."

He didn't exactly answer the question. From what Chaim had seen, Halévy was good at not exactly answering questions. Well, this one didn't matter much. That they could talk to each other, that was what counted.

Chaim was about to say so when Vaclav Jezek's monster rifle boomed, somewhere out there in no-man's-land. You couldn't mistake that report for anything else around here. Chaim wondered how the Czech kept that big, heavy brute from breaking his shoulder every time he pulled the trigger. Okay, it had a padded stock and a muzzle brake. Even so, anything that fired such a heavy slug so fat was bound to kick like a dinosaur.

Benjamin Halévy knew that boom for what it was. "Here's hoping he nailed at least a colonel," the French Jew said.

"*Alevai, omayn!*" Chaim agreed. They grinned at each other again. You had to know Yiddish to get that.

But then Halévy's handsome features soured into a frown. "If he did get a bigwig, Sanjurjo's *mamzrim*"—another Yiddish word knowing German wouldn't help you with—"will work us over for revenge."

"Let's have a look." It had been quiet around here. Chaim didn't think he was taking a horrible chance hopping up onto the firing step and peering toward the Nationalists' lines. Right at the front, everything seemed normal enough. But off in the distance, he saw something that put him in mind of a commotion in an anthill.

As soon as he did, he ducked down. Just as well, too, because an enemy bullet cracked by no more than a couple of seconds later. He didn't think it would have hit him—it sounded yards high—but that wasn't the kind of thing where you wanted to find out the hard way you were wrong.

"He got somebody?" Halévy asked.

"They're sure acting like it," Chaim replied.

And they were. The Nationalists' machine guns opened up in a minute or so. They lobbed mortars and some 77s at the Czechs' position, too. *Hate* was what the limeys called this kind of pounding. Chaim had picked up the word from an Englishman in the Internationals years ago—back before Hitler jumped Czechoslovakia, he thought.

As he crouched in the trench, he cradled his smashed-up hand under him. If it got hit again, they *would* cut it off. He knew that. There wouldn't be enough left to save.

After about ten minutes, the bombardment eased off. "Well, it couldn't have been a general," Halévy said, cautiously getting to his feet. "They stay mad longer for generals."

"They'd go *meshuggeh*—they'd fall on the floor and foam at the mouth like Holy Rollers—if our little Czech buddy really did blow Marshal Sanjurjo a new asshole," Chaim said as he stood up, too.

"Foam at the mouth like what?" Halévy asked.

"Holy Rollers. You don't have Holy Rollers over here?" Chaim said. When Halévy shook his head, the Jew from New York City explained: "Crazy Christians. Protestant Christians. They're mostly in the South, but not all of 'em. They roll around on the ground and they speak in tongues and . . . and like that." He realized he'd just told Halévy everything he thought he knew about them.

"Oh." After a moment, Halévy shrugged a very French-looking shrug. "No wonder I never heard of them. Not a lot of Protestants in France or Spain."

"No kidding!" Chaim said.

"Not a lot of Protestants in Czechoslovakia, either. Oh, I suppose maybe some of the Germans in the Sudetenland might have been Lutherans. But they didn't do any of that rolling around in church." Benjamin Halévy's face clouded. "They saved that kind of shit for Hitler."

"Yeah, I guess they would have."

He hung around with the Czechs till after darkness fell. Night was coming earlier all the time now as summer ebbed. Vaclav sneaked in from no-man's-land. No one challenged him till just before he reached the forward trenches. He was good at sneaking. He made his report in Czech, which meant nothing to Chaim. "He thinks it was a colonel he killed," Halévy said in Yiddish. "The prick had two aides with him, so he probably wasn't just a major."

Chaim held out his bottle of rotgut. "Here's to a dead Fascist colonel," he said.

"Hey!" Vaclav slapped him on the back—considerately, on the right side. He took the brandy and cradled it like a baby. "Good to see you again. And where did you get this?"

"Stole it—where else?" Chaim said. "Let's destroy the evidence." So they did.

Stories in the paper admitted the *Wehrmacht* was falling back in Russia, though they called it things like "consolidating our lines" and "forming strengthened defensive positions." What passed for news reports on Dr. Goebbels' radio admitted the same thing. While admitting it, they tried to deny it at the same time. They boasted in bloodthirsty fashion about all the Russians Germany was killing and all the Soviet panzers it was destroying.

If you believed Dr. Goebbels' radio, Stalin was scraping the bottom of the barrel when it came to manpower and machinery. If you believed the radio, he'd scraped the bottom of the barrel so many times, he must have scraped clean through it by now.

Of course, if you believed the radio and the newspapers, you were a bigger *Dummkopf* than Sarah Bruck hoped she was. She knew lies when she heard them. The only thing that kept her from hoping for a total collapse in the East was the thought that Saul was probably there. He was if he hadn't got killed by now, anyhow.

Sarah walked near the *Rathaus*. She carried a small cloth bag. The bag had woolen cloth inside it: some of a Jewish family's pathetically small ration of woven goods. It was going to be used to patch the shabby clothes she and her mother and father were already wearing, not to make anything new. Unless you were going to turn out a cap for a pinheaded baby, you didn't get enough to make anything new. Oh, that exaggerated, but not by a great deal.

She threw the Münster city hall a black look as she scurried by. The Party dignitaries who ran the town from there enjoyed making things as tough on Jews as they could. They were good at it, too.

An SS man strode past her, hobnailed boots clumping on the sidewalk. He scowled at her, but didn't ask—no, tell—her to stop and show her papers. She wore yellow stars in all the places Nazi regulations demanded.

"Stinking blackshirt!"

The cry made the SS man freeze for a moment with one foot off the ground, as if he were a frame in a newsreel. Then he whirled, amazement and fury warring on his hatchet face. "Who said that?" he shouted, an angry flush rising up from his collar, higher at every word.

He couldn't blame Sarah: the yell had come from a man. Several Aryans in worn clothes were possibilities. A couple of them looked to be fighting smiles. They were all past conscription age, but seemed in better shape than what they had on.

Then the SS man did round on Sarah. "Who said that, Jew?" he growled. "You must have seen. Tell me!"

"I'm sorry, sir, but I wasn't paying any attention," she said.

"Leave her alone, you lousy pigdog!" a woman yelled. Now that the SS man had turned, he couldn't tell for sure who she was, either.

He whirled again. He would have been a terror on a basketball court. "You are all under arrest! Every single one of you!" he bellowed. The back of his neck was even redder than his face. "Come with me to the *Rathaus* immediately—immediately, I say!"

"Lick my ass, peckerhead!" called one of the not-so-young men. The others laughed.

Sarah thought the laughter provoked the SS man more than the insult. He yanked a truncheon off his belt and walked purposefully toward the men.

One of them bent down and grabbed a beer bottle out of the gutter. With an economical motion that told of some practice, he broke the end on the edge of the curb. Sharp shards glittered there as he hung on to the handle. "Sure—come on," he said with a wolfish smile. "See how you like it."

By the way the blackshirt eyed the end of the broken bottle, he didn't like it at all. Instead of going on with his advance, he drew up a whistle that he wore on a string around his neck and blew a long, shrill blast. More SS men trotted out of the *Rathaus*.

But the whistle also made more ordinary people come hurrying up to see what was going on. They jeered and hissed at the SS men and shouted for them to go away. "Haven't you fuckers done enough to us?" a man yelled.

"You'd better clear out, you noisy old fool, or you'll really get what's coming to you!" the blackshirt closest to Sarah shouted.

She thought that was a great idea, and sidled away from the building dustup. If a Jew got caught anywhere near trouble, he—or she— would catch the blame for it. And Himmler's goons would be three times as rough on him—or her—as on an Aryan. She didn't want to give the SS men the least possible excuse to grab her.

Some of the Germans in the swelling crowd were too fed up to worry about such things. Half a brick arced through the air. Whoever threw it must have had plenty of practice during the last war, putting grenades right where he wanted them. It caught the first blackshirt a couple of centimeters in front of his right ear. He crumpled like a sheet of wastepaper. His truncheon clattered on the paving stones.

A great cheer rose from the crowd. They rushed toward the SS men who'd emerged from the *Rathaus*. More bricks and rocks and bottles flew. One of those SS men went down with a shriek, his hands clutched to his face and blood running out between his fingers.

The crowd let out another cheer. "Kill the bastards!" somebody cried, and in an instant they were all baying it together: *"Kill the bastards!"* Men, women, it didn't matter. As soon as that one fellow put it into words for them, they knew what they wanted to do.

Some of the SS men had pistols. They started shooting into the crowd, but they'd waited too long. They knocked down a few of the people in the lead, but by then the rest were on them. They screamed as they were overrun, but not for long.

By that time, Sarah had got around a corner, with a solid brick building shielding her from stray gunfire. More people were coming the other way. "What's going on?" a woman called to Sarah. If she noticed the Stars of David on Sarah's clothes, she didn't care about them.

"There's a mob by the *Rathaus*, and they're going after the SS," Sarah answered: just the facts, with no comments.

If any of them were convinced Nazis, they were liable to grab her for the blackshirts. Instead, they all clapped their hands and pumped their fists in the air. "Let's go help them!" the woman caroled, and they all did. Some paused to snatch up makeshift weapons. Interestingly, a mechanic was already carrying a stout spanner, while a man who wore the leather apron of a butcher or sausage-maker clutched a cleaver.

More pistol shots rang out from the direction of the *Rathaus*. Sarah wished she had the nerve to join the people going after their Nazi oppressors at last. But she didn't. They risked themselves, perhaps their families. She was too conscious that anything one Jew did endangered every Jew in the *Reich*. She didn't dare do anything but go home.

Somehow, news of the trouble had got there ahead of her. "Thank goodness you made it in one piece!" her mother exclaimed when she walked through the door. "They're shooting at people downtown!"

"I know. I was there when it started. How did *you* know?" Sarah said.

Hanna Goldman gestured vaguely. "You hear things."

"I guess you do." Could Mother have heard the gunfire from here? She might have been able to. With so little motor noise in the streets, sounds like that carried a long way.

Half an hour later, and closer to home, first one machine gun and then another opened up. Sarah had no trouble at all hearing them. More faintly, she also heard screams.

She breathed a sigh of relief when her father came in. Samuel Goldman was earlier than usual. His eyes snapped with excitement. "They've put the whole town under curfew," he said. "Münster's bubbling like a pot of stew somebody forgot on the fire. Who knows? Maybe the whole country will start bubbling, too."

"I don't believe it," Sarah said, both for the benefit of any hidden microphones and because, wish as she would, she truly didn't believe Germany would rise against the Nazis.

The Royal Navy hadn't tried to sneak a convoy from the British Isles to Murmansk or Archangelsk all through the long, light nights of far northern summer. The *Kriegsmarine* and the *Luftwaffe* had convinced them such efforts were only an expensive form of suicide at that season of the year. U-boats, destroyers, FW-200 long-range reconnaissance bombers ... The odds were stacked against freighters, even escorted freighters.

They got bolder as nights stretched longer, though. And so did Julius Lemp. Night gave freighters more chances to hide, but it also helped cloak stalking U-boats. Along with two other submarines, the U-30 helped scatter a convoy. He credited his boat with two freighters. One blew up with a roar that shook the submerged U-boat. The other burned and burned and burned. If it wasn't hauling high-octane avgas, he would have been amazed.

He was a happy man, then, or as happy as a dour man ever got, when he came into Namsos after that patrol. And he—and his men— were even happier when the base commandant ordered them down to Wilhelmshaven for a refit more thorough than they could get at the base in the far north of Norway.

Yes, they would be at sea a while longer. All the same, the advantages were obvious. In case they weren't, Gerhart Beilharz summed them up: "More booze. Better booze. More whores. Better whores."

"Maybe even a chance for some of us to take a furlough and see their families and friends," Lemp added dryly.

"That, too, skipper." By the way the engineering officer said it, it might be true, but it wasn't all that important. And, from what Lemp knew of U-boat sailors, Beilharz understood their priorities and made them his own. After a moment, he added, "More and better chow, too."

"Well, we can hope," Lemp said. "Even for servicemen, rations in the *Vaterland* are getting pretty dismal."

"Too right, they are," Beilharz said. "Suppose the *Bonzen* will hang a defeatism rap on us for saying so?"

"You know, Gerhart, I'm old enough that there are things in this world I can live without finding out," Lemp answered. And that, no doubt, explained why the two of them tossed the question around in whispers in Lemp's curtained-off cabin. Beilharz pondered the reply and seemed to find it good. Which was fine, unless he hung a defeatism charge on his superior—he wouldn't hang one on himself, of course.

When the U-30 tied up in the harbor at Wilhelmshaven, the men roared off to the town's fleshpots. After making his own report, Lemp had in mind a rather more upper-crust version of the same thing. Not to put too fine a point on it, he wanted to get drunk and he wanted to get his ashes hauled, not necessarily in that order. After a successful combat patrol, he figured he'd earned the right.

What he got instead was a summons to the office of the SS man who'd pulled his best electrician's mate off his boat for political unreliability the last time he was in Wilhelmshaven. The blackshirt was skinny and looked aristocratic; whether he was entitled to a *von*, Lemp didn't know. The man punctuated his conversation by blinking his eyes and by licking and licking and licking his lips.

Lemp eyed him with distaste he knew he didn't hide well enough. "Reporting as ordered," he said. He didn't say *Let's get this over with so I can get the hell out of here*, but his manner said it for him.

Blink. The SS man stared back at him. "I see your ship met no misfortune without Petty Officer Nehring," he said. Lick.

He still didn't know enough to call a U-boat a boat, not a ship. Odds were he didn't know enough to shake it before he stuck it back in his pants, but you couldn't tell him that. The SS knew everything—if you didn't believe it, all you had to do was ask them.

"No thanks to you," Lemp growled. If the pigdog had called him in to gloat about that, he'd . . . He didn't know what he'd do. What could you do to an SS man that God hadn't done already? "Have you got any other reasons for wasting my time today?" No, he wasn't hiding distaste at all well, was he?

"Do not play games with me, Commander Lemp." Lick. Blink. "The political situation is far more serious than it was when last we spoke."

"I don't know anything about that," Lemp replied. "I've been fighting the war since then. How about you?"

Anger turned the SS man's bony, sallow cheeks almost the color of a normal human being's. "I told you not to play games, Lemp." Blink. He didn't bother with the U-boat captain's rank any more. "Unrest is abroad in the land, and it is my duty to stamp out that unrest wherever it raises its ugly head. Believe me, I will do my duty."

"I'm trying to do mine, too," Lemp said. "If you help the *Reich* lose the war, is that doing your precious duty?"

"Stamping out unrest will help the National Socialist *Grossdeutsches Reich* win the war." Blink. "Now. Let us get down to business. Who in your crew is from in or near the rebellious city of Münster?"

"Rebellious?" Lemp said.

"That's right. Rebellious. In a state of resistance against the authority of the National Socialist *Grossdeutsches Reich*." The SS man brought out the clumsy phrase as if it were one normal people used every day. He punctuated it with another blink, then continued, "Answer my question, Lemp. Who in your crew is from Münster or close by?"

"You already took Nehring away for coming from around there and getting letters from his kin, didn't you?" Lemp said.

The look the blackshirt sent him was colder than winter water in the Barents Sea. "If you do not stop evading what I ask you, I promise"—lick—"you will be sorry. You have not the faintest idea of how sorry you will be."

What occurred to Julius Lemp was *With idiots like this in charge, no wonder Münster is up in arms*. He didn't say that; it would have landed him in water hotter than the SS man's eyes were cold. What he did say was, "I'm not evading you, dammit. Except by their accents, I don't know where they're from, and I don't care. All I know, and all I do care about, is who does what and how well he does it."

"Your uncooperative attitude will be noted." Blink.

"Oh, fuck your noting!" Lemp burst out. "If you want to know where they come from, go through their files. You don't seem to have anything better to do with your time. I damn well do." Visions of a perfumed blond *Fräulein* wearing a few wisps of silk capered lewdly across his brainpan. An officers' brothel would be a lot more fun than this. So would almost anything this side of a depth-charge attack.

"I have already made note of your unsatisfactory attitude," the SS man said.

"That's nice," Lemp answered blandly. "I suppose going out and fighting the war is what does it to me."

"I am fighting the war against treason and betrayal!" The blackshirt wasn't doing a lizard impression any more. Now he was really and truly steamed. The shrill fury in his voice showed it, too.

Lemp took off his cap. Even with it on, he looked less imposing than the Party functionary, because he didn't bother with the spring stiffener. No U-boat skipper did. But the white cloth cover said he *was* a skipper. The grease stain on the cover said he did some real work in that cap. Whether the SS man could read those signals, he didn't know.

Blink. "Get out of here!" the SS man said peevishly, as if Lemp had barged in without an invitation rather than in answer to a summons. Lemp got up and left before the fellow could change his mind. The brothel first, he decided, and then the officers' club.

Arno Baatz had talked with Russian-speaking Germans whose job was to intercept and translate Red Army radio messages. The Ivans had crappy security. They sent way too much in clear. The guys who monitored their signals said that when they started talking about the Devil's grandfather or his aunty, things had got screwed up but good.

Right this minute, Baatz felt like talking about Satan's second cousin once removed. Things in this part of Russia had got screwed up, all right, and they wouldn't unscrew any time soon. Rain poured out of the sky. Arno had yet to see a paved road in Russia more than a few kilometers outside a big city.

On German maps, the roads between Soviet cities had been marked as highways. In any self-respecting country, they would have been highways. In Russia, they were rutted dirt tracks. When the autumn rains fell, and when the drifted snow melted in the spring, they turned to mud. Baatz had never imagined such mud before he got here. It could suck the boots off a *Landser*'s feet. It could swallow a man up to his waist. It could drown a weary mule who let his head sag down into it. It could bog down a truck.

It could bog down a panzer, too. The sensible German engineers who'd designed the *Reich*'s panzer forces had no more dreamt of mud like this than Arno Baatz had himself. Russian T-34s plowed through glop that held Panzer IIIs and IVs the way spiderwebs held beetles. It was demoralizing. It could wreck your chances of living to a ripe old age, too.

Right this minute, there were no T-34s in the neighborhood. Baatz didn't think there were, anyhow. He looked over his shoulder, but he couldn't see much through the downfalling curtains of water. He couldn't hear much, either. The rain plashed all around. He wouldn't know Russian panzers were close by till one squashed him flat. That would be just exactly too late.

Adam Pfaff squelched through the mud a few meters away. Like Baatz, he wore his waterproofed shelter half as a rain poncho. It helped a little, but not nearly enough.

Pfaff managed a crooked grin. "You know what?" he said. "I wish we were Panzergrenadiers."

"Heh," Baatz said. "I've heard ideas I liked less—I'll tell you that." Panzergrenadiers didn't march into battle—or, as now, away from it. They rode armored halftracks so they could keep up with the panzers instead of wearing out shoe leather tramping along behind them.

Ten minutes later, the *Landsers* tramped past an SdKfz 251 that was buried in mud past the axle of its front wheels. The armored personnel carrier's two-man crew and the half-dozen glum Panzergrenadiers it had carried were all clumping around in the oozy muck, trying to excavate it or to get enough wood and brush under its power train to let it move again. Shelter halves or not, they were filthy and soaked.

"I take it back," Adam Pfaff said. "I don't want to be a Panzergrenadier after all."

Baatz eyed the struggling, cursing soldiers and their disabled mount. "Maybe you aren't as dumb as you look," he said.

"Hey!" shouted one of the profanely unhappy men wrestling with the SdKfz 251. "How about a hand, you clowns?"

Pfaff clapped and clapped, as if applauding a great save on a football pitch. Arno Baatz guffawed. The Panzergrenadier called them every name in the book, and a few that would have scorched the pages had anyone tried to set them down.

"I don't think he likes us," Pfaff said in tones of mild surprise.

"Too bad," Baatz answered. For once, the *Obergefreiter* didn't seem to want to argue with him.

A military policeman with a gorget on a chain around his neck—he wore it outside the shelter half he used for a rain cape—stood at a crossroads directing traffic. "Which regiment?" he demanded whenever another group of soldiers came up from the east.

Baatz told him when he barked the question yet again. "Which way do we go?" the *Unteroffizier* asked.

"Your lot heads southwest." The military policeman importantly pointed down the proper muddy track. He must have had the assignments memorized. Any list, except maybe one printed on a tin cup with crayon, would have turned to mush in short order.

"Damn chainhound," Pfaff said as soon as they got too far from the man to let him hear. The military policemen's emblem gave them the scornful nickname.

"He's just doing his job." Arno Baatz automatically respected authority. That was what authority was there for, wasn't it? It was to Arno. But, as soon as the words were out of his mouth, he saw he'd lost points with Pfaff. Any combat soldier with anything kind to say about the military police turned into a white crow.

Everybody in the squad was grousing by the time they got to a large village an hour and a half later. Another *Kettenhund* with a gorget stood at the edge of it. "What's your unit?" he growled. Again, Baatz told him. The military policeman looked disgusted. "Well, you buggered it up good and proper, didn't you? You clowns were supposed to take the other fork."

"What kind of *Teufelsdreck* is that?" Baatz said. He pointed back the way they'd come. "The fool with a gorget at the crossroads sent us down here."

"I don't care if the fucking Holy Ghost sent you," the military policeman said. "You've got to go back and do it right."

Baatz and Pfaff and the rest of the weary soldiers called him so many names, the Panzergrenadiers with the bogged-down halftrack would have listened hard. Back for an hour and a half and then on again for nobody knew how long? No wonder they swore!

For a little while, it rolled off the chainhound the way water rolled off the rubberized fabric of his shelter half. He was more patient than some military policemen Baatz had seen. Before long, though, that patience frayed. "Get moving," he said, a new sharpness in his voice. "Do you want me to call for an officer? You won't like it if I do, I promise."

Miserably, hopelessly, the *Landsers* turned away and headed back toward the crossroads. "What do you want to bet that other asshole tries to send us this way again?" Baatz said. No longer did he show any sympathy for military policemen.

"I hope the Ivans bomb the crap out of that place," Adam Pfaff said, jerking a thumb at the village they'd just left. "The chuckleheads there deserve it." Several of the other soldiers nodded. Even Baatz didn't reprove the *Obergefreiter*. Mud kept slopping into his boots.

Getting back to the crossroads took longer than going the other way had. The tired soldiers had to keep stepping off the road while men and vehicles moving the other way went by. Many of the vehicles were horse-drawn, local *panje* wagons the Germans had impressed into service—that being a fancy turn of phrase for *stolen*. The wagons had tall wheels and boat-shaped beds. They dealt with mud better than anything from the *Vaterland*.

A different *Kettenhund* stood at the crossroads when Baatz and his men returned. He didn't ask questions. He just waved them onto the other fork of the road. On a day without any large favors, Baatz gladly accepted the small one.

By the time he and his men made it to where they were supposed to go, night was falling. Other German troops filled every hut in the village. The weary *Landsers* ate their iron rations, fastened shelter halves together to make tents, and rolled themselves in blankets on top of more shelter halves to give themselves a quarter of a chance of staying dry. Baatz slept like a rock even so.

Chapter 9

Ivan Kuchkov didn't mind the *rasputitsa*, not even a little bit. He was happy to sit on his ass any old time, to roll cigarettes from *makhorka* and from newspapers he couldn't read, to eat black bread and sausage, and to drink his daily Red Army vodka ration and as much homebrew as he could get his hands on besides. He was happy to do that any old time, sure. But when the mud time slowed all motion to a crawl, he got the perfect excuse to stay lazy.

Officers got their dicks all excited about patrolling no matter what, about keeping the pressure on the Hitlerite hyenas. Well, they could get their knickers in as big a twist as they wanted. Yes, Red Army men were able to keep moving no matter how muddy it got. Yes, they were better at it than the damned Nazis. Just because you were able to do something, though, didn't mean you wanted to.

His section was holding a village somewhere in the western part of the Ukraine. The peasants who lived there disliked the Red Army less than a lot of Ukrainians Ivan had run into. For one thing, they'd found out that the Germans weren't such a hot bargain. For another, they could see that the NKVD would be calling the shots around here, and the *Gestapo* wouldn't. They might not be jumping up and down about it, but they could see their bread had lard smeared on the one side, not on the other.

This particular village had in it a wide-faced blond gal named Feodosiya. She gave Ivan one more good reason not to go out there and get his dick shot off when he didn't absolutely have to. She'd probably sucked some *Feldwebel*'s cock when the Germans held this place, but that didn't bother him. One lesson he'd had hammered into him was that you did what you had to do to get by. That went double for women.

For now, Feodosiya had latched on to him. She didn't worry about anything past whether what she did felt good and what she could get out of it. She could almost have been a man, in other words.

She saw the same directness in him. "You're all right," she told him one time after he slipped out of her. He thought that was what she said, anyhow. No, Ukrainian wasn't the same as Russian. When Feodosiya wanted to, she could talk so he couldn't follow her at all. She could get him to understand, though, too, when she felt like it. She did now: "You don't mess around the way a lot of guys do."

"Fuck, no, sweetie. Not me." They lay near the fireplace, on a couple of blankets and under a couple of more. Rain dripped through the thatching on the roof in a few places. A teacup caught a little one, a pot a bigger one. Over in the far corner of the hut, a mud puddle was forming because nothing caught that leak. All the dripping and splashing noises made Ivan want to take a leak himself.

He got out from under the blankets and, naked, walked over to a small birchwood table somebody in the village must have made— somebody who wasn't much of a carpenter. On the table sat a jar of *samogon*: homebrew, moonshine, unofficial vodka. Ivan knocked back a slug. *Samogon* came in every quality, from literal poison to stuff better than you could buy from the state distilleries. This was pretty good, and plenty potent.

"Here." He carried the jar back to Feodosiya. She sat up to take it. Her tits sagged a bit when she did; she had to be around thirty. Ivan didn't care. That just meant she knew how, as far as he was concerned.

"Here's some hot water for you," he said. Except for his cock, he couldn't think of anything that had as many nicknames as vodka.

She drank. She smiled. "*Tak!*" she said. That was one of the Ukrainian words Ivan understood. It meant *yes*. He would have said *da*—in Russian, *tak* was an out-loud pause for thought, something like *you know*—but it wasn't worth fussing over. Then she said something more, but he had no idea what.

He spread his hands. "C'mon, bitch," he said. "Talk so an ordinary fucker can follow you."

"I said, this tastes like the stuff Volodymyr makes." Feodosiya came closer to ordinary Russian. But the *samogon*-cooker's name reminded Ivan he wasn't in Russia. It should have been Vladimir, dammit.

"Tall, skinny guy with a pointy nose? Kinda looks like a German prick?" he asked. Feodosiya nodded. So did Ivan. "Yeah, that's who I got it from. Gave him some shchi from the stewpot." Shchi—cabbage soup—and borscht were Red Army staples. You took cabbages or beets: things you could get almost everywhere. You threw some spices or whatever else you could liberate into the pot with them. You boiled it. If you had any sour cream, you plopped that into the borscht. If you didn't, you managed without. Either way, you ate.

Feodosiya asked him something else. He frowned—he didn't get it. She tried again: "Aren't you cold, standing there with no clothes?"

"Oh, *cold*. That's what you meant. Nah, I'm fine," he answered.

She smiled again. "Probably because you're so hairy," she said. Ivan's frown darkened into a scowl. He knew how hairy he was: hairy enough so people called him the Chimp. They didn't do it much where he could hear them, though, because he walloped the shit out of them when they did. But then Feodosiya added, "I like my men hairy. That way, I'm sure I'm not messing around with another girl."

He got back under the blankets with her and guided her hand to his crotch. "Here's something else to give you a hint," he said, his good humor altogether restored as her grip tightened on him. They went on from there.

Every so often, he did have to go out on patrol. He didn't like squelching through the mud any more than anyone else would have.

And the Red Army helmet didn't do one damn thing to keep rain from dripping down the back of his neck. The German model, with its greater flare, had to be better for that.

"German pussies," he muttered as he slipped from one bush to the next. A squad of Germans, or a company, or a regiment, would still keep some survivors after taking on a like number of Russians. Everybody on both sides knew that. The Germans had better weapons and better tactics. But a German regiment couldn't knock out three Red Army units the same size, or five. There simply weren't enough Germans to win the war here.

By now, everybody on both sides knew that, too. Why else would the Fritzes be pulling back? Sooner or later, the Romanians and the Hungarians would jump ship on them. Ivan could see that, so he supposed Hitler also could. Then they'd get stretched even thinner.

Would the Poles bail out on them as well? There, Kuchkov wasn't so sure. Poles hated Germans. Who didn't, after all? But Poles hated Russians just as much. The bastards would have to be desperate before they cut a deal.

Motion. "Halt, fucker!" Kuchkov exclaimed, swinging the business end of his PPD toward . . . a stray dog. The skinny, dripping yellow beast looked even more miserable than he felt himself. But it ran away when he called it, which said it wasn't such a dumb son of a bitch.

The only sign of Hitlerites Ivan saw was a Nazi helmet with a bullet hole through the side. The Fritz who'd been wearing that helmet would be holding up a lily now—unless that sorry dog had fed on him. Ivan doubted it had; it would have been fatter in that case. Not even a German helmet would keep out a rifle round.

A carrion crow flew off, yelling at Ivan. Maybe it had got its share of carrion from the German who'd used that helmet. Ivan hoped so. He also hoped the crow wouldn't feast on him any time soon.

Not for a while, he thought. The *rasputitsa* meant his odds were better, anyhow. He slogged on for a while, then headed back to the village. Feodosiya would be waiting. Even if he didn't feel like flipping her legs up in the air as soon as he walked into the hut, keeping company with a friendly woman was something he hadn't done enough of for way too long. In the field, you almost forgot about such things. Almost, but not quite.

Plopped down in the Pacific between Kauai and Midway were assorted little rocks and atolls. In most of the ocean, they would have been nothing but menaces to navigation. For all Pete McGill knew, they remained menaces to navigation right where they were.

But, with the Americans at one end of that stretch and the Japs at the other, those rocks and atolls turned into important menaces to navigation. Most of them remained too small to matter to even the most megalomaniac military mind. Most, but not all. There was, for instance, the one called Tern Island.

Tern Island lay halfway between Midway and the main Hawaiian islands. It was nowhere near as big as Midway, but it was big enough to have its area measured in acres rather than square feet. It was also big enough so as not to disappear when the tide ran high.

Japan couldn't do, or didn't seem willing to do, anything with Tern Island (the name gave a hint about the place's usual natives). Even Midway lay at the very end of their logistics chain. The U.S. Navy, however, had taken a shine to the place. And the United States could do things with, and to, it.

Pete McGill watched from the deck of a baby flattop as construction battalions—Seabees, the Navy called them—leveled the top of the island and built a runway on it. Four escort carriers covered the freighters that had brought the Seabees and their equipment all the way up here to the middle of watery nowhere. Shark-graceful, shark-swift destroyers covered the slow, ugly carriers.

U.S. fighters from the baby flattops flew a continuous combat air patrol above the little fleet and above Tern Island. If Jap Bettys wanted to come down and bomb the construction work, they could try. The fighters were there to make sure they didn't have an easy time of it, though.

The powers that be had ordered Pete aboard the brand-new—but still not very shiny—USS *Block Island* for two reasons. That was how it looked to him, anyhow. For one thing, he knew all about the five-inch antiaircraft guns that were the biggest weapons the carrier mounted on a freighter hull carried. If Japanese planes got through the CAP and attacked the *Block Island,* he could serve the gun and try to knock them down.

For another, he was a trained paratrooper now. He had the badge to prove it. He didn't know why the Navy was building the runway on Tern Island. Nobody told a leatherneck sergeant shit like that. But he also didn't need to be a fancy-Dan admiral with stars on his shoulder boards and with his sleeves all encrusted in gold to make some pretty fair guesses.

That most of the other Marines aboard the *Block Island*—and, he figured, most of them on the other escort carriers, too—also wore tiny, shiny metal parachutes on their chests only solidified his guesswork. Nor was he the sole Marine doing the guessing.

They didn't have much else to do. The skipper sounded general quarters once or twice a day, just to keep people on their toes. He generally picked the most annoying times to start the klaxons hooting, too. But then, once you got to your post and you found out it was nothing but another drill, you stood down and went back to whatever you'd been doing before. And you went back to being bored.

Redistributing the wealth was against regulations, which didn't mean the Marines—and the swabbies—didn't do it. A deck of cards, a pair of dice: they helped make time go by. When you steamed round and round Tern Island and nothing happened, time needed all the help it could get.

A good bit of the available wealth ended up in Pete's pocket. He'd never make a great brain. He knew that. He was rather proud of it, in fact. But he could by God play poker. He'd learned, and paid for the privilege of learning, in the small, select Marine Corps garrison in Peking. Most of the men with whom he'd served were either dead or prisoners of the Japs. If that wasn't a fate worse than death, he didn't know what would be.

Another Marine put ten bucks in the pot after the draw. Pete took another look at his own hand: two pairs, fours and nines. He didn't rub his chin or do anything else to show what he was thinking or even that he was thinking. Such lapses got expensive. He just tossed in his hand. Rudy didn't bet like that unless he held something juicier than two crappy pairs.

That was how things seemed to Pete, anyhow. A sailor called Dusty had a different opinion. He saw Rudy's sawbuck and raised him another one. Rudy raised back. Dusty looked less happy then. He threw in another ten. "Call," he said.

Rudy showed a jack-high flush. Dusty said something filthy. He threw down three queens. Grinning, Rudy scooped up the cash. He glanced over at Pete. "I shoulda cleaned you out, too," he said.

"Ah, go clean under your foreskin," Pete told him. Everybody sitting on the circle on the deck laughed. Dusty started shuffling for the next deal. Pete had nothing but garbage in his hand, so he threw it away after the ante. Winning money was good, but not losing more than you could help counted just as much.

It wasn't that he never bet when he held nothing or raised on a busted straight. You had to do that kind of thing every so often, or you got predictable, and being predictable was death. But you also had to pick your spots, and this didn't feel like a good one to him.

He threw away another worthless hand. He lost with three kings the way Dusty had lost with three queens. He won a little pot. Then he bet a pair of tens as if they were a straight flush. He lost that one, too. Bluffing was hard here. The guys didn't care so much about money because they had so little to spend it on.

Win a little, lose a little, win a bigger hand, lose a couple of small ones. Then damned if he didn't draw two to three sevens and get back a pair of deuces. Not a mansion of a full house, but a full house just the same.

If the skipper calls an alert now, I'll strangle the son of a bitch, he thought. He didn't bet it the way Rudy had with his straight, with flags flying and trumpets blaring. He didn't want to scare people off. He wanted to keep them in, so he could take more of their greenbacks. If somebody else had something pretty good, so much the better.

And somebody else did: a broad-shouldered Marine corporal named Myron. He was one of those guys who got five o'clock shadow at ten in the morning. He had to shave twice a day. He raised a couple of times more often than he should have. When Pete kept raising back, he finally suspected a trend and called.

Pete showed off the boat. *"Malakas!"* Myron said. He slammed an ace-high flush down on the steel plate. Pete gathered in the pot. If he ever got back to Honolulu, he could have himself quite a spree.

One of the things you didn't do was walk out of the game right after you'd cleaned up. Now Pete wanted the *Block Island*'s captain to hit the switch for the klaxons. He wouldn't mind an excuse to run to his battle station with all that lovely moolah in his front pocket. (Peking duty had also taught him to carry his money there. Putting it behind you only tempted the pickpockets, and the thieves in Peking put Americans to shame.)

He lost a hand where he had nothing to speak of, then another one where he tried to fill a straight but didn't make it. He didn't raise so much on that one, not when Rudy made it plain he was holding something. And he was: a full house of his own. Myron didn't get burned so badly that time. Maybe he was learning, or maybe he just had bad cards.

Then the sirens did start screaming. Pete grabbed his helmet, hurried up to the flight deck, and ran over the planking there to the five-inch dual-purpose gun in front of the island. The gun could fight surface ships as well as planes, but if anything much more ferocious than a garbage scow attacked the *Block Island,* the baby flattop was in deep trouble.

No Jap bombers or fighters overhead: only the CAP. Another drill, nothing more. Over on Tern Island, the runway stretched. A bulldozer dumped rocks into the Pacific. Maybe that strip would end up longer than the islet, the way a carrier's flight deck overhung the hull. Pete didn't care one way or the other. He wondered if the poker game would start up again after the all-clear. He rather hoped it wouldn't.

Like the *Luftwaffe,* the Red Air Force was designed to have its planes fly from dirt airstrips near the front. To the *Luftwaffe,* Russia's *rasputitsa* came as a horrendous surprise. If Nazi troops on the ground needed air support but the Stukas couldn't fly because they'd got stuck in the mud, those foot soldiers would take a pounding. It happened again and again.

Of course, Soviet ground troops who needed air support during the *rasputitsa* also didn't get it. Soviet infantry and armor generals, though, mostly knew better than to put their men in spots like that during the fall rains and the spring thaw. Mostly. Like every other army since the beginning of time, Stalin's had its share of high-ranking donkeys.

Whether the generals knew he couldn't fly right now or not, Anastas Mouradian understood it perfectly well. So did every other pilot and copilot in his squadron. They caught up on their sleep. They ate like pigs. Some of them helped groundcrew men work on engines and controls and other things on their planes that needed repair.

Quite a few of them drank their way through the mud time. And when a Russian drank, he didn't drink to get a little buzz and to laugh louder than he would have sober. A Russian drank to get drunk, to drown himself in vodka.

Staying loaded for six weeks twice a year horrified Stas. He had but one liver to give for his country, and filling himself full of antifreeze like that wasn't his idea of fun. But the Russians who did drink like that seemed to manage fine. And when the fighting started up again and they had to go back to flying, they sobered up enough to do their jobs.

But the *rasputitsa* was a lonely season for him. Being sober when most of the people around you had got wrecked wasn't much fun. Ironically, the best companion he had was his copilot and ancient enemy, Isa Mogamedov. Whether he was a Muslim who clung to his faith's ban against alcohol or he was simply moderate like a lot of people from the Caucasus, he didn't make a hobby of getting shitfaced whenever he couldn't fly.

They played chess to kill time, which wasn't something you could do drunk. The Azeri won three or four times for every victory Stas managed to scratch out. He likely could have won more often than that. But, like any good wagon driver, he saw that the horse had to get a carrot every once in a while or it would simply refuse to go.

When they weren't playing chess, they talked. Each flavored his

Russian with a different accent: Mouradian's throaty, Mogamedov's more hissing. The old imperial language was the only one they shared. They talked endlessly about the Pe-2, how to make it bomb better and how to get away when the 109s and 190s zipped through the sky like hornets.

Stas would have liked to talk about other things. One of these days, the war would end. He was starting to hope he might live through it. What kind of country would the Soviet Union be afterwards? What kind of chances would a still-young veteran find in it? Would they know true Communism at last, or would things stay more complicated?

He would have bet Mogamedov wondered about such things, too. But if the Azeri did, he said no more about them than Anastas Mouradian. You might talk about things like that with your brother. If you were a trusting soul, you might even talk about them with the first cousin who'd grown up across the street from you. Either way, you'd do it late at night, behind doors not just closed but locked, and very likely in the dark.

Talk about them with your bomber crewmate? Yes, you kept each other alive every time you pulled back the yoke and brought the Pe-2 up into the air again. That was one thing. Trusting your crewmate not to sell you out to the NKVD? That was something else again. If the Great Terror of the 1930s proved anything, it proved you couldn't trust anybody not to sell you out.

And so they talked about cylinders and carburetors and keeping an eye on the armorers when they were loading the ammunition belts that fed the Pe-2's machine guns. If the bastards weren't careful, a gun would jam just when you needed it most.

Mogamedov said, "You have to make sure they're sober when they're putting the cartridges into the belts, too."

"Some people do take some watching, don't they?" Stas agreed. Neither of them said out loud that most of the groundcrew men were Russians, and that most Russians would get smashed on any day of the week that had *day* in it. Not in so many words, they didn't. But both of them looked at the most numerous folk in the USSR from the outside. Jews also did that. It was no accident that so many men from the Caucasus and Jews had risen to the top of the Soviet power pyramid. Outsiders were driven harder than those who had numbers on their side.

Back when the last war started, a lot of Russia's top generals had had German blood. But that had nothing to do with competence: only with noble blood. If those Russian generals with German names had known what they were doing, Stas knew he might be flying a plane with the Tsar's old red, white, and blue markings on it. But they hadn't, and the Red revolution swept them all away.

Not quite out of the blue, Mogamedov said, "We *will* beat the Hitlerites. I'm sure of it."

"Of course we will." Stas couldn't very well have said anything else. To doubt victory out loud was to ask for a bullet in the back of the neck; someone stupid enough to do that was too stupid to be worth anything in the gulag. The NKVD would think so, anyhow. He added, "The way the Nazis treat the lands they stole from us shows how well off we are under General Secretary Stalin."

"It does!" Mogamedov beamed at him. "That's very well put."

"*Spasibo,*" Stas said modestly. He felt like a man who had plenty to be modest about, all right. If it took a foreign invasion where the enemy destroyed everything he could and enslaved and brutalized everyone whose land he overran to make Stalin seem good by comparison, what kind of recommendation was that for the Soviet ruler?

But it did sound good, especially if you said it without audible irony. Stas appreciated irony in its place. He used it when he was talking about things where it wouldn't land him in trouble: unappetizing rations, say, or anything else where anyone would grouse. Sometimes even Russians smiled when he did.

If you aimed irony at the Soviet government, though, it would aim something back at you. One of those bullets in the back of the neck, maybe, in a Lubyanka basement. Or a twenty-five-year term at a camp north of the Arctic Circle. They rarely bothered with mere tenners any more. A term like that would also kill you, and might not take much longer to do the job than a pistol shot would. If they sent you off to Kolyma for twenty-five, you'd never see Armenia again—that was for sure.

"I want to bomb Berlin, that's what I want to do," Mogamedov said.

"They've dropped plenty on us. I want to pay them back, let the sons of bitches see what it's like."

"There you go!" Stas clapped his hands. "Blow that stupid, ugly toothbrush mustache right off Hitler's lip!" He'd started the war flying out of an airstrip in Slovakia, bombing the German invaders of Bohemia and Moravia. That was as close to hitting Germany as he'd come.

Some Russian flyers had bombed Berlin, as the English and the French had. But Soviet long-range bombers were slow and lumbering. No one talked about it in tones much above a whisper, but only a fraction of the ones that took off to strike the German capital made it back to the *Rodina* again.

Mogamedov lit a *papiros*. He offered the pack to Stas, who took one with a word of thanks. The Azeri said, "If we keep dropping shit on the Germans' heads here, sooner or later we'll push them back far enough so our Pe-2s can reach Berlin."

"After the mud dries out," Stas said. Isa Mogamedov nodded.

If there was a more backbreaking, filth-making job than replacing a thrown panzer track in Russian mud and rain, Theo Hossbach couldn't imagine what it might be. The job, in fact, was nasty enough to have pried several swear words out from between his usually tight-buttoned lips.

And what he said sounded like love poetry next to the fusillade of curses that poured from Adi Stoss. Most of what the driver said was aimed at himself. His tight left turn, after all, was what had made the Panzer IV shed the track in the first place.

"*Himmeldonnerwetter!*" he fumed. "A seeing-eye dog right out of driving school could have done that better than I did! I mean, a fucking *blind* seeing-eye dog could have."

"Take it easy, Adi," Hermann Witt said. "I told you to turn left, and you turned left."

"And this piece of shit went and came off," Adi snarled. "If I'd been a little smoother, it wouldn't have."

He gave a savage tug on the rope attached to one end of the thrown track. Little by little, the crew were wrestling the links over the return rollers and back toward the drive sprocket. Once they got the track onto the sprocket—if they ever did—they could reattach it to the other end, adjust the tension, and ride off into the sunset like cowboys in an American Western.

Sergeant Witt, perhaps incautiously, said as much. Adi clapped a muddy hand to his muddy forehead—he'd already used the gesture before, more than once. "Sure we can," he said. "If we don't bog down completely in the meantime. If the Ivans don't jump us. If—"

"If you don't quit pissing and moaning," Witt broke in. Just like the track, the panzer commander's patience had come apart.

Adi Stoss stared at him. Witt hardly ever barked like that. When he did, he had good reason to. Adi, luckily for him, owned enough mother wit to see as much. "Sorry, Sergeant," he said, his voice sheepish.

One of the things that made Witt a good panzer commander was not staying mad at the other guys in the crew. "All right," he said. "Let's get back to work, then." Another thing that made him a good commander was working hard and getting filthy like everybody else.

As they yanked and strained and swore, they all kept their Schmeissers where they could grab them in a hurry. Theo didn't think any Red Army men were in the neighborhood, but he wouldn't have sworn an oath in court. The Germans called their Russian foes Indians not least because of how they popped up where you least expected them. And thinking about riding off like cowboys naturally called Indians to mind.

In the distance, artillery grumbled and machine guns chattered. When you were cooped up inside your steel box, you never heard things like that. All you heard was the engine's growl and the rattle and clank of the suspension. Enemy bullets hitting the panzer sounded like gravel on a tin roof. Odds were you wouldn't hear the round that got through your armor. You'd just hear yourself scream—but not for long.

After a couple of hours of scraped knuckles and broken fingernails and a cut or two, they had the track back in place. Kurt Poske surveyed their handiwork and delivered the verdict: "Boy, that was fun."

"My ass!" Adi said.

The loader eyed him, then shook his head. "Sorry, sweetheart," he lisped in falsetto, "but it's not *your* ass I crave."

"Well, that's a relief," Adi told him. "If you talk that way, though, you're probably after Theo's instead."

Theo jumped. He hadn't expected to get dragged into the raillery. To make sure Kurt had no doubt where he stood on such things, he clapped a battered, protective hand to the seat of his grimy black coveralls. Everybody laughed.

"Come on, girls." Sergeant Witt lisped and shrilled, too. "Let's get back to business, shall we?" His voiced dropped into its normal register. "No chocolate-stabbers in this crew. That's one thing we don't have to worry about, anyway."

As Theo clambered into the panzer again, he was chewing on Witt's comment. By Adi's expression, so was he. Also by his expression, he wasn't so sure he fancied the flavor.

But Witt was all business after Adi fired up the Maybach engine and the panzer got moving again. At the sergeant's order, Theo radioed the company commander and regimental headquarters to let them know the crew had got the track back on. They both acknowledged the report. If they were delighted at the news, they hid it very well.

As the panzer chugged along, Adi glanced toward Theo and said, "I'm trying to drive like I'm on eggs. I don't want to have to do that again any time soon."

"I believe you," Theo said.

Adi smiled, as people often did when they got Theo to talk. Then he said, "I hope we stop in one of those Russian villages with the bathhouse where you throw the water onto hot rocks and you steam till you can't stand it any more—then you get a bucket of cold water in the kisser or jump in the snow if it's wintertime and whack each other with the birch-twig bundles. I've got all the dirt in the world on me right now."

"Not all of it." Theo spoke again. He held up his hands so Adi could see he was wearing a good bit of the world himself.

"Well, maybe you're carrying some, too." Adi dropped his voice so Theo could still hear but the three crewmates back in the turret wouldn't be able to: "You haven't been carrying yours for the past two thousand years, though."

Theo wondered what he was supposed to say to that. He said what he usually said: nothing.

"You know what the real bastard is?" Adi hadn't expected anything different, and went on without waiting for any kind of reply: "The real bastard is, if they come for me, it won't matter that I've spent a couple of years blowing up Ivans with you clowns. They won't care. And all of you are liable to wind up in deep shit if they decide you knew about me but didn't say anything."

"Knew what?" Theo asked, as if he hadn't the faintest idea what the driver might be talking about.

"*Ach, so.* Funny, Theo. I'm laughing, see?" The noises that came out of Adi's mouth might have sounded like laughter to him, but they wouldn't have to any normal human being. After those noises, he said, "Knew why—or one of the reasons why—I don't go to soldiers' brothels. The girls'd be too likely to remember me afterwards."

All this was as close as he ever came to naming his real—and serious—problem. Theo didn't think it was that big a worry. The girls German authorities dragged into soldiers' whorehouses in these parts rarely had a long *afterwards* in which to remember anybody, or any body part. Of course, that in itself was another reason both Theo and Adi stayed away from such establishments.

When they bivouacked, it wasn't in a village with a bathhouse. It was in the middle of a muddy field with the grass and weeds all torn up by panzer tracks and starting to yellow. There was a field kitchen in amongst the other panzers. Because their Panzer IV got there late, the stewed grain and turnips and sausage in the boiler were getting cold. Theo and his crewmates filled their mess tins anyhow. The stew spackled over the empty places between their ribs.

You hated to get under your panzer in weather like this. It was liable to sink down into the mud and squash you. If you used shelter halves to make a tent, you'd put your blanket on the mud. If you used the shelter halves for ground sheets, you'd get rained on. Theo slept sitting up inside the panzer. He was so tired, he didn't care about being uncomfortable. The other guys fought the rain. To him, that was their problem.

Chapter 10

During the summer, Spain got hotter than Czechoslovakia ever did. Vaclav Jezek bitched about that. During the winter, the cold of the central Spanish plateau pierced him to the root. He bitched about that, too.

During the fall, it rained. He really bitched about that. Any soldier hated being in the field while God pissed on him. A sniper, who had to stay in one place for hours at a stretch, hated it even more.

Benjamin Halévy was as sympathetic as usual: "You can always throw away your elephant gun and go back to being an ordinary soldier, you know."

Vaclav hated the antitank rifle's weight and clumsy length. He clutched the monster as if it were his beloved just the same. "I've lugged this fucker all over Western Europe," he said, exaggerating a little but not all that much. "I'll be damned if I get rid of it now. It's part of me."

"Like a wart. Or a tumor," Halévy said.

He might have been right. Vaclav was too stubborn to care. If he weren't, he wouldn't have wound up in the army of the Czechoslovakian government-in-exile to begin with. He gave Halévy a gesture that, to the American Internationals, meant everything was fine. To someone from Central Europe, it implied something else. Halévy chuckled. He never got stuffy about rank. And if he weren't a stubborn anti-Fascist himself, he wouldn't have ended up in Spain, either.

Out Vaclav went before dawn the next morning. If he caught pneumonia lying in a shell hole that slowly filled with water . . . then he did, that was all. He hadn't yet. He'd come down with the trots from eating bad food a few times, but that was about all. He didn't know anybody who'd fought for a while without having that happen to him.

On a day like this, he could get closer to the Nationalists' lines than he did most of the time. They wouldn't be able to spot him through the rain. How much he'd be able to see was another interesting question, though. He'd replaced the cardboard overhangs on his binoculars and rifle sight with ones he carved from scraps of wood, but he'd still be peering through the rain himself.

Strips of torn burlap and bits of foliage attached to his uniform and helmet and rifle broke up his outline. When he found a good hiding place, he'd rub mud on his cheeks and on his hands so he wouldn't show up against the background.

Nobody had taught him any of this business. He'd learned it or made it up as he went along. He wondered why no sharp-eyed German had killed him in France before he figured out what was what. A couple of them had tried—he knew that. He was still here, while the Fritzes' kin back in the *Vaterland* must have got wires to let them know their loved ones had died for the *Führer*.

Come to think of it, this morning he might need to do his face, but his hands would get plenty filthy crawling to his hidey-hole. He found a good one, and improved it with his entrenching tool so the water ran down to the bottom and didn't pool right under him.

By the time the gloomy day broke, he was ready for whatever might happen. He lay very still: he might almost have been a forgotten corpse himself. A sparrow certainly thought he was. The stupid little bird landed less than a meter from his face and started hopping around looking for seeds or bugs or whatever else it could pop into its beak.

"Hey, bird!" he said. "What d'you think you're doing, bird?" He spoke quietly. He thought it was the motion of his lips rather than the noise he made that scared the sparrow. Whatever it was, the bird let out a horrified chirp and took off as if it had a 109 on its tail. God tracked falling sparrows, didn't He? Well, here was one going up for Him to watch.

A few Nationalists started shooting at the Republican line. Each of them fired slowly, taking a long time to work the bolt on his rifle and load a fresh round. They had orders to shoot, but they weren't happy about them. Or, more likely, they hadn't had their first slug of espresso yet, so they were only half awake.

He could have killed them. They were spending way too long up on the firing step, too. But they weren't worth wasting ammunition on, not for a sniper like him. They weren't worth giving away his position for, either. *The small change of war*, Vaclav thought.

Sanjurjo's men would have been furious to know how he saw them. They were all heroes in their own minds. A lot of them truly were heroes. Spaniards didn't even worry about chances no sane German or Czech would take. They were the small change of war even so.

He swung his binoculars a few centimeters to the right and squinted through them again. He suddenly paid close attention to what he saw there: a fellow with binoculars of his own was looking back at him. Jezek didn't care for that, not even a little bit. He muscled his rifle over to bear on the Spaniard. Of itself, his right hand slid toward the trigger.

It wasn't just that the bastard might be searching for him. Anybody with binoculars was likely to be an officer. An officer might be worth killing. And an officer looking out from the forward trench would be easy to kill, too. From here, Vaclav figured he wouldn't have much trouble killing somebody over there with a Mauser.

Nationalist officers often painted their rank badge in gold on the front of their helmets. Part of the point of being a Nationalist officer was showing that you were. They were as aggressively boastful as Spanish Republicans were aggressively egalitarian.

He had trouble making out how big a wheel this brave fool was. The rain obscured whatever emblem he had above the outthrust brim of his German-style headgear. It did seem to have a lot of gold, though. That seemed promising, at least if you were a sniper.

The Nationalist lowered the field glasses and turned to say something to someone Vaclav couldn't see. He could see the man's round face and heavy jowls, his gray mustache, and the pouches under his eyes.

"Fuck me," the Czech whispered as he quickly centered the crosshairs on the target's head. He didn't *know* that was who he thought it was. He didn't know, no, but the shot was worth taking anyhow.

Stay in routine, he told himself, and he did. Target lined up? Yes. A couple of deep breaths, in and out. Don't hurry. Don't worry. If you hurry and worry, you'll miss. Don't think about who it might be. Don't think at all. Just aim and . . . shoot.

He didn't jerk the trigger. He brought his right index finger back hard enough to take up the slack, and then to fire the piece. The anti-tank rifle bellowed. Recoil slammed against his shoulder. Yes, he'd added to his collection of bruises. No, he hadn't done anything stupid like breaking his collarbone.

He hadn't done anything stupid like missing, either. If you dropped a boulder on a watermelon from the top of a five-story building, you might get an explosion of red mist and gunk like the one a fat, high-velocity, armor-piercing slug produced when it slammed into some luckless soldier's temple. Down went the Nationalist officer. He'd twitch for a minute or two, but he was already dead just the same.

Now—had the assholes in the trenches over there spotted the flash through the rain? Did they know where it came from? If they did, how excited would they get about it?

He didn't need long to realize it hadn't been some overage, over-weight major of artillery. The Nationalists started running every which way. Through his field glasses, he saw that they started pointing every which way, too. He breathed a little easier then. No, they didn't know which hole he was hiding in. They wouldn't start throwing mortar bombs this way or send out a couple of squads of pissed-off soldiers after him.

Rifle fire from the Nationalists' trenches picked up. Machine guns started their malevolent snarl. The enemy artillery bombarded the Republican lines. Wet and chilly in his shell hole, Vaclav lay without moving and began to think he really might have done it.

Peggy Druce fixed coffee and oatmeal for herself. While the coffee perked, she turned on the radio. It was eight o'clock straight up. She could catch the morning news while she got breakfast ready.

Well, she could after they tried to sell her soap and toothpaste and canned pork and beans. "A little bit less pork for the duration," the announcer said, "but just as much delicious goodness!" Undoubtedly just as much per can, too. They wouldn't lower the price because they'd cheapened the mix. That would be un-American.

NBC's three familiar chimes rang out. "Here is the news," a different announcer said. "American bombers gave Midway Island another pasting last night. Three planes are reported missing. One ditched in the Pacific, and most of the crew have been rescued."

Three planes were reported missing. That was what he said. Most people would take it to mean the United States had lost only three planes. If Peggy hadn't got stuck in war-torn Europe, she would have taken it the same way. But all the warring countries over there told as many lies as they thought they could get away with, and then another one for luck. Three planes reported lost could mean any number down in flames.

"President Roosevelt is delighted at industrial and agricultural production," the newsman said. "At a White House dinner last night, he said, 'We are getting the tools we need for victory, and when we have them we will finish the job.' The dinner menu included fried chicken, baked potatoes, and peas."

Peggy chuckled. That was the kind of plain food any American family might eat. FDR liked fancier recipes. When what he ate made the news, though, he kept it simple.

After what the President had for dinner came the foreign news. The Germans were denying a Russian breakthrough in front of Minsk. Goebbels claimed Stalin was obviously lying, because the ground in Russia was too muddy to let anyone break through. That sounded reasonable. Of course, when you were talking about the two biggest liars in Europe—a prize for which the competition was steep—who could guess whether sounding reasonable meant anything?

"And, in the long-running civil war in Spain so closely tied to the wider European struggle, Nationalist radio has at last admitted the death of Marshal Sanjurjo," the newsman went on. "A Nationalist statement says the marshal 'died a martyr in the unending struggle against atheistic Bolshevism.' No successor has been named. The Nationalists deny Republican reports of a power struggle among their generals."

That they denied it didn't mean it wasn't true. Peggy lit her first cigarette of the morning. The Spaniards didn't tell lies the size of the ones that came out of Berlin and Moscow, but it wasn't for lack of effort.

"Hitler and Mussolini have both expressed their regret over the loss of the man they have often called the liberator of Spain," the newsman said. "What will happen there now without him remains to be seen."

If Hitler and Mussolini missed Sanjurjo, Peggy didn't need to take out a slide rule to calculate that she didn't. The Spanish general's war had given the bigger Fascist dictators—and Stalin—the chance to test their weapons and let their soldiers earn some combat experience. They'd all gone on to bigger and worse things, too.

She left the radio on while she did the dishes. The sports news was that the Phillies had fired their manager. The A's were just as lousy. But, since ancient Connie Mack not only managed but also owned the team, chances were he wouldn't give himself the old heave-ho. It wasn't as if he hadn't wound up in the cellar plenty of other times.

Commercials followed the news, and then an interview show at a war plant. It was so stupid and saccharine, it soon made Peggy spin the dial. She felt embarrassed she'd listened to it for even a few minutes. Plenty of people must, she supposed, or they wouldn't leave it on the air. But if *that* was popular, the country had to be going to the dogs . . . didn't it?

She washed some clothes. She hung them out on the line behind the house. It wasn't warm any more. The wind blowing out of the north made the wet laundry flap. The clothes would dry fast, unless the wind brought rain with it.

When she went back in, she did some ironing, too. She thanked heaven for an iron you plugged into the wall, an iron that by God stayed hot. She'd learned to fight wrinkles with irons you had to heat on the stove, irons that cooled off to worthlessness by the time you carried them from the stove to the ironing board.

After the ironing, sweeping and dusting. Now that she had no one but herself for whom to keep the house neat, she did a better job of housekeeping than she had when Herb also lived here. She pictured him living in squalor in his apartment. She couldn't make herself believe the picture, though. Even living alone, Herb wouldn't be a slob. Any man who'd gone through the Army knew the basics of taking care of himself.

By the time she finished getting the place shipshape, it was almost noon. She stared at the clock on her nightstand as if it had done her wrong. And she felt it had. Didn't she just finish breakfast? It seemed that way, but she was hungry for lunch.

She'd had ham for dinner the night before. Wax paper–wrapped leftovers sat in the icebox. She sliced some ham thin, put it on bread, added sweet pickles and mustard, and ate the sandwich. Another cup of coffee washed it down. That was heated up from the pot she'd made for breakfast, and on the bitter side. Next to what they called coffee in Europe, it was the nectar of the gods.

After lunch, she started an Agatha Christie mystery. It was pretty good, but the Englishwoman's casual anti-Semitism grated in ways it wouldn't have before Peggy saw how Hitler treated Jews in the countries he'd overrun—and in his own. She sighed and put the book down. She'd changed, all right.

Her life had turned inside out because she'd been stranded on the wrong side of the Atlantic when Europe went up in flames. Well, sure, so did millions of other lives. But it wasn't even as if she'd got hurt. She'd just got stuck.

And, because she'd got stuck, she wasn't married to Herb any more. Her politics and her whole outlook on the world had changed. Why? Because she hadn't packed up and headed for home a week earlier.

How many other lives took turns just as big from causes just as trivial? It made you wonder. It really did. In some world where she *had* taken a train back to France and sailed for America, was another Peggy, one who still wore a wedding ring, rattling around this house right now? Was that Peggy wondering what things would have been like if she'd stayed in Czechoslovakia till the war broke out?

This Peggy's mouth twisted. "Trust me, kiddo—you wouldn't've had a whole lot of fun," she told the imaginary one, and tried to dismiss her from her own mind.

But, once summoned, that still-married Peggy didn't want to be dismissed. Neither did the idea that had spawned her, even if it seemed to belong to the lurid pulp magazines with the gaudy covers and the wildly titled stories. Because the real Peggy was sure she couldn't be the only one who conjured imaginary selves from the vasty deep. Everybody had places in his life where he could have done one thing but had done the other. Had he chosen differently, he would have had a different life story from then on out. How could you *help* wondering about the way that other movie would have run?

Peggy lit a cigarette to help herself think. It wasn't only people, was it? It was countries, too. What would Germany be like right now if Hitler had got killed in the last war? He could have, easily. He'd been a runner—from what Herb said, about as dangerous a duty as you could find. But he'd come through, and the *Reich* was what it was because he had. If you dug enough, history had to be full of crazy things like that. Peggy decided she didn't want to dig after all. She fixed herself a bourbon on the rocks. It helped, but not enough.

Louis Mirouze didn't look quite so miserable as a kitten you tossed into a puddle. But that was only because the young lieutenant's helmet kept his hair from going every which way like a soaked kitten's.

Aristide Demange was sure he looked every bit as soggy himself. He doubted he looked miserable, though. His guess was that he looked pissed off. It wasn't a wild guess. He usually looked pissed off, because he usually was pissed off. If you couldn't find something to get pissed off about while you were in the Army, you weren't half trying.

"Stupid *cons*," he muttered. Just then, a raindrop came down right on the coal of his Gitane. The cigarette quit drawing. He spat it out in disgust and fired up another one.

"Sir?" Mirouze said.

"Stupid *cons*," Demange repeated. "The cretins and syphilitic imbeciles who left us stuck in the mud here."

"Oh," Mirouze said. That would have been heresy to him not long before. Now he just shrugged. "Fuck 'em all."

"*Alors!*" Demange said in surprise. "I couldn't have put it better myself. You're learning, kid."

What showed in Mirouze's eyes was something on the order of *Fuck you, too*. He didn't come out with it. Demange might have laughed if he had. Or he might have coldcocked him, not because he outranked Mirouze but because only his friends could talk to him like that, and he counted his friends on the toes of both hands.

A German MG-42 spat a few short bursts over the French line, just to remind the *poilus* to keep their heads down. The Germans lived better in their trenches than the French did. The French seemed to think being miserable reminded you you were at war. The *Boches* made the best of things. In the last war, Demange had seen a deep German bunker with electric lights and with wallpaper over the timbers that shored it up. Except for being a good many meters underground, it could have been taken from an expensive flat.

"Here," Demange said. "You're a smart *cochon*, so I've got an arithmetic problem for you. If we advance ten meters every day, how long till we get to Berlin?"

"Long enough so I'm not holding my breath," Mirouze answered, which was close enough to the right answer to make Demange nod. The second lieutenant went on, "If we can push the Fritzes back to their old border, I'll be happy enough. As long as they don't shoot me, I will."

"Beats the crap out of '*On les aura!*' doesn't it?" Demange agreed. "And it's about as much as we can hope for on this side. Over in the East, the *Boches* have a little more on their plates."

"They've got the Poles over there to keep the Russians off them," Mirouze said. "Till the Poles turn their coats, anyhow."

"Heh! You mean the way we did?" Demange said. "I was over there when that happened, remember. And I'm goddamn lucky I'm back here now."

Off in the distance, German 105s woke up. Demange listened to the shells scream through the air. If that scream built and built till it sounded as if it were coming down right on top of you . . . then the chances were much too good that it was. That was when you wanted a deep bunker, like the German one Demange remembered. A direct hit from a 105 wouldn't bother that bunker one bit. You'd need something like a 240 to make it sit up and take notice, and those babies didn't grow on trees.

Mirouze was listening intently, too. His face cleared no more than a split second after Demange's. "They'll go wide of us."

"That's right," Demange said. "Some other sorry *salauds* will suffer, but not us. And you know what? The Germans shot me in the last war. If they don't get me this time, I won't mind. Let the next hero take his turn instead. Fine with me, by God!"

"If everybody thought like you, we couldn't have a war," Mirouze said.

"Everybody *does* think like me. You fucking *want* to get your family jewels blown off?" Demange said. "But when they tell you, 'We *will* kill you if you don't go, and the *Boches* may miss if you do,' what happens then? You damn well go, that's what."

Back behind them, French artillery started roaring. Demange carefully noted the flight of those shells, too. It was counterbattery fire, going after the Germans' guns. He relaxed, as much as he ever let himself relax. If his own side had started raking the enemy's forward trenches, the *Boches* might have felt obliged to return the favor. Some courtesies, Demange could do without.

Lieutenant Mirouze asked a new question: "What do you think of the antitank rocket the Americans have made, the *bazooka*?" He pronounced the name slowly and carefully, stressing how strange and foreign it was.

Demange thought the handle sounded idiotic, too, but that wasn't what the kid was talking about. "I've only seen a couple of them," he answered. "I've heard it can get through the armor on most German tanks—the Tiger still gives it trouble. If it can, I'm all for it. I'm for anything that gives the infantry a chance against *chars*. But what do you want to bet the Fritzes will start making their own as soon as they can get their hands on one? Then our tanks will start cooking, too."

"It could be." By Mirouze's expression, he hadn't thought of that. Also by his expression, he didn't much like the possibility now that Demange had pointed it out. What a shame! Whether he liked it or not wouldn't slow the Germans down a bit. Demange had no doubts there.

After a while, the shelling petered out. Only the rain and the chill and the machine guns to worry about then. Wasn't life grand? It was so grand, Demange took the water bottle off his hip and swigged from it. He had cognac in there, not water. It didn't do much about machine guns, but it sure made the rain and chill seem less annoying.

He offered Mirouze the aluminum bottle. "Thanks," the younger officer said, surprise in his voice: Demange wasn't usually so friendly. Mirouze started to cough when he found the bottle didn't hold water or even *pinard*. But he didn't choke and he didn't spew the stuff out his nose like someone who didn't know how to drink. He respectfully handed the bottle back. "Thanks is right."

"Any time. All part of the service." Demange stuck the bottle back into the cloth canteen cover.

"That'll put hair on my chest," Mirouze said. "Probably make me grow hair all over like King Kong."

"Just don't start pounding your chest and climbing the tallest building you can find. It wouldn't be beauty killed the beast—it'd be the fucking Fritzes and their damn buzz saws." As if to underscore Demange's words, an MG-42 sprayed more death at the French lines.

"I guess I won't." Mirouze sighed. "I'd make a crappy gorilla anyhow, wouldn't I?"

"Now that you mention it, yes," Demange said. The junior lieutenant was skinny and sallow, with a long, mournful face, not quite enough chin, and a sad little mustache that looked as if someone had put burnt cork on his upper lip and he'd washed off some of it but not enough.

"You know what else is funny?" Mirouze said. "Those biplane

fighters that got the ape were as good as anybody's ten years ago. They wouldn't last ten minutes now. Well, they would against King Kong, but not against real airplanes."

"You're right." Demange sounded surprised, mostly because he was. That a punk like Lieutenant Mirouze could come up with something worth hearing, something Demange hadn't thought of himself, had to come as a surprise. "What we had ten years ago was junk next to what we've got now."

"And who knows what we'll have in ten years more?" Mirouze said.

"Whatever it is, it'll probably kill you before you even get born." In his own twisted way, Demange had faith in mankind.

Every time Hideki Fujita woke up in the morning after a U.S. bombing raid, he thanked all the *kami* that he didn't wake up dead. He'd seen bombing raids from the Russians, but those were only an annoyance next to the pounding Midway was taking.

The island, bigger than any this side of the main Hawaiian group, took up several square kilometers. The only thing that let the Japanese garrison remain a going concern was that that was simply too much ground for a string of bombers to knock flat even with the worst will in the world.

Had they dropped incendiaries . . . Fujita imagined the devastation that kind of bombing could cause in Japan's lightly built cities, with so many walls of wood or paper. Yes, those would all go up in flames, and no one could guess how many people with them.

But the Americans were at the end of their reach here on Midway. The Home Islands lay thousands of kilometers to the west. No Yankee bombers could reach them. No Yankee bombers would ever reach them. Fujita was sure of it.

He walked over to the edge of the lagoon as soon as it began to get light. Bombs had fallen in the water there. The bursts killed the little silvery fish that took refuge in the shallows from bigger, meaner fish out in the Pacific. Some of them had washed ashore. They hadn't started to go bad.

A bayonet was rarely useful these days as a weapon of war. You fought the enemy at longer range than you could thrust with your bayoneted rifle. But a knife on your belt was still a handy thing to have. It was good for all kinds of things. Gutting little fish lying on the sand, for instance.

Another soldier was using his bayonet for the same purpose. A petty officer had a shorter knife that also did the job. He caught Fujita's eyes. "Well, the Americans went and got our breakfast ready for us, anyhow," he said, and ate the fish he'd just cleaned.

"*Hai.*" Fujita nodded. "I didn't have sashimi for breakfast very often before I came here, but there's nothing wrong with it." He ate a fish, too. "A lot better than no breakfast at all." He knew more about that than he'd ever wanted to find out. Anyone who'd been in combat for a while discovered more than he'd ever wanted to learn about missing meals.

The other soldier tossed some guts into the water. He crouched down and scooped out a fish that came up to the bait. Inside of two minutes, that one was inside him. "You won't get any fresher than that unless you eat dancing shrimp."

"I haven't done that since before I went into the Army." Fujita let out a sigh full of longing. What could be more delicious than a live shrimp peeled from its shell and still wriggling?

A gull swooped down, grabbed a dead fish, and swallowed it while flying away. The gooney birds here didn't care about people. The gulls knew enough to be wary of them. Some of the Japanese had eaten seagulls. The only reason they didn't do it more often was that gulls tasted bad.

One of the reasons they tasted bad was that they didn't care what they ate themselves. They were as bad as ravens. They would eat dead soldiers if you didn't get the bodies under the sand. Did that make you a cannibal if you ate them? Fujita hadn't, so he didn't worry about it.

He had other things to worry about. He went to work with pick and shovel so the G4Ms could try to pay the Americans back for their visit. Japan kept flying a few bombers in by way of Wake Island. The Americans had more, though, and could bring in planes and men and munitions more easily than Fujita's side. Their bases were closer to their homeland than this distant outpost of Empire was.

Rice. A little *shoyu* for flavor. Canned squid (the Americans had blown up a lot of food, but for some reason there was still plenty of canned squid). All things considered, sashimi from fish bombed in the lagoon was a step up from anything the cooks could do with what they had.

At the garrison's pitiful supper, everyone held the same thought uppermost in his mind. Would the Yankees come over again tonight? The only way to find out was to try to sleep and see if you made it through till morning without needing to dash for a hole in the sand. When U.S. air raids started, the soldiers and sailors used to give the antiaircraft gunners grief about not shooting down more American planes. Now the men saw the gunners did the best they could. The bombers flew high. The gunners had no searchlights to show them their targets. They had to fire at the engines' drone and hope for the best.

Fujita rolled himself in his blanket. After a day of hard labor on the runway—still nowhere near ready to take planes—he was ready to sleep hard for as long as anybody would let him. The Americans let him till a little past midnight. Then explosions woke him. He thought some of those booms would have woken the dead.

If he didn't want to be one of those dead, he needed to take what little cover he could find. He grabbed his belt and his rifle—ingrained military habit—and ran for a shallow, sandy trench. Bombs kept whistling down out of the sky. He didn't want to think about what would happen if one of them whistled down right here. But what else could he think about when the ground shook and the only light was the lurid flash of explosions?

Almost the only light. A couple of guns kept blasting away at the planes overhead. Their muzzle flashes and the ice-blue streaks from the tracers they fired also gave Fujita's eyes something to work with.

If you put enough shells in the air, sooner or later you were bound to hit something. So the gunners claimed. Other troops stationed on Midway loudly and profanely doubted it. But the gunners turned out to know what they were talking about after all.

Through the whistles and explosions and the rapid-fire booming of the guns, Fujita heard his countrymen cheering in their holes. He looked up into the night. Kilometers high in the sky, an American bomber was on fire. Flames spread up the wing to the fuselage. The plane plummeted toward the sea. When it crashed into the Pacific, wreckage and gasoline floated on the water, burning.

Rifles started going off. Fujita looked up again. Lit as if by flash bulbs, parachutes were floating down on Midway. He chambered a round in his own Arisaka and blazed away whenever he could see one. American flyers deserved whatever happened to them, especially if they didn't have the nerve to kill themselves instead of being taken prisoner.

One of the parachutes was coming down almost right on top of him. He fixed his bayonet. He might get some combat use out of it after all. When the flyer landed, Fujita scrambled from the trench and dashed toward him. He wasn't the only one, but he was the closest.

He could see and smell blood on the American, but the white man wasn't dead. He reached for something on his belt—a pistol, probably. Fujita fired from no more than a couple of meters away. The flyer groaned. Fujita gave him the bayonet, again and again. The Yankee screamed till his voice faded into a choking gurgle.

"Enough," another Japanese said. "You killed him, all right."

"I wish I could kill them all." Fujita stabbed the bayonet into the sand to get off as much of the American's blood as he could. If any other men from the burning bomber came down on Midway, he knew they would meet the same reception this fellow had.

As the rest of the enemy planes growled away, Fujita plundered the corpse. He took the pistol and a couple of magazines of cartridges. He also took the Yankee's emergency rations. They might not be good, but they'd be different, anyhow. He tossed the man's billfold aside— American money wouldn't do him any good. He didn't care if he slept the rest of the night or not. He'd hit back at the foe right here on Midway!

Chapter 11

One of the things Hans-Ulrich Rudel hated about the way the war had gone was that you couldn't ask questions any more. Well, you could, but you had to be careful about who heard them. Otherwise, you might get a visit from Major Keller, who would wonder whether your spirit was sufficiently National Socialist.

Or Keller might just decide you were hopeless. In that case, he wouldn't call on you. The SD or the *Gestapo* would. And if they took you away, who knew where you'd wind up or what would happen to you there?

No one knew, though almost everyone could make a good guess. That was another question you couldn't ask. It was bound to bring Major Keller or worse down on you if you did.

Hans-Ulrich could still talk to Sergeant Dieselhorst, and the non-com heard news long before he did himself. Picking a time when no one stood anywhere close, Rudel quietly asked, "What's the latest from Münster?"

"From where?" Dieselhorst said. "You mean that little town in . . . was it Bulgaria or Yugoslavia?"

"Bulgaria, I think." Hans-Ulrich matched dry with dry.

The sergeant rewarded him by hoisting one eyebrow. "Martial law is the last thing I heard. I mean, the whole *Reich* is under martial law, or as near as makes no difference, but this is the real stuff. Curfews, and they won't just arrest you if you get out of line. They'll shoot you."

"That's . . . harsh." Hans-Ulrich had supported the Nazis ever since he'd decided they were the ones to make Germany strong again. Now, for the first time, he started to wonder whether he'd made a mistake. "And how do the, ah, Bulgarians like that?"

Dieselhorst smiled a thin smile. "They're up in arms—literally, for the people who happen to have any. And I've heard they aren't the only folks in Bulgaria who are. I don't know that that's true. Bulgaria's a long way away, and you can't always trust the news that comes out of it. But that's what I hear."

"Huh." Rudel didn't like the way that sounded. "How can we fight a war if the home front falls apart on us? That's what happened in 1918."

After coughing a couple of times, Albert Dieselhorst made a small production of lighting a cigarette. The pause let Hans-Ulrich remember what a little boy he'd been in 1918, and that he didn't really know for himself everything that had gone on then. After said pause, Dieselhorst answered, "You know, if you build a house of cards outside and the breeze blows it over, that's one thing. But if you build it on the kitchen table and then you knock it down, you've got only yourself to blame. Or that's how it looks at me, anyway."

He waited. Hans-Ulrich realized he had to say something. "What do you suppose Major Keller would say to that?" he tried.

"Major Keller knocks down houses of cards for the fun of it . . . sir," Dieselhorst said. "If the Party had half as many people like Major Keller in it, we'd be twice as well off. That's how it looks to me, too."

Rudel opened his mouth. The speech about how, when enemies were everywhere, you needed National Socialist Loyalty Officers jumped to the tip of his tongue. But it didn't jump off. Foreign foes, yes—you needed to worry about them. When your own people started hating your government, though, how could you be so sure the people were the ones with the problem?

When Hans-Ulrich didn't come out with that canned speech, Sergeant Dieselhorst blew a stream of smoke up toward the sky. He didn't say anything like *You're learning* or *You're growing up*. The proof, as the geometry books put it, was left to the student.

Dieselhorst did say, "They would have been smarter not to mess with the bishop."

Again, Hans-Ulrich kept quiet. This time, it was because he didn't know what to say. He was no Catholic. He was the son of a Lutheran minister. He had no use for the Pope or his faith. But a Catholic bishop was a clergyman, too. What if the *Gestapo* had come for Pastor Rudel instead?

He had trouble imagining Johannes Rudel saying or doing anything that would make the authorities want to come after him. But if they did, he hoped the people of whichever little Silesian town he happened to be preaching in would be upset enough to try to do something about it.

So he said, "Yes, I guess they would. But we can't change any of that. All we can do is bomb the French and the English so they don't break through and invade the *Vaterland*."

"Well, you're right about that," Dieselhorst said. "It's bad when politics comes to the *Luftwaffe,* and it's bad when the *Luftwaffe* gets into politics." He ground out the cigarette under his boot heel. "And if we don't get more fighter support, we won't keep flying against the enemy much longer."

Hans-Ulrich grunted. The noncom was dead right about that. Without 109s or 190s flying top cover, Stukas that ventured far past the front were asking to get shot down. When the war was new, the *Luftwaffe* had more fighters and better fighters than the RAF or the *Armée de l'Air*. German fighters were still as good as any the Western democracies made, and better than the ones they bought from America. But there weren't enough of them here.

"Too many planes fighting the Russians," Rudel said. "Too many trying to keep the enemy from knocking our cities flat, too."

"I know," Sergeant Dieselhorst replied with what sounded like exaggerated patience. "You would have hoped the people who got us into this war wondered whether this would happen when they told us to start shooting."

"They thought we'd win in a hurry," Hans-Ulrich said.

"Yes, yes." Sure enough, the sergeant's patience showed more and more. "Winning in a hurry was Plan A. But they should have had Plan B ready ahead of time in case we didn't, and Plan C in case something funny happened, and Plan D in case something stupid happened, and . . . and on and on. That's why God, or maybe the Devil, made the General Staff, *nicht wahr*?"

"I don't think either one of Them would want to get blamed for it," Hans-Ulrich answered.

He surprised a laugh out of Sergeant Dieselhorst, which wasn't something he managed every day. "There you go!" Dieselhorst said. "You know, you can be dangerous if you give yourself half a chance."

"Who, me?" Rudel did his best to assume a look of wide-eyed in-nocence. For a minister's son, the look came naturally. The sergeant's snort confirmed that.

It started to rain then. That was another reason they weren't flying. The clouds in Belgium blew right off the ocean. When it was cloudy here, the ceiling was almost always low. You didn't want to go up in a dive-bomber when you might dive below the ceiling to drop your load and then not have time to pull up before you hit the ground.

The fellows in the level bombers didn't fret about such things. They flew above the clouds, not below them. They could bomb in any weather. But they were none too accurate even when they could see what they were aiming at. When they couldn't . . . Well, the bombs were bound to come down on something or other.

Up ahead of the airstrip, German guns started firing on the enemy positions facing them. Before long, French guns answered. Chances were none of the men serving the 105s could see their target, either. That didn't mean dropping shells on it wouldn't hurt the other side. Stretcher-bearers and ambulances would carry wounded men back to aid stations.

Gravediggers would be busy, too. Hans-Ulrich seldom thought about such things. When you were flying, you were too busy to worry about them. Only at times like this, when you couldn't go up, did they invade your mind.

It was also only at times like this that you got the chance to think about politics. And that was bound to be just as well.

Alistair Walsh had found one thing almost unchanged from the last war to this one. Wherever the front was in France or Belgium, *estaminets* would spring up right behind it. They'd sell you bad wine and watery beer, fried potatoes, fried eggs, and, if you were brave enough, fried sausages.

Somebody'd said you never wanted to know what went into politics or sausages. Was that Bismarck? Walsh thought so. The mustached old bugger might have been a Fritz, but he knew what he was talking about just the same. And you especially didn't want to know what went into sausages you bought at an *estaminet* within earshot of the guns.

Which didn't mean Walsh hadn't ordered a couple of them with his chips and his pint. Horse? Cat? Hedgehog? Ground-up inner tube? There was enough pepper and garlic mixed up with everything else to keep you from noticing how rank the meat (or possibly rubber) was.

He thought so, anyhow. A corporal sitting at the table next to his took a bite and pulled a face. "I think the landlord chopped up his granny and stuck her in here, like in the penny dreadfuls back when," the fellow said.

Walsh donned a contemplative look as he ate some more off his plate. "Not dry enough for granny," he said after he swallowed. "Maybe it's his maiden aunt."

"If she tastes like this, no bloody wonder she died a maiden," the corporal answered. He swigged from a glass of wine and grimaced again. "And this here is grape juice and vinegar."

"It could be worse," Walsh said. "The Army could be feeding us." The bloke with two stripes on his sleeve had no comeback to that. Walsh added, "I bet it's worse on the German side of the line, too. The *estaminets* there likely dish up turnip sausages and sawdust chips."

"How do you know these ain't?" the corporal asked, which was a better question than Walsh wished it were.

This wasn't one of those *estaminets* with pretty barmaids, or even homely barmaids, available *pour l'amour ou pour le sport*. The landlord's two strapping sons brought food and drink and took away dirty dishes. They weren't in uniform. They were ready to fight for their country's liberation to the last drop of English blood.

Well, it could have been worse. They weren't fighting in Hitler's Walloon Legion, either. The Fascist Belgians fought harder than the Germans did. They knew what the Allies would probably do to them if they got captured, so they made sure they didn't.

With a sigh, Walsh set a shilling and a little silver threepence on the table, grabbed his greatcoat, and walked out. English coins were valuable all out of proportion to the official rate of exchange. For all the veteran knew, the Belgians melted them down and made ingots out of them. He didn't care, as long as he could cheaply buy whatever he needed.

He shrugged on the greatcoat before he'd gone more than a few steps back toward the line. The wind blew out of the north, and warned that winter was on the way. For good measure, he pulled a khaki wool muffler out of his pocket. It was scratchy as all get-out—the Army worried as little about things like comfort as it could get away with—but it kept his neck warm.

Only a few trees still stood. As in the last war, hard fighting had smashed most of them to matchsticks and toothpicks. Leaves on the survivors were going, or had mostly gone, yellow. That sharp wind would soon blow off the ones that still clung to the branches.

Walsh hated bare-branched trees. Those skinny sticks thrusting up toward the sky put him in mind of bones with the flesh rotted off them sticking up from hasty, badly dug graves. You saw things like that after artillery tore up one of those burial plots. Walsh wasn't the kind to worry about unquiet ghosts, but he also saw those bones in his nightmares.

There was one stretch of ground on the way up to his position that the Germans could get a glimpse of. If they saw you, they'd fire a burst from one of their machine guns. The range was extreme. No one bullet was likely to hit you. That was why they fired the burst—they'd spend a dozen bullets, or a couple of dozen, in hopes of the hit.

When Walsh came to the couple of hundred yards where he might be in danger, he got down on his hands and knees and crawled so the *Feldgrau* sons of bitches wouldn't spot him. A couple of men were walking the other way. They didn't laugh at him—they did the same thing. The Fritzes were too good at hurting you even when you didn't give them any extra chances.

He sighed when he traveled up the zigzag communications trenches to the front line. The Germans had a better chance of hurting him up here, of course. But it was also a very familiar place. He'd spent a lot of time in trenches like this, through two wars and in training stints between them. He knew how to make himself at home, or as much at home as anyone could be in this low-rent district of hell.

At least it hadn't rained for a few days. The trenches were muddy. You couldn't get away from mud during a war, any more than you could get away from blood. But there weren't any reeking puddles or pools; the water had soaked into the ground. That made a difference. You hated to roll into a puddle in your sleep and soak yourself. The stench wasn't so bad after things had dried out a little, either.

He nodded to Jack Scholes, who took to this life the way any tough little creature would. "What's going on?" he asked.

"Not bloody much," Scholes said. "Germans must 'ave packed it in, loike."

"And then you wake up!" Walsh exclaimed. "That'll be the day. Chances are they're plotting something instead. Do you believe anything different, even for a minute?"

"Believe it? Nar." The young cockney shook his head. "But Oi can 'ope, roight, loike anybody else?"

"Should never take hope away from anyone," Walsh said, more seriously than he'd expected to. "Just don't get your hopes up too high for no reason, or they'll come crashing down, and you with 'em."

"That's the times when the Fritzes got tanks wiv 'em," Scholes said shrewdly. "Ain't seen none. Ain't 'eard none, neither."

"Well, good," Walsh said. It wasn't that he wanted the Germans to strike somewhere else along the line. He didn't wish that on any of his countrymen. He didn't even wish it on the French, not unless some froggy had gone out of his way to provoke him.

He wished the Germans would just turn around and go home. He was ready to follow them till they crossed over the border between Holland and their own country. He was ready to stop there, too, and wave good-bye as they vanished back inside Hunland. And as long as they stayed there and didn't bother anybody else, he was ready to let them stay there and go to hell in their own way.

The trouble with them, of course, was that they had the nasty habit of not wanting to stay there. Every so often, they burst out like locusts and tried to send everybody else to hell their way. They'd almost brought it off twice now. If they went back into Hunland now, would they decide third time was the charm along about, oh, 1962?

If they did, he wouldn't be the one who had to drive them back. He wouldn't be a Chelsea pensioner by then, one of the ancient, doddering soldiers who sometimes went to the football club's matches, but he wouldn't be ready to pick up a Lee-Enfield or even a Sten gun like the one he had now and go charging across a weedy field whilst machine-gun bullets cracked past him.

No, by then Jack Scholes would be a top sergeant, if he lived and if he stayed in. An East End street rat made as good a career soldier as a Welshman who chose the trade in place of going down into the mines till something caved in and smashed him flat. Both of them understood their other choices were worse. Why else would you want to soldier?

To kill things, people who weren't soldiers thought. But not even the Germans killed for the fun of it most of the time. It was part of the job, that was all. Only not right now, thank God.

The President of the Spanish Republic had breath like . . . Vaclav Jezek didn't know what he had breath like. He'd never smelled anything like that coming from a human being's mouth before. Coffee and harsh Spanish tobacco and brandy and rotten teeth and God only knew what all else. If you were digging a trench and you dug through a corpse that had been in the ground for only a couple of weeks, the stench from it would come pretty close to this.

If something like that happened, though, you could shovel dirt over the thing and go on about your business. Here, Vaclav had to stand next to the dignitary and take it. *Señor* Azaña was making a speech about what a wonderful chap he was, after all.

So Benjamin Halévy insisted, anyhow. The number of people reasonably good in both Spanish and Czech was severely limited. Halévy had come to Barcelona with Vaclav so he could explain what the President and the rest of the big shots were saying, and so he could also translate Vaclav's replies.

Photographers snapped pictures of the Czech and the Jew—not that the papers would say what Halévy was—standing next to the President as Azaña went on and on. "You did not despair of the Republic," Azaña declared, smacking one fist into the other palm. "After Rome was invaded from North Africa, that was the highest praise she could give her soldiers. After we too were invaded from North Africa, so it is with us as well."

Polite applause rose from the crowd as Halévy murmured in familiar, throaty Czech. Without the translation, Vaclav wouldn't have been sure his Excellency wasn't complaining about the paella he'd eaten the night before.

"And we have more than praise," the President went on. "We promote the grand hero Vaclav Jezek"—he made a horrible mess of Vaclav's name, as any Spaniard was bound to do—"to the rank of captain in the Army of the Republic. We pay him the reward promised for the death of the arch-criminal and traitor, the so-called Marshal Sanjurjo. And we grant him the citizenship of the Republic in addition to that which he enjoys in his own land. May Czechoslovakia soon be free again, as he has helped ensure the Republic's freedom! ¡*Viva* Vaclav Jezek!"

"¡*Viva!*" the people shouted.

Then Azaña stepped away from the microphone. Benjamin Halévy gave Vaclav a little shove toward it. He would rather have been out in no-man's-land facing a platoon of pissed-off Nationalists. All they would have done was kill him. Here, he was going to have to kill himself, and his death certificate would read *Perished of embarrassment.* He'd never talked in front of more than a classroom's worth of people, and thousands had to be staring at him here in this enormous plaza.

"Muchas gracias, Señor Presidente de la República de España," he said, in the process using up most of his Spanish. He went on in his own language: "Not many people have been fighting for freedom longer than us Czechs. But you have, here in the Republic. The President called me a hero. I'm only a soldier, doing my job. You folks, you're the heroes."

Halévy translated his words into Spanish. Then, showing himself a man of parts indeed, the Jew said them again, this time in Catalan. To Vaclav, it sounded like two parts Spanish and one part French. He could tell when Halévy switched languages, but still didn't know for sure what he was saying.

"Gracias otra vez," Vaclav added, and drew back. Yes, he would rather have stood next to a puff adder than a microphone.

"Good job," Halévy whispered to him as more stuffed shirts from the Republic came up to pump his hand and press their smooth cheeks against his. The crowd cheered and cheered, partly because he *was* the hero who'd killed Marshal Sanjurjo and partly, no doubt, because he'd kept it short. There were advantages to not being fond of public speaking.

One of the Spaniards handed him a glass of red wine and said something incomprehensible. *"No entiendo,"* Vaclav said. *I don't understand* was a handy phrase to learn in a language where you knew only a few handy phrases.

The Spaniard aimed his words at Halévy this time. The Jew obligingly translated: "He says the Nationalists are going after each other like half a dozen cats in a sack when you kick it."

"Well, good!" Vaclav exclaimed in Czech. He could have said that in Spanish, but as long as Halévy was here to do the heavy lifting, he'd let him. That thought sparked another one. Still in Czech, he went on, "Hey, guess what! Since they went and promoted me, I outrank you. How about that?"

Halévy came to stiff attention. He clicked his heels with a thump that would have gladdened the heart of a Hungarian colonel in Emperor Franz Joseph's extinct army. *"Zu Befehl!"* he exclaimed, as if he belonged to that army. Vaclav's father had. Maybe Halévy's father had, too, before he'd left Austria-Hungary for France. They'd used a smashed-down soldiers' German to let officers talk with their polyglot troops. It had worked, too, after a fashion.

The Spanish dignitary watched the two of them with no idea of what was going on. Benjamin Halévy said something to him in Catalan. Then the fellow laughed. Since Halévy had used Catalan, he did, too. If Vaclav knew only a little Spanish, he had next to none of the related language.

"He says anyone can tell we're old friends," Halévy explained.

"Are we?" Jezek considered that. He drained the glass of wine. "Well, hell, I guess we are. And which one of us is that a judgment on?"

"On both of us, I'd say," Halévy answered.

"I'd say you're right," Vaclav agreed.

They whisked him off to another banquet. Vaclav hadn't eaten so much since he got conscripted. The feast was in the Spanish style, with little plates of peppery this and garlicky that and pickled the other thing. Vaclav missed sauerkraut and creamed potatoes and dill and big slabs of boiled beef and all the other good things he'd grown up with. But he had plenty, and it beat the hell out of the crumbly sausage that came up to the trenches all the time and was an even-money bet to give you the runs.

After he'd had some more wine, and some more wine, and some more wine after that, he plucked up enough courage to say to Halévy, "Ask them if they think the Nationalists really will come to pieces without their big boss."

Halévy put the question into Spanish. He got back several impassioned responses—so impassioned, a couple of the men who made them almost came to blows. In due course, the French Jew reported, "They all hope so, but some think it's more likely than others do."

"Is that so? I never would've guessed." Vaclav laughed. He'd had enough wine to think almost anything was funny.

In due course, the President of the Republic got to his feet and raised his goblet. "Confusion to all Fascists everywhere!" he said. Everyone drank.

Then he looked to Vaclav. The sniper got to his feet, too. It took some effort; yes, he was feeling the wine. "Freedom for Czechoslovakia!" he said, first in his own tongue, and then, after more effort, in

Spanish as well. Again, everybody drank the toast. He knew he would have a head like a drop-forging plant tomorrow morning. Red wine would hurt you if you gave it the chance. But that would be tomorrow. *Mañana.* The next thing to never.

And in the meantime . . . He turned to Halévy. "They've given me this stack of pesetas and the medal and the promotion and this trip to Barcelona and everything. Now where do I go to get laid?"

"Ah! That's an important question!" The Jew conferred with the dignitaries. Then he gave Vaclav the word: "Go back to your hotel room after we finish here and they'll have someone for you. They're gentlemen—they said they'd get me a girl, too. On the house, courtesy of the Republic."

"They *are* gentlemen!" Vaclav said. Nice that Halévy would get some, too. Even nicer that he wouldn't have to pay for it. *I should kill Fascist marshals more often,* he thought, and reached for the closest wine bottle.

No English or French bombers had dropped their loads on Münster for a while now. They'd hit other towns not far away. The Nazis made propaganda out of that. They said the enemy planes stayed away because the people in Münster were also enemies of the *Reich.*

For all Sarah Bruck knew, the hacks who wrote for the Party papers were right. "Aren't they taking a chance, though?" she asked her father after a chilly night's sad supper. "If people think rising up against Hitler will keep the bombers away, they'll do it all over Germany."

"It could be." Samuel Goldman rolled one of his cigarettes built from scavenged butts. Maybe the latest propaganda piece was on the newsprint he used for cigarette paper. He lit the cigarette and blew out smoke. Then he went on, "But it may not work like that. Too many people remember all the noise about the stab in the back last time."

"It wasn't true," Sarah said.

Father nodded. "No, it wasn't. But what people think happened is just as much a part of history as what really did happen."

"That's too complicated for me," Sarah said. Off in the distance, a rifle barked. Unrest still simmered here, no matter what the rest of Germany was doing. A machine pistol snarled back at the rifle.

"Either he didn't get the one he was aiming at or the fellow had a buddy with him," Father said.

"Who was doing the shooting?" she asked.

"Somebody. Anybody." Samuel Goldman shrugged. "They didn't even want me back as an ordinary soldier, let alone for the General Staff." Another shrug. "Ah, well. I've never worn trousers with red *Lampassen,* and I guess I'm too old to start now." The strip of scarlet cloth along the outer seam of the trouser legs marked a General Staff officer's uniform.

"Too bad. I bet you'd do a better job than some of the fools who are wearing them," Sarah said.

"For one thing, you're wrong. To get on the General Staff, you have to know what you're doing," Father answered. "For another, even if you were right, what would I accomplish? I'd win victories for the *Führer,* that's all."

He didn't say anything like *And every Jew in Germany needs that like a hole in the head.* He didn't have to. Sarah could fill in the blanks for herself. "Well, you're right," she admitted. "You know what worries me?"

"No, but since you're going to tell me that doesn't matter so much, either," he said.

She made a face at him. Then she did tell him: "If they can't make people here feel like traitors, they're liable to try to make them feel like anti-Semites. If they're shouting 'The Jews are our misfortune!', they won't worry so much about shouting 'Down with the Nazis!'"

"It could be. The Nazis always play that card, or they do when they think of it," Father said. "And you want to remember that Cardinal von Galen complained about what Himmler's flunkies were doing to the feebleminded. He didn't say a word—not one single, solitary word— about what they were doing to us."

"Us?" Sarah said in some surprise. He never rejected his Jewish-ness, but he rarely made a point of it like that. He wanted to be a German, even though the Nazis didn't want to let him.

But he nodded now. "Us," he said again. "I'm not going to deny it. Even if I wanted to, I couldn't very well deny it." He touched the Star of David sewn onto the lapel of his threadbare tweed jacket.

There were more gunshots, these closer. Someone sprinted down the blacked-out street in front of the house. A minute later, several more people ran past after him. By the clump of their footfalls, they were wearing boots. That made them either soldiers or SS men.

I hope he gets away, Sarah thought. She didn't say that out loud. Except for the odd gunshot or odd fugitive sprinting by, it was eerily quiet. No telling how far a voice might carry.

"Never a dull moment," Father said dryly.

"I guess not," Sarah said.

Mother came in from the kitchen, where she'd been pickling cabbage. Sauerkraut would keep for a long time. It wasn't exciting, but it put food in your belly. Hanna Goldman clucked. "If anyone had told me a year ago I'd keep working while people were shooting off guns, I would have said he was crazy."

"You get used to anything. You get used to everything," Father said. "If people didn't get used to dreadful things, they couldn't have wars. You step on one mangled body, it's the most horrible thing that happened in your whole life. You step on three or four mangled bodies while you're walking to the field kitchen, you turn to your friend and go 'That last shelling smacked us pretty good, didn't it?'"

"That's—terrible," Mother said, which was exactly what Sarah was thinking.

"It is. I know it is. But you have to, or you do go crazy," Father replied. "A few men couldn't, and they did go *meshuggeh*." He smiled at the Yiddish word, but quickly sobered again. "The first time you shoot at somebody and the first time you know you hit somebody—those are bad, too. After you do it for a while, though, you just think *Well, all right, I got that one. Now he won't get me or any of my buddies.*"

"No wonder you never talk much about what you did in the war," Sarah said.

"No wonder at all," Father agreed. "Back before the Nazis took over, I'd go the the *Bierstube* with some of the other *Frontschweine*. We'd talk about things amongst ourselves. Why not? We understood—we were the only ones who did. But they got nervous about drinking with a Jew, and who could blame them? Besides, a lot of them are back in *Feldgrau* these days."

"You would have gone. You tried to go, only the fools who run things wouldn't let you. I was thinking about that a little while ago," Sarah said. "Why would anybody want to do that twice?"

"That's the wrong question, dear," her mother said. "The right question is, why would anybody want to do that once?"

"You will never have a closer comrade than the man who saved your neck during a trench raid." Father seemed to think he was explaining something. If he was, it was something that only made sense—that could only make sense—to someone else who'd been through what he had.

Sarah's reflections were interrupted when another rifle shot rang out. A bullet spanged off the bricks of the front wall a split second later. *"Gevalt!"* Mother said. Sarah couldn't have put it better herself.

"Hel-lo!" Father said. He wasn't horrified. On the contrary—he looked and sounded extremely alert. He also looked as if he wished he had a Mauser in his hands. The laborer, the professor, even the Jew dropped away, leaving only the old *Frontschwein*.

Whoever had the Schmeisser fired back in a long, stuttering burst. Then the rifle spoke again. Somebody let out a horrible shriek. It went on and on. Sarah wanted to stick her index fingers in her ears to blot it out. You weren't supposed to hear noises like that. Human beings weren't supposed to make noises like that.

Father bit his lip. He would have heard such cries before. He would have a better idea than Sarah about what would have to happen to somebody to force such cries from his throat.

After a while, the shriek became something more like a gurgle. Then silence fell again. "Poor devil," Father said. "Believe it or not, I wouldn't wish that on even an SS man. Well, he's not worrying about anything now." He began to roll another cigarette.

Chapter 12

"**K**eep in good order, you lunkheads!" Arno Baatz shouted as the men he led got into the train. They were lucky—this was a passenger car, even if it was one with hard seats. They wouldn't have to sprawl on the floor of a freight car that stank of horseshit from its previous occupants.

For once, the *Landsers* didn't grumble at him. One of them said, "Back to the *Vaterland*!" He might have been announcing miracles. They'd been fighting the Ivans for a long time. Being sent back to Germany probably felt like a miracle to them. It felt like something of a miracle to Baatz.

It was also a source of pride. "They figured we were reliable enough to help them clean out a nest of traitors," the *Unteroffizier* said importantly. "Our regiment, our company, our squad. We're not going to let them down, are we? Not when they're counting on us, we're not!"

He scowled at Adam Pfaff. The *Obergefreiter* looked back with an expression surely more innocent than the man who owned it. If Pfaff had thought he could get away with it, he would have sassed Arno about answering his own question. But he was cunning and sneaky enough to see he couldn't get away with it. So he acted all meek and mild instead.

He can't fool me, though, Baatz thought. Given half a chance, Pfaff turned into a barrack lawyer or a shirker. He was good enough against the Ivans. Even Baatz couldn't deny that. Politically reliable, though? Not likely! Not even a little bit likely.

Muttering, Arno took his own seat. His ass would be petrified by the time they got back to the *Reich*. No help for it, though, not unless he wanted to clamber up to the luggage rack about the windows and pretend to be a haversack all the way west.

With a series of jerks, the train began to roll. *"Dos vidanya, Rodina!"* somebody said—Russian for *So long, Motherland!* He didn't sound sorry to be heading out of the Soviet Union. Who would?

"Yob tvoyu mat'!" somebody else added. That was also Russian, and filthy. They'd all picked up little bits of the language: a phrase here, an obscenity there. Baatz hoped he never saw this place again. Then he could drop what he'd picked up.

Adam Pfaff was thinking along not altogether different lines: "Here's hoping the weather stays lousy. Then the *Sturmoviks* will leave us alone."

"Don't even talk about those bastards! You'll jinx us," Baatz said. Like any German soldier, he hated and feared the Red Air Force's ground-attack planes. The damned things were like flying panzers, so heavily armored they were hard to shoot down. They scooted along at treetop height, and pasted anything the pilot saw with cannon shells and machine-gun bullets.

They had been known to do horrible things to trains. In here, Baatz couldn't spot them and dive for a foxhole. He couldn't even shoot back. All he could do was add his hope to Pfaff's.

On the train rolled. He drank from his canteen and ate black bread and sausage he'd scrounged at the last village they'd camped in. He tried to sleep. After a while, he did. Hard seat with a straight back? So what? He could have slept hanging by his knees like a bat.

He knew exactly when they passed out of Byelorussia and into Poland. All of a sudden, he could read the lettering on the signs. The words still looked like something off an eye chart—they were in Polish. But he could try to sound them out.

The other thing that made Poland look different from the USSR was that it hadn't been fought over so much or so recently. The farther west they went, the better the countryside looked. The landscape was flat and boring and the trees had shed their leaves, but they were intact. So were farmhouses and villages. The people who stared at the train as it rattled past looked and dressed like Western Europeans, not like dirty Russian peasants out of a novel from the last century.

Warsaw was a real city. It had taken some bomb damage, but not much. Women in overalls worked alongside old men on repairs. Most of the young men wore Poland's dark, greenish khaki and fought the Ivans along with the *Wehrmacht*.

Excitement in the car built as the train neared the German frontier. At the border, Polish guards waved good-bye bare moments before German railway workers waved hello. Some of the soldiers waved back. Arno didn't. He would have for a pretty girl, but didn't waste his time on friendship for men in uniforms that weren't military.

They rolled through Breslau, the center of the recruiting district from which almost everybody in the regiment had come. Baatz posted men to make sure no one tried to jump off the train and sneak home.

Catching his eye, Pfaff said, "Good thing they didn't stop us on a siding here. We would've lost half the guys."

"Well, we might have," Baatz allowed.

Way off in the east of the *Reich*, Breslau hadn't been hit hard by either Russian or English bombers. When they got to Berlin a few hours later, Arno saw a city that had been bombed. Before the war started, Göring said you could call him Meyer if even a single bomb ever fell on the capital. These days, the *Luftwaffe* chief had to be used to his new Jewish name.

Things didn't improve when the train steamed west out of Berlin. The RAF and the *Armée de l'Air* seemed to have hit every ten-pfennig town along the tracks. Here a train station lay in ruins, there a block of flats or a factory was nothing but charred beams and broken bricks.

The soldiers talked among themselves in low voices as they got a good look at the destruction. Arno would have liked to hear what they were saying, but no one said anything in that tone of voice close enough for him to make out the words. That in itself fanned the flames of his suspicions. If talk wasn't defeatist, you didn't care who heard it.

People from units conscripted from this part of the *Reich* said that letters from their loved ones let them know things weren't so good at home. Baatz had thought those letters were bound to be tinged with treason. Now, seeing the beating this part of the country had taken, he didn't find it so easy to make such flip judgments.

A few kilometers outside of Münster, bandits in the bushes fired at the train as it passed. A window in the car blew in, spattering soldiers with broken glass. The bullet broke a window on the other side going out. Only dumb luck it didn't hit anybody.

"Nice to know we're loved and welcomed," Adam Pfaff remarked.

"We're here *because* they're traitors to the *Führer*," Arno answered. "We're going to whip them into shape, and we're going to whip them into line." He looked forward to it. If whipping people into line wasn't what an *Unteroffizier* was for, what would be?

But the whipping had to wait, because the train stopped at the edge of town instead of going on to the station. Word filtered back that somebody had messed with the switches. If an alert policeman hadn't spotted it, they might have derailed.

Little boys in short pants scampered by the track, yelling things at the soldiers. Baatz couldn't make out what they were saying with his window closed. He opened his, even though that let in the outside chill. It helped less than he'd hoped. The local dialect was so far from his, it hardly sounded like German to him. But then one of the kids shouted *"Arschloch!"* at him and held up his right hand with thumb and forefinger making a circle and the other three fingers raised. The curse and the gesture that went with it would have been perfectly clear from Munich all the way to Königsberg.

He almost shouted back something about the little bastard's mother, but decided that was beneath a noncom's dignity. But he did take a good, long look at the punk. If he ever saw him again, he'd make him sorry, twelve years old or not.

With a wheeze and a groan and a series of jerks, the train got moving again. And that was their welcome to Münster.

Chaim Weinberg moved forward cautiously. That was partly because, with only a hand and a half, he wasn't as quick with his rifle as some of the bastards he might run into. And it was partly because, having fought in Spain since 1936, he had caution ingrained in him by now. That line about old soldiers and bold soldiers held all too much truth.

But it looked as if the Nationalists really were on the ropes. Or rather, they were too busy fighting one another like the Kilkenny cats for the ever more worthless top spot in their territory to care a great deal that the Republicans were taking it away from them, more of it by the day.

Somewhere not far from here, Vaclav Jezek had blown out Marshal Sanjurjo's brains. From what Chaim had heard, the Czech had blown off most of the *Caudillo*'s head. The Fascists had had to bury him in a closed coffin because nobody in the funeral business could make him look even as much like a human being as he had before he got killed.

The Nationalists had pulled out of these trenches so they could go after other Nationalists who fancied a different general. Most of them had, anyhow. A few diehards still figured they wouldn't be fighting over anything before long if the Republicans overran their positions.

Muddy, smelly, full of trash, the Nationalists' trenches looked even worse than the ones from which the Abe Lincolns and their International brethren had emerged. The Nationalists were retreating. And they were sloppy Spaniards. Chaim had seen some of the trenches the Spanish Republicans fought from. They were no tidier than this mess.

Up ahead and to the left, a brief firefight broke out: rifles and a Tommy gun or two. Chaim trotted toward it. If cleaning up the Fascists and cleaning them out was easier than it had been, he wanted all the more to get in on it. But the shooting had stopped by the time he drew near.

A Republican with one of those Tommy guns led three gloomy Nationalists toward the rear. Their hands stayed high. The Republican grinned at Weinberg. "We'll reeducate these *putos*," he said. "Or I'll finish them now if they want to run."

"*Bueno,*" Chaim answered, and gave a thumbs-up. It wouldn't be so good for the captured Fascists, though. Republican reeducation camps owed a lot to their models in the USSR. The only thing the Spaniards couldn't duplicate was Siberian weather. Up in the mountains, they even came within screaming distance of that.

He scurried along a communications trench toward the rear. It wasn't straight—nobody in his right mind left a long, straight stretch of trench waiting to be raked by small-arms fire or lethal fragments from a shellburst—but it didn't have enough bends to make him happy. He hoped nobody from the other side would lob any artillery this way. He hadn't heard the Nationalists' big guns at all today. He didn't miss them a bit.

The ground at the far end of the trench was as full of shell holes as a sixteen-year-old's face was full of pimples. A sixteen-year-old's face, however, didn't present the spectacle of a burnt-out truck that had taken a direct hit. It didn't have bushes growing on it, either, only peach fuzz that was trying to turn into whiskers.

One of the other Abe Lincolns waved to him. Chaim waved back. "Hey, Luis!" he called. Luis was from Madrid. He was a pretty good guy. He'd joined the Americans a couple of years ago now, and had picked up a lot of English.

"We've got the fuckers by the short hairs," he said now. When you learned English from soldiers, that was the kind of English you learned.

"Bet your ass we do," Chaim said. "Now we twist." He illustrated with a graphic gesture. Luis laughed. So did Chaim, but only for a moment. Then his face clouded. "I wish like hell Mike woulda lived to see the day."

"*Sí.*" Luis nodded. "*Señor* Carroll, he was a good comrade."

"The best," Chaim said. He and Mike had been in Spain together since not long after the civil war broke out. They'd saved each other's skins more times than anybody could count. Chaim remembered his buddy every time he did anything with his smashed and much-repaired left hand. Sometimes remembering was all you had left. Too goddamn often, in fact.

"Only thing we can do now is pay back the cocksuckers," Luis said. "Pay them back for what they do to *Señor* Mike, pay them back for what they do to the whole country. We pay them plenty."

Through long stretches of the fighting here, neither Republicans nor Nationalists had bothered taking prisoners. Spaniards were in terrible earnest when they fought. They weren't always good at it, but sincerity and ferocity did duty for skill. Maybe reeducation camps were a mercy by comparison. On the other hand, maybe they weren't.

Behind the smashed truck were two hastily dug graves. One of them had a cross made from two boards nailed together at right angles. Only a bayoneted rifle thrust into the ground with a helmet on the stock marked the other. That surprised Chaim. They talked about people who were more royal than the king. Well, the Nationalists were more Catholic, or more ostentatiously Catholic, than the Pope.

Before too long, Chaim and the rest of the advancing Republicans got into hill country their artillery had hardly touched. He gave the neat, prosperous-looking farmhouses fishy stares. Anybody could hide in places like that, and you wouldn't know it till he started shooting at you from a window or something.

Other men saw the problem, too. They solved it with revolutionary directness: they torched farmhouses and barns and even chicken coops. Farmers and their wives and children stared with terrible eyes as smoke and fire rose from their homes.

"Are you sure this is a good idea?" Chaim asked a Spaniard with a torch. "You'll make the people hate you."

"Screw the people in these parts," the Republican answered, scowling. "They're all Fascist sympathizers, anyhow. Who do you think they've been selling their produce to?"

"But it will all be one country—your country—again pretty soon, I hope," Chaim said. "Shouldn't you make peace with somebody who wasn't actually trying to kill you?"

All he got was a nastier scowl from the other man. "You sound like a counterrevolutionary," the fellow said suspiciously.

"Oh, *fuck* you." Chaim held up his left hand. Wounds and surgical scars made it enough of a twisted horror to widen the Spaniard's eyes no matter how hard he tried to hold his face straight. Chaim went on, "When you've got a souvenir like this, you can bitch about my ideology. Till then, just shut up, you hear?"

In the Republic, everybody said *tu* to everybody else all the time. The familiar *you* was egalitarian. *Usted,* the formal word, signaled class discrimination and pro-Fascist politics. But *tu* was also the word you used with dogs, with children, with servants, and with people you wanted to insult. Chaim used it here in the last sense. It was all in the tone of voice. He might not have a great handle on Spanish grammar, but insult he could handle.

The Spaniard flushed. He angrily turned away from Chaim. That didn't stop him from tossing the torch into a pile of hay next to the barn here. The hay began to burn. Before long, so did the barn. If the farmer didn't like it, what could he do? Count himself lucky the men from the Republic hadn't shot him and gang-raped his wife.

Or he could find a hatchet, wait in the trees, and kill the next Republican soldier who came by. Chaim wouldn't have done that, or he didn't think he would. He came from a long line of people who'd survived pogrom after pogrom without getting their own back . . . till the Russian Revolution, anyhow. And his folks were in the States by then. Spaniards were different. They took vengeance seriously, and often killed without calculating cost.

He was sure the Spanish Republic was worth fighting for, worth dying for. He never would have come here if he weren't. Whether it would be worth living in after victory came, that didn't seem so clear. But he had an advantage over the Spaniards. If he didn't like it, he could go home. They already *were* home, and stuck with whatever the Republic dished out to them.

Machine guns chattered. Rifles yelled. Alistair Walsh nerved himself to dash around a stone fence taller than a man. The English had pushed forward a couple of hundred yards, into a Belgian village. By the way things worked these days, that was good progress. Anything could be waiting on the far side of that fence, though. Anything at all.

And *anything*, around here, would include men in field-gray uniforms and coal-scuttle helmets. They would have Mausers and Schmeissers and MG-42s. Well, no help for it. This was one of those times that made him wish he were back in Wales, hundreds of feet underground, grubbing away at a coal seam with a pick.

"Ready, boys?" he asked the soldiers who huddled in a smashed-up house with him. Nobody said no. It was too late for that, however much they might wish it weren't.

He held a Mills bomb in his right hand. He'd already pulled the grenade's pin. He kept his thumb on the detonator. They told you not to do that—you could ruin yourself by mistake. But they weren't here, and he was. All kinds of rules went out the window in wartime.

"Let's go, then," he said. He sprinted, all hunched over, to the end of that wall. He chucked the Mills bomb around behind it without showing his hand for more than a split second. As soon as the bomb burst, he sprayed the other side with bullets fired blindly from his Sten gun. That only added to the guttural cries there.

He and his men dashed around the wall then, firing as they did. Several Germans were down. Others gaped in horrified amazement. *"Hände hoch!"* Walsh yelled. The Master Race didn't always want to fight to the death.

Sure enough, these Fritzes had had enough and then some. They threw away their weapons and raised their hands. Some of them shouted *"Kamerad!"* And one added "We surrender!" in excellent English.

That made things easier. Walsh's German was limited to the phrases you needed to tell prisoners what to do, and he rarely understood what the Germans answered. So he was smiling as he said, "Tell 'em we won't hurt 'em if they do what we tell 'em."

The German spoke in his own language. Then he asked, "May we tend to our wounded, please?"

"Right. Go ahead. Then we'll take you back," Walsh said. The Germans dusted antiseptic powder on wounds and bandaged them. They gave a badly hit man one morphine shot, and then another. Walsh wasn't sure he'd make it. If they let him die comfortably, it was the last and not the smallest favor they could do for him.

"I am glad to be out of the fighting," said the man who spoke English. He had a cut on the back of one hand and another on his cheek from grenade fragments. Neither was much worse than a scratch. He'd been lucky.

"Bet you are," Walsh said with rough sympathy. "Want a fag?" He held out his packet of Navy Cuts.

Danke schön," the German said. "I am Eberhard Rothmann. I am a *Gefreiter.* My pay number is—" He rattled it off. After lighting the cigarette, he went on, "I am very glad to be away from this. Twice now in twenty-five years our leaders have taken us into losing wars."

"So why did you Germans go, then?" Walsh asked. The lads in Field Intelligence would be happy to get their hands on this bird. He sang like a canary.

"Because they told us what to do, first the Kaiser and then the *Führer,* and then we did it," Rothmann said. "And look what we have for doing it." He gestured at his dead and injured countrymen. "But now, from what I hear, we have had a bellyful of this stupidness."

One of the other Germans must also have spoken English, or at least understood it. He said something sharp in German. Eberhard Rothmann answered in the same tongue. Then he went back to English.

"What I say is so, even if it likes Klaus not," he said. "The people, they have had enough of foolishness."

"He is liar!" Klaus said. His English had a much thicker accent than Rothmann's.

Walsh cared nothing about that. He told off Jack Scholes and a couple of other men. "Don't let anything happen to them," he said. "Don't shoot them unless they run or they try to jump you. Get their wounded to an aid station. Got all that?"

"Roight, Staff," Scholes said impatiently. He gestured with his bayoneted Lee-Enfield. "Come on, you filthy buggers. 'Op it, loik."

Hop it they did. Walsh and the remaining Englishmen warily pushed forward. He peered around the smashed, charred carcass of a German armored car, then hastily jerked his head back. "There's a Tiger a hundred yards down the path," he whispered. "Stay low, for Christ's sake."

No one had seen him peek out. If the Tiger crew or the other Fritzes who were bound to be close by the monster realized the Tommies were so close, exterminating him and his pals wouldn't take long.

"Shall we send 'em a flying 'ard-on?" one of the men asked. The bazooka's phallic rockets hadn't needed long to get a dirty name pasted to them.

But Walsh shook his head. "He's front end-on to us," he said. "It won't get through his armor." The bazooka was a better antitank weapon than anything the infantry had had up to now. It beat the stuffing out of the PIAT. It had its limitations, though. A Tiger's thick frontal armor was more than it could handle.

"What do you want to do, then?" the soldier asked—a reasonable enough question.

"Wait," Walsh answered. "Let's see what the Germans have in mind. If they pull out on their own, we don't have to drive them out." They wouldn't kill any enemy soldiers that way. On the other hand, the Germans wouldn't find the chance to kill any of them, either. Walsh approved of not getting killed. He wasn't even especially keen on getting wounded. He'd done it before, and found it overrated.

If the Germans decided to come forward again . . . That might not be very enjoyable. He flattened himself out, wiggled forward, and looked ahead from under the dead armored car. He didn't see any approaching jackboots. Not seeing them suited him fine.

Dusk began to descend. The Tiger's engine noise got louder. Walsh's heart leaped into his mouth. The tank could squash the armored car and him with it and never break a sweat.

But why would it bother? A couple of rounds of HE and a burst or two from the machine guns would finish him with ease, thank you kindly.

He risked another peep around the armored car's mudguard. The Tiger was backing up—backing away, in other words. The tank commander stood head and shoulders out of the cupola so he could see where he was going. Two or three German foot soldiers standing nearby waved and pointed to steer him away from obstacles. Walsh wondered why they bothered. What was a Tiger made for, if not for grinding obstacles under its tracks?

Sure as hell, its retreating rear end took out the corner of a house. The house fell in on itself. The Tiger, unfazed, backed over and through the wreckage. The infantrymen pulled back with it.

"Bugger me blind," Walsh said as he pulled his head in once more. "I think it'll be all right—till tomorrow, anyway."

He had ration tins in pouches on his belt. The first one he grabbed was steak and kidney pie, without a doubt the best ration the Army made. One of the men carried a cooker that burned methylated spirit with an all but invisible flame. They brewed tea. Life might not be ideal, but it looked a lot better after grub and char.

Snow came later in the Ukraine than it did in Russia proper, but come it did. Ivan Kuchkov and his men put on white snow smocks and whitewashed their helmets. The smocks would get dirty soon enough. Well, so would the snow. They'd stay camouflaged for a while.

Sasha Davidov was putting on a fresh coat of whitewash when Ivan came up to him. The skinny little Jew looked up before Ivan got very close. You couldn't sneak up on him. Nobody could—certainly not Ivan, and he was pretty good at sneaking. Those hair-trigger nerves made Sasha such a good point man.

"What do you need, Comrade Sergeant?" he asked.

"Not a fucking thing, not right now," Ivan answered. "Tomorrow . . . Tomorrow I hear we get some tanks."

Davidov nodded. "Yes, I heard that, too." With his beaky nose, he looked like a sparrow—a sparrow that badly needed a shave, but even so.

"Did you? I just now found out, so fuck your mother," Kuchkov said without heat. "Who told you? One of your clipcock buddies?"

"You keep your ears open, you hear things," Davidov said, a *yes* that wasn't a *yes*.

"You keep your mouth open, somebody'll stick a dick in it," Kuchkov said. Then he got back to the business at hand: "So we'll be going forward again."

"Seems pretty likely," Davidov agreed.

"Yeah. It does. So you take your sorry kike ass out before sunup and see what kind of cunts we've got in front of us," Ivan told him. "The more we know, the better the chances we fuck them and they don't fuck us."

"I'll do it, Comrade Sergeant," the Jew said. "But I'm pretty sure they'll be Germans."

Ivan was pretty sure of the same thing. "Goddamn Hitlerite dickheads," he said in disgust. "Always those Nazi pricks. Never the Hungarians any more. Never the shitass Romanians and their stinking cornmeal mush." His scowl made him even uglier than he was already. "And I fucking know why, too."

"Because there are more Germans—and a lot more front-line Germans—than anybody else?" Davidov was a rational, sensible man. Except for being a hell of a good scout, he was wasted in the field. He should have gone back to Stavka and helped the generals decide how to move armies around.

Of course, rational and sensible didn't necessarily mean right. Ivan laughed a nasty laugh. "No! Shit, no! That doesn't have one single fuck to do with it. The NKVD cunts, they've got it in for us. They didn't throw our sorry asses in a penal battalion after Vitya plugged the prick of a *politruk*. They didn't bother. Keep sending us up against Hitler's bitches for a while and we get used up any which way, know what I mean?"

Sasha Davidov rubbed his narrow, pointed chin. No, he didn't look like a Russian. No wonder Jews got it in the neck all the goddamn time. All you had to do was see them to know them for outsiders. "I don't like to think things work that way," he said slowly.

"Well, how the fuck else are things gonna work?" Kuchkov asked in honest amazement.

The T-34s came up during the night. They'd been whitewashed, too, to make them harder to spot. Ivan would have been amazed if the Germans didn't know they were there, though. Their diesel engines belched and farted as if they'd been gobbling beans and cabbage for the past hundred years. When daylight came, the exhaust pipes would throw up black smoke you could see for kilometers. Just being able to see them coming, though, didn't mean the Nazis could stop them when they did.

At least it wasn't one of those attacks where everybody linked arms and charged the Germans yelling *Urra!* Machine guns did horrible things to attacks like that. Sometimes even Russians broke before they got to their target. Sometimes, though, the men the MG-34s and MG-42s didn't slaughter jumped down into the Fritzes' foxholes and cleared the bitches out.

Here, the Red Army soldiers trotted through the misty dawn by ones and twos and in small groups. Yes, the T-34s spewed smoke through the mist. Yes, loping along behind them meant breathing all that smelly crap. Ivan didn't care, even if he coughed. For one thing, he'd had his hundred grams of vodka, so he didn't care about much of anything. For another, attacking with tanks beat the hell out of going in without them. They smashed things for you. And they drew fire that would be aimed at *your* miserable ass without them.

The Germans had sown mines in front of their positions. Signs with a skull and crossbones and the warning *ACHTUNG! MINEN!* made sure that was no secret. Kuchkov couldn't have read the words even in Russian. He knew what they meant, though. They meant trouble, to say nothing of danger.

Either the tank commanders didn't see the signs or they didn't give a piss. Maybe they thought only antipersonnel mines lay under the snow, and they didn't need to worry. They found out they were wrong when something went *ba-blam!* under the lead T-34. The tank slewed sideways and stopped, its left track blown off the road wheels. The crew bailed out on the side away from the Fritzes and huddled behind the crippled machine.

Ivan passed them with a certain sour sympathy. Pretty soon, some officer or NKVD man would see them and decide they could best serve the Soviet Union as infantrymen for a while. If they lived, maybe they'd get another tank. Or they might not. Nobody'd tried to put Ivan in another bomber after he bailed out of his burning SB-2.

A foot soldier tripped a different kind of mine. With a small boom, it kicked a package of shrapnel balls and more explosives up to about waist high. Then the package blew up in midair. The shrapnel balls tore the Russian almost in half. They didn't kill him right away anyhow. He lay in the snow, thrashing and bleeding and screaming, till someone running by shot him to shut him up. Ivan nodded. That guy was doing the poor mutilated fucker a favor.

Trust the Fritzes to come up with a mine made to blow off your dick and your balls. Ivan wanted to cup his hands in front of his crotch as he ran through the minefield. It wouldn't help, but he wanted to do it anyhow.

One of Hitler's saws started spitting out death. The MG-42's muzzle flashes came so close together, they made almost a continuous tongue of flame. Kuchkov threw himself down on his belly in the snow and crawled forward from then on out. Even so, some of the rounds cracked past just over his back.

A T-34 halted. Its cannon swung to bear on the machine-gun position. The Germans fired everything they had at it. Bullets sparked off its armor plating. But they didn't seem to have any antitank guns in the neighborhood. The T-34's gun boomed. The German machine gun fell silent.

"*Urra!*" the Red Army men yelled. Some of the ones who'd flattened out like Ivan got up and started running again.

"No, you stupid fucking dingleberries!" he screamed.

Too late. The MG-42 came back to malevolent life. Half a dozen Russian soldiers fell in the blink of an eye. The T-34 fired again, and then once more. The Nazis' machine gun stayed quiet after that. Kuchkov kept crawling just the same.

By the time the Russians got to the German forward trenches, the Fritzes had pulled out of them. A dead man stared blindly up at the sky. Snowflakes grizzled the dark stubble on his cheeks and chin. Ivan fumbled through his belt pouches for food and tobacco. The Hitlerite had a nice flint-and-steel cigarette lighter. Kuchkov stuck it in a pocket of his snow smock.

"Come on! Chase them harder!" Lieutenant Obolensky yelled.

The men obeyed . . . to a point. If the Germans were pulling back on their own, a sensible Red Army soldier didn't want to stick his neck out too far. Like a careless turtle, he might lose his head. Yes, the Nazis could wind up in a stronger position that would have to get cleared out next week. But next week lay a million years away, and it could damn well take care of itself.

Chapter 13

The *Block Island*'s launch put-putted toward Tern Island. A strong swell was running down from the north. Pete McGill had always had a pretty strong stomach. He'd been seasick a couple of times, but only a couple. Now, gulping, he wondered whether this would make one more.

Another Marine from the escort carrier leaned over the gunwale and noisily fed the fish. That did nothing to calm Pete's queasy insides. "Take it easy, boys," said the potbellied CPO at the rudder. "We'll be there in a few minutes." His cheeks were still bright pink. By the way he looked and sounded, he would have been happy as a clam if King Neptune and Davy Jones started playing ping-pong with the launch.

A stubby pier stuck out from the end of the runway the Seabees had built on Tern Island. The launch put in alongside it. Sailors helped the leathernecks scramble out of the launch and up onto the planking. The Marine who'd puked got down on his hands and knees and kissed the creosoted wood. Pete didn't go that far, but he knew how the poor guy felt.

At the end of the runway, a flock of C-47s crouched under camouflage netting. More Gooney Birds circled overhead. They'd land for refueling as soon as the first bunch took off. More Marines would file into them. Then they'd get airborne again, too.

Pete ducked his head as he climbed into the plane to which a sailor with a clipboard beckoned him. He took his seat with his back against the C-47's aluminum skin. He'd be fifth in the drop order. *Good*, he thought. *Not long to wait once the jumping starts. Not long to think about anything.*

Not long once the jumping started. But Tern Island was still two or three hours away from Midway. Till the jump light started going green, he'd have plenty of time to brood about this, that, and the other thing. He figured he'd come up with more ways for this operation to get fubar'd than the Japs ever could.

A scraping noise. A leatherneck across from Pete twitched. "What's that?" He'd already started brooding.

"That's your crabs playing hopscotch," Pete said. The other Marine gave him the finger. Chuckling, Pete went on, "Nah, that's just the netting coming off. They'll fire up the motors soon—you wait."

They did. First the starboard engine roared itself awake, then the port. The thunderous roar filled Pete from the soles of his boots to his helmet pressing against his hair. It seemed to come from inside as much as from without. If you had a loose filling or something, that roar would shake it right out of your tooth.

Before long, the C-47 taxied down the new runway. It bumped a few times, but what did you want—egg in your beer? One last bump and it was airborne. More noises from below meant the landing gear was retracting up into the wings. Pete unslung his rifle and cleaned it. *No jams today,* he thought. *Better not be.*

He wondered if they would have done better to take off in the middle of the night, so they got to Midway around daybreak. He shrugged. He was only a sergeant. He didn't make choices like that. Hell, he didn't even get asked about choices like that. They told him to get into the airplane, jump out of it, and start killing Japs as soon as he hit the ground.

He'd do it, too. All he wanted was to kill as many Japs as he could before they killed him. He figured they would, sooner or later. He just wanted it to be later. He was still paying them back for Vera, killed in Shanghai before the USA and Japan were even officially at war. He was paying them back for his own smashed shoulder and leg, too, but those were details.

The Marine next to him pulled his canteen from its pouch and took a swig. Then he offered it to Pete. The way he'd drunk told Pete it probably didn't hold water. He took his own cautious swallow. Sure as hell, that was vodka or raw corn or torpedo juice or something else that would pour clear and look harmless but would get you crocked in nothing flat.

"Thanks, man," he said as he gave back the canteen.

"Sure. All part of room service, y'know?" The other leatherneck grinned.

"Yeah, well, I wish I was in a room in some crib on Hotel Street with somebody prettier'n you," Pete answered.

"This ain't exactly the Ritz, is it?" the other Marine said.

"Only compared to where we're going," Pete said. That held enough truth to have sobered them if they'd drunk a lot more than the small knocks they'd poured down.

Somebody sitting up near the front bulkhead liberated a harmonica from a pocket and started blowing on it. A civilian DC-3 would have had enough soundproofing to let Pete listen to whatever he was trying to play. A military C-47 didn't bother with such frills, except maybe in the cockpit. Anybody back here was strictly cargo. Pete wasn't going to complain. If he had to choose between engine noise and harmonica music, he'd take engine noise any time.

On and on they went. The plan was for high-altitude bombers to plaster Midway before the C-47s got there. That way, the Japs would already be groggy by the time the Marine started falling out of the sky on top of them. It sounded good. Whether it would actually work . . . Well, they'd all find out pretty damn quick.

After what seemed like either ten minutes or three years, depending, the pilot spoke over the intercom: "Midway comin' up. Jumpmaster, open the door. Marines, good luck to y'all." His drawl said he was from somewhere between South Carolina and Mississippi.

Wind howled into the plane when the jumpmaster undogged the

door. Pete got his first look outside since takeoff. The Pacific wasn't nearly far enough below. He got a glimpse of a real gooney bird—an albatross—gliding along looking for fish.

Then the jumpmaster yelled, "There's Midway, dead ahead!" He could see it. Pete couldn't, not from where he was sitting. He just watched the light over the door. Red meant they were still out to sea. When it went green . . . That was when the picture show started.

Green! The first Marine went out before the jumpmaster could scream at him. Red. Then green again, much sooner that it would have come on a practice run. Another leatherneck out. Red. Green. Another. Everybody slid toward the door at each jump. Red. Green. Red.

Green. Pete stepped forward and stepped out. Sand and scraggly grass not far below. A bullet snarled past him. Not all the slanties were dead or stunned, then, dammit. *Wham!* The chute opened. Down he went. He was a sitting duck, but he wouldn't hang up here for long. That was why the C-47s came in so low.

His boots thumped on the sand. He cut himself out of the parachute—no saving for a rainy day now. He just missed cutting off the top of his left thumb as he slashed through the tough webbing. He was looking around for his fellow paratroops when there was a tremendous explosion overhead. One of the Gooney Birds had taken a direct hit from a flak gun. It tumbled out of the sky in burning chunks. He hoped the Marines had already got out, but he had no way of knowing.

He had to worry about staying alive himself. Midway was full of broad, shallow bomb craters—the sand didn't lend itself to deep ones. Marines sheltered in some of them. Others held Japs. The small-caliber Arisakas they carried sounded different from the Marines' Springfields. The Japs didn't seem to have any Tommy guns, though a couple of Nambu machine guns and their pale blue tracers added to the chaos.

There! That bastard was wearing the Japs' faded khaki. Pete brought his rifle to his shoulder. It bucked as he pulled the trigger. The Jap folded up on himself. Then something tugged at Pete's sleeve. When he looked down, he saw a bullet had torn his tunic without tearing up his arm. Sometimes you'd rather be lucky than good.

Most of the enemy fire seemed to be coming from the east. That was where the main American base had been. Hirohito's boys must have taken it over when they seized the island. Now they'd die here.

"Come on!" Pete called, and waved his men forward. Before long, his bayonet had blood on it. All that training he'd done with the damn thing, and here he'd finally used it. But the revenge still didn't feel like enough.

When the air-raid sirens began to howl in the middle of the morning, Hideki Fujita laughed and swore at the same time. The officers had their heads up their back passages. Who would take a drill seriously when it came at a time when American bombers were most of the way back to Oahu?

Only it turned out not to be a drill. The antiaircraft guns pounded away. Bombs began bursting on Oahu and in the ocean around it. The Yankees had lousy aim. When enough came down, though, how much did it matter?

All Fujita could do was huddle in a trench and hope none of those badly aimed bombs came down on top of him. None of them had yet, or he wouldn't be here huddling. He dared hope he'd stay lucky one more time.

One of the bombers got hit and plunged toward the Pacific. That was what they got for having the nerve to come over in broad daylight! Fujita wasn't the only Japanese fighting man to raise a cheer.

Another bomber got hit, and then another one. The Americans weren't buying anything cheaply today. But the bombs kept raining down, too. A near miss knocked Fujita over onto his back, half buried him in sand, and left his ears too abused to hear anything much below a shout.

Air raids always seemed to last forever. Digging a finger into one ringing ear, Fujita scrambled out of the trench when the American planes finally flew off to the southeast. Unless an officer grabbed him and told him to do something else, he intended to go over to the lagoon and fill his belly with fresh-killed fish. Even bombs brought some good with them.

He saw that the airstrips had taken another beating. It would be a while before the G4Ms on Midway could even try to repay the Yankees for what they'd done here today. If you didn't count the potency of germs, it was an uneven fight. Japan was at the very end of her reach here, while American strength in Hawaii kept growing and growing.

Fujita had almost got to the lagoon when the air-raid sirens began to screech again. He heard them as if from very far away, but hearing them at all made him swear. The Americans wouldn't be coming back, and they wouldn't throw two separate waves of planes at Midway . . . would they? Why? What point to it?

But those were more planes coming in from the direction toward which the bombers had flown. These were much lower, and differed in shape. Fujita rubbed his eyes, not to get sand out of them but in disbelief. These airplanes had a familiar outline. On his journeys across the vast reaches of the Japanese Empire, he'd flown in more than one Showa L2D3-1a. How could he not recognize them when he spied them now? What were they doing coming up from the southeast?

Only they weren't Showas. Somebody'd told him once that the Japanese transport was a license-built version of the U.S. DC-3. These were the American originals, with stars on wings and fuselage in place of the Rising Sun. They'd come close enough for him to spy such details now—and to give him a good look at the men parachuting out of them one after another after another. The sky was full of silk.

He didn't hang around to admire the spectacle. Instead, he unslung his rifle and started to fight. He'd never dreamt Midway might be invaded from above. But even though he hadn't, the Americans had.

Some Japanese soldiers were already firing at the paratroopers, and at the planes that carried them. One transport blew up in midair, showering Midway with blazing wreckage. *"Banzai!"* Fujita whooped.

He quickly emptied one clip, then another. He took more from a countryman's corpse. The dead man didn't need the rounds any more, while Fujita could still kill Americans with them.

He fired again at the men wafting down. Then a Yankee already on the ground sent a bullet that kicked up sand by his feet. He dove for cover. Standing up to fire at the parachutists wasn't safe any more.

Everyone was running every which way, Americans and Japanese alike. The Yankees had mostly come down in the less garrisoned western part of the island, but not all their drops put them where they were supposed to go. The Japanese had trained against invasion from the sea till Fujita was sick of it. Anybody with eyes in his head could tell that the Americans would want Midway back if they could get to it.

But no one—at least no one with the authority to give orders here—had dreamt the Americans would come by air. No one had planned what to do in case that happened. Without planning, the Japanese were at a disadvantage. They never had been great improvisers.

"We will defend the barracks and the desalinization plant and the special unit!" shouted an officer—Fujita presumed the man was an officer, anyhow—with a loud, authoritative voice. "They will give us the best cover. And we'll see how the Yankees do with only the water they brought along."

Whether the fellow with the loud voice was on officer or not, the command made good sense to Fujita. If the Americans had to come straight at defensible positions, they'd pay a high price for every centimeter of sandy soil they seized. Maybe other Japanese forces would be able to relieve the garrison. Or maybe it would be able to dispose of all the paratroopers and go on harassing Hawaii.

An American machine gun spat funny-looking red-orange tracers not far enough above the ground. The Yankees fed their machine guns from belts, not aluminum strips, so they could fire longer continuous bursts. And for every tracer you saw, there were all the ordinary rounds you didn't. You also had to hope none of those rounds saw you.

Japanese soldiers whom some of those rounds had seen lay sprawled in the sand. A dreadfully wounded man pulled a grenade off his belt, yanked out the pin, and rolled onto the little bomb. His body took the full force of the burst. Not the perfect form of seppuku, but it would serve. He wasn't suffering any more, and he wouldn't need to worry about disgracing himself and his family by being captured.

By the way the Americans kept pushing forward, they didn't think the garrison could stop them. As the sun slid down the sky toward the western horizon, Fujita began to believe they were right. More of them had landed than he'd guessed, and transports kept flying in to drop reinforcements and supplies. They wouldn't have to fight with just the water they'd brought.

"Sergeant!" a captain called. "Can you take a squad and drive the Yankees off that little bit of high ground there?" He pointed to show the position he meant. "It gives them too good a firing position—they can rake these trenches if they bring up machine guns."

"*Hai!*" Fujita saluted. What was he going to do, tell the captain no? He didn't think a whole company could drive the Americans off that swell of ground, but the garrison didn't have a company to commit in the first place. He grabbed a squad's worth of soldiers and sailors and told them what they had to do.

No one told him no, either. The men just nodded. They hefted their rifles. One attached a fresh magazine. Then they were up and scuffing over the sand toward the low but dangerous hillock.

Like autumn leaves, they began to fall. Had Fujita been a samurai, he would have used the line in his death poem. But he was only a sergeant trying to do a job. He knew he would fail, but the trying somehow mattered.

He made it farther than he thought he would—all the way up the swell. He was wounded once before he reached the top. His leg hurt, but he kept going. And he shot an American there before he caught two more rounds in the chest. He fell as if in slow motion in a film. A Yankee with three stripes on his left sleeve brought up his rifle to finish him off. Flame from the muzzle. And then, as in that film, final fade-out.

Theo Hossbach missed the radioman's position in the old Panzer II for one very good reason. The wireless set in the obsolete little machine sat back by the fireproof—everyone hoped!—bulkhead separating the fighting compartment from the one that held the engine. It was the warmest place in the panzer to sit. Even on the worst Russian winter days, it wasn't too bad . . . once you persuaded the engine to start, anyhow.

He had a much better chance of staying alive in this Panzer IV. He also felt he had a much better chance of freezing to death. Up here at the front of the chassis, he was as far from the nice, warm engine compartment as he could get. His breath smoked. His teeth chattered. The Panzer IV had a heater, but it didn't do much.

Adi Stoss' breath smoked, too. The driver didn't seem to care. "How'd you like to play football in weather like this?" he said. "The pitch'd be frozen hard, and the ball would bounce like it was out of its mind."

"No thanks!" Theo might have put more expression into his answer than he'd intended.

Adi laughed. "Yeah, it'd be even worse for a 'keeper, wouldn't it? Us outfield players, we're running around and banging into each other. We stay warm that way. 'Keepers, you've got to stand in front of your nets and turn into ice cubes. Well, everybody knows you guys are nuts."

"Your mother," Theo said, which made Adi laugh some more. As far as Theo was concerned—as far as any goalkeeper was concerned—the notion that their position attracted eccentrics was a slander perpetrated by ten-elevenths of the footballing world. That in itself went a long way toward proving the outfield players' point.

Then a sharp order blared in Theo's earphones: "The regiment is to assemble at once in the birch forest in the northwest corner of map square Green-17. All units acknowledge immediately."

"Acknowledging," Theo said, and gave the panzer's number. As soon as he'd done that, he gave the news to Adi and to Hermann Witt.

"That's not where we were going," the panzer commander said with commendable calm. "Who'll plug the hole we're leaving in the line?"

"Don't know," Theo said: the truth, but not a helpful truth.

"Something's fucked up somewhere," Witt said. Theo thought that was very likely, as it was on every other day since the creation of the world. The sergeant went on, "Well, if we lose the war because the Ivans pour through the hole, nobody can blame us for obeying orders."

"Who says?" Adi put in, and he too had a point. Nevertheless, he swung the panzer to the southwest and chugged toward the rendezvous.

They got there a couple of hours later. By then, Adi was muttering darkly about how close to dry the fuel tank had got. Theo had yet to meet a panzer crewman who didn't mutter about fuel every once in a while . . . or more often than that. Panzers didn't sip gas. They gulped it. They all but inhaled it. And getting more was never as automatic as it should have been.

Other worries first, Theo thought as he climbed out of his steel shell. It was even colder in the open air. He had on a wool sweater and long johns under his black coveralls. He was cold anyway. He lit a cigarette. It didn't warm him up, but he enjoyed it anyhow.

More Panzer IVs, and a handful of beat-up IIIs, clattered into the woods. More crewmen in panzer black got out and started loudly and profanely wondering what they devil they were doing there. Theo thought it was too cold and too Russian out for such important philosophical questions, but what did he know? He knew he didn't have the answer, which put him one up on most of his comrades.

"*Achtung! Achtung!* Gather around me, dedicated soldiers of the *Grossdeutsches Reich!*" That loud voice belonged to Major Stähler, the National Socialist Loyalty Officer. Theo and the whole crew had as little to do with him as they possibly could. With Adi driving their panzer, even that little seemed like too much.

"Maybe he knows something," Witt said.

"That'd be a first," Adi remarked. Theo heard him, but he didn't think the sergeant did.

"Our regiment—our brave and reliable regiment—has been chosen for an important military honor," Stähler went on as the crewmen gathered around him. "You will have heard certain lying rumors about disaffection, even rebellion, within the boundaries of the *Grossdeutsches Reich.*"

As a matter of fact, Theo had heard those rumors. He didn't suppose anyone in the regiment hadn't. Adi seemed to know an awful lot about what was going on in and around Münster. He never got mail from home, but he damn well did keep his ear to the ground. And, from what he said in a low voice when no one untrustworthy could overhear, a hell of a lot was going on around there.

"We must ruthlessly stamp out treason without mercy so the war effort can proceed to our certain final triumph," Major Stähler said. "Rebels against the state, the Party, and the *Führer* must be suppressed.

They must be, and they shall be. And our regiment has been chosen as one of the instruments of suppression."

He sounded proud to announce that. The panzer crewmen's hum of low talk suddenly rose. Some of them were bound to be proud, too—like any German outfit, the regiment had its share of enthusiastic Nazis. Some, yes, but far from all.

Stähler went on, "Since the police and the security services have not been able to bring order to certain regions in the western areas of the *Reich*, the *Wehrmacht* will insure that obedience to our beloved *Führer* is restored. As I said, we are part of that effort."

If the *Führer* was so beloved, why did he need a regiment of panzers to restore obedience? Theo wondered about things like that. He also wondered how many other soldiers wondered likewise. But then something else the National Socialist Loyalty Officer said lit up inside his mind like a searchlight. So they were bound for the western part of Germany, were they? Surely it was no accident that most of this regiment came from Breslau, not far from the Polish border. The Nazis might be bastards, but they were sly bastards. They knew better than to send a unit where the men might have to open fire on their cousins and sisters and mothers and granddads and kid brothers.

"And so," Major Stähler finished up, "tomorrow we shall proceed to the nearest railhead. From there we shall return to our dear *Grossdeutsches Reich* and cleanse it once and for all of the filth of treason and betrayal." He looked out at the assembled panzer crewmen. "Any questions?"

No one said a word. You had to be the world's biggest *Dummkopf* to ask questions of someone like Major Stähler. You wouldn't find out anything worth knowing, and whatever you said would land you in trouble. The major was just trolling for suckers. He didn't catch anybody this time. Theo wondered why he bothered trying.

But Theo didn't wonder for long. Stähler bothered because some people were at the same time rebels and natural-born damn fools. If you offered them half a chance, they *would* give themselves away. The loyalty officer was just doing his job.

"Germany," Hermann Witt said in wondering tones. "Been a devil of a long time since I last saw Germany."

"Me, too," Lothar Eckhardt agreed. The gunner went on, "Not my part of Germany, exactly, but a lot closer to what I'm used to than this Russian garbage is." He nodded at Adi. "We *are* heading back to your part of Germany, aren't we?"

"Sounds like it," Adi answered. "I'm the same as you are, only more so. I haven't seen the old stomping grounds in a hell of a long time. I wonder if I remember what things look like." He shrugged broad shoulders. "Doesn't matter, I guess. We'll figure out what to shoot at."

He didn't say whether that should be rebels or people like Major Stähler. Theo had opinions on that score. No doubt Adi did, too. No doubt everybody in the crew did. Whether all those opinions matched . . . Well, that was an interesting question, wasn't it?

"This is Douglas Edwards with the news." Even coming out of a radio speaker, the newsman's voice sounded as if he belonged on the stage. Peggy Druce had always thought so. Edwards went on, "President Roosevelt has announced that the Stars and Stripes fly once more over Midway Island."

Peggy nodded as she spread butter and jam on her toast. The *Inquirer*'s edition yesterday had had a great photo by some wire-service cameraman of a group of Marines stabbing a flagpole with Old Glory flying from it into the sandy soil of what passed for high ground on Midway.

"A few stubborn Jap holdouts still skulk on the little island like sand crabs," Edwards said solemnly. "They cause casualties every now and then, but cannot hope to change the result of the battle. The Marines hunt them down one by one. Soon no more will be left to hunt. And what comes next for Uncle Sam in the Pacific? I'll be back with a look at that right after the following important messages."

If you found yourself in desperate need of cigars or laundry soap and had no idea where to turn, the messages might have seemed important. Otherwise, they just helped the network pay its bills. Douglas Edwards was bound—was more than bound: was paid—to think that important. It didn't matter a hill of beans, or even a single bean, to Peggy.

When Edwards came back, he delicately suggested that the United States might look to Wake Island next. "Thank you, Field Marshal Model!" Peggy exclaimed. You didn't need to belong to the German General Staff to figure that one out. Peggy'd done it for herself while the sultry chanteuse sang the praises of White Owls. Wake was now the closest Japanese-held dot on the map to the main Hawaiian islands. It legally belonged to the USA. Once it fell into American hands again, nobody could even dream about dropping any more germ bombs on Honolulu.

In the Atlantic, a German U-boat had fired two torpedoes at a U.S. destroyer. Both missed. The destroyer depth-charged the U-boat, but didn't sink it. FDR had sent Hitler a stiff protest note. Hitler'd told Roosevelt where he could stick that note. All of which was done diplomatically, of course, but that was what it boiled down to.

On the Eastern Front, the Russians kept moving up and the Germans kept falling back. Marshal Antonescu loudly denied that Romania was thinking about bailing out of the war. Of course, the louder a dictator and his henchmen denied something like that, the truer it was liable to be.

Take Dr. Goebbels, for instance. He was now loudly denying there was any such thing as unrest inside the *Reich*. Douglas Edwards played a recording of Lord Haw-Haw—otherwise an Irishman named William Joyce who'd lived in the States for a while and who could put on a plummy, aristocratic British accent—saying, "The German people stand united behind Adolf Hitler!" Goebbels had also announced that anyone who didn't stand united behind the *Führer* would stand alone in front of a firing squad.

In Spain, the Nationalists really did seem to be falling to pieces now that Marshal Sanjurjo had bitten the dust. The Republic had regained more ground the past few weeks than in several previous years. Peggy had read *For Whom the Bell Tolls*. It made her admire the Spaniards. It also made her think that the parts of Spain the Republic took from the Nationalists wouldn't be much happier now than Nationalist-conquered chunks of the Republic had been before. A civil war was a filthy business no matter who wound up on top.

When Edwards started talking about tornadoes in Oklahoma and

Arkansas, Peggy stopped listening. She thought of places like that the way a smart, well-connected Englishwoman would have thought of Scunthorpe, a Frenchwoman would have thought of Périgueux, or a Russian woman would have thought of Irkutsk. She supposed people had to live in such places, but she was mighty glad not to be one of them.

A train wreck in Wisconsin and a strike at an aluminum plant outside of Los Angeles didn't much interest her, either. She got up and turned the radio to a station that was playing music. She kept it on while she did the breakfast dishes. The jazz was hotter than she usually enjoyed, but she found herself washing the frying pan in time to the sax's propulsive rhythm.

After the dishes were done, she changed the station again. She didn't want to be jitterbugging while she swept the floors. Music that made you get up and dance was all very well in its place, but she didn't think cleaning the house was that place.

Once she got things clean enough to suit her, she paused to smoke a cigarette. American tobacco tasted so much better than the hay and horseshit they had in Europe, it wasn't even funny. She sometimes wondered why she hadn't quit while she was stuck over there. Hanging on to the habit with the crap they were stuck with hardly seemed worth it.

But she had, and she was glad of it. For one thing, the Nazis disapproved of women who smoked. They claimed it was unhealthy. The prejudice seemed as irrational to her as their hatred of Jews. Anything they disapproved of, she was all for.

And, for another, what else besides a cigarette gave you the perfect excuse to do nothing for a few minutes? Oh, there were coffee breaks, too, but those weren't the same. They were bigger. You couldn't take coffee any old place, the way you could with a cigarette. A lot of the time, you had to go to the trouble of making coffee if you wanted some. A Chesterfield or an Old Gold was always there.

"Unhealthy, my ass," Peggy muttered as she stubbed out the butt. Now that Herb wasn't here, she could talk to herself as much as she pleased. No one would think she was crazy. Well, not on account of that, anyhow.

She was thinking about lighting another one when the telephone rang. She answered it. "Hello, Peggy. Ned Altrock here," said a hearty voice.

"Oh, hello, Ned. How are you?" Peggy said. He was a good-sized wheel in the Pennsylvania Democratic Party. She didn't know what his precise title was. It amounted to fixer.

"I'm busy," he replied. "Only a year till the election, you know."

"Uh-huh," Peggy said. Till she'd got involved in politics, a year away from an election might as well have been forever. She knew different—she knew better—now. A year was nothing. The wheels had already started spinning behind the scenes. Ned sounded as if he were doing a good many RPMs, all right.

"I hope we can count on you to do your part again this year," Altrock said. "People still talk about what a tiger you are on the campaign trail."

"Do they?"

"They sure do. And we can use some more of that, you know," the fixer said. "The war news isn't everything we'd want it to be, even if we've got Midway back. You can bet the Republicans will try and beat us over the head with it. Anything you can do to make people be sensible, that'd be terrific. Things are liable to get tight this time around."

By *make people be sensible,* he of course meant *make people do what we want and vote our way.* Peggy said, "Well, why not? It's not like I don't have some time on my hands nowadays. You'll pay the usual expenses, right? Train tickets, hotel bills, food, that kind of stuff?"

"Oh, heck, yes," Altrock assured her. "Hey, we'll throw in a stipend, too. I know things are a little tighter for you now."

That meant he'd heard about the divorce. "Thanks," Peggy said. Nice to be wanted, even if he was only interested in her for what she could do for FDR.

Chapter 14

People who fought on the ground said the Germans were easier to push back than they ever had been. They'd pulled so much out of the Soviet Union to hold off England and France in the West that they didn't always have enough left to keep the Red Army from going forward.

Anastas Mouradian only wished things were like that in the air war, too. The problem was, the air frontier above the Low Countries was narrow. The *Luftwaffe* had taken some planes out of the USSR to fight over there, but not all that many. Plenty of 109s and 190s still prowled the frigid air over the workers' and peasants' paradise.

"It will work out however it works out," Isa Mogamedov said when Stas muttered about that in the cockpit. With the ground frozen hard, the Pe-2 squadron was back in business. Unfortunately, so were the Messerschmitts and the Focke-Wulfs.

"So it will," Stas said, and sent the copilot and bomb-aimer a quizzical look. Mogamedov hadn't quite come out with the Arabic *Inshallah*, but he'd come about as close as a secular New Soviet Man was ever likely to. A Russian probably wouldn't have noticed anything out of the ordinary in the reply. Then again, Russians hadn't spent the past nine hundred or a thousand years living next door to Azeris.

Groundcrew men used a truck-mounted starter—a device borrowed from the Americans—to make the bomber's engines turn over: first the port, then the starboard. Mouradian studied the instrument panel. Everything looked the way it was supposed to. He waved to the boss sergeant on the airstrip. The noncom waved back.

One after another, the Pe-2s took off. The target today was one of the railroad lines leading west out of Minsk. Stas couldn't remember hitting targets on the far side of the Byelorussian capital. Not in this phase of the war, anyhow.

He released the brakes and taxied down the dirt runway. The bomber got airborne and climbed over the pale-barked birch trees in the woods past the end of the airstrip. The birches looked as if they'd been whitewashed like the squadron's planes. Any Nazi fighter pilot would have a hard time spotting the Soviet aircraft against the drifts below them.

As he got closer to the front east of Minsk, more monuments of man's inhumanity to man made themselves known in spite of the snow. There was a burnt-out tank, with soot spread over whiteness. From this height, he couldn't tell whose tank it had been. That didn't matter any more. It was nothing but scrap metal now. Sooner or later, he supposed, the Russians would haul the carcass to a foundry and make something new out of it.

Here was a burning village that had been on the German side of the line for a long time but now found itself in Soviet hands once more. Stas couldn't see any of the human dramas down there, either, but this scene had played out many times before farther east. Some of the peasants would have cozied up to the Nazis, either because they liked Hitler better than Stalin or just because they thought that was the best way to keep their bellies full and their wives and daughters unraped.

And now they would pay for guessing wrong. Their neighbors would want revenge. The NKVD would want to pay back treason. If the peasants were lucky, they'd go straight into punishment battalions. There, at least, they had a small chance of coming out in one piece. If they weren't so lucky, they'd go to the gulags instead. Or they'd simply meet a noose or a bullet to the base of the skull.

Their wives and daughters still might get forced. Only the uniforms of the men holding them down would be different.

The squadron didn't fly over Minsk. The Pe-2s took a dogleg to swing south of the city. The Red Air Force had found out by painful experience that the Fascists had packed the place with antiaircraft guns. German gunners had both skill and enthusiasm. You didn't want to give them a shot at you if you didn't have to. For that matter, you didn't *want* to give them a shot at you even when you did have to.

But skirting the flak guns took the squadron straight into a swarm of marauding FW-190s. Stas hated the new German fighter. A Pe-2 had a fair chance against a 109. Odds when you ran into 190s were worse. They had more speed, heavier guns, and a cockpit that gave their pilots terrific all-around vision. They were Trouble with a capital T.

"Dump the bombs!" Stas shouted into the speaking tube that carried his voice back to the bomb bay.

"I'm fucking doing it," Fyodor Mechnikov answered. The bomb-bay doors opened. The explosives would come down on somebody, with luck on somebody German. Mouradian wasn't inclined to be fussy. Designers always claimed that their brainstorms were fighting bombers. They always lied. Fighters were made for just one thing: shooting down other planes. Bombers had to do other things, too, and couldn't fight back so well.

Suddenly lighter by upwards of a tonne, the Pe-2 got faster and more nimble. All the same, Stas stayed low and gunned the bomber for every kopek it was worth. The best way to deal with German fighters was not to hang around anywhere close to them.

But then the machine gun in the dorsal turret chattered. "Eat shit, you whore!" Mechnikov shouted at the fighter he was trying to drive off.

Bullets slammed into the Pe-2. There was no fire. The engines kept running. When Stas cautiously tried the controls, they worked. No hydraulic lines punctured. No wires cut. That was all luck, of course—nothing else but. The German pilot who'd put the burst into the Pe-2 had to be cursing his. He'd done everything right. He just hadn't managed to knock the bomber out of the sky.

Stas fired a burst at the FW-190 as it streaked past. He didn't do it any harm, either. It zoomed away to go after some of the other planes in the squadron. That suited Mouradian fine. "We scared off the son of a bitch, anyhow," he said.

"That's right. Fedya must have taught him respect." Mogamedov spoke with perhaps less irony than he'd intended.

"If he hadn't been up there banging away, that burst the Hitlerite hit us with would have been longer. It might have done us a lot of harm." Stas kept eyeing the gauges. Everything was jammed up hard against the emergency lines. Fair enough. If almost getting shot down didn't qualify as an emergency, what in blazes would?

Mogamedov kept checking the instrument panel, too. It didn't seem to satisfy him . . . or he might have had trouble believing it. "The engines sound good, don't they?" he said, as if by putting it in the form of a question he didn't have to sound like someone who believed it.

"Pretty good." Stas didn't want to admit any more than he had to. A New Soviet Man ought not to believe in outmoded superstitions like tempting fate. Sometimes, though, the unreconstructed old Armenian peeked out from behind the New Soviet mask he wore.

Behind Mogamedov's goggles, an equally unreconstructed old Azeri checked to make sure the 190 was really gone. So Stas thought, anyhow. He might have been wrong, but he didn't think so.

Then bursts of flak, black with angry, fiery cores, began buffeting the Pe-2. In his wild efforts to escape the German fighter, Stas had come too close to the rings of antiaircraft guns girdling Minsk. He swung the plane hard to the south once more, away from the city.

"Where did the rest of the squadron get to?" Mogamedov asked.

"Good question. My guess is, we're scattered over fifty kilometers of sky," Stas answered. "As long as we see each other again back at the airstrip, we can worry about the details some other time." Mogamedov thought that over, then nodded.

Off in the distance, a German stuck up his head to see what the French in front of him were up to. Aristide Demange took a shot at the *Boche.* He didn't think he hit the *con.* He did make him disappear in a hurry, which was what he'd wanted to do.

He also hopped down off the firing step from which he'd fired. A few seconds later, the Fritzes turned loose a burst from a machine gun. Maybe all those rounds would have missed him. It was nothing he cared to find out by experiment.

A *poilu* coming into the trench from the smashed Belgian village behind it grinned sympathetically. "You were lucky, Lieutenant, getting down when you did," the fellow said, his southern accent nasal and grating in Demange's ears.

"Lucky, my left one," Demange said, focusing his usual scorn for all humanity on one human in particular. "Listen, Marcel, I don't care how stupid you are. Even a Provençal clodhopper like you should be able to see that, when you try and kill somebody, he's gonna try to kill you, too. So maybe you shouldn't give him the chance, eh?"

Marcel pondered that. Demange could see, or imagined he could see, the gears going round in the soldier's head—going round . . . very . . . very . . . slowly. *"D'accord,"* Marcel said at last.

Demange suppressed the urge to clap a hand to his forehead in theatrical despair. The only thing that could have made Marcel act any dumber than he did now would have been for him to chew gum like a cow or an American. The worst of it was, Demange couldn't ride him as hard as he would have liked. When it came to smarts, Marcel wasn't the highest card in the deck, no. But he was easygoing and he fought all right. You didn't expect or even want brains in all the privates.

The ruined village in back of them was the one that had been in front of them a few weeks before. They didn't need to measure their advance in centimeters per day, but they didn't need to measure it in kilometers per day, either. At this rate, they'd cross the Low Countries and push on into Germany about when Demange died of old age.

Of course, if he stayed at the front, old age was the least of his worries. He didn't take idiotic chances, the way fools fresh from basic training and hotheads did. He remembered that the sons of bitches on the other side carried rifles and other tools of mayhem. The less they got to use them on him, the better he liked it.

Some chances, though, you couldn't help. If some fat general's secretary told him she wouldn't suck him off one morning, he was liable to order his brigade to attack the Germans out of sheer spite. That kind of shit never got into the history books. It happened all the time, though.

He stuck up his head to see if some frustrated German general whose secretary wouldn't put out was going to get a regiment's worth of the *Führer*'s finest slaughtered on account of pique. The Fritzes seemed quiet. Demange hadn't come up in the place he'd fired from. He also didn't stay up longer than a second or two. Yes, he knew the ropes.

Nobody was supposed to go between the lines. They called the battered ground out there no-man's-land for a reason. But a Belgian farmer in a worn felt hat, baggy corduroy trousers, and stout Wellingtons ambled along as if he had not a care in the world. Little smoke signals rose from the pipe clenched between his teeth.

Demange had seen such types before, in the last war and in this one. They came out of their holes whenever things quieted down. Sometimes they were harmless. They'd arrange to trade your tobacco for the other fellow's schnapps, or to take a letter from a granny on one side of the wire to her granddaughter on the other.

Sometimes they were anything but harmless. They'd spy for one side or the other or sometimes for both. While they were going through the motions of trading, they'd scout out the other side's positions and report back to whoever was paying them. Or the sweet letter from grandmother to little girl would be chock-full of coded messages. You never could tell.

And Demange distrusted Belgians on general principles. Half the Flemings wished they were Germans. The Walloons—even the ones who weren't Rexist bastards—spoke French with a funny accent, even worse than what a Provençal like Marcel used.

"Hey, you!" Demange yelled at this Belgian. The man slowly looked back toward him, as if uncertain he was being addressed. Demange had seen it done better. Hell, he'd done it better himself. "Yeah, you, shit-for-brains! Get your ugly ass back here so I can talk with you!"

The farmer did his best to pretend he was deaf. His best didn't impress Demange. Up came the rifle. He wasn't particularly trying to hit the Belgian, but he wasn't particularly trying to miss, either.

If a rifle bullet cracking past a meter or two in front of your snoot didn't draw your attention, chances were you'd already bought a plot. The Belgian decided he might do better to come back to the French lines after all. A good thing for him, too. Demange would have aimed the next round with care.

A lot of people would have had trouble getting through the drifts of barbed wire in front of the French lines. The farmer knew the secret ways at least as well as Demange did. *Have to change our routes,* Demange thought irritably.

Down into the trench slid the Belgian. He wore a bushy gray mustache. He might have fought in the trenches the last time around. Now he'd gone into business for himself.

"What d'you want?" he asked in his peculiar French.

"What were you doing out there?" Demange returned. "And don't fuck with me, either. You give me crap, I'll knock your teeth down your throat." He sounded as if he looked forward to it. Well, he did. It would turn a boring day halfway interesting.

The anticipation in his voice and on his narrow, nasty face got through to the Belgian. Some people, you did better not to mess with. "I was going to sell the *Boches* some applejack," the farmer said slowly.

He did not visibly have any. "Where is it?" Demange snapped. "And if you say you were gonna bring it later, you're in more trouble than you know what to do with."

"I'll show you." The farmer unbelted his pants and let them drop. He wore long johns under them—it was cold out here. He also wore rubber bands around the ankles of the long underwear. He reached into the long johns and pulled out two fat rubber hot-water bottles. He handed Demange one. Demange unscrewed the stopper and sniffed. That was applejack, all right. Demange held out his hand for the other one. Sourly, the farmer passed it to him. He checked. Applejack in both of them, all right.

"Well, it is what you say it is," Demange allowed. "And since it is, I'll give you a whole franc for it."

"A franc!" The Belgian's mustache quivered with fury. He must have known he'd get screwed, but he hadn't expected to get screwed that royally.

Because Demange was feeling generous, he said, "Oh, all right—a franc for each bottle." He tossed the Belgian not one but two coins of yellow aluminum-bronze. "Out of my own pocket, you see."

"No wonder some of us think the Germans are a better deal," the farmer said. "You . . . You . . . !" Words failed him, which was his good luck.

"Get lost, *cochon,*" Demange said coldly. "I ever see you again, we'll talk about it with the undertaker."

Away the Belgian went. If looks could have killed . . . But you needed a rifle for that.

"Gather round, boys!" Demange told the soldiers he led. "We'd better destroy the evidence, in case he complains to a brass hat or something." Destroy the evidence they did, and they had a hell of a time doing it, too.

Hans-Ulrich Rudel understood that Stukas had had their day—literally—as dive-bombers. Without fighter cover, they wouldn't, and didn't, last ten minutes. And giving them the cover they needed tied up Bf-109s and FW-190s that could have been doing more useful things.

Logically, the *Luftwaffe* should have scrapped them all and given their pilots hotter planes to fly, planes that could fight or flee well enough on their own to get by without escorts. But the higher-ups didn't want to junk any weapons of war that still had use to them. And so some egghead decided to turn the Ju-87s into night raiders.

It made a certain amount of sense. Even Hans-Ulrich had to admit that much. Planes aloft in the dark were hard to spot and hard to shoot down once spotted. That French bombers built before the war, bombers even more spavined than Stukas, kept coming back from night attacks over the *Vaterland* proved as much.

Finding targets in the dark was also an adventure, of course. But the Ju-87s were no more inaccurate than any other German bombers. You couldn't dive-bomb when you couldn't judge when to pull up. You could fly on the level and drop all those hundreds of kilos of explosives where you hoped they'd do your side the most good.

You could, and the Stuka pilots were doing it. They'd struck at ammunition dumps and railroad yards close to the front. They'd also ventured deeper into France. Hans-Ulrich had hit Caen twice and Paris once. He'd bombed them, anyhow. He hoped he'd hit them.

Here he was again, droning along toward Paris. To guide his plane, he had a compass, an airspeed indicator, and a wristwatch with luminous hands. Fortunately, Paris was a big place. Some of the bombers that had been built with this kind of mission in mind—He-111s and Ju-88s, for instance—could be guided toward their target by radio beams. The Stuka carried no such receivers. Maybe groundcrew men would install them one of these days. Hans-Ulrich wasn't holding his breath.

Before long, he stopped having any doubts about where Paris lay. Flak guns on the ground threw cascades of shells at the *Luftwaffe* planes above them. Muzzle flashes marked thicker concentrations of guns—and, Rudel supposed, thicker concentrations of targets worth hitting.

Tracers climbed up to and past the Ju-87. Their glowing trails and the shell bursts all around put Hans-Ulrich in mind of fireworks displays. Fireworks displays didn't fill the sky with sharp fragments, though.

From the rear-facing seat, Sergeant Dieselhorst used the speaking tube: "I think they may have an idea we're here."

"Do you?" Hans-Ulrich said. "Well, you could be right. Just in case, I'll give them something to remember me by." He yanked on the bomb-release lever. The large bomb under the fuselage and the smaller ones under the wings fell away. Big flashes of light down below said other German bombs were already bursting on the capital of France.

He didn't stick around to watch them. He hauled the Stuka's nose around and headed back toward Belgium. The plane was friskier without its load. No Ju-87 would ever be either fast or maneuverable, but it came closer than it had.

Not far off to the side, an enemy night fighter ambushed another Stuka. Machine-gun tracers stabbed at the German plane. It caught fire. Stukas carried good defensive armor, but you couldn't stop everything. Flame licked across the Ju-87's wing. The plane began to fall out of the sky. Hans-Ulrich hoped the pilot and rear gunner/radioman were able to use their 'chutes. Hope was all he could do.

No—he could do one thing more. He could mash down the throttle and scoot away from there as fast as he could go. He could, and he did. The farther from the busy French defenses over the capital he got, the less likely he was to meet a shell with his name on it or an enterprising enemy pilot peering into the darkness to spy a shape against the stars or the telltale glow of flames from the exhaust pipes.

Finding the airstrip from which he'd taken off was another adventure. Only dim lamps marked it—anything more would have invited a call from English or French planes. Landing when those lights were all he could see was nothing he'd trained for.

A couple of pilots in the squadron had already had to write off their Stukas. One was still in the hospital with burns and broken bones. Hans-Ulrich got down with no worse than a jolt. Still, this wasn't a business for the faint of heart.

When he went to the commander's tent to report on the mission, he was glad to find Colonel Steinbrenner sitting behind his little folding table. Only a paraffin lantern and the colonel's cigarette coal shed any light on things. They made Steinbrenner's face look older and wearier than it was.

"Yes, I saw it, too," the squadron CO said when Hans-Ulrich mentioned the Stuka shot down over Paris. "That was Rolf Wutka and Sergeant Schmidt."

"*Aii!*" Hans-Ulrich said, and covered his eyes with one hand. "I went to flying school with Rolf." They hadn't got on that well, then or later, but even so . . . "I feel like a goose walked over my grave. Not many of us left who've been going up since before the war."

"No, not many," Steinbrenner agreed. He was one—he'd been doing it longer than Rudel. After a moment, he went on, "Things could be worse, you know. We could be bombing our own cities instead of the enemy's."

"Have *Luftwaffe* units started doing that?" Hans-Ulrich asked. He'd always been a man stolidly loyal to those set in authority over him.

Past that, he was about as political as an apricot tree. Even someone like him, though, couldn't help knowing how restive the *Reich* had got these days.

"If they have, I haven't heard about it, and I think I would have," Colonel Steinbrenner said. He might have added more, but stubbed out the cigarette instead. The way he shook his head seemed to tell Hans-Ulrich he'd thought better of whatever it was. Maybe it didn't matter. Maybe it mattered so much, he didn't trust Hans-Ulrich with it. Sighing, he went on, "Anything else about your return flight?"

"Only the adventure of landing." Rudel gave back a lopsided grin. "But you already know about that, don't you?"

"For a second there, when I was getting my nose up, I wished I were wearing a diaper under my long johns," Steinbrenner said. "About the only worse thing I can think of would be coming in on an aircraft carrier's flight deck at night."

Germany had started building a carrier. When the war broke out, the *Graf Zeppelin* got shelved. All those tonnes of steel went into other things instead. Hans-Ulrich tried to imagine landing on a rolling, pitching deck with only lanterns to guide him in. "You're right, sir. That would be worse. I didn't think anything could be," he said. "Still, I'd like to try it, you know?"

"From most people, that would be bragging. From most people, it'd be *Quatsch,* is what it'd be," Steinbrenner said. "From you, though, from you I believe it. I remember how you won your *Ritterkreuz.*"

Hans-Ulrich touched the medal he wore at his throat. He was the one who'd thought of mounting panzer-busting cannons under a Stuka's wings. He was the one who'd taken them up and tried them out, too. He shrugged. "I didn't do it for the Knight's Cross, sir."

"I didn't say you did," Steinbrenner answered quietly. "That makes it more likely you'd want to fly onto a carrier, though, not less."

"All I want to do is hit the enemy as hard as I can, however I can, wherever I can," Rudel said.

"I know that." Colonel Steinbrenner sighed again. "Life would be simpler if everyone were more like you." He gestured. "For now, get out of here. Grab some sleep if you're not too wound up. We'll go out again tomorrow night as long as the weather's not too beastly."

"Zu Befehl, mein Herr!" Hans-Ulrich said. One advantage to following the soldier's trade was that you could always find the right answer.

Julius Lemp had taken the U-30 east through the Kiel Canal before. This time, though, he had men on the flak gun on the platform at the back of the conning tower. RAF raiders were growing bolder day by day. Yes, there were antiaircraft guns on both sides of the canal. Yes, a couple of Bf-109s buzzed overhead. Chances were he was worrying too much.

He kept men on the gun even so. If an enemy fighter-bomber did come after his boat here, he couldn't dive to escape it. The canal wasn't deep enough. He had to try to fight it off, or at least to make the flyer too anxious to be accurate.

No fighter-bombers roared in out of the west. Lemp relaxed when the U-boat came out into the broader waters of the Baltic. Now he could dive. He could dodge, too. Somehow he was sure that, if he hadn't manned the gun, the English *would* have strafed him. There was an old joke about snapping your fingers to keep the elephants away. He knew about it. He just didn't care. A U-boat skipper had better not care about jokes. Suspenders, belt, binder twine, a cummerbund . . . Whatever could possibly hold up his trousers.

Kiel wasn't far from the eastern edge of the canal that bore its name. As the U-30 neared the port, Lemp saw smoke from two or three fires rising into the gray, hazy sky. He tugged at his beard in perplexity. "What's going on there?" he said, pointing to the smoke plumes. "Do you suppose the RAF has started making serious daylight raids?"

Behind him, Gerhart Beilharz shrugged. Before the engineering officer could answer, what sounded like a cannon fired inside the city: once, twice, three times. Another column of smoke started going up. "I think we're doing it to ourselves, skipper," Beilharz answered sadly.

"That's—madness," Lemp said. But just because it was mad, that didn't make it any less likely. The uprising that toppled the Kaiser at the end of the last war had started here, when sailors from the High

Seas Fleet mutinied against their officers. A lot of them were Reds, but every one of them was sick of the hopeless, losing fight.

Lemp couldn't imagine a Bolshevik uprising in Kiel today, or anywhere else in Germany. But millions of people all through the *Grossdeutsches Reich* were sick of this hopeless, losing fight.

When Wilhelm II saw the jig was up, he went into exile in Holland and stayed there quietly for the rest of his life. Of all the things Lemp could imagine Adolf Hitler doing, going quietly into exile stood last on the list. Hitler would hang on to power as long as he could, and then another twenty minutes besides.

Naval infantrymen in *Stahlhelms* on the wharf aimed an antipanzer cannon at the incoming U-boat. The U-30's deck gun was bigger and more powerful than that door-knocker on rubber tires, but it wouldn't be the only piece aimed at the boat. It was just the only one the sailors could spot. And for a U-boat, which had no armor, any fight with artillery was a losing fight.

"Nice to see we're welcome," Lemp said, his voice frigid with fury.

"Sir, I think we would have got a friendlier hello if we put in at the quays by London Bridge." Lieutenant Beilharz sounded disgusted, too.

"One good thing, anyhow," Lemp said. "That damned SD pigdog with the manners of a wall lizard is still back in Wilhelmshaven—or I hope like blazes he is, anyhow." Beilharz nodded. He'd spent plenty of time listening to his skipper vent his spleen on the subject of the security-mad *Sicherheitsdienst* man.

A petty officer with a megaphone bawled, "Continue your slow approach. Make no sudden, dangerous-looking maneuvers. Your crew will be taken off the boat for interrogation and evaluation before being released for liberty."

Lemp waved to show he heard. Somebody from the boat would get fed up and tell the interrogators where to head in. He could see that coming like a rash. Then the blackshirts would jug the poor, pissed-off fool, and they'd sneak a spy aboard to take his place . . . assuming they didn't already have one or several on the boat (an assumption Lemp didn't hold).

Unless he felt like making a mutiny, he couldn't do anything about this. What the goons who gave that petty officer and more men like him their orders didn't understand, though, was that such orders were almost an open invitation to making a mutiny. And when it came—oh, not from the U-30, not now, but from somewhere, and soon—the goons would have the gall to act surprised.

Or perhaps they wouldn't. Those smoke plumes climbing into the sky argued that the nation had already mutinied against the government, regardless of whether the armed forces had.

One of the armed sailors who boarded the U-30 to take off the crew had an accident. All kinds of fittings on the boat stuck out or hung down where a careless man could bang his head on them and knock himself cold. So Lemp assured the excitable ensign who was thinking more along the lines of felonious assault.

Since the ensign couldn't prove anything, and since Lemp outranked him and was almost old enough to be his father, he calmed down. He had to. Lemp smiled, but only behind the puppy's back.

His men went off for their grillings. He expected to face the usual board of senior officers himself. They might not quiet down so fast about the poor naval infantryman's "accident"—they were harder to con than an ensign not dry behind the ears.

Instead, Lemp found himself escorted into the presence of Admiral Karl Dönitz. He saluted less sloppily than he had in years. "Sir!" he said to the commander of the U-boat force.

"At ease, Commander," Dönitz answered, his voice mild. His cheeks and forehead were broad, his chin narrow and pointed. But for a blade of a nose, he had flattish features. Most of the time, he was among the calmest of men. He tried to use that now, but in spite of himself his voice held a certain edge as he asked, "And how did you like your reception?"

Because Lemp trusted the admiral, he answered honestly: "Sir, I think the Royal Navy would have been friendlier." It was Beilharz's line, but it summed up what Lemp thought.

Dönitz's narrow, gray-blue eyes assessed him. "The Royal Navy would know what you are," the admiral said. "At the moment, all we have in Germany are suspicions."

"Yes, sir. I can see that," Lemp said. "And if you keep showing them this way, plenty of people will decide they should give you something to suspect."

"*Et tu, Brute?*" Dönitz murmured.

Lemp hadn't trotted out his schoolboy Latin for years. He would have thought he'd forgotten it all, but he understood what that meant, both literally and in the words behind the words. "Sir, if the government is trying to make everyone in the *Reich* hate it, it's doing a good job," he said.

"The government is *trying* to win the war." Dönitz sounded as if he'd had this argument many times before, certainly with others and possibly with himself as well. "If treason springs up, the state has to put it down so the fight against the foreign foe can go forward."

"If the government makes things so bad that no one wants to fight for it, how can it win against England and France and Russia, sir?" Lemp said.

Admiral Dönitz's arched nostrils flared. "And you've been out at sea on patrol," he muttered, more to himself than to the man standing in front of his desk. What did he think Lemp might have done had he been ashore all this time? Pulled a grenade off his belt and chucked it into the officers' club? That was what it sounded like, that or something worse. Dönitz went on, "You need to be careful with that kind of talk, you know."

"Oh, yes, sir," Lemp replied. "But if you're going to report me to Himmler's bully boys, we're already ruined past the hope of fixing." Dönitz waved him out of the office. He felt as if he'd just survived a depth-charging.

Chapter 15

Chaim Weinberg heard a man wailing behind a barn. He trotted over to see what was going on. Two Republican soldiers were kicking the farmer here and slamming him with their rifle butts. If nobody stopped them, they were plainly going to beat him to death.

"What's going on?" Chaim didn't quite point his rifle at them, but the idea was there.

They scowled at him: a couple of kids, one with a wispy excuse for a mustache. "Who are you?" that kid asked.

"And what business is it of yours?" the other one added.

"I'm an Abe Lincoln, that's who I am," Chaim answered. Saint Paul could have sounded no prouder when he said *I am a Roman citizen*. Chaim added, "I've been fighting over here since before you punks had hair on your balls. I guess that makes it my business. So, one more time—*¿qué pasó?*"

"We're punishing this rotten counterrevolutionary," the soldier with the mustache said. "He was feeding the reactionary forces until we liberated this area."

"And so? What was he going to do? Tell them no, he couldn't do that? Tell them he was a Marxist-Leninist?" Chaim rolled his eyes. "They would have given him what you're giving him, only they would've done it sooner."

"He did it for years," the kid with the mustache said, only now with uncertainty in his voice.

"Who was running things here all this time?" Chaim returned. "We only just got here, you know. And you really went and made him love the Republic, didn't you?"

"*¡Viva la República!*" the farmer said, staggering to his feet. He was about fifty. He had a big mouse under one eye. Blood ran down his forehead and face from a scalp wound. More dripped onto his collarless shirt from another.

No matter what he said, chances were he wished the Devil would stick his pitchfork in the Republic's ass. But he had sense enough to know saying that *would* get him killed. In Spain, you had to be for or against. Lukewarm was right out. With great dignity, the man wiped his face on his sleeve. He grimaced at the bloodstains.

"Go on. Get lost," Chaim told the Republican soldiers. "You've done your good deed for the day." He gestured with the rifle to put some oomph in the order.

He didn't think he would have plugged them had they said no. But they weren't so sure about that. They also weren't sure, however, that they'd been doing what they were supposed to when they started stomping the farmer. So they did take off, leaving only black looks and an obscene gesture to remember them by.

"*Muchas gracias, Señor,*" the farmer said. "You have saved my life, for whatever it may be worth to you." He put a hand on his ribcage and winced. If he didn't have a busted slat or two, Chaim would have been amazed. The kids hadn't been playing when they punted him—not even close. His life might not be worth much even to him for the next little while.

"*De nada,*" Chaim answered. "I wanted you to know that not everybody from the Republic is a son of a whore."

"*Bueno.* That is worth knowing," the farmer said gravely. "Now it appears the Republic will be in charge here."

"It does look that way," Chaim agreed.

"I am going to drink wine to restore myself," the farmer said. "You will allow me to give you some?"

"Try and stop me from allowing you." Chaim grinned.

When the farmer had worked that through, he allowed himself the ghost of a smile. He led Chaim into the farmhouse. By his limp, they'd kicked him in the thigh, too, probably going for his *cojones* but missing. The farmhouse didn't look as if he lived there alone. It was too neat, but not with a stern bachelor neatness.

"My wife is with my daughter, a few kilometers from here," the farmer explained as he poured red wine into two mugs. "My daughter is having a baby. I am glad Luisa did not see this. She would have tried to stop them, and she had no rifle." He raised his mug. "*¡Salud!*"

"*¡Salud!*" Chaim drank. It was strong and rough. The farmer might have made it himself or traded a couple of chickens to a neighbor for a jug's worth. You wouldn't want to pay much for it. For drinking a toast, it was fine.

Cautiously, the farmer held out his hand. "I am called Diego Lopez," he said.

"*Con mucho gusto, Don Diego,*" Chaim replied, and gave his own name.

Lopez gamely tried to pronounce it. Having heard before what Spaniards did to *Chaim Weinberg*, the Abe Lincoln hid a smile. The farmer said, "You told those others you were a foreigner. Your name shows it, and your Spanish. You speak very well, but you are no native."

Along with being compulsively brave, Spaniards were compulsively polite. They would inquire after your health while they carved up your liver. Laughing, Chaim said, "My Spanish is crappy. I try, and I can make people understand me, but it's crappy all the same. I know that."

"I have not seen many foreigners before. Please excuse me for a moment." Lopez poured water from an earthenware crock onto a rag. He used it to clean more blood from his head. Eyeing the stains on the rag, he sighed. "Is this what we have to look forward to under the Republic?"

"I hope not," Chaim answered. "There are *putos* in every army in the world, though, *¿verdad?*"

"Yes, that is true," Diego Lopez said. "Some of them fought for Marshal Sanjurjo, too—it is not to be doubted."

"Every army, every side," Chaim said. "They think it's fun to beat up on people who can't fight back. And it's much safer than going after the enemy's soldiers."

"I believe that." Lopez held out the jar of wine. "Would you like me to fill that again for you, *Señor*?"

"*Muchas gracias*," Chaim replied. The farmer also poured more for himself. They wished each other good health before they drank. No, it wasn't great wine, but any wine was better than no wine at all.

"Ahh," Lopez said. "Yes, that does take some of the pain away. I have not seen any Nationalist soldiers here lately, not since just after Marshal Sanjurjo, ah, passed away."

Got his head blown off, Chaim edited. But saying that to his host would have been rude. Lopez might have fed the Spanish Fascists because he had no choice. He might also have sympathized with them. A depressing number of people did, or the fight never could have dragged on so long. That was the sort of thing Chaim didn't want to know officially. If he didn't know, he didn't have to do anything about it.

He said, "The Nationalists seem to be fighting among themselves more than they're fighting the Republic now."

"Marshal Sanjurjo was a strong man." Lopez seemed to pick his words with care. "No one left on the Nationalist side has the power of character to bring everyone else with him." He didn't say he approved of the cause under which he'd lived. That would have given Chaim a handle on him. You had to be careful with someone you hadn't known for a long time, even if that someone had just saved your life.

"You should make friends with the Internationals—bring 'em food or something," Chaim said. "They'll keep ordinary tough guys from giving you trouble."

"I had heard that no one has to do things like that in the Republic," Lopez said.

"People hear all kinds of things, don't they?" Chaim replied, his voice bland. "Wherever there are people, it's a good idea to make friends."

"So it is things as they are, and not things as the ones in charge wish they were?" the farmer asked shrewdly.

Chaim came to Spain on the strength of his idealism. He still had some: enough to think the Republic was better than the reactionaries who fought against it. He nodded anyhow. "It's things as they are, all right."

"Here." Hermann Witt held out a paper and a pencil. "One more thing for you to sign."

The form assured *Wehrmacht* headquarters that everyone in the crew of this particular Panzer IV had been vaccinated against small-pox. Almost of its own accord, the pencil scrawled *Adalbert Stoss* on the line at which Sergeant Witt pointed.

"Thanks," Witt said, and went off to bother the couple of men who hadn't yet done their bit for the *Reich*'s paperwork.

Saul Goldman looked down at his right hand as if it belonged to someone else. As a matter of fact, it did, or it seemed to more often than not. That hand was convinced he was Adi Stoss, and would scribble Adi's illegible signature wherever anyone said it needed to go.

He answered to *Adi,* of course. He had no idea what he'd do if somebody were to call him Saul. That name was gone, forgotten by everyone except his family (if they still lived—he had no idea) and the various Nazi security services. *They* still lived, and to them he was not just a wanted man but that even more dangerous creature, a wanted Jew.

Saul had done his best to think of himself as Adi so he wouldn't hang himself by slipping up. In Poland and Russia, days or even weeks could go by without his being reminded of who and what he really was. That he made such a good soldier only showed what rubbish the *Führer*'s rules against letting Jews into the military were.

But these days the regiment was stationed just outside of Münster. He hadn't expected to see his hometown again till after the war ended and the Nazis no longer ruled Germany—assuming that happened and assuming he lived to see it, which didn't seem likely.

Here he was, though. Münster had had a bellyful of National Socialism. And National Socialism had also had a bellyful of Münster. If
the SS couldn't keep the town obedient to the *Reich*, Hitler was ready
to use the *Wehrmacht* to take care of that.

For now, the panzer regiment remained on the outskirts of town.
No self-important officer or politico had ordered in the machines.
Maybe the Party *Bonzen* hoped the threat of armor would keep Münster in line. Or maybe some worried colonel feared that street fighters
would chuck a Molotov cocktail through an open hatch from some
upper-story window and then get away unpunished.

Staying out of town didn't break Saul's heart, not even a little bit.
He was glad that, if and when the panzers were ordered into Münster,
he'd sit in the driver's seat, looking out at the world through his vision
slits and armor-glass vision blocks. He was even gladder the locals
would be looking in on him the same way.

That was what you got for making yourself a reputation on the
football pitch. Not just his neighbors would recognize him if he stuck
his head out the hatch the way drivers sometimes did when things
seemed safe. No. Hundreds, maybe thousands, of people would.

When you were wanted for murder, that wasn't the ideal situation.
His large, callused hands folded into fists. He remembered swinging
his shovel at the labor-gang boss who kept yelling that he was a rotten
kike and hitting and kicking him every time he got the chance. He
remembered the thrill that ran up the shaft when the flat of the blade
caved in the bastard's skull. And he remembered running farther and
faster than he ever had on the pitch to get away from all the sons of
bitches who were chasing him.

One of his footballing friends passed him the identity papers with
his new name on them—and without anything to show he was a Jew.
In the Nazis' *Reich,* greater friendship than that no man had. The
photo didn't look a whole lot like him, but who worried about such
things? Besides, the documents he'd got since joining the *Wehrmacht*
bore his authentic mug shot.

By now, at least half the people in the regiment knew he was a Jew.
The National Socialist Loyalty Officer wasn't one of them. Of course,

there were a great many things Major Stähler didn't know. To Saul, at least, that was one of the more important ones, though.

"Hey, Sergeant!" he called.

"What's cooking, Adi?" Witt came back.

"Got a question for you," Saul said.

"I'm all ears."

"Suppose we get an order to start shooting canister at the civilians in Münster. What do we do then?"

Panzers carried only a few rounds of canister. You didn't use it very often. It was like an overgrown shotgun shell full of shrapnel balls. If the Russians charged arm in arm, the way they sometimes did, a canister round could get rid of a couple of dozen of them at once. It could smash a crowd of civilians into red ruin in nothing flat, too.

Hermann Witt made a horrible face. "Don't ask me shit like that, all right? If they're trying to set fire to the panzer or something, I'm entitled to try to stay alive myself. If they're not . . . *Der Herr Gott im Himmel,* who would give an order like that if they're not?"

Saul scratched his head. Actually, he scratched his service cap. It bore the regime's embroidered eagle clutching a swastika in its talons. Not quite by accident, his forefinger brushed the fylfot several times. If Witt got it, fine. If not, Saul hadn't said anything that could land him in hot water.

Witt got it—Saul had thought he would. The panzer commander sighed and rolled his eyes. "I hope they don't, that's all," he said.

"But what happens if they do?" Saul asked.

He'd pushed it too far. He saw as much right away. "We won't worry about that till the time comes—*if* it comes, and I hope like hell it doesn't," Witt said sharply. "Till then, we're *not* going to worry about it. We won't bang our gums about it till then, either, all right?"

"All right, Sergeant," Saul answered. Had he been an Aryan, he might have kept pushing. Since he wasn't, since he had his own secrets to guard, he needed to walk soft.

Lothar Eckhardt felt no such limits. "Know what I heard?" he said after a trip to the spare-parts depot to pick up a new and allegedly improved reticle for the gunsight.

"Something juicy, by the way your tongue's hanging out," Saul said. "You look like a hound in front of a butcher's shop."

"Do I? Wouldn't be surprised," the gunner said. "They're saying the generals have started plotting against the *Führer* again."

"They've been saying that since the war started," Saul reminded him. "And whenever it looked like it might come true, the *Führer* went out and shot himself some generals."

"Yes, but—" Eckhardt protested.

Saul cut him off. "But, nothing. When the *Führer* needs the *Wehrmacht* inside of Germany, of course they're going to start saying that kind of stuff again. Saying it doesn't make it so."

"But—" Eckhardt tried again.

"No buts, dammit." Saul stopped him again, too. "Don't you think the SS and the SD are listening to hear exactly who's spouting that shit? Use your head for something better than a hat rack, Lothar. You're no dope. Don't you figure the SS and the SD are starting rumors like that so they can find out who likes them? You go running your mouth, you're just handing them the excuse to get their hooks into you."

"Oh," the gunner said in a small voice. "Thanks, Adi. No, that hadn't crossed my mind."

"Well, it should have. Don't take chances, man." Saul knew all about not taking chances. Maybe Lothar's rumors were even true. He could hope so. The generals would have to be better than the Party *Bonzen* . . . wouldn't they? But whether the rumors were true or not, he had no intention of passing them along.

Arno Baatz knew how to handle troublemakers in territory the *Reich* had occupied. If they gave you any lip, you smashed them in the head with your rifle butt. If they still showed fight after that, you shot them or hanged them. If you hanged somebody, you put a placard around his neck so his friends and relations would get the message. It was all simple.

Now he and the men he led were back in Münster, though. He still wanted to clobber anyone who squawked, and to kill anyone who squawked twice. *He* was loyal to the *Führer,* even if the people here weren't.

But things weren't so simple here as they had been in fleabitten Russian villages. These people weren't Ivans. They were as German as he was. And, while shooting them wouldn't have bothered him one bit, the idea plainly did bother a lot of soldiers.

"We put on the uniform to protect these people," grumbled a private named Bruno Gadermann. "We didn't put it on to shoot them down like dogs or Russians."

"We put on the uniform to protect the state, the *Grossdeutsches Reich,*" Baatz explained. "That's what we swore our oath to the *Führer* to do. Sure, we have to fight against our foreign enemies. But we have to fight against treason at home, too. Treason is what ruined the *Reich* in 1918—the stab in the back."

He believed what he said. He was too young to remember those days himself, but that was what people had said ever since he started noticing what people said. Adolf Hitler said it. The National Socialist Party—to which Arno was proud to belong—said it: thundered it, even. Why wouldn't he believe it, then?

Not everybody did, not quite. Adam Pfaff stirred when he spoke of the stab in the back. Pfaff's politics had always been suspect, at least as far as Arno Baatz was concerned. But the *Obergefreiter* only stirred. You couldn't gig a man for that. He might have had an itch or something. Baatz didn't believe it for a minute, but an officer, even the loyalty officer, would want more in the way of proof than he could give.

"It doesn't seem right, that's all," Gadermann said.

"Following your superiors' orders doesn't seem right?" Arno asked, his voice ominously calm.

He was disappointed when Gadermann saw the rapids ahead before he crashed into the rocks and turned over. "I didn't mean that, Corporal," the soldier answered quickly.

"Well, what did you mean, then?"

"Nothing, Corporal. I didn't mean anything." Gadermann made a production of charging his pipe with tobacco, tamping it down, and lighting it. Baatz thought pipes looked faggy and the stuff guys smoked in them smelled foul, but they weren't against regulations or anything.

Questioning your superiors' authority was. The National Socialist Loyalty Officer would be very interested to hear about it. What happened to Bruno Gadermann after that wouldn't be pretty. Unlike Pfaff, he didn't know when to keep his big trap shut.

On the other hand, he'd probably be scared enough to shut up and do as he was told from now on. If he disappeared, the rest of the men in the squad would understand why. That might scare them, too. Or it might make them sympathize with Gadermann and with the rebels in Münster, and leave them unreliable when they were needed most.

If you couldn't count on the men you led . . . If you couldn't count on them, you were screwed. Your country was screwed. After the stab in the back, the Kaiser couldn't count on his men to keep order any more. And that was why the Kaiser—well, it would be his son now, wouldn't it?—wasn't running Germany any more. So it seemed to Arno, anyhow.

He glanced over at Adam Pfaff again. Pfaff didn't say boo. He was too sly a barracks lawyer to lay his neck on the chopping block. *What a shame,* Arno thought. Pfaff was good enough in the field. Baatz still wished he weren't stuck with a troublemaker like him.

The squad moved out again the next morning to check people's papers and generally keep a lid on things. As they tramped toward the couple of blocks they could call their own, Pfaff remarked, "Boy, the RAF has knocked the snot out of this place, hasn't it? You don't see ruins like this farther east."

Baatz wanted to come down on him for that. It sounded too much like defeatism. But how could he, when every word was the plain and simple truth? Münster *had* been bombed halfway back to the Stone Age, and you *didn't* see so much damage where enemy bombers had to fly farther to strike.

Then Bruno Gadermann said, "No wonder people around here aren't happy with the government. I wouldn't be, either, if it let me get clobbered like this."

"That will be enough of that, Gadermann," Arno snapped. He rounded on Adam Pfaff. "You see what you're doing? You're encouraging him to think disloyal thoughts. That's a military offense."

"It would be if I were doing it," Pfaff said. "But you're really reaching today, aren't you? If I bitched about the weather and then Bruno complained it was raining, too, you'd blame that on me."

"The weather is fine today," Baatz said. And it was—it was chilly, only a degree or two one side or the other of freezing, but the sun was out and just a few clouds scudded across the sky.

He waited for Pfaff to accuse him of missing the point on purpose (which he was) or of being an idiot. Either way, he could jump on the *Obergefreiter*'s corns. But Pfaff kept quiet. How were you supposed to hang a man when he wouldn't give you any rope?

A labor gang cleared rubble from the streets with push brooms and spades. Several of the men in it wore the yellow Star of David. One of them, a gray-haired little guy with a limp, came to attention when the *Wehrmacht* troops tramped by.

"Look at the sheeny, pretending to be a soldier," Arno said scornfully.

"I bet he was, in the last war. He's got the look," Adam Pfaff said. "They took Jews then. They took everything that could walk on two legs and wasn't a chicken." He chuckled. "The soldiers took all the chickens."

"Funny. Funny like a truss," Baatz said. "Even if they did stick a uniform on him, odds are he found some cushy slot away from the trenches, the way kikes always like to do."

"Where'd he hurt his leg, then? Catching a packet's the easiest way to do that," Pfaff replied.

Arno almost asked the laborer. But how could you trust a Jew's answer? And he had the uneasy feeling the old bastard might show he was wrong. Now staying quiet served his purpose, so he did it.

"Go fight the Russians, you stinking sacks of shit!" someone shouted from one upstairs window or another. "Go fight the Russians, and leave us alone!"

Had Baatz carried a Schmeisser or a Russian PPD instead of his rifle, he might have hosed down the whole block of flats. Things were out of hand, sure as hell!

Someone had painted FREE THE BISHOP! and HIMMLER TO DACHAU!

on a wall. The corporal stared in astonished outrage. The nerve of these people! He pointed at the graffiti. "Why don't they have a cleanup crew getting rid of those?" he demanded.

Worse was yet to come, right around the corner. He found himself gaping at PEACE! and THE TRUE CROSS, NOT THE HOOKED CROSS! *Hakenkreuz* was German for *swastika*.

"I don't think the Catholics here like the Party much," Adam Pfaff remarked. Once more, Baatz would have come down on him if only he could have. Was Pfaff a mackerel-snapper himself? Arno couldn't remember. *Have to find out,* he thought.

Getting to the checkpoint was nothing but a relief. He could browbeat civilians, which was almost as much fun as browbeating soldiers. If he hadn't been so angry with the Catholics in Münster, he would have given a pretty young Jewish woman a harder time. Her papers were in order, but he might have felt her up anyway, just for the fun of it. As things were, he let her go with no more than a growl. Only after she'd got half a block away did he wonder if he was going soft.

Sarah Bruck didn't need long to decide she liked German soldiers better than blackshirts. Oh, the corporal who checked her papers had a mean face and piggy eyes, but you couldn't blame a man—too much— for the way he looked. He examined her documents and handed them back with no worse than, "Well, all right, get the hell out of here."

For once, the Nazis in Münster weren't shrieking about the Jews. The Jews here weren't up in arms against the government. There weren't enough of them, and they knew too well what the SS would do to them if they did have the nerve to rise.

There were lots of Catholics in Münster, lots and lots. They had the sort of safety numbers gave. Not even the Nazis could snuff out a whole German city, no matter how much they might want to. Himmler had to find other ways to scare the locals into submission. No doubt he had spies planted among them. But Sarah would have bet the Catholics had spies in the SS and the SD, too. Not everybody put the *Führer* ahead of the Savior.

None of which should have had anything to do with her, since she couldn't stand the *Führer* and didn't believe Jesus was the Savior. But Jews could get caught in the crossfire like anybody else. Regardless of her likes or beliefs, she also had to worry about other people's: an ancient lesson for Jews.

She came to another checkpoint a few blocks later. Again, she presented her papers. Again, they passed muster. But as she went on, one of the *Wehrmacht* men patted her on the behind.

She kept walking, her back stiff. Anything else would have been worse. This way, they just laughed. If she provoked them . . . She didn't want to find out what would happen if she provoked them. All at once, though, she didn't like ordinary soldiers so much.

Only a couple of pharmacies still let Jews buy, even during the restricted hours they could use for shopping. She'd never imagined getting a bottle of aspirins could turn into an adventure. Of course, she'd never imagined all kinds of things that had happened since the war started.

Marrying a baker's son? Being widowed a few months later? Being widowed by bombs from England, which was Hitler's enemy and should have been the German Jews' friend? More mystery in any of those than in the familiar bottle with the white tablets with the familiar BAYER stamped on them crosswise.

Had the Nazis pressed the Bayer company to change the shape of their stamp to a swastika? Sarah supposed they wouldn't have. They made noises about tolerating Christianity . . . as long as the people who professed it did what the regime told them to. German Christians, so called, seemed eager to blend their beliefs with Nazi ideology.

Catholics went along less readily. Some of them conformed where they could. Others, not so much. If they'd conformed more readily, Münster wouldn't lie under martial law now.

A rifle cracked, once, twice, back in the direction from which she'd come. A moment later, a machine gun snarled an angry reply. Someone screamed, a voice faint in the distance. The shrieks went on and on. Sarah wanted to stick her forefingers in her ears to block them. A badly wounded human sounded too much like a big dog hit by a car.

Heading home, she went around the checkpoint where the soldiers had handled the merchandise. She realized she took the same kind of chance at every checkpoint she came to. Maybe the new troops she met would be even worse. But maybe they would leave her alone.

"Why are you out?" asked a sergeant she'd never seen before after he inspected her identity documents.

"I needed some aspirins." She showed him the bottle.

He made a thoughtful noise halfway between a cluck and a grunt. "All right. Münster's a headache for everybody, I guess. But go on home now, and stay there till you really need to come out."

"Thanks," she said in glad surprise.

"You're welcome," he answered. Then he spoiled it by adding, "*Heil Hitler!*"

Or did that spoil it? Sarah wondered as she hurried away. He'd just been decent to a Jew, or as decent as a German soldier was likely to get. Wouldn't he need to give his men a signal that he remained loyal to the regime and that what he'd done didn't mean anything?

The harder you looked at things, the more complicated they got. Her father had said as much. But he was talking about things like how closely the speeches in Thucydides matched what the speakers really said or why Brutus joined the plot against Julius Caesar. If it was true everywhere, what did that mean?

What is truth? Pilate asked. It was a good question in New Testament days, and it remained a good question now. Truth was something like whatever remained after you looked at a question from every angle you could.

Sometimes, of course, nothing was left after you did that. Hitler's speeches sounded splendid, but he hardly ever said anything but *I want it because I want it*. A three-year-old would have got his bottom warmed for that. The *Führer* got thousands of people yelling *Sieg heil!*

Sarah wondered what would have happened if the war had gone the way Hitler wanted, if Paris had fallen in the early days of 1939. Would people here be up in arms against him now? She didn't think so. England would have made peace then—what choice would she have had? And the German flag might be flying over the Kremlin right this minute.

As things were . . . As things were, she made it through the rest of the checkpoints without getting groped again. She supposed it was a triumph of sorts. When you were out of sorts, though, you wished for bigger triumphs than that.

"I hope it wasn't too much trouble," her mother said when she got home.

"It could have been worse," Sarah said. If it could have been better, too, she didn't spell that out.

She also didn't need to. "Oh, dear," Hanna Goldman said. "Maybe I should have gone myself. They wouldn't have bothered me."

"I'll live." Sarah suspected her father would tell her it was only soldiers being soldiers, which was to say, men being men. The really scary thing was, that might well be true. Men could get annoying enough any time if they thought you were attractive. Men with rifles at hand, she was discovering, could be worse. How were you supposed to say no if one of them insisted that you say yes?

But when Samuel Goldman came home, he was excited about other things than man's inhumanity to woman. He pulled a tinfoil tube out of one of the inside pockets of his jacket. "Look at that! Will you look at that?" he exclaimed. "It's half full—more than half full—of butter! Butter! Can you believe it? A soldier just threw it away, as if he didn't have a care in the world. And if he could afford to throw butter out, he didn't. When's the last time we saw any?"

"Before the war," Sarah said. "Has to be." They'd cut Jews' rations sooner and harder than those of Aryans.

"I thought so, too," Father agreed. "With this"—he tapped the tube with his finger—"we could fry some eggs if we only had some eggs."

"Maybe a soldier will throw them away," Mother said. Father looked so wounded, she backtracked: "Well, I'm glad you got it any which way. It will taste good on bread, and we have got some bread."

Samuel Goldman seemed happier. "I don't think even the Party *Bonzen* get butter very often any more. And the soldiers throw out cigarettes they've hardly smoked, too. They've got it soft in the Army." He paused. "People would have said the same thing about us in 1918. But soldiers helped make the Kaiser leave." His eyes twinkled. "We can hope, anyhow."

Chapter 16

So this was what victory looked like. Vaclav Jezek had never seen it before, not in all the days since the Czechoslovakian Army conscripted him. He'd lost in his homeland, fought to a draw in France but then had to leave when the politics shifted under his feet, and now he'd spent a good long stretch in the trenches here in Spain.

No more. The war, what was left of it, was out in the open now. Here and there, the Nationalists would try to make a stand, but regiments seemed to distrust the men on either side of them even more than they hated the Republic. As often as not, they would surrender, especially when they saw they were facing foreign troops and not their vengeful countrymen.

Vaclav was glad when it was easy. He was especially glad when he didn't have to do a lot of marching. Carrying upwards of ten kilos of antitank rifle in the trenches was one thing. He could take it off his shoulder or his back a lot of the time. When he sneaked out into no-man's-land, he was down on all fours or on his belly. Tramping along with it from sunup to sundown he could have done without.

Benjamin Halévy watched a section of Nationalists stack their arms after giving up. The Czechs searched them, more to get rid of holdout weapons than in hopes of loot. The Spaniards were a poor and raggedy lot. They had nothing worth stealing, not any more.

"Poor bastards. They don't know what they're getting into," Halévy remarked. "The Republicans will send them to reeducation camps, and who knows how many will come out, or when?"

"They would've been just as nasty if they'd won, or even worse," Vaclav said.

The scrawny, dirty, shaggy Nationalist prisoners nudged one another. *"Russos,"* one of them said, pointing to Jezek and Halévy.

Even with his rudimentary Spanish, Vaclav got that. "They think we're Russians," he said, laughing.

"Czech has to sound as foreign to them as Spanish does to you," Halévy answered. He didn't say *to us*. He was fluent in Czech, French, and German, and could manage Catalan, Spanish, and Yiddish—and maybe other tongues, too, for all Vaclav knew.

Off the prisoners went, hands clasped on top of their heads. When they got to the rear, Republican Spaniards would take charge of them. Then their fun would really start, as Halévy had said. But the Republicans weren't—for the most part—killing prisoners out of hand these days. Both sides had done too much of that. They meant it when they said they hated each other.

Vaclav hated Fascists and Fascism. He rather liked Spaniards. They were so different from people he'd known before he got here, they fascinated him. They sometimes drove him crazy, too, but he suspected that worked both ways.

As the Czechs started marching again, he said, "Remember how some of our guys went back to France again after the alliance against Stalin fell apart?"

"I'm not likely to forget," Halévy replied. "The French Army tried to recall me, too, you know."

"I was thinking, now that this war's pretty much won, I'd like to get up there and give the Nazis some more."

"I wouldn't mind so much, either," the Jew said. "Chances are I could tell them I never got their stupid recall letter."

"Would they believe that?" Vaclav asked.

"I doubt it. But they couldn't prove I was lying. That would be enough to keep them off my back," Halévy said. He touched the lieutenant's badge painted on his helmet. "I'd have to get used to being a sergeant again. My own country won't let me stay an officer—God forbid!"

"Wasn't that Dreyfus guy a captain back when?" Vaclav inquired, perhaps less cautiously than he might have.

He didn't faze Halévy—or if he did, Halévy didn't let on. "He sure was, and look what that earned him. Devil's Island, no less! And when it was all sorted out at last and he got his rank back and everything, what then? Why, he won the right to get shot at in the last war. Lucky fellow, Dreyfus!"

"Some luck! Did he make it through? I never knew how the story came out," Vaclav said.

"As a matter of fact, he did," Halévy replied. "He ended up a lieutenant colonel. If he hadn't been a Jew, he might have commanded a brigade." He shrugged a very French shrug.

They passed a boulder that faced the road. A graffito in Spanish defaced the ancient gray stone. " 'Death to traitors,' " Vaclav said. It wasn't the first time he'd seen that threat. Every Nationalist faction thought all the others were traitors.

"Hell of a slogan, isn't it?" Halévy remarked. "All it means is 'Death to everybody who doesn't agree with me.' "

"That's what politics comes down to, isn't it?" Vaclav said.

"No, no, no, no!" Benjamin Halévy said it in French, so it sounded even more negative than it would have in Czech. He went on, "Politics isn't about killing the other fellow. It's about getting him to go along with you so you can get rich off of him. You only kill him when you see he won't go along with you."

"Ah, thanks. Now I get it," Vaclav said. They grinned at each other, for all the world as if they'd both been joking a moment before.

Planes buzzed high overhead. The Czechs looked up anxiously, ready to jump off the road and dive for cover if the fighters belonged to the enemy. But the planes were marked with the Republic's red, gold, and purple, not the black X in a white circle the Nationalists used. They might have attacked by mistake—such things had happened before. This time, the fighters kept on flying north.

A woman in a long dress weeded a vegetable plot by a roadside farmhouse. She wasn't a witch, but she was a long way from a beauty. If she had a pretty daughter, the younger woman stayed out of sight. Vaclav didn't see any livestock, either. Maybe the animals were hidden, or maybe the Nationalists had already eaten them. Soldiers could be worse than locusts: locusts didn't carry rifles.

A body hung from one of the higher branches of an olive tree half a kilometer farther on. He wore a yellowish khaki Nationalist uniform. Around his neck hung a placard. "What's this one say?" Vaclav asked.

" 'I betrayed my friends,' " Halévy answered. His arched nostrils flared. The dead Spaniard had been hanging for a few days, by the way he smelled and looked. The carrion birds would go to work on him in earnest before long.

"Some friends," Vaclav said. A moment later, he spoke again, this time in musing tones: "I wonder how many trees will sprout fruit like that when we clean up Czechoslovakia."

"Quite a few. Lampposts will grow that kind of fruit, too," Halévy said. "You may not want to do too much of that, though, or all the trees and lampposts will sprout again twenty years from now."

"Huh," Vaclav said. "Plenty of people back there deserve hanging. You do what the Nazis tell you, you suck up to the Germans who're holding you down, what do you expect? A big kiss?"

"No, but people have to live with each other afterwards," the Jew replied. "I don't think the Republicans have figured that out yet. They want to pay back everybody who wasn't on their side."

Vaclav had seen Spanish notions of revenge. He said the worst thing about them he could: "These people are worse than Hungarians." For people from his part of Europe, Magyars were the touchstone of touchiness.

He made Benjamin Halévy smile. "My mother comes out with things like that," Halévy said.

"Well, good for her!" Vaclav exclaimed.

They tramped on. A few Spaniards fired on them from rocks up ahead. The Czechs spread out and moved forward in short rushes. The Spaniards fell back to keep from getting outflanked. The advance went on.

It was bloody cold. Snow and sleet fell together. Aristide Demange swore at the miserable weather in Belgium. It wasn't so bad as it had been in Russia, but nothing was *that* bad, the last circle of Dante's hell included. Before long, it would be Christmas, and then 1944.

A little farther east, the Germans were holed up in a village they'd held for years. They were comfortable there, and warm. Half the kids under four had probably come out of their mothers making the Nazi salute.

Crouching in a miserable, freezing hole in the ground wasn't the same. Demange wanted either to take the village ahead away from the Fritzes or fall back to the last one the French had liberated.

His superiors didn't feel like listening to him. Regimental head-quarters lay a couple of villages back. The colonel there was plenty comfortable. "Your zeal does you credit, Lieutenant, but the weather militates against a successful attack, I fear," he said, spreading his clean, well-groomed hands in regret. "It is a pity, isn't it?"

"The Germans didn't think this kind of weather was too shitty in 1938," Demange pointed out.

"And they failed," the colonel said placidly.

They'd failed to take Paris. They'd sure taken everything from the Dutch border to the suburbs of the capital, though. Demange re-frained from pointing that out; he could see it wouldn't help. Instead, he said, "Well, how about letting us fall back a kilometer or two, then, to get into warmer quarters?"

"Give back even a millimeter of liberated Belgium? Give it up?" The colonel shook his head. "*Pas possible!* You will stay where you are and accommodate yourself to your circumstances."

"Right, sir. I see you've accommodated yourself to *your* circum-stances mighty well," Demange said. He didn't know this had been the mayor's house before the colonel ensconced himself in it, but that was the way to bet. It was the biggest, most comfortable house in the village. He knew that, all right.

The colonel's graying mustache quivered. "Why should I not demote you for insubordination?" he asked, no doubt thinking the mere idea would reduce Demange to a quivering slice of gelatin.

To the colonel's unhappy amazement, Demange laughed in his face instead of quivering. "Because I'd thank you for it, that's why," he snarled. "I never wanted to be an officer in the first place. I got stuck with it, is what happened to me."

He left without saluting. He also left without waiting for permission. If *Monsieur le Colonel* wanted reasons to demote him, now the stinking *con* had a whole raft of them.

But *Monsieur le Colonel* turned out to be made of subtler and more vindictive stuff than that. Not long after Demange came back to his cold, wet hole in the ground, a runner brought an order forward. Demange's company was to attack and seize the village in front of them. By tomorrow. Or else. The order said nothing about artillery support or any other help from the rest of the regiment.

"*Merde*," Demange muttered, and the Gitane in the corner of his mouth twitched as he spoke.

"Could it be that you succeeded in provoking our brave and aggressive regimental commander?" Lieutenant Mirouze asked—he was learning how to talk to Demange, all right.

"Yeah, I fucking provoked him," the older man replied. "But I did too good a job. The old bastard doesn't want to break me down to sergeant, dammit. Not even down to private. The *con* wants me dead. And if the rest of the company buys plots behind mine, he doesn't give a fart."

"What do we do, then?"

"I'll think of something. Bastard's cute, is he? I'll show him." Demange figured he would, too—or die trying. The colonel hadn't left him any other choices.

Going straight at the village in broad daylight with the *Boches* watching and waiting would generate the slaughter the regimental CO had to expect. That would also be the kind of attack the unimaginative son of a bitch would make himself if someone ordered *him* to take the place.

So Demange gathered his men together and plotted a night attack instead. Then he asked, "Any of you dopes from Alsace or Lorraine?" As he'd hoped, a couple of soldiers were. He tried another question: "Can you talk enough German to get by?"

They both nodded. He'd hoped they would. Those provinces had been history's football, kicked back and forth again and again between France and Germany. Most people knew some of both languages. He stuck the German-speakers up front with *Stahlhelms* on their heads and captured Nazi greatcoats on their backs. With luck, they'd fool the Fritzes' sentries long enough. Without luck . . . Without luck, *Monsieur le Colonel* would get what he wanted no matter how cute Demange played it.

The men slithered forward an hour before midnight. It had warmed up enough to turn sleet into icy rain. You had to be crazy to try anything in weather like this. Demange hoped the Germans thought so, too, and that they were all busy screwing their Belgian whores.

Wire twanged as cutters snipped it. The plashing of the rain helped hide the noises. It also helped keep the sentries from spotting the approaching Frenchmen till they were almost on top of them. Then a German called, "Halt! Who comes?" Demange knew enough of the language to get that.

"*Gott im Himmel!* Is this the front?" His Lorrainer sounded convincingly surprised.

"You shithead!" the sentry said, and went on from there, telling the man what a jerk he was. He squawked when the Lorrainer's bayonet went home, but not for long, and not loud enough to alert anyone else. The French soldier got his own helmet and greatcoat out of his pack and put them on in a hurry so his own side wouldn't shoot him by mistake.

Somewhere not far off to one side or the other—no, to one side *and* the other—there'd be more sentries. Nobody raised the alarm, though. The other German-speaker must have done his job, too. Whispering in excitement, the French company sneaked into the village.

Most of the *Boches* seemed to be in the church. Guttural singing came from it. Christmas carols. Wasn't that sweet? Demange whispered to the Lorrainer: "If we bust in there, can you tell 'em to give up? Tell 'em we'll kill 'em all if they fuck around?"

"You bet, Lieutenant," the soldier answered.

"All right. That's what we'll try, then. And if the assholes do fuck around, we damn well will kill 'em," Demange said.

It wasn't quite so simple, though. Nothing was ever as simple as you wished it would be. A German sentry paced the streets. He was caroling, too, along with the men in church. He wasn't doing it very loud. He might not even have known he was doing it. But he warned the French troops he was there before he came around the corner. They slid into cover. With the rain, it didn't have to be great.

That was the last mistake he ever made. Demange hid in a doorway, knife in his right hand. As soon as the German walked past, Demange silently slipped up behind him, clapped his left hand over the sentry's mouth, and pulled his head back. He drew the knife across the Fritz's throat. If you did it right, the guy you were killing hardly let out a peep. Demange had practice. He did it right. The German slumped to the cobbles with no more than a muffled grunt.

On to the church. Demange's men surrounded it. In case of trouble, they could shoot through the windows and chuck in grenades once they broke the glass.

Demange and the Lorrainer and a couple of squads of his toughest men went up the stairs. The rain helped dull their footfalls. So did the racket the carolers were making. He tried the door and grinned nastily. It wasn't even locked.

He threw it open. They rushed inside. The Lorrainer gave forth with his spiel in German. The Fritzes were staring in horror. The candlelight in there exaggerated shadows and made them look all the more appalled. *"Hände hoch!"* the Lorrainer finished. If any French soldier knew the tiniest bit of German, that would probably be it.

One by one, the Germans raised their hands. Demange and his men took charge of them. Their officer—a captain, by his shoulder boards—glared at Demange. "On such a night, this is not sporting," he said in fair French.

Demange was inclined to agree with the Fritz, but so what? "We get orders, too," he answered with a shrug. After a beat, he added, *"Joyeux Noël."*

Poilus led the Germans out of the church and into captivity. A few *Boches* in the houses came out to see what was going on. They got scooped up, too; the French had to shoot only one of them. A pretty blond Belgian woman wept for him. *Too bad,* Demange thought. *You'll be blowing someone else soon enough.*

He sent a message back to the colonel: *Village captured. No casualties on our side.* With luck, the messenger would wake him up delivering it. An ordinary officer would win a medal for this. Demange hoped the colonel wouldn't try to kill him again for a little while. Past that, he expected nothing.

Theo Hossbach had heard that the RAF wasn't bombing Münster any more. German radio and newspapers claimed England was going easy on the place because it was full of traitors to the *Reich*.

The RAF hadn't come over the first few nights after the panzer regiment camped outside of Münster. But then the bombers did show up. Maybe they were striking at Münster itself. Maybe they were going after the troops sent there to restore order instead. Bombs fell on both impartially.

Inside a panzer, or in a foxhole under one, you were safe from anything short of a direct hit. That didn't mean the bombing was fun. The Panzer IV rocked on its tracks again and again. Twenty-plus tonnes of steel tried to rear up once. "Even more fun than Katyushas!" Adi said as bombs burst all around.

"And they said it couldn't be done!" Theo was dismayed into a complete sentence. If this was the beating he took inside so much armor plate, what were things like for civilians and their homes? How did they go on through pounding after pounding like this? They were the ones who deserved the Knight's Cross, not the men who'd actually been trained for war.

"I hope my family are all right," Adi said tightly. Most of the regiment might come from Breslau and its *Wehrkreis,* but he'd grown up around here.

And, of course, he had more to worry about with his family than most people did. Theo didn't know what to say about that. He didn't know anything he could say that wouldn't make Adi think his secret was under assault. So he did what he did best: he kept his mouth shut.

Next morning, the radio net crackled with reports of fresh unrest inside Münster. Some of the gray-haired sausage-makers and book-keepers and mill hands still seemed to remember the stunts they'd learned when they went to war a generation earlier. Some of them had pistols and hunting rifles, too, toys they'd managed to keep hidden in spite of all the searches the security services had made.

They'd managed to pin down some foot soldiers. They fired from upper stories and rooftops, and slipped away before the troops could pay them back. One exasperated infantry captain complained, "The bastards might as well be Ivans, the way they disappear!"

Before long, the panzer regiment got orders to move out. "We have to put the fear of God in them," the CO declared.

Theo relayed the command. "They make a desert and call it peace," Adi said. Theo recognized the quotation, though he doubted anyone else in the panzer would have. The name people usually called him by was short for Theodosios; his father had been wild about Edward Gibbon. He knew more Roman history than he knew what to do with.

Back in the turret, Lothar Eckhardt said, "These people could be our fathers and mothers and sisters. I don't know that I want to shoot at them."

"Is that mutiny, Lothar?" Hermann Witt asked.

"I don't know, Sergeant," the gunner answered unhappily. "Do *you* want to shoot at them?"

"Do I want to? Of course not," Witt said. "But I've done all kinds of things I didn't want to since I put on these coveralls. That's what war's about."

"You've never done any of that stuff to Germans, though," Eck-hardt said. "Only to the enemy."

"If these people are enemies of the government—" the panzer commander began.

"Then maybe the government is the one with the problem, not the people," Adi broke in.

Several seconds' worth of silence followed. Then Witt said, "Adi, I understand why you're saying that, but—"

Adi interrupted again: "I'm not saying it because I'm a Jew, Sergeant." Theo's jaw dropped all the way down to his chest, and he would have bet everyone back in the turret was just as gobsmacked. Adi'd never called himself a Jew before. He'd never come close. Now he went on, "Besides, it's not Jews in Münster rising up against the stupid Nazis. It's Germans, like Lothar said."

"We swore an oath to the *Führer*. All of us did. Even you, Adi," Witt said.

"I know. But we didn't swear to be lemmings and follow him over the cliff," Adi answered.

"He's right," Theo put in. He knew that might win him the attention of the SS and the SD. He didn't care now, though he also knew he might care very much later. He felt like a free man. He hadn't remembered how good that felt.

He looked out through his vision slits. Some of the other panzers around them were starting up. Some weren't. If that didn't mean the same argument was raging inside of them, he would have been amazed.

Witt saw the same thing. Since he could look out through the cupola, he was bound to see more of it than Theo. Plaintively, he said, "Do you want us to start shooting at each other right here in the encampment?"

"No, Sergeant." Adi kept military respect, which made him more persuasive, not less. "The other poor conscript bastards aren't the enemy. Himmler's blackshirt goons are."

"Adi, start the engines. We can go into Münster," Witt said. "We'll see what kind of orders they give us when we get there. If we can honorably carry them out, we will. If we can't . . . We'll burn that bridge when we come to it. We don't have to burn it yet."

That sounded more like a plea than an order, but Adi said, *"Zu Befehl!"* and stabbed the starter button with his forefinger. The engine roared to life. He put the panzer into gear and rolled out of the encampment. He didn't go very fast, and Witt didn't try to hurry him.

Maybe Witt thought that, once people started shooting at them, he could get his crew to shoot back. Maybe he was right, but Theo wouldn't have bet on it. He knew *he* didn't intend to fire on any of the locals no matter what happened.

They'd just reached the outskirts of town when the radio crackled to life again. "All panzers! All panzers! Halt and return immediately to your encampment!" a sharp, unfamiliar voice ordered.

"On whose authority?" someone asked—probably a captain in charge of a company.

"I am Colonel Joachim von Lehnsdorff, of the General Staff. I have relieved your regimental commander because he has issued orders beyond his competence. Return to your encampment at once, I tell you!" That Prussian-accented voice carried the snap of command.

"*Zu Befehl, Herr Oberst!*" The man who'd questioned him gulped before getting his acceptance out.

Hermann Witt said, "I never heard of the General Staff canning a regimental CO before."

"What do you want me to do, Sergeant?" Adi asked.

"Oh, go back. Go back. I'm not sorry to get an order like that, not even a little bit," Witt answered. "But it's like even the *Wehrmacht* can't make up its mind what it wants to do."

"It's probably just like that," Theo said. After that sentence, he spent another one: "The *Wehrmacht* has to decide whether it belongs to the Nazis or to Germany."

Beside him at the front of the panzer, Adi grinned crookedly. "What you mean is, the *Wehrmacht* has to decide whether Germany belongs to it or to the Nazis."

That was the question, all right, much more than *To be or not to be.* Theo found himself nodding. But it was more complicated than Adi made it out to be. The armed forces were divided against themselves. A good-sized chunk of the *Wehrmacht,* from the rank and file up into the officer corps, favored the Nazis.

Hermann Witt said, "I wonder what the *Führer* will do when he finds out about this."

"We'll all find out," Adi said. By then, the panzer was clanking away from Münster. Theo was content with that. He'd worry later about whatever came next.

The man in the white coat—the doctor, Pete McGill supposed he was—shook his head. "No, I'm sorry, Sergeant, but no one who retook Midway will be leaving the island right away."

"That's a crock . . . sir," Pete said. He had to remind himself that military doctors carried officer's rank. "I'm healthy as a horse. All the guys who were gonna get sick, they've gone and done it by now."

"We don't know that for sure," the man in the white coat replied. "We won't know that for some time to come. If it makes you feel any better, I'm stuck here along with you."

"It doesn't make me feel one goddamn bit better," Pete said. "Uh, sir."

And yet, however little he wanted to admit it, he had to grant that the sawbones had a point of sorts. Leathernecks on Midway had died of plague and of anthrax. One poor bastard had died of smallpox. Pete had never seen that before, and hoped to heaven he never saw it again. It was a hell of a nasty way to cash in your chips.

"This island may never be safe for human habitation again—certainly not for anyone who hasn't been thoroughly immunized," the doctor said. "We can give it back to the gooney birds. They don't seem to come down with any of the human diseases here."

"So what did we go and take it back for, then?" Pete growled. "Way you sound, the Japs would've dropped dead by themselves pretty damn quick."

"Anyone who wasn't thoroughly immunized, I said," the doctor answered. "The Japs were. So were you men. So am I. Things would have been much worse if that weren't true."

"It's 1944 now," Pete said. "When do we get turned loose? In 1946? Or 1950? Or 1960? Or is this a waddayacallit—a life sentence?"

"I'm sorry, but I have no idea," the doc said. "Can you imagine the stink if you guys leave Midway and start an epidemic somewhere?"

Pete could imagine it, all right. What he couldn't do was care. He scowled. "Terrific . . . sir. Least people could do for us is bring in some broads who've had all their shots. By the time they could leave, they'd be richer'n anybody else on the island. Bet your ass they would."

"Good for morale but bad for morals, I'm afraid," the doctor said primly. "You'll just have to imagine you're on a warship on an extended cruise. In effect, you are."

The Japs had been stuck out here without any whores, too. That was probably one of the reasons they'd fought almost to the last man. They'd got so mean, they hadn't cared whether they lived or died. And die they had. On an island with no place to hide, everybody on one side or the other was going to. The Japs didn't surrender, and the Marines didn't try to get them to.

"It's all a bunch of crap, you ask me," Pete said. "And if we're here till summer, we're gonna have half the landing craft in the Navy."

He exaggerated, but not by much. C-47s flying off Tern Island delivered some supplies to Midway by airdrop. More, though, came by sea. A freighter would fill up a landing craft with food and fuel and whatever else the leathernecks needed. The crew would hop into a launch and go back to the mother ship. A motorboat would bring a replacement crew out from the island to bring in the landing craft. The scheme worked, but more and more big square boats crowded the beach.

"We can afford that," the guy in the white coat said. "As far as the whole war goes, it's just pocket change."

"Yeah, that's what they treat us like, sure as hell," Pete said. "Pennies, maybe nickels if we're lucky. Not dimes. Dimes are worth a little something."

The doctor shrugged and walked away. If being marooned here bothered him, he didn't show it. Maybe he couldn't get it up. Maybe he played with himself all the time. Or maybe he was a fairy, and spending months on an island with a bunch of Marines was hog heaven for him.

Pete had no way of knowing about that. All he knew was how much he wanted to get back to Honolulu and Hotel Street. Any place with no booze and no babes wasn't worth living in. None of the landing craft had brought in hooch yet, not even the horrible unofficial stuff that got cooked up on every warship ever launched. Life wasn't fair, dammit.

It was warm. It was a little humid. Every so often, it rained for a while. Pete didn't need long to get bored. He smoked like a chimney—they did have enough sense to send plenty of coffin nails. He fished in the lagoon and on the beach. What he caught tasted better than the rations they brought in.

He played poker. Everybody played poker except for the guys who shot dice and the handful of eggheads who played bridge instead. The eggheads insisted bridge stayed interesting even when you didn't bet on it (though they did). Pete thought playing cards where no money changed hands was about as much fun as kissing your mom.

He won a little more than he lost. He was no human slide rule, able to figure odds like an insurance salesman. But he'd played a lot. He knew good hands, not-so-good hands, and hands that looked good but would let you down like a cheating cocktail waitress. And, most important of all, he knew how to lie with a straight face.

"Fuck you, McGill," another leatherneck grumbled when Pete raked in a pot. "I can't tell when you're bluffing, and I'm sick of getting my ass burned on account of it."

"Aw, gee, Edgar, you say the sweetest things," Pete lisped in shrill falsetto. He batted his eyelashes at his victim. That broke up the whole table (though actually they were sitting on a couple of blankets). For some reason, nothing on God's green earth seemed funnier than an unshaven, smelly Marine mincing like a fruit.

Even Edgar laughed, though he looked pained when he did it. "Whose deal is it, anyway?" he asked, trying to shift attention away from himself and Pete.

The game went on. Pete didn't win all the time—nowhere close. The cards wouldn't let you. The trick was to win as big as you could when you won and not to throw away too much when you lost. And Edgar might have been disgusted, but Pete disguised the truth when he delivered it fairy-style. If Edgar admitted he couldn't read Pete, that gave Pete a serious edge.

Not everybody came equipped with a poker face. Pete had played against one guy whose eyebrows jumped every time he got a hand worth betting. The guy didn't know he was doing it, which didn't help him. Good cards made another fellow turn pink, as if he'd got caught peeking down a girl's blouse. Pete didn't think even a doctor could keep anyone from blushing. But that fellow's color changes cost him money.

You studied the people you played against. You tried not to show you were doing it, but you did. You knew they were casing you, too, casing you like a bank vault. You gave away as little as you could by the way you acted and by the way you played.

If you were a sucker, if you bled money the way a bayoneted Jap gushed blood, the smartest thing you could do was get the hell out of the game. Some guys had the sense to see that. They threw a baseball around or read magazines. Others wondered where this month's pay had disappeared to, and last month's, and next month's, too.

No Japanese planes bombed them. Bettys from Wake Island could have reached them, but the slanties didn't bother. They had to realize they might not hang on to Wake much longer, either.

Then what? Not back to where they'd started, not with Guam and the Philippines still in Japanese hands to shield the Home Islands and the Dutch East Indies. But at least Honolulu would be able to take a deep breath and not worry so much about coming down with anthrax if it did.

No. The Marines on Midway were the ones who had to worry about that. Which was one big reason they couldn't get off Midway, dammit.

Chapter 17

Julius Lemp wished the U-30 were out patrolling in the North Sea or the North Atlantic. He even wished his U-boat were hunting Russian freighters and warships in the Baltic. Any time a man wished he were out in the Baltic, he had to hate wherever he was.

Where he was was Kiel. He and his men remained confined to the naval base. The powers that be didn't trust them to attack the enemy. The powers that be also didn't seem to trust them not to attack their own comrades.

After a lot of wire-pulling, Lemp finally secured another audience with Admiral Dönitz. The commander of the German U-boat fleet gave him a stony stare. "I hope this will be interesting," he said.

"So do I . . . sir," Lemp answered. "Do you really think that if you turn us loose we'll head up the Rhine and start sinking barges and tugboats? Or shell our own fortifications here?"

"Certain people . . . have wondered about these things," Dönitz said, plainly choosing his words with no little care. "The political situation is, ah, increasingly delicate."

"Is it?" Lemp said. The radio and the newspapers admitted no such thing—but then, they wouldn't. No one in the officers' club admitted any such thing, either. But then, you had to be an idiot to speak freely in the officers' club these days. By now, Himmler's various security services had swept up most of the fools who couldn't dog their hatches.

"It is." Dönitz spoke with chill certainty. "There are at the moment certain, ah, unfortunate disagreements over some policies between the *Führer* and, ah, a faction within the General Staff. And if you tell anyone I told you that, I will call you a liar to your face and I will make sure you envy the fate of a destroyer that hits a mine. Do you understand me?"

"Yes, sir," Lemp replied. "You have a way of making yourself very plain, sir."

He hoped to make the admiral smile. No such luck. Dönitz's eyes stayed as cold and gray as the North Sea at this season of the year. "And you and your men have a reputation for raising trouble, here and up in Norway. So is it any wonder some people don't want to let you out of port in a U-boat stuffed with torpedoes and 88mm shells?"

The unfairness of that took Lemp's breath away. "Sir," he said stiffly, "the only reason the lads kicked up their heels a little in Namsos was that it made an impossible liberty port. No girls, hardly any beer . . . You know what a U-boat patrol is like, sir. You know how the men want to blow off steam afterwards."

"They almost blew up the town," Dönitz said. "Twice."

Lemp had wondered whether that would come back to haunt him. He'd never dreamt it would come back to haunt him like this. "Sir, what happened in Namsos had nothing to do with politics," he insisted.

"And, no doubt, you will also tell me your desire to keep on your boat an electrician's mate the SS found unreliable had nothing to do with politics, either." Dönitz was, or affected to be, implacable.

"Nehring was a good electrician's mate. He was the best one in the boat, in fact. I didn't want some thumb-fingered idiot screwing with my batteries. Was it his fault he came from Münster?"

"Ah, so that was why the SS didn't trust him, is it?" the admiral said. "Münster is . . . Münster is a running sore. I don't know what else to call it, and I wish I did."

"Sir, Nehring was about as political as your ashtray," Lemp said, which was nothing less than the truth. "They pulled him off the boat because they had the vapors, not on account of anything he did."

"Right now, Lemp, coming from Münster is a political act," Dönitz replied. "You may not like that. The people who come from Münster may not like it, either. But they will not be trusted by the present government, any more than they would be if they were Jews."

What he said came from his mouth as if he were reading from an official report. How did he feel about the present government and its politics? How did he feel about that General Staff faction he'd mentioned? He had to have opinions. God didn't issue human beings without them. What they were, though, Lemp couldn't divine.

He did say, "Right now, I'd take a Jew who was as good an electrician's mate as Nehring. The rating they gave me isn't terrible, but he's not that good. Jews served in U-boats in the last war, didn't they?"

"They did." Dönitz bit off the two-word admission. "They do not now. They will not now. And have you any idea how thin the ice is under your feet, Lemp? I have but to repeat what you said now and you will end up envying whatever happened to your Nehring."

"If I thought you were the kind who repeated such things, sir, I wouldn't have said it," Lemp answered. "But I thought you were someone who wanted people to tell him the truth. Maybe I was wrong."

"Maybe you were," Dönitz agreed, which made frigid chills run up Lemp's spine. The admiral continued, "In politics, truth is whatever those in power say it is. As military men, we have to recognize that."

"Even when the truth looks different to us?"

"Even then. If the truth looks different to you, the leaders will think that is because you are betraying them."

Even when what they see as the truth leads us into a two-front war, and one we're losing? Lemp wondered. No wonder Münster was a running sore, in that case. He'd got away with one piece of frankness, just barely. Dönitz's scowl said he wouldn't get away with two. All he said, then, was, "Please send us out to sea, sir."

The commander of the U-boat fleet read his mind entirely too well. "That is not necessarily an escape for you, either," Dönitz said.

"No? Then I'd always be sure who the enemy was." Lemp decided to poke again after all.

To his disappointment, he didn't faze the admiral. "Maybe not. But you might leave me with the feeling that I had blood on my hands."

"I joined the *Kreigsmarine* to fight, sir," Lemp said. "If the Royal Navy sinks me, they get the credit. You don't get the blame."

"At the start of the war, I would have agreed with you," Dönitz answered. "Now . . . Now I'm not so sure. Our losses have gone up alarmingly the past few months. I feel as if I have blood on my hands every time I send out a U-boat."

He was a cold-blooded, cold-hearted Navy officer, not Lady Macbeth. That he should say such a thing amazed Lemp. All the same, the U-boat skipper came back with, "Anyone can have a run of bad luck, sir. And we've handed the limeys more grief than they've given us."

"I am not quarreling with your courage. I am quarreling with your equipment," Dönitz said. "England has ways to detect and attack our U-boats for which we've found no good countermeasures. Our slide-rule pushers are not even sure they understand all of them." He held up a broad-palmed hand. "None of that is to leave this room."

"Yes, sir." Lemp was too worried by the admission even to think of protesting. "I know their hydrophones beat the devil out of anything they had in the last war, but—"

Dönitz cut him off: "It's more than that. It's worse than that. Any time a U-boat surfaces, it seems, an enemy plane or warship rushes at it. It has to be radio detection. We have that, too—we use it to watch for enemy bombers. But we have not been able to build a detector to sense whatever they're using. It may as well be black magic."

Lemp thought about some of the RAF and Royal Navy attacks he'd been through. They'd come out of nowhere—or so it seemed to him—and they'd come straight at the U-30. Without a good crew and some luck, he wouldn't be standing here to listen to the U-boat force commander's lament.

"None of *this* is to leave the room, either," Admiral Dönitz added.

"I wouldn't think of it, sir," Lemp answered honestly. He couldn't stay, and now he couldn't go out, either. He was in as much trouble as the rest of the *Reich*.

Staff Sergeant Alistair Walsh crouched in some bushes. He had a chicken-wire cover on his tin hat with branches stuck up in it, so he looked something like a bush himself. His uniform, khaki to begin with, was splotched with mud and grass stains. From more than a few feet away, no one who didn't already know he was there would have had the slightest idea.

The only trouble was, the Germans didn't care. They had a couple of MG-42s in the ruins of the Belgian farm buildings ahead, along with what seemed like all the ammunition in the world to feed them. They'd fire a burst, traverse a little, and fire another one. They weren't particularly aiming, or Walsh didn't think they were. They just wanted to kill anyone who might be in front of them, whether they could see him or not.

Jack Scholes crawled over to Walsh. Only the buttons on the front of his battledress tunic kept him from getting lower to the ground than he was. A snake would have been proud to own him as a cousin. Without raising his head even a quarter of an inch, he said, "Captain 'ammersmif says we've got to tyke out them bloody MGs."

"Jolly good," Walsh answered sardonically: it was anything but. "And does he say how we're supposed to do it?"

The tough little Cockney shook his head without getting it any higher off the ground. "'E wants you to 'andle it."

"He would," Walsh said without heat. This was what he got for being a veteran staff sergeant. Subalterns, lieutenants, even captains were suppose to lean on men like him. Men like him kept junior officers from making too many mistakes that got them and a raft of soldiers killed.

It wasn't even as if Captain Hammersmith were wrong. They did need to take out those machine guns. Otherwise, the Fritzes would go on murdering Tommies within a two-mile-wide semicircle in front of their position for as long as they had ammo. And, being Fritzes, they would have piles of it.

But attacking the MG-42s would get more men killed. They had plenty of open ground in front and on both flanks, and more soldiers in field-gray to the rear. Coming straight at them, you needed to have made out your last will and testament beforehand, because chances were you wouldn't stick around to take care of it afterwards.

"Have we got trench mortars? Can we get trench mortars?" Walsh asked. If he could drop bombs down on top of the Germans, he'd solve the problem on the cheap. The new company commander should have been able to figure that out for himself, no matter how unweaned he was.

"Oi'll arsk 'im," Scholes said, and slithered away.

"Don't come back if we have got them," Walsh called after him. "Don't give the Germans the chance at you."

He pulled his entrenching tool off his belt and started digging the best scrape he could while flat on his belly. He piled the dirt up in front of him and behind the bush. You commonly needed four sandbags' worth of dirt to stop a rifle-caliber round: somewhere between a foot and a foot and a half, all well tamped together. Moving that much earth took a while. Well, he had nothing better to do with his time.

And damned if Jack Scholes didn't come crawling back. "Ain't got no fuckin' mortars," he reported.

"Bloody hell," Walsh said. As soon as he finished with this scrape, he was happy enough to stay here till, oh, 1953. Maybe the *Boches* would die of old age by then or something. Anything was better than changing that nest in broad daylight.

Anything . . . He whistled softly. "Wot yer got, Staff?" Scholes asked. He sounded sure Walsh had something. Coming up with things was what a staff sergeant was for—or he thought so, anyhow. In that, he differed little from the captain.

"Tell him we'll try a night attack to settle them," Walsh said.

"'E wants it done now," Scholes said dubiously.

"Then he can take care of it himself, and I'll write his next of kin a kind letter about what a brave bloke he was—if I'm still here to do the writing," Walsh answered. "Tell him just like that. And say nights are still long—he won't have to wait till ten o'clock for the show."

"Oi'll tell 'im." Scholes snaked off again. This time, he didn't come back. Walsh hoped that was because Captain Hammersmith saw reason, not because Scholes stopped something going back or moving forward. Since the captain didn't order an attack on his own, Walsh thought he had some chance of being right.

The Fritzes stopped hosing down the landscape with bullets as twilight began to deepen. They were an orderly, predictable people—except when they went off the rails and started another world war, of course. They'd packed it in at dusk the night before, too, and the night before that. Nighttime was for rest and food, not for fighting. So they seemed to think, anyhow.

Most of the time, Walsh agreed with them. All kinds of horrible things could go wrong with a night attack. But at least you might take the Germans by surprise with one. And anything seemed better than rushing forward into the storm of lead. They'd tried that at the Somme, and lost a small city's worth of dead the first day—which didn't count the wounded, or what happened over the next few excruciating weeks. This would be a smaller slaughter, but not necessarily in proportion to the number of men engaged. Head-on slogging wouldn't go. A night attack might. And so, a night attack it would be.

Walsh told off two attacking parties. Both would be armed with Sten guns. They'd need to get close, and they'd need to throw around a lot of bullets when they did. They had Mills bombs, too, lots of them, and a bazooka for whatever bunker-busting they'd need to do.

And they had compasses with radium-painted needles that glowed in the dark. With luck, they'd get close to where they were supposed to go. Without luck . . . Without luck, the captain or someone else would write Walsh's kin one of those kind letters. Or maybe they'd just get a wire from the Ministry of War.

He didn't worry about that. He worried about getting where he was going in spite of the cold, nasty drizzle that started coming down. The Germans who served those MG-42s would be nice and dry. They might even be warm. All the more reason to hate the buggers.

Once your eyes got used to it, you could see amazingly well in the dark. Not fine details, no, but plenty well enough to get around. Well enough to navigate, too, if you were careful. And the rain's dank dripping kept the Germans in their nests from hearing the enemy coming until he was right on top of them.

That turned out to be literally true. Walsh stuck the muzzle of his Sten into the Germans' firing slit and emptied the whole magazine. The screams that came from inside were at least as much from shock and horror as from pain. He yanked the pin off a grenade and chucked that through the slit, too. One of his men added another. That took care of that.

It did for one MG-42, anyhow. The Germans in the other position fired off a flare and started shooting at whatever the hateful white light showed. But, because of the rain, it didn't show as much as usual. It also didn't alert their friends farther back that they were in trouble. And some of the Tommies had already got round behind the second machine-gun nest. They quickly finished it with grenades and subma-chine guns.

They threw off enough sandbags to get into the nests, plunder the dead, carry off the machine guns, and booby-trap the positions with trip wires and Mills bombs. Then they got out of there. "'Ere you go, Staff." Jack Scholes handed Walsh a prize: a tube of liver paste. "An' if anyfing'll 'appy up the captain, loike, this 'ere little game will."

"If anything will," Walsh said. "For a little while." Scholes laughed. Walsh wished he'd been joking.

When a Pe-2 taxied to takeoff, the engines stayed pretty quiet. When you gave them full throttle to get airborne, the roar filled your head. Anastas Mouradian wore a leather flight helmet. He had earphones so he could hear radio messages from his squadron commander and fellow flyers. The roar filled his head anyhow. It seemed to swallow him whole. He often marveled that it didn't shake his molars right out of his jaw.

By the way Isa Mogamedov's lips drew back from his teeth as the bomber started its climb, the Azeri was feeling the same way. Seeing Stas' eyes on him, he said something.

Whatever it was, that all-consuming roar made it unintelligible.

Stas cupped a hand behind his ear to show he didn't get it. Mogamedov obligingly tried again. He shouted and used exaggerated mouth movements so the pilot could read his lips: "Poland this time."

"*Da.*" Mouradian nodded to show he'd heard. "We're moving forward." He also mouthed the words, feeling much like a ham actor as he did. There were things he didn't say, too. For instance, he didn't remark on how long it had been since the squadron could bomb any country other than the USSR. When you said something like that, you put your life in the hands of the person to whom you said it.

Yes, a bomber pilot and copilot/bomb aimer already had their lives in each other's hands. But that was different. If the Germans—or even the Poles—got one of them, they'd get both of them. The NKVD could pick and choose. Better, far better, not to give the Chekists the chance.

Flak came up at the Pe-2s. Mouradian's plane bounced in the air like a truck rattling over a rutted road. But no clangs told of steel ripping through the thin aluminum skin. All the gauges stayed steady. The Germans still held part of Byelorussia and the Ukraine. The Red Army hadn't cleared them out of Latvia and Lithuania yet, either.

But the Pe-2s could hit Poland even so. They could, and they would. Marshal Smigly-Ridz needed to be reminded there was a price for choosing Hitler over Stalin. The Soviet Union had already paid an enormous price because Smigly-Ridz didn't care to cough up Wilno when Stalin demanded it. That was one more of the things you said to nobody unless you happened to own a death wish.

On they droned. It was a longer flight than most, so Stas kept a wary eye on the fuel gauge. They'd have plenty to get where they were going and back again unless something went wrong. He eyed the gauge anyhow. Getting hit was the most likely way for something like that to go wrong, but far from the only one. A cracked line, a clogged line . . . The longer you'd been flying, the more possibilities like that you could think of.

He and Mogamedov both spent a lot of their time peering out every which way at once through the cockpit glass. Bf-109s, FW-190s, whatever outdated junk the Poles were flying—if you didn't spot them before they saw you, you'd go down in flames before you could complain about how obsolete the fighters were. Stas wished he had eyes on stalks like a crawfish so he really could look in two directions at the same time.

The squadron commander's voice sounded tinnily in his earphones: "That's Wilno dead ahead. We'll aim at the railroad yards and the steel mills."

Railroad connections and factories had made Stalin want the town in the first place. Now his minions would try to wreck them. If you thought about it, it reminded you of a spoiled five-year-old. *If I can't have them, you don't get to use them, either!* The scary thing was, that was probably just what was going through Stalin's beady little mind.

Yet another thing you couldn't say. Mouradian could say "Acknowledged," so he did. He also called into the speaking tube: "Lower the bomb-bay doors, Fedya. We're almost there."

"I'm doing it," the bombardier answered. And Mechnikov did. The wind howled in a new way as it whipped around inside the bomb bay.

Flak started coming up from the guns in and around Wilno. The fire was fierce and accurate. Whether those were Poles or Germans down there, they knew their business.

Stas tipped the Pe-2 into a shallow dive all the same. "A little to the left, Comrade Pilot," Mogamedov said. "We're coming up on the train station."

"A little to the left." Stas adjusted their course.

"Let them go, Fedya!" the Azeri called to the bombardier. The explosives fell free. The bomb-bay doors closed. Stas yanked the Pe-2 around in a tight turn and scooted for home.

Just in time. Messerschmitts tore into the Red Air Force bombers. One dove past Mouradian's plane and was gone before he could open up on it. He did see that it was marked with Poland's two-by-two red-and-white checkerboard rather than the German swastika. So the Poles weren't flying junk any more, then. Hitler'd sold them fighters worth having.

The machine gun in the dorsal turret chattered furiously. Fyodor Mechnikov saw something worth shooting at, or thought he did. Better to blast away at something that wasn't there than to let a Fritz—or even a Pole—shoot you from behind.

Two planes trailing smoke and fire spun toward the ground: a Pe-2 and a smaller 109. Mouradian gunned his machine till all the performance gauges cranked well into the red. The groundcrew men could fix the engines later. Or they could if he bought himself a later for the mechanics to fix them in.

He wondered if he should try to get higher. If he did, he and his crewmates would have a chance to bail out in case a 109 shot up the plane. But climbing would cost him speed, and speed was what would get him out of here. A Pe-2 was just about as fast as a Messerschmitt, and had far more range. Going flat out would bring him back to the airstrip with less gas in the tanks than he'd expected, but that was the least of his worries now.

Another bomber from the squadron went down. What made a fighter pilot go after one plane but not another? The size of the red stars on its wings? The way the sunlight shone off the cockpit or the turret and drew his notice? Being in the right place to dive on the Pe-2? Or nothing more than dumb luck? Stas had no answers. He'd never had any answers to questions like those. All he knew was, he was still around to ask them.

Ten minutes put ninety kilometers or so between him and the Polish 109s waspishly defending Wilno. One more check showed only a few scattered Pe-2s close enough to see. When he eased back on the throttles, the engines seemed to sigh in relief. The pointers on the dials fell back to safe levels.

"Another one down," Mogamedov said, and then, "A few more like that and we don't come home from one."

"Afraid you're right," Stas said. "But it's not as if we haven't known that for a while, is it?"

"No." After a beat, Mogamedov added, "No wonder so many Russian pilots drink like fish, is it?"

"Mm, maybe not," Stas said. "But do they drink because they're pilots and they know they're going to catch one, or just because they're Russians? Some of the Russians in the groundcrew pour it down every bit as hard, and they never get off the ground."

"And some of the pilots would drink like that if they didn't fly," Mogamedov allowed. "Not all of them would, though, or I don't think so."

"It could be. I may do some drinking myself today once we get down," Mouradian said.

"Some drinking? Most people do some drinking. Drinking till you can't see any more—that's different," Mogamedov said.

He hardly ever did even some drinking. But, as you didn't say some things, so you didn't ask some questions. If he admitted he was a believing Muslim, he would be giving Stas a hold on him. If he denied it, he might be lying. The two of them were all right in the cockpit, and in the officers' tent. For an Armenian and an Azeri, that would do, and more than do.

Hans-Ulrich Rudel stood to stiff attention in front of the folding table that served Colonel Steinbrenner as a desk. "Reporting as ordered, sir," he said, saluting. "What do you need?"

"To ask you a question," the squadron CO said. "Whatever you tell me, I promise it won't be held against you."

Whenever somebody told you something like that, he didn't mean it. Even a preacher's son like Hans-Ulrich got that. "One of *those* questions, is it?" he said with a wry grin.

Steinbrenner, though, wasn't grinning. "Yes, I'm afraid it is," he answered, and his voice sounded as somber as if he were officiating at a graveside service.

"Well, then, you'd better ask me, hadn't you?" Rudel said. Any trace of amusement vanished from his voice, too.

"All right. Here goes." But the colonel paused to light a cigarette and drag deep before he continued, "If you were ordered to bomb a German city in a state of rebellion against the *Führer* and the *Grossdeutsches Reich*, would you do it? Could you do it?"

No wonder he hesitated! That wasn't what anybody would call a small question. Hans-Ulrich knew what the proper military answer was. *Zu Befehl, Herr Oberst!* Anything else was less than his duty, less than his oath to Adolf Hitler. All the same . . . No, it wasn't a small question. He tried to come back with a question of his own: "Is that what you are commanding me to do, sir?" You were—just barely—permitted to make sure you clearly understood your orders.

But all Steinbrenner said, in a voice like stone, was, "Answer what I asked you, please."

"Bomb German civilians?"

"German civilians revolting against the government of the *Grossdeutsches Reich.*"

"Sir, I—" Rudel came to an unhappy stop. Fighting Germany's enemies was an honor, a privilege. Telling him who Germany's enemies were was the *Führer*'s job. But if the *Führer* told him the German *Volk* were Germany's enemies . . . Had he been a pinball machine, his eyes would have read TILT. "Sir, I just don't know," he finished after that stop.

"Thank you," the squadron CO said. "You're dismissed."

"Sir?" Too much was happening too fast.

"Dismissed." Steinbrenner cut off the syllables as if with a scissors. In case two-syllable words had suddenly got too hard for Rudel, he chose some shorter ones: "Get the fuck out of here."

Hans-Ulrich left. Not to put too fine a point on it, Hans-Ulrich fled. Mere combat didn't faze him—he had its measure. If you lived, you lived. If you died, you died. You did your best to live. But the unknown terrified even the bravest.

A lot of men would have gone to the officers' tent and got smashed. If you couldn't think straight, you didn't need to worry about what you couldn't—or didn't want to—understand. But drowning his sorrows had never been Rudel's style. Obeying orders no matter how he felt about them had never been a problem before. Now, all of a sudden, it was.

The trouble was, the airstrip didn't have many places where someone could go to be by himself. The first one he thought of was the revetment that sheltered his Stuka. But when he got there he found Albert Dieselhorst fiddling with the trim tabs on the plane's tail.

"Morning, sir. What's cooking?" Dieselhorst took a longer look and found a different question: "Good God! Who stepped on your tail?"

"Colonel Steinbrenner did," Rudel answered.

"Why?" the radioman and rear gunner demanded. "You haven't even screwed any *Mischlings* I know of since we got to Belgium. You're a *good* boy . . . uh, sir."

"*Danke schön*," Hans-Ulrich said in a distinctly hollow voice. "No, I wasn't naughty—not that way, anyhow."

"What *did* you do, then?"

"I didn't do anything. It's what the colonel asked me." Hans-Ulrich explained just what that was.

Sergeant Dieselhorst stared at him. "*Der Herr Gott im Himmel!*" he burst out, and then added several comments even more pungent. Once he'd got those out of his system, he asked, "And what did you answer?"

"I said I didn't know whether I could do it or not."

"Huh." The sergeant eyed him thoughtfully. "I'll tell you one thing, so you know. If they ever give you orders like that, I sure as hell don't want to sit in the back seat."

"You'll end up in all kinds of hot water if you try to refuse," Hans-Ulrich pointed out.

"I understand that. Believe me, I do. I've been in the service a lot longer than you have." Dieselhorst hawked and spat on the dirt near the Stuka's tailwheel. Shaking his head, he went on, "I don't think they'll give you orders like that, though."

"Why not? Why would they ask me something like that if they aren't serious about it?"

"Oh, I'm sure they're serious about it. Matter of fact, I'm sure they're crapping their drawers about it." The veteran set a hand on Rudel's shoulder. "But Colonel Steinbrenner asked *you*. If you aren't the guy in the squadron who's most loyal to the people in power, fuck me if I know who is. And *you* told him you weren't sure you could bomb your own people. Suppose somebody who doesn't like the Party so much takes his Stuka up. Where will he put his bombs? On the rebels? Or on the shitheads who tried to make him bomb them?"

"That would mean civil war!" Hans-Ulrich yipped.

"Very good," Dieselhorst said, with the air of a teacher congratulating a short-pants kid who'd aced an exam. "But doesn't it seem to you like we've already got a civil war? Why would they be asking you about bombing Germany if we didn't?"

Hans-Ulrich opened his mouth. Then he closed it again. He realized he had no good answer for that. He didn't even have a bad answer for it.

Sergeant Dieselhorst patted him on the back. "You're doing fine," he said, still as teacher to student, or maybe more like father to son. The age difference between them wasn't that large, but the difference in worldliness probably was. Dieselhorst went on, "Keep going down that road and you'll make it to grown-up yet."

"Oh, fuck you!" Hans-Ulrich shook off the sergeant's hand. Dieselhorst laughed like a loon, which only irked the younger man more. He said, "You're so smart, what would you have told the colonel if he asked you something like that?"

"You gave him a good answer. And he knows how honest you are, so he has to take it seriously," Dieselhorst replied. "I might have said the same thing. Or I might have told him there's no way I'd do anything against my own people, because there isn't."

"The SS might make you change your mind," Hans-Ulrich remarked.

"Sir, the blackshirts can make anybody promise anything—I give you that," Dieselhorst said. "But they can't make you keep your promise once you take off. There's no room in the cockpit for some asshole to hold his Luger to your head. They know it, too. They're not all stupid. Only lots of them."

That was also heresy or disloyalty or insubordination or whatever you wanted to call it. Or maybe it was just the attitude of a man who saw what he saw and knew what he knew and tried to get along as best he could.

"Like I say, sir," he went on earnestly, "I don't think it'll come to that, honest to God. If you don't want to start dropping bombs inside of Germany, nobody wants to."

Was that faint praise? Or was it faint damn? Hans-Ulrich decided to take what he could get. "Thanks," he said, and left it right there.

Chapter 18

Somewhere up ahead, there were Germans. Somewhere up ahead, there always seemed to be more Germans. Ivan Kuchkov had started to think the Hitlerites stamped out soldiers in a factory somewhere near Berlin. He shared the conceit with the men in his section. He gave them orders; they were stuck listening to him unless they really wanted to get the shit piled on their backs.

"They turn the fuckers on a lathe," he said, warming to his story, "and then they spray on the gray uniforms the way we paint trucks."

"I almost believe it, you know?" Sasha Davidov said.

"What? They don't make kikes the same way?" Ivan gibed.

The scout shook his head. "Afraid not, Comrade Sergeant. If they did, there'd be more of us. No, we fuck like everybody else."

"Like hell you do," Kuchkov said. "You've got those clipped cocks. Probably shortens the recoil when your gun goes off."

As the Red Army men laughed, Davidov said, "I knew there had to be some kind of reason for it." He didn't sound pissed off or anything. That was good. Ivan had no use for him as a Jew, but he made a damn fine point man. And somebody who could see trouble before it saw him was a better life-insurance policy than even a full drum on your PPD.

"Where was I?" the sergeant went on. "Oh, yeah. They machine the fucking Fritzes. They paint the uniforms on the cunts. And then . . . You guys ever seen a bottle factory? One where the bottles trundle by on a fucking belt and this machine stamps the caps on 'em, bang, bang, bang? You know what I'm talking about, assholes?" He waited for them to nod, then finished, "Well, that's how Hitler's pricks get the helmets on their knobs."

"It's cheap work," Sasha said. "A bullet goes right through one of those things."

Kuchkov picked up his own helmet. While he wasn't in action, he just wore a forage cap. He hefted the ironmongery. "Sure, bitch. And this'll keep out everything up to a goddamn 105, right?"

Sasha Davidov didn't answer. Everybody knew a German helmet was better than the Soviet model. Ivan had had that thought himself, too many times to count. Never mind the steel—even the leather and pads that made the thing tolerable to wear—were of higher quality than their Red Army equivalents. It was *such* a fucking shame that wearing one would make his own side put holes in it.

One of his men asked, "Comrade Sergeant, are you criticizing Soviet production?"

The guy was a new replacement. His name was Mikhail . . . Mikhail Something. Ivan couldn't remember his surname or patronymic. But he knew danger when he heard it. "Not me," he answered without missing a beat. "Nobody's helmet keeps out bullets. Anything that could'd be so goddamn heavy, it'd make your stupid head fall off."

He waited. Mikhail didn't say anything else. The prick was on the lean side, and kind of pale. By the way he talked, he came from Moscow. Piece by piece, none of that meant anything. But when one of your boys shot a political officer . . . The NKVD could build a case any way they pleased.

Sasha Davidov sat there by the fire, not quite looking at Ivan. The skinny little *Zhid*'s cheeks hollowed more than usual when he sucked in smoke from a *papiros*. He needed a shave. The dark stubble on his cheeks and his big nose made him look like a blackass from the Caucasus.

Jews were different, though. Get in trouble with a blackass and he'd come after you and cut your liver out. Get in trouble with a Jew and two years later you'd be in a camp somewhere north of the Arctic Circle and never quite sure how you wound up there. Jews liked revenge cold, not hot.

But they and blackasses had one thing in common. They were mostly too goddamn smart for their own good. Sasha could see that this Mikhail was trouble, same as Kuchkov could. And the two of them had been together for a long time now. Sasha could probably see what Kuchkov had in mind to do about it, too.

Whatever the Jew saw, he didn't say anything about it. He didn't even raise a dark, ironic eyebrow. He just sat there, leaning toward the flames and smoking the *papiros* till he'd burnt every milligram of tobacco in the paper cigarette holder.

He won't rat on me, Ivan thought. In the USSR, that was the touchstone of trust. *Zhid* or not, Sasha passed. He and Ivan had saved each other's nuts plenty of times. Mikhail, on the other hand . . .

Soviet officers used up men the way they used up machine pistols and tanks and planes. Ivan had joked about the Germans' manufacturing soldiers. His own superiors behaved more as if they thought their side did. Doing this or that would cost so many men, so many machines. So when they did this or that, they didn't care a bit if they lost that many tanks and that many soldiers. They even had a word for that; Ivan had heard them use it. The troops and the equipment were *fungible,* was what they were.

And if Soviet officers had an attitude like that, what kind of attitude was a hard-nosed Soviet sergeant likely to have?

Next morning, Ivan booted his men out of their bedrolls before any light showed in the eastern sky. "C'mon, you whores," he growled. "We're gonna shove ourselves up the Fritzes' cunts before they've pissed away their morning hard-ons." Somebody laughed. Ivan rounded on him. "What's so fucking funny?"

"Nothing, Comrade Sergeant," the soldier said quickly. "I serve the

Soviet Union!" It was as soft an answer as he could give. If he'd tried to explain about mixed metaphors, Ivan would have knocked the crap out of him.

They ate black bread and sausage. Some of them gulped their hundred-gram vodka ration to keep from worrying about what might happen pretty soon. Kuchkov drank some of his, but not all. Sasha Davidov didn't touch any. At the point, he needed to stay alert as a hunted rabbit.

Mikhail swallowed his vodka dose, every drop of it. The Red Army men moved out in a ragged skirmish line. More of them carried PPDs like Ivan's than rifles. At close quarters, all you wanted to do was spray a lot of lead around. A machine pistol was terrific for that.

They moved cautiously, hunching low. The sun coming up behind them could silhouette them against the horizon and throw their moving shadows a long, long way.

Somewhere up ahead sat a farm village. The Germans didn't seem to want to pull back from it. Maybe one of the cunts there was an extra good lay. Boot the Hitlerites out and the next village was six or eight kilometers farther west. It seemed worth doing.

Sasha hit the dirt a split second before the MG-42 in the village started spitting out death. Ivan didn't know what kind of animal instinct the little Jew had, but Davidov had it, all right. And, because Ivan kept an eye on him, he also hit the ground before bullets snapped through where he'd been.

Some of the other Red Army men went down on their own as soon as the lead started flying. Others had 7.92mm help in falling. The Russians fired back, though they were still too far outside the village for submachine guns to do much good. Well, that was why you still needed to bring along some riflemen.

"Flank them out!" Kuchkov yelled. "You pussies—yeah, you over there! Go get 'em!"

They tried. They feared him more than they feared the Fritzes. But they started too soon. Hitler's fearsome buzz saw swung around and knocked them back before they could knock it out. No, the Nazis really didn't want to leave this place. And, as long as they fed belts into that MG-42, they could kill a regiment's worth of Russians here.

Ivan knew a lost cause when he saw one. "Back!" he shouted. "We'll have to shell them out or bomb them out or something, the fuckers."

The Russian soldiers who could retreat did. Kuchkov wasn't altogether astonished when he saw that Mikhail wasn't one of them. The new guy had been part of the flanking party the German machine gun savaged. Wasn't that a shame? Ivan rolled some coarse *makhorka* in a scrap of newsprint and lit the homemade cigarette. *Fungible* wasn't *mat*, but it still turned out to be a handy word to know.

Brakes chuffing, the train pulled into Broad Street Station. Peggy Druce looked out the window at the familiar platform. Another political trip down—this one to Altoona. That was about as far west as she usually went. Somewhere around there, Philadelphia's gravity or influence or whatever you wanted to call it began to fade and Pittsburgh's to grow.

Even Pennsylvania's roads reflected the split between the state's two biggest cities. In the southeast, they looked like a segment of a spider web with Philly sitting where the spider would. Pittsburgh occupied a similar position in the southwest. Geography had something to do with that. Some of it, though, was attitude and who your friends were.

"Broad Street Station! Philadelphia!" the conductor shouted, in case you were too dumb to know where you were.

Peggy was already on her way to the door. She'd scoot back to the baggage car to snag her suitcase. Then she'd splurge and take a cab back to her house.

Only she didn't. There on the platform waiting for her stood Dave Hartman. The master machinist sent her a crooked grin. "Hey, good-lookin'," he said.

"What are you doing here?" Peggy asked, more surprised than pleased. "Why aren't you at work?"

"They're doing a changeover—gotta retool a little on account of we'll be making a new model," Dave answered. "So I had me the afternoon off, and I figured I'd pick you up."

"That was sweet," Peggy said as she went back to the baggage car.

Dave walked beside her. She gave the colored redcap her claim check, and handed him fifteen cents when he set her suitcase at her feet.

Dave grabbed the suitcase. "Your back!" Peggy squawked.

"Hush your face, doll," he said. So she did.

When they got to his old Ford, she said, "Honest, Dave, you didn't need to bother. I know what the gas ration is these days."

"Hush your face," he repeated as he threw the suitcase in the trunk. Only after he'd held the door open for her did he go on, "Don't hardly drive it any which way. Gotta give it a go every once in a while or the tires'll flatten out and the battery'll die on me."

Peggy knew that protesting too much was a losing cause. All she said was, "Well, thank you very much. I was going to grab a taxi."

"Waste of money when you've got your own private chauffeur." Dave started the car. You could hardly hear the engine, no matter how old it was. Yes, he took care of it better than any garage was likely to. He put it in gear. "I do hope the tires hold out. You really gotta have connections to get your hands on new ones, way things are these days."

"I may be able to take care of that if you need them," Peggy said.

"Through the guy who was dumb enough to dump you?" Dave shook his head. "No offense, but I don't want anything to do with him."

Herb probably could get new tires when he needed them. No denying he was a well-connected man. But Peggy answered, "I wasn't thinking about him. Remember, I just came back from a political trip—and I've made a lot of them. Plenty of Democratic big shots who owe me a favor or two. I could promote some Firestones or Goodyears, I expect."

He laughed. "Never thought I'd get to know a fixer, not in a month of Sundays I didn't. See what happens when you go to a ballgame?"

"All kinds of crazy things," Peggy agreed with a fond smile. She had no idea whether this was love or just a rebound. People who'd been through divorces said you were commonly crazy the first couple of years after your knot got untied. If it ended up not working, she'd chalk it up to experience and try to go on from there. In the meantime, she'd enjoy it for as long as it stayed enjoyable. It had so far.

Not many cars were on the streets. Compared to Philadelphia before the war, they seemed deserted. Compared to Hitler's Germany . . .

The only civilian vehicles that still operated in the Third *Reich* were fire engines, ambulances, and doctors' cars. Yes, whether this glass was half empty or half full depended on how you looked at things.

Shops here still had clothes and beer and radio sets and toys and noodles in them. The variety wasn't as big as it had been before Uncle Sam started fighting the Japs, but you could mostly get what you needed, even if not just what you wanted. Somebody from Berlin plopped down in the middle of Philadelphia would die of shock, or possibly of greed.

Because traffic was so light, they got up to Peggy's house in nothing flat. "Want to come in for a drink?" she asked.

"Twist my arm." He held it out. It was firmer and harder than Herb's; he kept himself in fine shape. Peggy gave a token twist. Dave yowled like a cat with its tail under a rocking chair. "Mercy! Mercy and bourbon."

"Bourbon is a mercy," Peggy said. She was going to carry her bag into the house, but Dave didn't give her the chance. Men could be most annoying when they acted most chivalrous.

Ice cubes clinked in highball glasses as she built the drinks. Dave raised his in salute. "Mud in your eye."

Idly, she turned on the radio. Once it warmed up, music started coming out. But the record cut off abruptly—so abruptly that somebody at the studio scraped the needle across the grooves. "We interrupt this broadcast to bring you a special news flash!" the announcer said in portentous tones.

"Uh-oh," Dave said, halfway down his drink. "Wonder what went off the rails this time." He might have meant that literally; along with factory explosions, railway disasters often caused we-interrupt-this-broadcast announcements.

Not this afternoon, though. "Adolf Hitler, the Nazi *Führer*, has announced that, from this time forward, the Greater German *Reich* considers itself to be at war with the United States of America. At the same time as his announcement, German U-boats attacked American merchant ships and naval vessels without warning. Some have been sunk, and American lives have been lost."

"Holy Jesus!" Peggy said hoarsely. She finished her drink at a gulp.

Then she poured more Jim Beam over the rocks. She needed a refill. Dave drained his glass and held it out for more, too.

"American diplomats in Berlin and their German counterparts in Washington will be exchanged through neutral nations," the announcer went on. "In an early statement from the White House, President Roosevelt said that he did not want this fight and did not go looking for it. He also said, however, that, while the Nazis may have started the war, the United States will finish it."

"Yeah!" Dave put down his drink so he could smack one fist into the palm of his other hand.

Peggy, who followed politics more closely than her new boyfriend did, knew FDR wasn't putting all his cards on the table. The way America had armed and encouraged England and France meant she was already close to being at war with Hitler's Germany. But why would Hitler want to make things official when FDR couldn't because he didn't have the political backing?

Hitler, of course, had problems of his own in Germany. No matter how hard Goebbels tried to keep things quiet, word of the unrest kept leaking out. Maybe the *Führer* had decided declaring war on America might unite the country behind him. If he did . . .

"He doesn't know what he's messing with," Dave said. "Kaiser Bill didn't, and Adolf doesn't, either. But I bet we show him, same as we did the last time around."

"I bet we do," Peggy agreed. And that seemed to call for more drinks.

Posters sprouted in Münster like toadstools after a rain. Most of them, of course, came from the government. People who didn't like what the Nazis were up to took their lives in their hands to print broadsheets with their message, and risked them again when they went out under cover of darkness with paste pots. They did it, though. The regime didn't have things here all its own way on the propaganda front—not quite, anyhow.

But these latest posters came straight from Goebbels. Sarah Bruck winced when she saw them. One showed FDR and Eleanor Roosevelt sitting side by side in fancy dress—only the American President's face was just a false front, behind which you saw a bearded Jew with a great hooked nose and flabby lips. Eleanor was saying, "Franklin! Your mask is slipping!"

The other showed a German eagle, complete with swastika, striking down the one that represented America. FORWARD THE *REICH*! that one shouted. FORWARD TO VICTORY!

Sarah didn't want to be at war with the United States. Or maybe she did, if that would bring Hitler and the Nazis down faster. But if the USA and its allies knocked Münster flat and killed her . . . Well, in that case she'd have a thing or two to say to them in the afterlife. If there turned out to be an afterlife.

In spite of the war, in spite of the uprising, in spite of the jumpy German soldiers on the streets, Sarah smiled. Here she was, piling one if on top of another. *Piling Pelion on Ossa,* her father would say. Being the daughter of a professor of classics and ancient history, Sarah even knew what that meant. Those were the mountains the Titans of Greek myth had stacked when they tried to storm the gods on Mt. Olympus.

Some ways, she knew more about the ancient Greeks' religion than she did about her own. She'd studied theirs more thoroughly. She'd just grown up with hers. She'd grown up with scraps and pieces of hers, anyhow. Till Hitler came to power, her family had been happily secular. Only after he showed how much he hated Judaism did her folks decide there had to be something to it after all.

"Hey, Jewigirl!" a soldier called. "Why don't you come over here and—" He gave forth with a lewd suggestion.

Cheeks aflame, Sarah walked on as if she hadn't heard him. The soldier and his buddies laughed, but they didn't come after her. Ignoring soldiers had always worked up till now. When it stopped working, if it stopped working . . . She didn't want to think about that, so she didn't.

Someone had painted a slogan on a wall: NAZIS ROT IN HELL! Nobody'd whitewashed over it yet. That was one of the things labor gangs did these days. Her father sometimes came home with his clothes dappled with whitewash.

Sarah read the slogan out of the corner of her eye. She knew better than to turn her head to look at it. Doing that got you in trouble, the same way screaming back at the dirty-minded soldiers would have. Somebody was always watching you. Whenever you went outdoors, you had to act as if somebody was, anyway.

She ducked into the grocer's shop. It was late in the afternoon, of course. The grocery wouldn't have had much when it opened hours ago. It had even less now. Before the war, sheep would have turned up their noses at the mangy turnips in the produce bin. Now Sarah was glad to see them. She could bring *something* home.

There was a difference between bad and worse. She picked some of the less diseased-looking turnips. In a bin farther back, she found rutabagas. Kale and spinach remained, too. And they had powdered mustard. She hadn't seen any for a long time. Some of the powder would probably be yellow chalk, but what could you do? She got a couple of packets.

The grocer took her money and the required ration coupons. He still had a double chin. What kinds of things did he get that he didn't sell? No, you wouldn't expect people who dealt in food to go hungry. Her baker husband and in-laws hadn't. She hadn't, either, not while she was married to Isidor. These days, the worm gnawed her stomach again.

She chose a different way back to her house. She didn't want to pass that bunch of soldiers again. They already had ideas. If they saw her one more time, they might decide to do something about them. The fewer chances you took, the better off you were.

A blackshirt at a checkpoint demanded her papers. She produced them. They were in order. "Well, go on, kike," he growled: the small change of insult.

She hadn't gone more than a few steps before gunfire rang out in the center of town. That dreadful ripping snarl could only come from an MG-42. German soldiers were hosing down a building from which rebels had fired—or maybe just a building from which they thought rebels had fired. If they shot a few people who had nothing to do with the uprising, they wouldn't lose any sleep over it.

"You stinking Jews!" the SS man shouted after Sarah. "This trouble is all your fault!"

She wanted to argue with him. Himmler had got Münster up in arms against him by seizing the Catholic prelate, Cardinal von Galen. The cardinal hadn't said a word about Jews; all the signs were that he couldn't have cared less about what happened to them. He'd protested the "mercy killings" of mental defectives. Other people sick of the way the government was botching the war joined the anti-Nazi movement and swelled its ranks. Jews had nothing to do with any of that, either.

But talking back to an SS man was stupid for any German, and suicidally stupid for a Jew. As she had with the soldiers, Sarah kept walking. As long as the blackshirt stuck to talk, she wouldn't worry. Talk was even cheaper and more worthless than kale, which was really saying something.

He sent a parting shot after her: "After we beat the Americans, we'll give all the Hebes over there what-for, too!"

Again, Sarah kept her mouth shut. She had to bite down hard on the inside of her lower lip to manage it, but she did. The *Reich* hadn't been able to beat England and France and torment their Jews, though horrible things were supposed to have happened to the ones they'd caught in Russia. The SS man must have pulled his vision of triumph over the United States out of an opium pipe. Or maybe you needed to smoke something stronger than opium to get that kind of hallucination.

She managed to escape. No one was shooting around here right this minute. But a rifle or machine-gun bullet could fly a couple of kilometers and kill somebody who chanced to be in the wrong place at the wrong instant. There hadn't been any funerals like that on the block where her parents' house stood, but the next block over had seen one, and a little girl in the hospital with a hole in her leg. Bad luck? God's will? Sarah had no idea. She wasn't even sure there was a difference.

A cigar butt lay on the sidewalk: three centimeters or so of stepped-on tobacco, soggy at one end. As casually as if she'd been doing it all her life, she bent and picked it up. She had no use for it herself—she'd never got the smoking habit. But her father would mix it in with his own scroungings. Jews got no tobacco rations. If Father was going to smoke, he had to make do with other people's leavings.

Or, sometimes, he managed to steal unsmoked cigarettes he found in bombed-out houses—another kind of scrounging. He'd even got American cigarettes that way, from the home of a Party *Bonz* whose connections let him latch on to things ordinary people couldn't even dream of. Those connections, though, hadn't kept his fancy place from getting blown to smithereens . . . or a Jew from enjoying things for which he had no further use.

When Sarah came home at last, her mother asked, "How did it go?"

"Could have been worse." Sarah displayed the produce in her stringbag. "And I found part of a cigar for Father."

"That's good. He'll be happy," Hanna Goldman said. "What have you got there? Mustard? When was the last time they had any?"

"I don't know. It's been a while. If only we had some meat to put it on," Sarah said.

"Well, it won't go bad," her mother said—they didn't. All you could do was try to get by and hope the war ended before you did. Did America's entry into the European fight make that more likely or less? Sarah didn't know. Like everyone else, she could only wait and find out.

Arno Baatz puffed out his chest. The *Unteroffizier* knew something most people didn't. He'd heard it from a *Gestapo* officer. The secret policeman hadn't been talking to him, and might not have talked at all had he known Arno was eavesdropping. But that had nothing to do with anything. Arno had heard. He knew. He felt proud. He felt important. He liked feeling important.

Part of the fun of knowing something other people didn't was getting the chance to tell them. Then they knew, too, of course, but they also knew you'd known before they did. That was how you scored points with your fellow men.

And so Baatz gathered his squad together and said, "Listen, you clowns, you'd better behave yourselves and keep all your gear better than new for the next few days, or else you'll catch hell."

"Since when did they appoint you God?" Adam Pfaff inquired.

"Might've known you'd be the one to piss and moan. But it won't have anything to do with me. You'll catch hell from everybody," Arno said loftily.

"Oh, yeah? How come?" the *Obergefreiter* asked.

"How come? I'll tell you how come. Because the *Führer's* coming to Münster to make a big speech, that's how come." There. It was out. What Arno knew, he'd spread. Whether it was something he was supposed to spread, he simply didn't worry about. He could no more keep it quiet than he could do without eating or drinking or breathing.

Some of the soldiers gaped at him. He hadn't convinced all of them, though. Speaking for the unconvinced, Pfaff said, "Sure he is. And when he decided he would, the very first person he phoned up to tell him was *Unteroffizier* Arno Baatz. In your dreams!"

"No, of course the *Führer* didn't phone me," Baatz snapped. "Don't be a bigger *Dummkopf* than you can help."

"So how *do* you know, then?" Pfaff said. "Or are you just talking to hear yourself talk—again?"

"Doubt all you want. You'll find out," Baatz answered. "And when you get your ass in a sling, don't come crying to me and say I didn't warn you. Us and the SS guys, we've got to make sure the *Führer* stays safe while he's in town and the rebels don't kick up any fuss." By the way he said it, the forces protecting Adolf Hitler would include Himmler's police and prison guards and praetorians . . . and this one squad of *Landsers*.

"You really believe this shit, don't you?" Pfaff sounded less skeptical himself now.

"I believe it because it's true," Arno said. "And I want to see you clean yourself up—all of you, in fact! You look like pig sties in marching boots. Oh, and Pfaff, when we line up for the *Führer's* inspection, you'd damn well better be toting a rifle with a varnished stock, you hear me?"

The *Obergefreiter* unslung his gray-painted Mauser. Arno Baatz had hated that nonregulation piece since the second he set eyes on it. Pfaff started to say something, then had second thoughts. At last, he answered, "If the *Führer* inspects us, I'll do it. But he was a *Front-schwein* himself. I bet he'd understand."

"He'd understand what a square peg you are, that's what he'd understand," Baatz retorted. Adam Pfaff clung to a wounded, dignified silence.

For the next couple of days, nothing out of the ordinary happened. The soldiers began to give Arno funny looks when they didn't think he could catch them doing it. But he had what might as well have been a radio antenna to pick up such things. He noticed, all right.

He noticed, and he worried. What if he'd heard wrong? What if the *Gestapo* officer had been talking through his high-crowned cap? Arno knew he would never live it down if he'd made a mistake. The men didn't respect him enough as it was (they would have had to treat him like a field marshal to give him the respect he felt he deserved). They wouldn't respect him at all if the *Führer* didn't show.

But then things started tightening up. Parties of soldiers and labor gangs full of convicts and Jews went to work cleaning up Münster. The city hadn't taken as much of a beating as some Russian town that went back and forth between the *Wehrmacht* and the Red Army three or four times, but it wasn't in what anybody would call great shape.

Grudgingly, Adam Pfaff said, "Well, maybe you were right, Corporal. Otherwise, we wouldn't be putting mascara and rouge on this corpse."

"Bet your ass we wouldn't," Baatz agreed, also grudgingly. Neither Pfaff's rank nor his own, which shielded them from most fatigue duties, kept them from shoveling and hauling as if they were kikes or jailbirds. His hands were getting blisters in places where they didn't already have calluses.

Even more galling was the ironic glint that sparked in the dark eyes of the big-nosed bastards with the yellow stars on their clothes. *See?* they might have been saying. *You like Hitler, and what has it got you? You're doing the same kind of shit we are.*

If one of them *had* said anything like that to Arno, he would have knocked the pigdog's teeth down his throat with an entrenching tool. The Jews knew better than to open their big yaps. Whether or not they said anything, though, their eyes spoke for them.

The SS began moving in in droves: *Gestapo* men, SD men, hard-faced troopers from the *Waffen*-SS. The looks they gave ordinary German soldiers were even more scornful than the ones the *Landsers* got from Jews. To the SS functionaries, soldiers were only cowflops under their boots. Medieval barons must have looked at peasants the same way.

Every so often, the peasants had risen up against their noble over-lords. They'd killed all the barons and counts and princes they could catch. Arno had never sympathized with the peasants till now. He finally understood.

He still got angry when he saw Jews eyeing him in their sneaky, snotty way. His understanding wasn't all that flexible. It stretched only so far.

SD men—faggots if he'd ever seen any—started hanging red-white-and-black bunting and swastika banners all over town. They wanted to give the impression that Münster loved the National Socialist German Workers' Party and the *Führer*. Even Arno knew better than that. Why were soldiers and panzers holding the place down under martial law if everybody in it was such a contented citizen of the *Grossdeutsches Reich*?

Well, everybody in it except the Jews. They weren't citizens of the *Reich*. They were only residents. Most Germans—most good, moral, upright Germans—wished they weren't even that.

A few RAF bombers came over by night. In the confusion of the air raid, someone with matches and a can of kerosene torched a lot of banners and bunting. The soldiers had more important things to worry about. For Arno and his men, staying alive stood pretty high on the list.

By contrast, the blackshirted fairies pitched conniption fits when the sun came up and they discovered how their artistic handiwork had been vandalized. They started screaming and wailing and demanding house-to-house searches to smoke out the culprit. Some of the things they wanted to do to him once they caught him made Arno's blood run cold. For somebody who'd spent so long on the Eastern Front, that was saying something.

"Boy, they're sweethearts, aren't they?" Adam Pfaff said.

"At least," Arno answered. He wasn't used to agreeing with the miserable *Obergefreiter*, but they saw eye-to-eye on this one.

The artistic SS men raised such a hue and cry that it finally took a *Wehrmacht* colonel general to tell them to shut up and to make it stick. Along with Himmler's elite, high-ranking Army, Navy, and *Luftwaffe* officers were coming into Münster to hear what their chief of state had to say. Some of them eyed the SS paladins the way the blackshirts looked at *Landsers*. An interesting time was had by all.

Chapter 19

Pete McGill handed the Marine Corps quartermaster sergeant his helmet. He'd worn one like it ever since he became a leatherneck. So had a zillion other Marines, and even more doughboys and dog-faces. Any English soldier who'd gone over the top at the Somme in 1916 would have recognized them: they were nearly exact copies of the limeys' tin hats. Tommies wore them to this day.

Marines and soldiers had worn them to this day, or something close to it. But Progress with a capital P was now reaching even the garrison on Midway. In exchange for Pete's steel derby with its broad brim, the quartermaster sergeant handed him a pot-shaped plastic helmet liner and a helmet that fit tightly over it. You could adjust the straps and padding inside the liner so it gave a good fit to your particular noggin.

When Pete started to do that, the quartermaster said, "One thing at a time, if you don't mind. You've got to sign for this baby first."

As a matter of fact, Pete had to sign twice: once for the helmet and once for the liner. He said, "You sure there's not an extra form for the goddamn chin strap?"

"No, that's included on the form for the helmet proper, to which it attaches," the quartermaster sergeant answered automatically. Then, a beat slower than he should have, he realized Pete was being sarcastic. He jerked his thumb at the tent flap. "Funny guy, huh? Get the hell outa here, funny guy."

Grinning, Pete got. He looked out at sand and at the Pacific, which from Midway seemed to stretch to infinity in all directions. The island still stank faintly of dead Japs. The Marines hadn't taken more than a handful of prisoners, most of them captured too badly wounded to die fighting or kill themselves. As far as Pete was concerned, if Hirohito's boys hadn't caused so much trouble from this place, they would have been welcome to it.

Come to that, if Midway hadn't been a place from which you could either cause trouble or try to stop it, no one in his right mind would have wanted to set foot on it. It could have stayed as it was in the beginning, all sand and thin grasses and crash-landing gooney birds.

But on the Pacific's vast, watery chessboard, islands were important squares. You could put garrisons on them. Even more crucially, you could fly planes off them.

They still hadn't told him when they were going to let him and the rest of the Marines who'd recaptured Midway get off the island and go somewhere with more civilized comforts. They also still hadn't imported any vaccinated hookers. As far as Pete was concerned, that was really a goddamn shame.

He barked sudden laughter. The quartermaster sergeant who thought he was God's anointed because he doled out the spiffy new helmets . . . They wouldn't let that sorry son of a bitch off Midway any time soon, either. Pete wondered if they'd told the guy yet. He would have bet against it. The quartermaster was too full of himself to have got that kind of bad news.

An American flag fluttered near the chugging desalinization plant. And, Pete saw, a new banner had gone up alongside: a smaller, plainly homemade one. MIDWAY—HOME OF THE TYPHOID MARY PARACHUTE BRIGADE, the flag declared.

Pete laughed again. You could laugh or you could cuss or you could go Asiatic: grab a rifle or a Tommy gun and do as much shooting as you could till they got you. Nobody here had actually done that. More than one Marine had talked about it, though. Some were just blue-skying. Others sounded honest-to-God tempted.

They said that when you talked about crap like that you never actually went and did it. Pete never had worked out who *they* were supposed to be. He had seen that a lot of what they said was pure bullshit. This once, he hoped the mysterious *they* knew what they were talking about.

One way to keep from going Asiatic was to take your mind off your troubles. As soon as things like prunes and canned apple juice started getting to the island, a couple of enterprising Marines rigged up a still and started turning out joy juice. It wasn't what you'd call good hooch—it wasn't within miles of what you'd call good hooch—but hooch it was. With no good hooch closer than Kauai, the customers weren't inclined to be fussy.

Navy ships were supposed to be dry, but Pete had never served on one that didn't have some unofficial alcohol available. As long as the producers didn't get greedy, didn't get blatant, and did grease the proper palms, they could go about their business without much trouble.

So things went here. Nobody got too curious about the tent way off by itself. Nobody got too curious about the steady trickle of men who visited it, either.

Pete came back with a couple of canteens' worth of the enterprising corporals' firewater. They claimed the stuff was cognac. Pete thought any Frenchman who brewed up such nasty stuff would kill himself for shame—which, of course, didn't keep him from drinking it. A leatherneck from Mississippi called it stump-likker. That came closer to truth in advertising.

After he'd drunk enough to take the edge off his own gloom, he wondered what would happen if you got an albatross toasted. Would a cop pull the bird over for reckless flying? Would a drunken albatross land any worse than a sober one? *Could* a drunken albatross land any worse than a sober one?

The only problem with finding out was, he had no idea how to inebriate a gooney bird. The sole fresh water on Midway was the stuff the desalinization plant turned out. He'd never seen albatrosses drink. Maybe they got everything they needed from the fish they ate. Or maybe they drank from the Pacific. Pete had no idea. Someone who studied the birds might know, but he didn't.

Another way to assassinate some hours was with a deck of cards. Yes, the poker games on Midway had started before the last Japs got hunted down. They hadn't stopped since. Back in Peking, Pete had learned the expensive way not to mix booze and poker. Booze turned you into an optimist. It also turned you into a sucker. Better, or at least smarter, to wait till you had a clear head and to fleece the fools who didn't know enough to do that.

Games here got insanely expensive. Guys had nothing else to spend their money on. They didn't know when, or even if, they'd ever escape Midway. And so they bet as if there were no tomorrow.

For one poor leatherneck, there *was* no tomorrow. He'd won for a while. Then he started losing, and losing, and losing some more. He went through all the money he had. He went through a year and a half's pay he hadn't earned yet. He wrote IOU after IOU, figuring he'd start winning again pretty soon.

Only he didn't. And, one dark, moonless night, he walked down to the edge of the ocean and blew his brains out. The note by his body read *Well, I guess I'm square now, and my folks will get my insurance.*

That was sobering. It didn't stop the games, but it did make people cut back on the stakes and not allow gamblers down on their luck to pledge money they hadn't made yet. Pete liked the changes. Gambling was all very well, but the only way anyone needed to risk his life was in action against the Japs.

Or, now, against the Germans. Pete still held his grudge against the slanties, but he wouldn't have said no if someone sent him storming ashore on some Belgian beach. Hitler's would-be supermen thought they were hot shit. Their daddies had, too, till U.S. Marines taught them better in France. Some of those old Marines were still in the service. Lots of them had taught Pete the soldiering trade. Giving the Nazis what-for would be a way to show them how well he'd learned his lessons.

Would be. He was about as far from the *Wehrmacht* as a human being could get. He had no idea when the brass would decide Midway was decontaminated enough to make shipping people off it safe. In the meantime, he had stump-likker and poker games. Oh, it was one hell of a life, wasn't it? Wasn't it just?

Spring was in the air. Aristide Demange surveyed it with the same jaundiced gaze he turned on summer, fall, and winter. So birds were singing? So flowers were blooming?—at least till artillery fragments cut them down to size. So bright green grass sprouted in shell holes and on the parapets of entrenchments?

So what?

Demange scowled at his men, too. "You think the *Boches* can't kill you because the sky is blue and you've got a stiff bulge in your pants? The Germans don't care. They're just waiting for you to do something stupid so they can blow your balls off. Then you won't have to worry about hard-ons any more." His voice rose to a shrill, mocking falsetto.

"It's spring for them, too, *n'est-ce pas?*" one of the *poilus* ventured.

"Oh, sure. It's spring. But they're professional about it, you know? And you'd better be the same way, Émile, or you'll be sorry."

"Yes, sir," Émile said, which was never the wrong answer. Maybe he knew what Demange was talking about. He'd seen some action, and he hadn't disgraced himself.

"All right, then." Demange paused to light another in his long string of Gitanes. It had started when he was eleven or twelve and would stop only when they shoveled dirt over him: say, a thousand years from now, or maybe an hour and a half. He went on, "Listen to me, you dumb cocksuckers. I'm not trying to get you killed, because if you get killed, chances go up that I get killed, too, and I'm not ready to die just yet. You got that?"

Their heads bobbed up and down. The only thing wrong with them was that their superiors kept trying to use those heads—and Demange's along with them—to bang through reinforced concrete.

Émile spoke up again: "If you look at it that way, sir, what we ought to do is, we ought to sit tight here and wait for the Americans."

Demange thought so, too. That was pretty much what France had done the last time around. After the mutinies of 1917, France couldn't have done much else then. Even so, Demange had mixed feelings about it. He would rather see Americans dying for liberty than die for it himself. But wasn't it monotonous and even a little embarrassing to get your chestnuts pulled from the fire twice in a row by the same country? If God was writing the script, He could have used some help from a competent dramatist.

Daladier and his kind, of course, would defend France to the last drop of American blood. But the French generals didn't mind killing off Frenchmen. When had they ever?

"Tell you what, Émile," Demange said. "When they give you a field marshal's baton—and I promise you won't get yours a day later than I get mine—you can tell people what to do. In the meantime, we're both stuck with following orders from the fat, white-mustached fucks who've already got theirs."

Émile grinned at him. Some of the other soldiers muttered among themselves. Sure as the devil, one of those sniveling little rats would report him. That would be pretty goddamn funny. What was the worst the brass could do to him? Demote him? He'd thank them. He'd kiss them on their talcumed cheeks. Send him to the front? He'd already logged more time at the front than any other three men you could name. Not fearing consequences gave a wonderful sense of freedom.

He might have invited the *poilus* to tattle on him, but the German loudspeakers chose that moment to come to life. Both sides had them. They were something new, something modern, something to make war even more awful than it had been for the past five thousand years.

"Soldiers of France!" the loudspeakers boomed. Whoever was talking through them, he spoke perfect Parisian French. A prisoner reading a script? A French Fascist who'd gone over to the other side? Probably not someone from Alsace-Lorraine, at home in German and French—the accent would be different. Whoever this *cochon* was, he went on, "Soldiers of France, why spill your blood for Jew Bolsheviks and Jew capitalists? Do you want your towns full of nigger American troops cuckolding you and leaving you with black babies to raise?

When you fight the *Reich* and your fellow white men, you fight the wrong enemy!"

He might speak perfect French, but he mouthed German propaganda. "I wish they'd drop leaflets with that garbage printed on them," Demange said. "With leaflets, at least we could get the shit off our asses."

The French loudspeakers shouted back a few minutes later. Plenty of anti-Nazi German-speakers, Jews and others, had taken refuge in France. Demange's German was sketchy, but he got the drift here. They were going on about how even the German people couldn't stand Hitler any more, so what was the point of stopping a bullet for him?

"Is that true, sir?" Émile asked. "Are the Germans really up in arms against the Nazis?"

"Beats me," Demange answered cheerfully. "Our papers say they are, and of course you know everything you read in the goddamn newspaper's got to be the straight goods, right?"

"*Mais certainement*," Émile said, cynically enough to squeeze a short chuckle out of Demange.

"All right, then," the lieutenant said. "But I'll tell you this—as long as both sides want to fight the war with loudspeakers, that's fine by me. Yeah, they're annoying as shit. But even if you shoot a loudspeaker full of holes, it won't squirt blood all over the place and it won't start screaming for its mama."

The *poilu* contemplated that. "Well, you aren't wrong," he said in due course. "Uh, sir."

Truth to tell, Demange barely noticed his near-omission of the courtesy. He felt happier about Émile's measured praise than he had about anything in . . . he couldn't remember when. *I'm getting soft,* he thought. He barked at some other soldier the way a man might kick a dog after quarreling with his wife.

Before too long, the powers that be on one side or the other—for all Demange knew, it might have been the powers that be on both sides—decided war by loudspeaker was too peaceable to suit them. Howitzers and mortars started hitting the front-line trenches.

Huddling in the mud—the *springtime* mud—Demange called

down curses on his generals' heads. Artillery duels always hurt the French worse than the *Boches*. As they had been in the last war, the Germans were masters of field fortifications. His own countrymen . . . weren't.

And the Nazis had been sitting on Belgium for years. The Belgian frontier had been the effective border between Germany and France since their unsuccessful truce and alliance against the USSR. What German soldiers took refuge in around here hardly deserved the insulting name of field fortifications. They'd had enough thought and reinforced concrete poured into them to be something else again, something more on the order of the Maginot Line.

Somebody not far enough away started shrieking. He kept on shrieking till the stretcher-bearers carried him away. French fieldworks were just that: scratchings in the dirt. The French brass didn't think their men would stay in any one set very long, so they didn't bother strengthening or improving them. *Poilus* got carved up for their stupidity.

After the sun went down, the Germans staged a trench raid half a kilometer south of Demange's position. They shot half a dozen men and captured half a dozen more for grilling. "We would've chased 'em off if they tried that here," Émile said stoutly.

"*Peut-être*," Demange answered. *Maybe* was the most he could say. He tried to keep his men alert, and more afraid of him than they were of the *Boches*. But anybody could get caught with his pants around his ankles.

Those captured soldiers were probably singing like nightingales. Demange hoped they didn't know too much. *The Germans should have grabbed some generals*, he thought. *Generals never know anything at all.*

Spaniards were big on ceremonies. Chaim Weinberg had had to get used to that when he came over here. Americans went the other way. They did up Independence Day and Memorial Day and Armistice Day after a fashion, but only after a fashion. A ceremony over something that didn't already have a day set aside for it? Americans mostly didn't bother.

With Spaniards, though, if something wasn't celebrated and wasn't seen to be celebrated, it might as well not have happened. Maybe it had to do with the Mass and other Catholic rites. Any which way, the Nationalists didn't just surrender. They and their Republican counterparts staged an elaborate ceremonial to show they were surrendering.

Chaim got invited to the surrender (which took place outside of Seville, the last major city the Nationalists held) because he was one of the longest-serving American Internationals still in Spain. So they told him, anyhow. He wondered whether La Martellita had anything to do with the invitation. He would rather she'd invited him back into her bed, but that wouldn't happen. Little by little, he'd got resigned to the idea. Oh, well—it sure had been fun while it lasted!

He rode a bus down to Seville. All the way there, he wondered whether he ought to go into town and find a barber. When he finally came out with that, most of the other Internationals on the bus groaned. But two of them—a Magyar and an Estonian—said they'd been thinking the same thing. That made Chaim feel better. Other people could be crazy some of the same ways he was.

It wasn't a perfect surrender ceremony, even if the Nationalist soldiers stood there in neat ranks under the old red-and-gold Spanish flag. They'd stacked their arms in front of those ranks. The rifle barrels gleamed in the bright sunshine.

The men were there, yes. Most officers above the rank of major weren't. They'd slipped over the border to General Salazar's Fascist Portugal . . . or they'd been captured, tried at summary courts-martial, and died—for the most part with exemplary courage—in front of Republican firing squads.

Still, the Nationalists did have a general at their head. Millán Astray had founded the Spanish Foreign Legion, which held many of the other side's toughest troops. He was the one who'd given them their *Long live death!* motto. He himself had paid death on the installment plan. He was missing his left arm and his right eye.

But he was here, where so many of his comrades had chosen exile.

He had the courage of his convictions, all right. He was bound to know what would happen after he gave himself up to the Republicans. He could expect no more mercy than he would have given had he won.

He was the bull in this arena, not the matador. He had not even the bull's chance to gore. Yet there he stood, sour, hateful, and brave. Peering at him, Chaim saw that he'd even donned a red-and-gold patch over his empty eye socket for the occasion. Was that loyalty to the cause? Or was it just mockery of the victors? Either way, Chaim found himself reluctantly admiring the tough, mutilated little man. Millán Astray might be a son of a bitch, but he was a son of a bitch with style.

A Republican color guard advanced toward him. The flag of the Spanish Republic—red, yellow, and purple—flew from a taller staff than that of the vanquished Nationalist banner. No one was going to miss any symbolic tricks today.

Some of the Republican bigwigs following the color guard wore uniforms not very different from those of the rebels. Others clung to the overalls that had been a de facto Republican uniform for so long. That was revolutionary chic. General Astray glowered at them, but he could do no more than glower.

He glowered again when the Republican military band played the *Internationale*. The Spanish Foreign Legion went into battle singing songs like "Death's Fiancé!" This was a different tune both literally and metaphorically.

Once the music stopped, a Republican general strode up to Astray. The Nationalist commander saluted. The Republican returned the compliment. Millán Astray reached into his holster and pulled out the pistol it held: no fancy automatic with mother-of-pearl grips, but a beat-up revolver that had plainly seen much use.

Before handing it to the Republican, General Astray said, "You know I would rather kill you with this than give it to you. I know what you would do to my good men, though, so I will go through with what the two sides have agreed."

"There has already been enough killing. There has already been too much killing," the Republican officer said. Newsreel cameras whirred, recording his image and his words. He went on, "Spain is one once more. The killing is over."

Millán Astray wagged a finger at him, as if to say they both knew better. And so they did; the Nationalist general had but hours to live. If that bothered him, he didn't show it. Yes, he had style. With another salute, he presented the revolver to the Republican. Then he asked, "May I have the privilege of addressing my soldiers one last time?"

The Republican general stirred and frowned; maybe that wasn't in the script to which the two sides had agreed. "Briefly," the Republican said at last, "and without inflammatory sentiment."

General Astray's bow was a skeletal parody of the one a dandy might give. "You have my oath," he said, and crossed himself to show he meant it.

"Go on, then," the Republican said gruffly.

Turning, Astray also bowed to the Nationalists standing at wooden attention. "Well, boys, we did the best we could. We thought we'd cut revolution out of Spain the way you cut a cancer from the body. Instead, revolution's gone and cut us out. You don't know ahead of time what will happen in a war. You wouldn't need to fight it if you did. We wouldn't have given them a big kiss if we'd won. I don't expect they'll kiss us, either, now that we've lost. You're men—you're proved it. Be strong. Sooner or later, you'll come out the other side." He saluted them. "¡Viva la España! ¡Viva la muerte, amigos!"

"¡Viva la muerte!" the Nationalist soldiers shouted.

Millán Astray turned back to the Republican general. "Do what you want with me—you will anyway," he said. "Go easy on them. They're just soldiers."

"We will do what we will do," the Republican answered in a voice like iron. Chaim suspected he had a better idea himself of what that would be like than General Astray did. The Nationalists would go through reeducation camps, all of them. The ones who were just soldiers, and not too bright, would get out after a few months. They'd be watched the rest of their lives, of course. They'd have trouble getting good jobs. Their sons wouldn't be likely to get into good schools. But, after a fashion, they'd get along.

The sergeants, the lieutenants, the captains . . . They wouldn't get off so lightly. They'd do hard labor on short rations for a long time. None of them would come out of the camps for years. A lot of them wouldn't come out at all, unless they did it feet-first.

In Yiddish, he whispered to the Magyar who'd also thought about the barber of Seville: "Those Fascist bastards are gonna have a rough time."

"After everything they did, they deserve a rough time," the Hungarian International replied in Bela Lugosi–flavored German.

"Well, yeah." Chaim couldn't let such a challenge go unanswered. He was asking to get reported if he did. Then he'd get to find out about reeducation camps from the inside. He found a question to distract from his last comment: "What'll you do now that the war here is over?"

"Go fight the Nazis—*aber natürlich*," the Magyar replied. "You?"

"Maybe I'll do that," Chaim said. "Or maybe I'll go home, then come back and fight 'em in my own country's uniform."

That shut the Hungarian up. Soldiers in *his* country's uniform marched side by side with Hitler's men. Pleased with himself, Chaim watched the Nationalists trudge off into captivity.

Vaclav Jezek stood with the rest of the soldiers of the Czechoslovakian government-in-exile as a Spanish Republican brigadier general harangued them. The general spoke no Czech—as far as Vaclav could tell, you could count the number of Spaniards who did speak Czech on the fingers of one hand, and you wouldn't need to worry about the thumb or the pinkie. The officer delivered his speech in lisping Spanish.

Like most of his countrymen, Vaclav understood at best one word in ten—not even enough to catch the drift. He turned to Benjamin Halévy. "What's he going on about?" Halévy could make sense of Spanish, along with several other languages.

He could, and he did: "He's telling us what a bunch of heroes we are. Tigers of valor, he calls us."

"Does that sound as stupid in Spanish as it does in Czech?" Jezek asked, genuinely curious.

"Just about," said the Parisian Jew with the parents from Prague. The Republican general gave forth with a gesture straight out of grand opera. It must have signaled a change of subject, because Halévy went on, "Oh—now he's going on about how many Hitlerite Fascists we're going to kill once we get to Belgium."

"Happy day," Vaclav said. With the fighting in Spain over and done with, the foreign contingents that had fought for the Republic were heading home if their homes happened to be free, or into battle against the Nazis if their homes remained occupied.

"You've paid your dues and then some," Halévy said. "You could probably find a way to get a discharge."

"Sure—I could go to a whorehouse," Vaclav said. The Jew sent him a severe look. Ignoring it, he continued, "What I really want to do most is go home. And that's the one thing I can't manage."

He'd grown up in Prague. His family had lived there for as long as anybody could remember. And Prague had lain under the Germans' muscular thumb for the past five and a half years. Of all the lands Hitler had overrun, Bohemia and Moravia would be the last ones he coughed up. The Red Army might march into Berlin before it marched into Prague. And even if it did march into Prague, the Russians would make landlords almost as nasty as the pigdogs with the swastika-clutching eagles on their tunics.

Benjamin Halévy set a hand on his shoulder in mute sympathy. A moment later, Vaclav jerked off the hand, not from anger but from surprise. The Republican general had just come out with a very Spanish version of his name. He wouldn't have recognized it if he hadn't heard the like before.

"What's he want?" he hissed to Halévy.

"Go up to him," the Jew answered, also sotto voce.

Vaclav did. The Spaniard shook his hand and did the double cheek-brush so beloved by Latins (and by old-fashioned Austrians and Magyars pining for the lost days of the Dual Monarchy). Then the man switched from his own language to trilled, lisped German: "Can you understand me?"

"Yes, sir," Vaclav said.

"Good. You are much to thank for our victory. You shot the enemy of the people, Franco. Then you shot the bigger enemy of the people, Sanjurjo. Spain never forgets you for this."

"Thank you very much, sir."

"Remember, we make you for this an honorary citizen of Spain. If you ever need help, a Spanish ambassador gives it to you, same as if you were born here."

"I do remember, and I thank you for that, too, sir," Vaclav replied. It might even actually mean something, especially since the brigadier handed him a scroll and a passport that made it highly official. Czechoslovakia, these days, was more a defiant state of mind than anything else. Having connections with a country that really existed could be useful, all right.

His own countrymen gave him three cheers as he returned to the ranks. The Republican general went back to Spanish to finish his speech. Most of it, Vaclav realized, was for local consumption. The Republic was showing its own people how nice it was to its foreign allies.

When they got on the train that would take them up to France, the Republic showed its gratitude in a real way. It put them in second-class cars with padded seats, not on the hard benches of third class. Vaclav wiggled in his. "I could get used to this," he said.

"Don't," Halévy told him. "As soon as we cross the border, it's liable to be 8 HORSES OR 36 MEN."

"A box car!" Jezek made a face. That was what the French painted on the sides of each one so nobody could mess up the carrying capacity. "They really know how to show they care, don't they?"

"They care that we can kill some *Boches* for them. They care that they can use you up—and me, too—instead of some genuine Frenchmen," Halévy told him. "Don't worry about it, *mon vieux*. Pretty soon, the Spaniards won't care, either."

"You know how to make me feel good, don't you?" Vaclav answered his own question before the Jew could: "Nah. If you were a blonde with no morals, then you'd know how to make me feel good."

"Funny guy." Halévy glanced over at the antitank rifle leaning against the wood paneling of the second-class car's wall. "I wish Hitler would come within a couple of kilometers of the front. Then you could do unto him as you did unto Sanjurjo. But from what I hear, Hitler didn't take chances like that even before you plugged the Marshal."

"Too bad." Vaclav cocked his head to one side and studied Halévy. "How do you hear shit like that?"

"I keep my eyes open." Halévy paused for effect. "My nose sees all kinds of interesting things, too."

"Will it see my fist if I punch it?" Vaclav didn't bother to find out. He was just joking around.

When they got to the border in the Pyrenees, a Spanish military band played a farewell for them even though it was the middle of the night. The French soldiers on the other side seemed much less interested. They herded the Czechs to the next train. They didn't thrust them into box cars smelling greenly of horseshit. They did give them third-class cars with hard benches jammed too close together. Vaclav would have been more annoyed had he been more surprised.

No one on the French side of the border cared at all about the Czechs' Spanish rank badges and medals. The French attitude was that foreign badges on foreign men meant nothing in their country. Three officers with fancy kepis did take Benjamin Halévy off to one side and question him for more than an hour before they finally let the troop train roll out of the station.

"What was *that* all about?" Vaclav asked. "They think you were smuggling hashish or something?"

"Worse than that—much worse." Halévy rolled his eyes. "They said I was wearing rank badges I wasn't entitled to. That a sergeant should become an officer while they weren't looking . . . Not so long ago, it would have been a matter for Devil's Island. We spoke of this before, and about how they wouldn't let me stay promoted."

"Uh-huh. Like I told you then, fucking good thing your name isn't Dreyfus," Vaclav said.

"You've got that right. But he was already an officer. Not me! They accept no such improper promotions, as they made ever so clear," Halévy said. "So I'm just a noncom again, and lucky to be that. They also made it clear how lucky I am. They could have court-martialed me for going on with the war while they were busy sucking up to Hitler."

"Sucking him off, you mean," Vaclav said savagely.

Halévy waved a forefinger at him: a very French gesture. "You can talk about them like that. They aren't your superiors. They are mine, and I'm stuck with them. They did finally admit I still enjoy the privilege of dying for my country. Isn't patriotism grand? Oh, and have you got a cigarette?" They smoked while the train clattered north and east, toward the bigger war.

Chapter 20

Colonel Steinbrenner climbed up onto a wooden crate so everybody in the squadron could see him. Hans-Ulrich Rudel was up near the front of the crowd anyway, as usual. Even by German standards, he was compulsively punctual. And he wanted to hear what the squadron CO had to say.

Sergeant Dieselhorst stood behind Rudel and to his left. A cigarette dangled from the corner of Dieselhorst's mouth. That and his elaborately uninterested expression made him look like an American gangster. Hans-Ulrich didn't own enough of a death wish to tell him so.

Steinbrenner raised a hand. The flyers and groundcrew men fell silent. Everybody wondered what was going on. The colonel had summoned them all, but he hadn't said why.

"The *Führer's* going to talk tonight," Steinbrenner said. "Some of you will already know that, but I want to make sure nobody misses it. This is supposed to be one of the most important speeches he's given since the war started. You'll want to hear it for yourselves instead of getting it by bits and pieces from the newscasts and the papers." His arm shot up and out in the Party salute. *"Heil* Hitler!"

"*Heil* Hitler!" the men echoed, returning the gesture as they shouted the slogan.

Hans-Ulrich wanted to hear Hitler speak. Part of what made the *Führer* so marvelous was that, while you listened to him, all your doubts disappeared. Rudel had plenty of doubts he needed to exorcise.

"Good," Steinbrenner said. "I hope that, after he speaks, we'll have a better notion of where we're going and what we've got to do to get there. Whatever it is, for Germany's sake, we'll do it."

"*Heil* Hitler!" the *Luftwaffe* men chorused again. Along with most of the others, Hans-Ulrich gave the Party salute once more. The squadron commander returned it.

As the men drifted apart, Albert Dieselhorst came up alongside Hans-Ulrich. "Well, that was interesting," the radioman and rear gunner remarked.

"Interesting how?" Rudel asked.

"Mm, for one thing, the colonel talked to us about this speech himself. He didn't give the job to Major Keller. I would've guessed the National Socialist Loyalty Officer would have told us about political stuff."

"That's true. I hadn't thought about it, but it is," Hans-Ulrich said. "Whatever the *Führer*'s going to say, then, it must be important—especially since he's speaking from Münster."

"Yes. Especially." Sergeant Dieselhorst's voice was dry. Neither of them seemed to want to take that any further. The less you said about a place where rebellion still bubbled, the better off you were. After they walked on for a few more steps, Dieselhorst added, "And the colonel didn't say anything about what'll be in the speech."

"I guess he doesn't know," Hans-Ulrich said.

Dieselhorst nodded. "I guess you're right. But that's interesting, too. Most of the time, when the big cheese is going to come out with one of these fancy speeches, the brass has a pretty good idea of what he'll say ahead of time. They need to know which way to jump, and they need to get us peasants ready to jump that way."

"Huh." That hadn't occurred to Hans-Ulrich, either. He eyed his worldly crewmate. "All these things you know, all these things you think about, how come you're not a Party *Bonz* yourself?"

The sergeant started to say something, then plainly decided not to. After a few more steps, he took another shot at it: "I never much wanted to have anything to do with politics, sir. You have to tell too many lies to too many people. Doesn't matter a bit which side of the fence you're on. You just do. It's part of the game, the same way dive brakes are part of the Stuka's game."

"Huh," Rudel said again. "I never looked at it like that."

"Of course not, sir. You think telling a lie's a sin." Dieselhorst sounded amused and indulgent, the way a father might while talking about his little boy's antics. "I'm just not very good at it, and I don't think it's much fun. So I'm better off here in the *Luftwaffe* than I would be working in some *Gauleiter*'s office."

Hans-Ulrich started to deny that he thought lying was sinful. As Dieselhorst had before him, he caught himself. He couldn't deny it unless he felt like lying himself—which would indeed be a sin. You could put a preacher's son in the cockpit of a warplane. You could even turn a preacher's son into a good National Socialist. What you couldn't do was make him forget who his father was, and what his father stood for.

All he did say, then, was, "I guess I wouldn't make such a great politician, either, then."

That got a laugh out of Sergeant Dieselhorst. "Maybe not. Each cat his own rat, or that's what they say."

"Is it?" Hans-Ulrich hadn't heard it before, but he'd long since decided that Dieselhorst had done and heard all kinds of things he hadn't.

He realized Germans wouldn't be the only ones listening to this speech. It would go all over the world by shortwave. It would be history in the making. That made him want the sun to speed across the sky and set so he could find out what was on the *Führer*'s mind.

It gave Dieselhorst different ideas. "What do you want to bet every *Luftwaffe* pilot who flies anything faster than a Stuka will be over Münster and its approaches while Hitler's talking to make sure the RAF doesn't drop any bombs on him?"

Hans-Ulrich hadn't thought of that, but he nodded. "Makes sense to me."

He ate supper without paying much attention to what went into his mess tin. Considering the stews the field kitchen turned out, that might have been just as well. After he cleaned up the kit, he joined the crowd of *Luftwaffe* men gathered in front of a radio hooked up to a truck battery. At the moment, someone was playing Bach on a piano. Some of the flyers and groundcrew men looked bored. Rudel enjoyed the music; he'd been listening to it since he was a baby. That was another souvenir from his father.

Then the Bach program ended. The radio played "*Deutschland über Alles*" and the "*Horst Wessel Lied*": national anthem and Party anthem. That was what they always did before they broadcast anything important.

"Here is the beloved *Führer* of the *Grossdeutsches Reich,* Adolf Hitler, speaking to the German *Volk* and to the world from the city of Münster," gabbled an announcer with an excited voice.

"People of Germany, I have come to Münster to tear up treason by the roots," Hitler declared. "It is because of treason that our war against the Jew Bolsheviks of Moscow and the Jew capitalists of London and Paris and New York City has not gone as well as we should have hoped. They are not content with corrupting the peasant *Untermenschen* and mongrel factory workers they exploit. No! Instead, they whisper their filthy venom into German ears as well."

He had an Austrian accent and an Austrian habit of peppering everything he said with particles: little words that added emphasis but that many, maybe even most, German-speakers would have left out. But his voice was such a splendid instrument that even such tics seemed not to matter—no, seemed to disappear—after a sentence or two.

"When Germans seek to rise against the German state and seek to hinder the struggle against Bolshevist barbarism, they cannot be doing this on their own. No, they must be incited by outside agitators, and by the filthy, wicked Jews still resident in the *Reich*. And they must be punished for their betrayal of *Volkisch* ideals. They must be, and they shall be!" Hitler's voice rose and grew more urgent. "We will make them bend the knee! We will make them tremble in fear. We will—"

The speech abruptly broke off. There was a noise that might have been a shot or might have been an explosion. Then only the soft, staticky hiss of the carrier wave came out of the radio.

Theo Hossbach sprawled on the grass with the other crewmen from his panzer and the rest of the regiment, listening to the *Führer* telling the world about what he was going to do to Münster and the people who lived there. The radio was turned up loud so everyone could hear in spite of the noise from all the airplanes overhead.

And then, all of a sudden, the speech stopped. Theo heard a kind of a bang from the radio. At almost the same time, he heard kind of a bang from the direction of Münster.

"*Scheisse!*" one of the men in black panzer coveralls said loudly. He got up and whacked the radio with the heel of his hand. It went on hissing, but the *Führer*'s speech didn't come back. He said "*Scheisse!*" again, even louder than the first time.

Adi Stoss leaned toward Theo. "The trouble's not in the set, is it?" he murmured.

Since Theo was a radioman, he supposed he was the logical one to ask. He hadn't checked out the radio, though, and he hated being wrong even more than he hated talking in general. All the same, some kind of answer seemed called for. "I . . . wouldn't think so," he said reluctantly.

That hiss went on and on, probably for two or three minutes. More bangs and booms came from the direction of Münster, though not from the radio set. That might not have meant anything much. You could hear bangs and booms from Münster almost every night. The people in town who didn't fancy the regime used darkness as a camouflage cloak to help them strike at its backers. The timing now seemed intriguing, though.

"Change the frequency," someone suggested. "See if we can pick up something somewhere else."

"No, leave it." Hermann Witt spoke up with a panzer commander's authority. "Something funny's going on. The *Führer*'s station wouldn't crap out for no reason at all."

There was another interesting point. Had Hitler's station crapped out not for no reason but for some reason? If it had, what would that reason be?

No sooner had that thought crossed Theo's mind than a voice started coming out of the radio. It wasn't Hitler's voice. Instead of sounding like a professional rabble-rouser, this fellow seemed tired unto death and had a harsh, abrupt Prussian way of talking.

"Good evening, people of Germany and people of the world," he said. "I am Colonel General Heinz Guderian. I find myself heading the Committee for the Salvation of the German Nation."

"The *what*?" Several people there in front of the radio said the same thing at the same time.

"As I speak to you, Adolf Hitler is dead," Guderian went on. "We have removed him from power because he led Germany into a war that did not succeed, and because he threw away any chance of a fair result by bringing the United States of America into the European conflict. We took this step with great reluctance, but we also took it with great resolution. Even more than in the last war, the United States is an enemy Germany cannot hope to overcome."

"Sweet Jesus Christ!" a panzer crewman exclaimed not far from Theo. "What do we do now?"

"Some people may not be happy that we have assumed authority in this way," Guderian continued, which had to rank as one of the champion understatements of all time. "This being so, we need to make it very plain that the Nazi Party is no longer the ruling party in Germany, and is no longer the only party in Germany. As I speak, forces loyal to the Salvation Committee are arresting Göring, Goebbels, Hess, and Himmler."

"Sweet Jesus!" That same voice rang out again.

"Soldiers of the *Reich,* sailors of the *Reich,* flying men of the *Reich,* obey your officers and carry on. We have taken this action to secure an honorable peace, and we believe we can," Guderian said. "Men who would not confer with Hitler because of his endless lies will do so with our trustworthy officers and civilian representatives. All sides must see that peace is preferable to the past five and a half years of slaughter and destruction. God will surely bless our cause. Thank you, and good night."

"Deutschland über Alles" rang out again. The *"Horst Wessel Lied"* didn't. That told Theo the Salvation Committee was running the radio station, anyhow.

More Bach poured out of the radio set. It was good, calm, peaceful, churchgoing music, music that advertised a good, calm, peaceful, churchgoing Germany to the listening world. Theo hoped the listening world was paying attention. He also hoped the Salvation Committee could get away with the coup—and that Guderian hadn't been lying through his teeth when he talked about the Committee's program.

And he hoped Germany itself and the German armed forces were feeling good and calm and peaceful, whether churchgoing or not. Hitler and the Nazis had been running the country for more than eleven years. They'd had plenty of time to plant their doctrines in people's heads, plenty of time for those doctrines to flower and fruit.

Off in the distance, a Schmeisser opened up. An MG-42 answered it. Yes, not everyone would be thrilled to see the *Führer* overthrown. Which side was the Schmeisser-toter on, and to which side did the machine gunner belong?

Before Theo could do more than frame the question, somebody right here in the crowd of panzer crewmen shouted, "They can't get away with plotting against the *Führer!*"

"The hell they can't!" somebody else yelled. Yes, the chickens were coming home to roost, and they weren't wasting any time doing it.

With a meaty thud, somebody's fist connected with someone else's jaw. Somebody yelled "Death to the traitors!" at the same time as somebody else yelled "Down with the Nazi swine!"

In an instant, the panzer crews were flailing away, sometimes one against another, sometimes man against man inside a single crew as some showed they were for Hitler and others against him. Theo stuck out a leg and tripped a man he knew to be a loudmouthed Nazi. When he scrambled to his feet, one boot just happened to connect with the back of the loudmouth's head. It was only an accident, of course. Of course.

He wasn't astonished to discover that Adi had flattened another Party sympathizer. If you were sitting next to somebody like that, what were you supposed to do? Wait till he flattened you? Not likely!

"Back to the panzer!" Sergeant Witt shouted. "My crew, back to the panzer!"

Theo couldn't remember the last order he'd liked better. Inside the Panzer IV, they'd be safe from the slings and arrows of outraged National Socialists. And they could do some slinging and arrowing of their own if they had to.

On which side would they do it, though? Theo was sure of where he and Adi stood. He was pretty sure about Hermann Witt, too. Eckhardt and Poske, though . . . They'd never shown any sign of wanting to give Adi grief. That argued their hearts were in the right place.

Someone got in front of Adi and fell down quite suddenly. Whoever he was, he didn't get up again. They scrambled into their panzer, slammed the hatches shut, and dogged them.

"Fire it up, Adi," Witt said. "I won't shoot first, but this is liable to be a big mess. We'll take cover and figure things out later."

"I'll do it, Sergeant," Stoss said. "That sounds like a terrific plan." The engine rumbled to life.

Theo put on his radio earphones just in time to hear somebody say, "Our regiment stands behind the Committee for the Salvation of the German Nation. We will obey orders coming from the Committee."

Schmeissers started barking, almost surely inside the encampment. As Adi put the Panzer IV in gear, another panzer's main armament bellowed. Not all the regiment seemed ready to stand behind the Salvation Committee. Theo had wondered whether the coup would touch off a civil war. He wasn't wondering any more.

Julius Lemp had always admired Colonel General Guderian. From everything he could see, the man got as much out of his panzers as anybody was likely to get. With every country's hand—and factories—raised against the *Reich*—what could be more important?

He'd wondered about that for a long time. Now he had an answer. The Committee for the Salvation of the German Nation could be. Or the forces fighting the Committee could be, depending on who won.

They were going at it hammer and tongs. Kiel sounded as if it were in the middle of the world's biggest fireworks display. If you looked out the window, you might think it was. Tracers and shell bursts lit up the night sky, now here, now there, now suddenly all over the place.

Of course, if you looked out the window you were also liable to get killed. Plenty of bullets that weren't tracers were flying around. Rifles, submachine guns, and MG-34s and MG-42s added to the hideous cacophony. And a barracks hall across the courtyard from the one where Lemp was staying had taken a direct hit from a 105 round—or maybe it was a 155. Whatever it was, it had knocked down half the building and set the wreckage on fire. Sailors were hosing down the burning rubble and pawing through it, looking for people who might still be alive.

The really scary thing was, Lemp had no idea which side had shelled that barracks, or why. If something had come down over there, something could come down on this hall, too. He could die without having any idea why, or even who'd killed him.

He hadn't signed up for that. (He'd signed up so he could surprise people on the other side and send them to the bottom, but he didn't dwell on such things right this minute.)

Most of the *Kriegsmarine,* he judged, would go along with the Salvation Committee. Naval officers tended to be conservative professionals who had no great love for the Nazis.

Naval officers, yes. Ratings? Ratings might be another story. Or they might not. With a small start, Lemp realized he knew less than he should about what kind of politics ratings had. Some of them liked Hitler—he knew that. The ones who didn't . . . The ones who didn't commonly had sense enough to keep their mouths shut about it.

Someone knocked on the door.

The knock on the door in the middle of the night. Everyone's worst nightmare, in the *Reich* no less than in the USSR. In ordinary times, at least you knew what to say when they came for you. Chances were a thousand to one it wouldn't do you any good, but you tried. How could you even try, though, when you weren't sure which faction the goons out there belonged to?

Lemp thought about pretending not to be there. But if they broke down the door (or just opened it—it wasn't locked), things would go worse for him afterwards. The Committee or the Party? The lady or the tiger? He'd know in a second.

He opened the door.

Two petty officers with Mausers and a lieutenant with a Schmeisser scowled at him from the hallway. "Which side are you on?" one of the petty officers growled.

They didn't tell him which side they were on. He'd either be right or he'd be dead. "The Committee," he said. If not for the *Gestapo* man with the lizardy blinks and tongue licks who'd plucked Nehring from his boat for no visible reason, he might well have answered the other way. He hated the idea of going against duly constituted authority. But when duly constituted authority was a pack of hooligans, he hated giving in to it even more.

Had he answered the other way, he would have been lying in a pool of his own blood a few seconds later. As things were, the armed men grinned like fierce baboons. "There you go, sir!" the petty officer said. Now he gave Lemp his title of respect. *Now I've earned it,* Lemp thought dizzily.

"Have you got a weapon?" the lieutenant asked.

"No. It's back in my cabin on the U-boat," Lemp answered. "I didn't think I'd need to go shooting things up."

"Here. Use this, then." The lieutenant pulled a Walther pistol from his belt. Gingerly, Lemp took it. The lieutenant went on, "Come with us. We're cleaning out the Nazi turds."

"They're trying to clean us out, too," Lemp remarked as stuttering machine guns dueled outside.

"That's why I gave you the Walther, sir," the lieutenant said patiently.

Lemp had no idea how he'd do, shooting it out with the other side through doors and around corners. This wasn't the kind of warfare he'd trained for. Regardless of whether he'd trained for it, it was the kind of warfare he had.

They'd started down the hall toward the next room when a tremendous blast of noise staggered them all. "Good God!" Lemp exclaimed. "What the devil just blew up?"

"Nothing," the lieutenant answered. Lemp could barely hear him; his ears were stunned. The younger man went on, "That was *Gneisenau's* broadside. She's with us."

"Good God!" Lemp said again. He'd known the battle cruiser was in port, but it hadn't meant anything special to him. Why should it have? He'd had nothing to do with battle cruisers—not till civil war broke out, anyhow. But the *Gneisenau* mounted nine 280mm guns. They could throw their enormous shells at least thirty kilometers. Nothing on land could stand up to that kind of bombardment. Nothing anywhere could, except for the thickest armor on a few battleships. "What are they shooting at?"

"Beats me," the lieutenant said cheerfully. "Whatever it was, it isn't there any more."

He was bound to be right about that. Bombs from a Stuka might do for the warship. Lemp couldn't think of anything else that would. The *Gneisenau* ruled as far as its great guns would reach.

They knocked on the next door. A captain opened it. "Which side are you on?" the petty officer demanded.

The captain's answer was proud and prompt: "I am loyal to the legitimate government of the *Grossdeutsches Reich*." In case anyone doubted what that was, his right arm shout up and out. "*Heil* Hitler!"

His answer was proud and prompt—and wrong. Both petty officers shot him, one in the chest, the other in the face. He shrieked and crumpled. Lemp's stomach tried to turn over. No, this wasn't the kind of killing he was used to.

Gunfire inside the barracks made a couple of officers stick their heads out into the hallway to find out what was going on. One of them hastily ducked back into his room and slammed the door behind him. The other man fired at Lemp and his comrades with a service pistol.

He was only ten or twelve meters away, but he missed. He missed three times in quick succession, as a matter of fact. He probably hadn't won a marksman's badge when he qualified with the pistol back in the day, and chances were he hadn't fired it more than two or three times in all the years since.

Combat was the hardest school around. The officer never got a chance for his fourth shot. The lieutenant loosed three quick, professional bursts from his Schmeisser. You didn't really need to aim the machine pistol. You just had to point it, which was much simpler. Down went the pro-Nazi officer.

He wasn't down for the count, though. He groped for the pistol, which he'd dropped when he fell. One of the petty officers shot him through the head. He kept thrashing even after that, but to no purpose, not with his brains splashed on the linoleum and the white-painted wall.

"Come on," the lieutenant said. "We'll clean up this floor and go on to the next." Lemp numbly followed. He hadn't fired a Walther for quite a while himself. *Have to get my hands on a Schmeisser,* he thought.

Ivan Kuchkov had seen a lot in his days fighting the Hitlerites. One of the things he'd seldom seen, though, was a German coming forward under a large flag of truce. Oh, every once in a while one side or the other would ask for a cease-fire to pick up the wounded. But that was just a little pause in the business of killing one another. This felt different.

The approaching German here wasn't a sergeant, or even a captain. He was a colonel with a gray mustache. And he spoke Russian, something not many Fritzes did.

"I would like to be taken back to your high command!" he called as he strode forward. "I am here to ask for a truce along a broad stretch of front. Perhaps we can have peace."

Beside Kuchkov, Sasha Davidov looked as if his eyes were about to bug right out of his head. "I never heard a German talk that way before," the *Zhid* whispered. "I never knew Germans *could* talk that way."

"Me, neither," Ivan said. "'Course, chances are it's all moonshine and horseshit."

"I wouldn't be surprised," his point man answered. "What'll you do, though?"

"I'll fucking well take him back to Lieutenant Obolensky, that's what," Ivan said. "Let him figure it all out. That's what officers are for."

He stood up, showing himself amidst the tall grass and bushes. The

German colonel turned to come straight toward him. "Good day, Sergeant," he said in that accented schoolboy Russian.

"*Yob tvoyu mat*'," Ivan answered with a nasty grin. The Fritz turned red, so he understood it. Well, tough luck. Ivan gestured with his PPD. "Come along with me, bitch."

He didn't have far to go to find Lieutenant Obolensky. The young company commander was only a couple of hundred meters to the rear. He slid out from behind some bushes and said, "Well, Comrade Sergeant, what have you got here?"

"Prick's a Nazi colonel, Comrade Lieutenant," Ivan said, which was obvious anyhow. "Wants to fucking parley with our brass."

"Does he always talk like that?" the German asked plaintively.

"*Da*," Lieutenant Obolensky said. That made the Fritz blink. Obolensky went on, "Tell me who you are and what you want."

"I have the honor to be Karl-Friedrich von Holtzendorf. I am a staff officer attached to Army Group Ukraine," the German said. "As you may have heard, there has been a change of government and a change of policy in the *Reich*."

"Hitler screwed the pooch, so you got rid of him," Ivan said. Obolensky held out his hand with the palm flat to the ground, trying to shush him. Ivan made a disgusted face. He didn't want to waste politeness on a bastard who wore *Feldgrau*.

To his surprise, Colonel von Holtzendorf nodded. "That is about the size of it, Sergeant, yes. We are trying to find reasonable terms to end these unfortunate conflicts."

"One man's reasonable is another man's outrageous," Obolensky observed. Kuchkov would have said the same thing, but he would have put more oomph into it.

"I understand that," von Holtzendorf said. "I have come to find out what terms your military and your government believe to be reasonable. Can you please radio your army-group—no, you say your front—headquarters and let them know I am coming?"

"I'll send you back to regimental HQ," Obolensky said. "They should have a radio, if it's working. If it's not, they'll take you back farther. Sooner or later, you'll get where you want to go."

Karl-Friedrich von Holtzendorf's left eyebrow jumped toward the bill of his high-crowned cap. If he'd been wearing a monocle in that eye like a Nazi officer in a movie, it would have fallen out. Ivan understood why the Fritz looked so scandalized. He was sure every company—maybe every section—in the *Wehrmacht* had a radio set. He was also sure almost all of them worked almost all the time. The Germans were great for using lots and lots of fancy equipment.

It helped them only so much. The Red Army was great for using lots and lots of Russians—and every other folk in the Soviet Union. Had it had the Hitlerites' fancy gear, it might not have had to spend so many men. *Fungible*, Ivan thought once more. But you did what you could with what you had. The Red Army had soldiers, and used them . . . and used them up.

"Comrade Sergeant, tell off three men. You and they will take Colonel von Holtzendorf"—Obolensky pronounced it *Goltzendorf*, since Russian had no *h* sound—"to regimental headquarters. About four kilometers that way." He pointed northeast.

"I serve the Soviet Union!" Ivan said. He nodded to the German. "Don't get your pussy lost, sweetheart. I'll be back fast as a fart."

He grabbed two tough guys and Sasha Davidov. "I don't want to have anything to do with that goddamn Nazi shithead," the Jew said.

"Not even to tell him how many knots you feel like tying in his dick?" Ivan asked slyly.

"Well, when you put it that way . . ." Davidov came along with no more backtalk. Ivan chuckled to himself. If you knew what made somebody tick, you could get him to do anything you wanted.

Grubby Red Army Jew and aristocratic *Wehrmacht* officer eyed each other with undisguised suspicion and loathing. Kuchkov had Colonel von Holtzendorf keep carrying the white flag. "Wouldn't want one of our fuckers shooting you by mistake. That'd be such a cocksucking shame," he said.

"I think so," the German agreed. "I would not want that, either."

"No—way better they should shoot you on purpose," Sasha said.

"I am trying to stop the fighting," von Holtzendorf said. "I don't know if I can, but I am trying."

"And how much did you try the last few years?" the Jew returned.

"They don't give medals like that to peacemakers." The colonel wore the German Cross in Gold and the Iron Cross First Class on his chest, as well as the ribbon for the Iron Cross Second Class and two wound badges. No, he hadn't always been a peacemaker. Germans usually wore their medals in the field, even if it gave their foes a better shot at them. Pride came in all shapes.

Von Holtzendorf shrugged. "I fought in the last war, too. I have two sons in the *Wehrmacht,* one north of here and the other in Belgium. They would be about your age. If I succeed in this, maybe none of my grandsons will have to find out what sleeping in a trench is like."

"Alevai," Davidov said. That wasn't Russian or, evidently, German either. He didn't explain it. Instead, he went on, "Did you people really get rid of Hitler?" Unlike Lieutenant Obolensky, he could say *h.*

"We did. We had to," the colonel answered. "He went too far."

"He got you into this cunt of a war, and you didn't fucking win it," Ivan translated.

"Among other things," von Holtzendorf said. "Finally, among too many other things."

"Is Himmler dead, too?" Sasha asked.

"I . . . think so. There are conflicting reports," Colonel von Holtzendorf replied. "It is certain, though, that the SS still resists the Salvation Committee."

Ivan laughed, but only to himself. If the Germans had bought themselves a civil war, how were they going to fight the foreign enemies they'd made for themselves? He chuckled again. If he could see that, he was sure people like Stalin and Molotov could, too.

They got to the tents housing regimental headquarters in less than an hour. The sight of a Fascist colonel made the place bubble like a forgotten kettle of shchi. Ivan wasn't thrilled about turning von Holtzendorf loose, but he did. And what would come of it . . . well, who the hell could say?

Chapter 21

Saul Goldman snuggled the Panzer IV into a corner so it was shielded by a house on one side and a stone wall in front. He wasn't just worried about the pro-Hitler panzer crews from his regiment. Some of the *Waffen*-SS men who'd failed to protect their precious *Führer* drove Tigers. It would have taken a lot more stone than was in that wall to shield the Panzer IV from one of their rounds.

His family lived only a few kilometers away. He hoped they were all right. Hope was all he could do right now; he hadn't yet dared go see them. The Salvation Committee hadn't done anything about the Nazis' anti-Semitic laws, but no one on that side went around screaming *The Jews are our misfortune!* Still, he wasn't just a Jew. He was a Jew with a murder charge hanging over his head.

But, no matter what else he was, he was also a German soldier fighting for the people trying to overthrow the Nazis. No matter what he did with the rest of his life, the way it looked to him was that he could live a long time on the credit he was piling up in these few hectic days.

If he could live at all. Hermann Witt spoke a warning to the crew:

"Keep an eye peeled for ordinary infantrymen, too. A lot of the clowns they've got around here still think they ought to be going *Sieg heil!*"

"That goes double for you, Sergeant," Saul said. "You're the one who's got to keep sticking his head up out of the cupola to find out what's going on."

"Don't worry about me," Witt told him. "You tend to your job, and I'll tend to mine."

"Yes, Mommy," Saul said sweetly. Everybody in the panzer laughed. Everybody knew he was kidding on the square just the same.

"I only wish the two sides had different colors," Kurt Poske said. "I hate the idea of shooting at somebody who's with us by mistake."

All the panzer crewmen agreed with that. Even Theo nodded. But Sergeant Witt said, "What can you do?" and no one had a good answer for him. The Salvation Committee's colors were black, white, and red, just like the Nazis'. The Nazis, of course, slapped swastikas all over everything. The Salvation Committee had gone back to the flag of the German Empire, a horizontal tricolor.

Saul did think the Salvation Committee was smart to steer clear of the Weimar Republic's black, gold, and red. Few Germans had happy memories of the Republic. If more had been happy with it, Hitler wouldn't have found it so easy to overthrow.

And, of course, if more people had been happy with the present regime, Hitler would still be running things. But the German generals, faced with the idea of a two-front war against two industrial powers that each outclassed and outmanned the *Reich* (plus England and France, which between themselves and their colonies also outproduced and outmanned Germany), decided that they had to find a peace even if—especially if—Hitler didn't want to.

Out of nowhere, Theo spoke up: "You know what's really crazy?"

"You mean, besides you?" Saul said. He couldn't let something so unusual pass unremarked.

Theo ignored him. "What's really crazy is, so many stupid fools want what's left of the Nazis to keep running things."

Weeks went by when Theo didn't say so much of his own accord. He'd hit on something important here, though, or Saul thought he had. Everything Hitler had done since the war started had pushed Germany straight toward the cliff. The *Wehrmacht* hadn't taken Paris. France fought on. So did England. Joining Poland's war against Russia hadn't knocked out the Bolsheviks. Now the *Reich* was falling back or being driven back on all fronts. Why would anybody with a working set of marbles want to see more of that kind of performance?

"Hello!" Witt said suddenly. "We've got what looks like a couple of companies of foot soldiers moving across our front. Now—which side are they on?" Saul couldn't see them from the driver's seat; the stone wall blocked his view. After a moment probably spent raising binoculars to his face, the panzer commander grunted. "Ha! They've got swastika armbands! Kurt! Canister!"

"Canister!" Poske echoed. After a couple of seconds, the round clanged into the breech. The loader had to reach down and out to grab it, then bring it back and slam it home. The panzer carried only a handful of canister rounds. The crew didn't need them very often, and naturally stowed them in the most out-of-the-way ammunition racks.

When you did fire one, though, it could do horrible things. The panzer's canister rounds were basically 75mm shotgun shells. They were full of lead balls, and at short range they could ruin a crowd like nothing else on God's green earth.

The turret traversed a little. The gun came down to shoot just over the wall. "Fire, Lothar!" Witt yelled. "They know we're here. The motion must've tipped them."

"On the way!" Lothar Eckhardt said, and the gun boomed. Then the gunner muttered, "Oh, dear Lord!" Saul couldn't see what the round had done to the pro-Nazi foot soldiers, but that told him everything he needed to know.

Almost everything—a second later, a rifle round rang off the turret. It hadn't a hope in hell of punching through, but it showed the canister shell hadn't killed or maimed all the *Landsers* out there or broken their spirits.

"Another round of the same, Kurt," Witt said, and then, "Lothar, while he's loading it hose 'em down with the turret machine gun."

"Another round of canister," Poske said at the same time as Eckhardt was replying, "I'm doing it, Sergeant."

As the MG-34 mounted alongside the panzer's big gun spat death, Saul wondered how many times they'd chewed up Russians like that. Quite a few, even if he couldn't put an exact number to it. No matter how often it was, he'd never imagined they would be using the machine gun the same way against rebellious German soldiers.

No, that isn't right, he thought as the cannon roared again. *We're the rebellious German soldiers.* He grinned ferociously, liking the idea.

Then Sergeant Witt spoke to him: "Back us out of here, Adi. I don't want them coming through the house and jumping us with grenades or Molotov cocktails. Let's get out into the open, where we can see trouble coming."

"Backing us out, Sergeant." Saul put the panzer into reverse. Ivans who drove T-34s often carried a mallet to whack the shift lever and make the transmission do what they told it to. German engineering was of a higher order . . . even if the USSR kept turning out ungodly swarms of crude but deadly panzers.

After Saul had backed away, Witt sent the panzer out around the end of the wall. That showed Saul what the two rounds of canister had done to his countrymen. Even if they were committed Nazis, the sight made him gulp. The only difference between Russians and Germans after they got blasted to pieces and strings was the color of the bits of unbloodstained cloth covering corpses and bits of corpses.

More bullets rattled off the panzer, these probably from a submachine gun. Theo fired a quick burst from the bow machine gun. He raised the thumb on his left hand, which told Saul they wouldn't need to worry about that fellow till the Judgment Day.

"Good job," Witt said. "I don't think this mob will give us any more trouble, anyhow. Any orders on the radio, Theo?"

"Nope," Hossbach answered laconically.

"On my own. I wonder if I can stand that much freedom." The panzer commander paused thoughtfully. "I wonder if Germany can stand that much freedom." It was one of the better questions Saul Goldman had heard lately. He wished he didn't have to worry about the answer, too.

. . .

Over on the far side of the barbed wire, the Germans were going out of their minds. To Alistair Walsh, that meant they were going further out of their minds than they already were. When soldiers wearing the same uniform but different armbands started shooting at one another, something was rotten in the state of *Deutschland*.

Only one thing could make all the Fritzes shoot in the same direction these days. When the English or French tried to push a little deeper into Belgium, the Germans turned from distracted lunatics in the middle of a civil war back into, well, Germans.

That was the last thing any of their foes wanted. Distracted lunatics were exciting, even entertaining, to watch. Germans were dangerous. All the *Reich*'s neighbors had two wars' worth of experience—France had three—about just how dangerous Germans were.

So Walsh and his men sat tight. They didn't shoot at the Fritzes. The Fritzes mostly didn't shoot at them even if they showed themselves, as long as they didn't look as if they were about to attack. It was a funny kind of war. Any kind of war that turned ordinary soldiers into would-be striped-pants diplomats struck Walsh as pretty funny.

But that was what this war was doing. Jack Scholes came up to Walsh and demanded, "'Ere, Staff, wot kind of peace d'you reckon the Germans'll figure is cricket?"

"Haven't the foggiest," Walsh answered; he wasn't ashamed to admit he had no notion of what would happen next. "Hell's bells, Jack, we don't even know whether the generals can beat the Nazis, or whether somebody like Himmler—no, they say Himmler's dead: somebody like Heydrich, then—turns into the next *Führer*. If that happens, the fighting'll be on again for real soon enough."

"Say the generals win." Yes, Scholes was like a terrier; he didn't want to let go of what he grabbed on to.

"It would have to be something close to the *status quo ante bellum*, I expect," Walsh said, sucked into the argument in spite of himself.

"To the wot?" Latin was Greek to Scholes. "Blimey, you throw the fancy talk around like a toff, you do."

"Bugger off! There. Is that plain enough?" Walsh said. The private grinned at him, showing off snaggled yellow teeth. The only reason

Walsh knew the sonorous Latin phrase was that he'd heard it a lot the last time around. He explained: "To the way things were before the war."

"Oh." Jack Scholes pondered, then nodded. "Makes sense. Can't let 'em fink they turned a profit on the deal, can we?"

"I hope not," Walsh said. He lit a Navy Cut, offered one to Scholes, and let out a long, smoke-filled sigh. "Of course, if we don't flatten them right and proper now, chances are we'll have another dustup with them fifteen or twenty years down the road."

Scholes sent him a sly grin. "Chances are, eh? Chances are it won't be your worry then, too."

"I hope not. I've already got shot in two wars—three would be too bloody many. But you'll be a staff sergeant yourself by then if you stay in."

"Roight. And then you wake up." The kid reacted with automatic mockery. A moment later, though, his gray-blue eyes narrowed. "D'yer really fink Oi could?"

"Why not? The other soldiers respect you, and you've picked up a lot since we first bumped into each other," Walsh said.

"Since you first got stuck wiv me, you mean," Scholes said, not without pride.

"You said it—I didn't."

"A staff sergeant? Me? Cor! Wouldn't me mum bust 'er buttons?" But Scholes' eyes narrowed again, this time in a different way. " 'Course, I've got to live through this little go-round first, eh?"

"It would help," Walsh admitted dryly. The younger man grunted laughter. Walsh went on, "Your chances now are a hell of a lot better than they were a few days ago, at least if the German Salvation Committee wins its scrap with the Nazis."

"You've got that right, I expect," Scholes said. "But if peace goes an' breaks out, 'oo says the Army'll want to keep a scrawny West 'Am supporter loike me?"

He had a point. East End Cockneys weren't always the first choice of the powers that be for promotion or for anything else that didn't involve the risk of sudden death. They weren't calm and reliable and obedient, the way country boys were supposed to be. Like their counterparts from Mancunian and Liverpudlian slums, they had the nasty habit of doing as they pleased, not as they were told.

Still, Walsh said, "I would have gone back to digging coal if they hadn't decided to keep me in khaki in 1919. There are ways to get them to do what you want—and I'll be glad to put in a good word for you. We need blokes who can tell privates what to do . . . and who can look a subaltern in the eye and let him know he's a goddamn fool."

Jack Scholes laughed again. "Oi'd 'ate that, Oi would."

"I daresay." Walsh chuckled, too. "You can't let them know you enjoy it, though. You can't let them know you're laughing at them. Mm, most of the time you can't, anyhow. They need that every once in a while."

"When you can't get 'em to pull their 'eads out of their arse'oles any other way?" Scholes guessed shrewdly.

"Something like that, yes." In a few years, Walsh wouldn't have wanted to be the junior lieutenant who rubbed Scholes the wrong way. No subaltern would make that mistake more than once. The experience might be educational. It would definitely be traumatic.

A sentry called, "German coming this way with a white flag!"

Walsh got up onto the firing step to look east into Belgium. "We've seen more flags of truce since the Fritzes did for Adolf than in the whole war up till then," he remarked.

This German looked like . . . a German: boots, *Feldgrau,* Schmeisser, coal-scuttle helmet. He had an Iron Cross First Class on his left breast pocket. After a moment, Walsh noticed he wore his shoulder straps upside down. Noncoms and officers often did that so snipers wouldn't spot their rank badges and single them out.

"Far enough!" Walsh yelled to him. "Put down the weapon! *Hände hoch!*"

The German obediently set the machine pistol on the ground and raised his hands. "I carried it to protect myself from my countrymen, not to attack you," he said in excellent English.

That Walsh believed him was a sign of how much and how fast things had changed. "Come on, then," he called.

Still holding up his white flag, the Fritz did. His unloving country-men started shooting at him before he made it to the English trenches. He hit the dirt with professional speed and crawled the last few yards before slithering down into what Bruce Bairnsfather had so memora-bly tagged "a better 'ole" during the last war.

"I hope they won't start throwing mortar bombs at us because you got away," Walsh said.

"I likewise," the German agreed. "I am Ludwig Bauer. I am a major." He rattled off his pay number, adding, "And now I am well out the war."

"Which side were you on?" Walsh asked. When the officer hesi-tated, Walsh said, "I won't throw you back either way—I promise. But I do want to know."

"May I say I am on Germany's side and leave it there?" Bauer re-turned. "Other Germans may want to shoot me, but I do not want to shoot them. I would rather a prisoner of war become than hurt my own *Volk*."

As a military coup ousted England's pro-appeasement govern-ment, some nasty Scotland Yard men hadn't worried at all about hurt-ing Walsh, who opposed them. "Well, I can understand that," he said, and meant it. He turned to Jack Scholes. "Take the major back to regi-mental HQ. They'll carry on from there. We don't have to fight him any more—just feed him."

"Roight." Scholes gestured with his rifle. "Come along, you." Bauer came. He seemed as happy as a sheep in clover. And why not? Unless choking on the slop POWs ate killed him, he'd live to go home again.

The clock over the stove said it was coming up on seven o'clock: time for the morning news. Peggy Druce turned on the radio. She didn't want to miss anything. The *Inquirer* sat on the kitchen table, but the news it held was several hours old by now. Things had been changing so fast, she wanted to stay up to the minute.

Along with the paper, she had her first cup of coffee on the table. Her first cigarette of the day sat in an ashtray, sending a thin, twisting ribbon of smoke up toward the ceiling. She hadn't worried about breakfast yet; she wouldn't starve before she found out what was going on.

She suffered through a singing commercial for a brand of cigarettes she couldn't stand and another one for an oleomargarine that promised it was just as good as "the costlier spread." She snorted and tried without much luck to blow a smoke ring. The oleomargarine makers couldn't call it butter because dairy farmers didn't want the competition. A lot of places, it wasn't even legal to add yellow coloring to oleomargarine.

But the dairy farmers weren't the only ones trying to grease the people who bought things. Peggy'd tried oleomargarine, which had a much more generous ration allowance than "the costlier spread" did. She'd tried it once, that is. To her, it tasted more like machine oil than butter.

"This is Douglas Edwards with the news," the familiar voice announced. "The German Salvation Committee continues to make progress in its fight against diehard Nazis. There are reports of panzer battles in the Ruhr and others outside of Berlin pitting the *Waffen*-SS against *Wehrmacht* units loyal to General Guderian and the Committee. SS casualties are said to be very heavy."

Peggy stubbed out the cigarette. Some of that was in the *Inquirer*, but not all of it. She thought about lighting another one, but decided to wait till after breakfast. She sipped her coffee instead.

"German Salvation Committee members are discussing peace terms in London, Paris, and Moscow," Edwards went on. "Certain broad outlines have become plain. Germany definitely will evacuate the Low Countries and Denmark and Norway. Her forces will also leave the western areas of the Soviet Union that they still occupy. The Salvation Committee agrees to all of this without complaint."

The Salvation Committee had agreed to all of that a couple of days earlier. The *Inquirer* had already reported about it. Peggy waited to hear some of the new news she'd been hoping for, or at least to hear there was no new news.

"There seem to be a few sticking points in seeking a general European peace. One involves Austria, another Czechoslovakia, a third the district around the Polish city of Wilno, which is also claimed by the USSR, and the last the fate of the Baltic countries of Estonia, Latvia, and Lithuania.

"German diplomats point out that the other great powers had accepted the *Anschluss* joining Austria to Germany in 1938, and that England and France were on the point of conceding the Czechoslovakian Sudetenland to Germany when the assassination of Sudeten German leader Konrad Henlein by a Czech nationalist touched off the Second World War. They also point out that the Slovaks are happier in an independent Slovakia than they were as, ah, country cousins in the former Czechoslovakia.

"These same German diplomats object to Stalin's claims against Wilno and the Baltic states. They plainly don't want to let down their Polish allies, who have also suffered severe losses against Russia. Stalin's attitude seems to be that, if Germany can come out of the war with more than she began it with, the USSR should be able to do so, as well.

"Talks, then, continue. It seems as though neither England nor France is sure of how hard a line to take. It also seems that President Roosevelt has not yet made up his mind how hard to push them—or how hard he can push them, since America so recently entered the European war. More after these important messages."

These messages were important only if you had dentures or were constipated. Peggy turned on the burner under the coffee pot to heat it up. Maybe Douglas Edwards would have more to say about the European situation after the commercials. She wanted to find out whether the Salvation Committee intended to start treating Jews like human beings again. If it did, and if it was willing to say it did, she figured she would have to take it seriously.

But the next story was about an American bomber raid against Jap-held Wake Island. There was also a story about a naval battle somewhere in the South Pacific where both sides claimed to have mauled their foes' aircraft carriers. And there was a story about how all the American soldiers and sailors in Australia were popularizing baseball there.

As soon as that one started, Peggy realized she wouldn't hear any more serious war news. She poured herself the second cup of coffee and fixed her breakfast eggs and toast. After she did the dishes, she went after the *Inquirer*'s crossword puzzle. The guy who put the clues together thought he was cute. As far as she was concerned, he gave himself too much credit. *Gigantic trouble (2 words),* for instance, turned out to be MELOTT. You wanted to throw something harder and heavier and pointier than a horsehide at somebody who did something like that.

She'd been in Czechoslovakia when the Germans invaded it, going on six years ago now. She didn't think they deserved to keep any of it. They'd started doing horrible things to the Jews there as soon as they invaded, and as far as she knew they hadn't stopped since. They didn't exactly give the Czechs a great big kiss, either. As for Slovakia, the thugs running it were a pack of cheap imitation Nazis. One of them was a priest, but he still acted like a cheap imitation Nazi.

Of course, what she thought the Germans deserved had nothing to do with the price of beer. Great-power diplomacy was what it was, not what you wished it would be. As Douglas Edwards had pointed out, in 1938 England and France let Germany swallow Austria and were ready to sell Czechoslovakia down the river. Hitler attacked it without even giving them the chance. The world hadn't seen peace since.

When Chamberlain and Daladier went to Munich to try to talk Hitler into letting them hand him the Sudetenland on a plate instead of running into the kitchen and grabbing it himself, Czechoslovakia's diplomats hadn't even been allowed in the room. They'd had to sit and wait while foreigners decided their country's future.

Would anybody pay attention now to what the Czechs wanted? Peggy tried to hope so. Try as she would, she had trouble bringing it off. England and France hadn't been eager to fight over Czechoslovakia to begin with. They'd done it, but with no great enthusiasm. They still had none for the war. Hitler had shown himself to be full of deadly dangerous ambition. If General Guderian and his friends didn't want to lie down with the lamb and get up with lamb chops, the European democracies would deal with them.

By the same token, no one outside the area was likely to get excited about which country the people in and around Wilno wanted to belong to. No, the question was, who got to have it? Right this minute, Stalin looked like the odds-on favorite. For that matter, who outside the Baltic region would notice or care if the USSR quietly gobbled up Estonia, Latvia, and Lithuania? They'd belonged to the Russian Empire for a long time.

The Estonians, Latvians, and Lithuanians liked independence? They didn't want to belong to the Soviet Union? What had Chamberlain called the 1938 Czechoslovakian crisis? *A quarrel in a faraway country between people of whom we know nothing.* Yes, that was it. And that was how almost the whole world would feel about this quarrel, too.

After Peggy finished the crossword puzzle, she fixed herself a stiff bourbon on the rocks. She didn't usually start off so early—that was for lushes. But she'd gone and thought herself sad. As long as you didn't drink yourself blind, bourbon made a pretty good medicine for that.

Anastas Mouradian was trying to explain the current status of the war to Isa Mogamedov. "Suppose you have a cat in a box, a box where you can't see or hear anything inside," he told his copilot.

"I have a cat, *da.*" Mogamedov nodded agreeably. "Is it a good Soviet kitty or a nasty, hissing, biting Fascist fleabag?"

"Bear with me. Suppose you want to find out whether the cat in the box is alive or dead."

"You open the box," Mogamedov said.

"Suppose you want to find out without opening the box, though."

"Can you smell inside, to find out whether the cat is shitting or rotting?"

"Not that, either."

"Well, how *do* you tell, then?" the Azeri asked with the air of a man humoring a lunatic.

"I've thought a lot about it, and the way it looks to me is, you *can't* tell till you open the box and you see whether a live cat jumps out or something's in there stinking that you've got to chuck on the rubbish pile. Till then, you just don't know. As far as you're concerned, the cat is alive and dead at the same time . . . until you open the box and see," Stas said.

Mogamedov muttered a few words in Azeri. Stas didn't understand them, but the tone left something to be desired. Then Mogamedov switched back to Russian: "And this has what, exactly, to do with the war?"

"Well, mostly that we don't know what will happen—we have no way of knowing—till either it happens or it doesn't," Mouradian answered. "Maybe we'll go back to bombing the Fritzes and they'll go back to trying to shoot us down. Or maybe it will be peace, and we start figuring out what to do with our lives from then on. In the meantime, though, the war is alive, but it's dead, too."

What he said made sense to him—a peculiar kind of sense, but sense even so. Whether it made even a peculiar kind of sense to anyone else . . . he was about to find out. If Mogamedov laughed in his face, he thought he really would have to look for another crewmate, no matter if putting in the request meant a black mark on his record.

The Azeri looked as if he were about to laugh. Then he stopped looking that way. Quite visibly, he thought it over. After a minute or so, he said, "Well, you're not as crazy as I thought you were when you first came out with it. Or I don't think you are, anyhow."

"Thanks," Stas said. "I know it's loopy, but it's interesting to play with in your head, too, isn't it?"

"It is." Mogamedov nodded "Not a dead war, not a live war . . . That's what we've got, all right."

He must have liked the conceit well enough to pass it along to other flyers and groundcrew men. Pretty soon, people all over the air base were talking about "Mouradian's cat." Isa hadn't stolen the credit for it. Or he might have decided he wanted to stick Stas with the blame.

That was another one of those cases where you couldn't know the answer till after you asked the question. You might not know even then. When you opened the imaginary box, a live cat either would or wouldn't hop out. A dead cat couldn't lie about being alive. But Isa Mogamedov could lie.

Stas didn't give him the chance. He didn't ask.

Some of the Red Air Force men teased him about "Mouradian's cat." A few seemed interested in the paradox. He was more proud than otherwise to have his name attached to something people were talking about.

He was for a little while, anyhow. Fighting men being what they were, they didn't talk about "Mouradian's cat" for long. Pretty soon, they started going on about "Mouradian's pussy." That might have been funny once—to him. To a lot of the guys, it got funnier every time they said it.

"Hey, Stas," another lieutenant called at supper, "how's your pussy?"

"Well, Volodya, why don't you step outside the tent here, and I'll show it to you," Mouradian answered calmly.

Everyone whooped as they strode out together. Half a minute later, Stas came back in. He sat down and returned to the kasha and mutton in his mess tin. Some of the knuckles on his left hand were skinned. His right ankle was sore from kicking Vladimir Ostrogorsky in the belly so hard, but that didn't show.

When the Russian didn't come back in right away, a couple of men went out to see what had happened to him. They came back staring at Stas. "*Bozehmoi*, Mouradian," one of them said. "Volodya won't ask about your pussy again any time soon."

"That was the idea," Stas answered, and returned to his supper without another word.

He did wonder how many friends Lieutenant Ostrogorsky had, and whether they'd try to pay him back. He dared hope they wouldn't. Ostrogorsky had been asking for it. Anybody could see that. Well, Stas hoped anybody could see it.

At last, Ostrogorsky did walk in. By the shaky way he moved, he might have downed a liter of vodka. His eyes didn't quite track, either. He had a bruise on the side of his jaw; a trickle of blood ran down his chin from one corner of his mouth.

"You don't fight fair," he told Mouradian.

"Too bad," Stas said. "You want an engraved invitation, go join a boxing club. And tell your jokes somewhere else."

"If I tell a really funny one, you'll probably murder me." Ostrogorsky rubbed his midsection. Stas' kick had caught him right in the solar plexus. After that, the Russian couldn't have fought back no matter how badly he wanted to.

Stas only shrugged. He wanted to say he was done with it if Ostrogorsky was. He didn't, though. He worried the other man would take it as a sign of weakness. Someone from the Caucasus surely would have. Russians didn't ritualize revenge the way southern men did, but Mouradian wanted to keep the edge he'd won for himself.

After supper, Isa Mogamedov said, "I'm sorry. I should have known they would turn it into something filthy. I didn't mean for that to happen."

"*Nichevo,*" Stas replied. Yes, that was a useful Russian word.

"I didn't know you were such a tough bitch, either." Mogamedov brought out *blyad* with the self-consciousness anyone who hadn't grown up speaking Russian showed when he took a mild stab at *mat*.

"Partly luck," Stas said, adding another shrug. "Partly I surprised him. He must have thought I was going to spend a while cussing before I started fighting. But why waste time?"

"Remind me not to get you that mad at me," the Azeri said,

The squadron commander called Stas in on the carpet the next morning. Lieutenant Colonel Leonid Krasnikov was a squat, blond, wide-faced man, about as Russian-looking as any Russian could get. Silver-framed glasses only made his gray eyes colder. But all he said was, "Did you have to hit him that fucking hard, Mouradian?"

"I'm sorry, Comrade Colonel," Stas answered, which was true . . . up to a point. "I hoped that, if I did a proper job of it once, I wouldn't have to do it over and over."

"Is that what you hoped?" Krasnikov's stare got no friendlier. He sighed. "Well, except for a broken tooth you didn't do any permanent damage. And you *were* provoked. So get out of here."

"I serve the Soviet Union!" Stas saluted and left. The squadron commander had some humanity lurking in him after all. Who would have guessed that? Maybe there wouldn't be any more fighting in the air or on the ground. Maybe the cat was alive. Maybe.

Chapter 22

Major Keller looked earnestly, even urgently, into Hans-Ulrich Rudel's face. "We need you," the National Socialist Loyalty Officer said. "The State needs you. The Party needs you. The *Grossdeutsches Reich* needs you."

"Needs me to do what, sir?" Hans-Ulrich knew the loyalty officer thought he was very loyal to the *Führer*. Keller wasn't wrong, either. He had been loyal to Adolf Hitler. That kind of feeling was harder to come by, though, when you tried to attach it to Rudolf Hess or Reinhard Heydrich or the other top-ranking National Socialists who headed the fight against the Salvation Committee's forces.

Keller had no doubts about where his own loyalty lay. "To bomb a column of traitors and rebels moving from Münster toward the Ruhr," he answered.

"Sir, that's a mighty long flight. All the way across Holland, into the *Reich* . . . And how much company would I have?" Hans-Ulrich didn't flat-out refuse the order. He just pointed out the difficulties.

"You will not fly alone. I promise you that. And you would be able to land in the Ruhr. Loyal forces there hold several airfields. Remember, Rudel, you swore a sacred oath of loyalty to the *Führer*. Are you a man of honor, or some other kind of man?"

"Major, the *Führer* is dead," Hans-Ulrich reminded Keller.

The loyalty officer turned red. "Yes, he is. But *Reichsmarschall* Göring is his legitimate successor, or the deputy *Führer* or the *Reichsführer*-SS if the *Reichsmarschall* cannot take up his duties." No one knew what had happened to Göring, not for sure. No one knew if he was alive or dead. If he was dead, no one was sure which side had killed him, or precisely why.

Rudolf Hess, the deputy *Führer,* wasn't exactly a nonentity, but he wasn't a charismatic leader, either. And *Reichsführer*-SS had been Himmler's title. Himmler pretty definitely was dead; the title belonged to Heydrich now. The other title that stuck to Heydrich was Hitler's Hangman. Such people were useful—what state didn't need a security chief?—but he also wasn't a leader for whom men would charge, singing, into battle.

"Sir, before all this really got started, Colonel Steinbrenner asked me if I was ready to bomb other Germans," Hans-Ulrich said. "I told him I didn't think I could do that. I'm telling you the same thing."

"Colonel Steinbrenner's loyalty is not above suspicion—far from it," Keller said darkly. "And you wouldn't be bombing Germans here. Traitors do not deserve to be called by that glorious name."

"You are not in my chain of command, sir." Rudel kept grasping at straws, grabbing for time. "If someone who is tries to give me that order, well, I'd have to think about it, anyway. In the meantime, it's been good talking with you." He ducked out of the National Socialist Loyalty Officer's tent before Keller could do anything but stare.

None of the flyers or groundcrew men now at the Belgian airstrip had opened fire on men who disagreed with them . . . yet. No one here had even tried to arrest anyone else, which might have started the shooting. Nor had England or France attacked the base. If they had, they might well have smashed it. But they would have united all the surviving *Luftwaffe* men against them.

They were smart enough to see that. By all the signs, they were smarter politically than anybody playing the game on the German side.

Hans-Ulrich hadn't gone far before Sergeant Dieselhorst appeared at his side out of nowhere. "Well? What's the latest from the major?" Dieselhorst asked.

"He wanted me to start bombing the Committee's forces inside Germany," Rudel answered baldly.

"What did you tell him?"

"Basically, that I might do it if Colonel Steinbrenner told me to, but that he wasn't my commanding officer and didn't have the authority to send me out."

"That's pretty good, sir!" Dieselhorst gave him a thumbs-up. "The colonel won't give you that order in a million years. He's behind the Salvation Committee all the way, Steinbrenner is."

"Is he?" Now Rudel's voice held no expression whatever. The news wasn't a surprise, but it hurt just the same, the way finding out the girlfriend you suspected really was unfaithful would.

Dieselhorst heard that emptiness. "*Ja,* sir, he is. If we'd stuck with what we had, what would've happened? We'd've gone down the shitter, that's what, ground to powder between the Ivans and the Americans."

"Or we might have won in spite of everything. We still might." Hans-Ulrich had believed in the Party and the *Führer* as long as he could, and then a little longer besides. *Mein Ehre heisst Treue,* the SS motto said. *My honor is loyalty.* He was no blackshirt. He didn't even like them. But that idea resonated with something deep down inside him.

"I am, too, you know," Dieselhorst said. "You can turn me in to the major if you want."

Wearily, Rudel shook his head. "Give me a break, Albert. I wouldn't do that." Hearing that the sergeant had no use for the Nazis surprised him not a bit. "You know I lean the other way. If your side wins, turn me in to whatever takes the *Gestapo*'s place if you want to."

"Something will, sure as houses. Can't hardly run a country these days without something like that. And if that's not a judgment on us, screw me if I know what would be." Dieselhorst sighed, then brightened. "I *am* glad you didn't get the plane bombed up and take off for Germany with somebody else in the back seat."

"I have no stomach for killing Germans, even in the middle of a civil war," Hans-Ulrich said. "I told that to Steinbrenner. I told Keller the same thing."

"Your father raised you the right way." Had Dieselhorst said it mockingly, Hans-Ulrich would have tried to deck him. But he sounded as if he meant it.

"Thank you," Hans-Ulrich said, acknowledging that. "Thank you very much. Plenty of other Germans don't seem to have any trouble with it at all. Otherwise, we wouldn't be where we are."

"No, we wouldn't. We'd be gurgling down that stinking shitter instead. Everybody would goose-step after the *Führer* till he led us right over the cliff. And that's where we would have gone. This way, maybe, just maybe, we get another chance."

"A chance to do what? We're supposed to be the masters of Europe—"

"Says who?" Sergeant Dieselhorst broke in.

Hans-Ulrich gaped at him. He'd taken the idea for granted for so long, he had no idea where he'd got it. It was all over *Mein Kampf,* of course, but that wouldn't impress Dieselhorst.

And the sergeant repeated, "Says who? We've tried to conquer the damn thing twice now in my lifetime, and look what it's got us. If we snag a peace without reparations and without sanctions, we can make like an ordinary country for a change. I'm sorry, sir, but I'll be damned if I can get a hard-on about being part of the *Herrenvolk.* I'd sooner go to a tavern and drink beer."

"But what about the Bolsheviks?" Hans-Ulrich asked.

"Christ, what about 'em? They're in Russia, and they're welcome to the goddamn place, as far as I'm concerned. I don't want to go back there again—I'll tell you that," Dieselhorst said. "The Bolsheviks in Germany and the ones in Hungary and the ones everywhere else but Russia got stomped after the last war, and just what they deserved, too."

"There's Spain. Spain's turned as red as a baboon's behind."

"And it's fucked up the same way Russia was: a few rich people on top and a big old swarm of hungry ones on the bottom." Dieselhorst paused a moment before adding, "You ask me, the Nazis were taking Germany down that road."

Rudel automatically looked around to see who might have heard the dangerous crack. He shook his head in wonder. If the Salvation Committee won, you wouldn't have to worry about speaking your mind . . . for a while, anyhow. That might make the change worthwhile.

Or, of course, it might not. But he was sure of one thing. He didn't need to worry about standing in a bread line. Even if peace broke out, whoever ran the *Reich* would need bomber pilots. Like security men, bomber pilots were a vital part of the modern state.

Arno Baatz peered out a second-story window in Münster's *Rathaus*. Just the quickest of glances, and then he pulled away. The soldiers out there wanted to kill him—and the rest of the *Wehrmacht* men and *Waffen*-SS soldiers and prison guards and secret policemen still holding this part of town against the traitors and bandits who'd murdered the *Führer*.

Somewhere out there was Adam Pfaff, with his goddamn gray-painted Mauser. The stinking son of a bitch sneaked away even before everybody knew for sure Hitler had died. So did two other men from Baatz's squad. He wanted to kill them, and he didn't want them to kill him.

He glanced down at the swastika armband he wore. Part of him wished he could take it off and slip away himself. Things didn't look good for National Socialist supporters in Münster. The perimeter kept shrinking. Arno had always backed authority. Now, though, he looked to have guessed wrong about who authority was going to be.

A 105 fired not far away. The shell slammed into a building his side still held. Part of the stonework front fell in. But an MG-42 kept snarling from the ruins. A lot of the people who still wore the swastika were stubborn indeed.

Which looked to mean they would wind up stubborn and dead. No reinforcements had come in; the other side held all the territory around Münster. Arno glanced down at the armband again. If he took it off so he looked as if he could belong to either side . . .

If he did that and the SS caught him, they would shoot him out of hand. One redheaded bastard with a Schmeisser specialized in executing anyone suspected of halfheartedness. The way he shot people, they took a long time to die.

So if you were going to do a bunk, you had to make sure you made it. Otherwise, you were better off sticking tight. The traitors were out to kill the people still loyal to the Party, yes, but they weren't especially out to kill them slowly.

That 105 blasted the nearby building again. More of it collapsed. A fire sent black smoke into the sky. The MG-42 barked more defiance at the men who'd chosen the Committee for the Salvation of the German Nation.

An SS top sergeant stomped into the room where Arno sheltered. "Come on with me," he said. "We're going to counterattack. We've got to take out that 105. It's slaughtering us."

Arno gulped. If the traitors had two brain cells to rub together, they'd protect their artillery with machine guns and machine pistols. Any try at taking it out would be suicidal. He couldn't say that, not unless he wanted to meet his own side's redheaded executioner. He did ask, "How good do you think our chances are?"

The SS man just looked at him. With those gray eyes and rocky cheekbones, the fellow might have stepped straight off one of Mjölnir's recruiting posters. "We've got to try," he said, which told Baatz everything he needed to know. "They'll kill us for sure if we don't get rid of it. If we do, we can hold out a while longer."

Worst of it was, he was right. Arno fell in behind him. They went through the *Rathaus,* combing out men who could join in the assault. When they had a couple of squads' worth, the SS noncom seemed satisfied. Arno still didn't think the force was big enough. He kept his mouth shut. He had no more idea than the soldier from the *Waffen*-SS about where they could scrape up more fighters.

They were about to move out when two shells from the 105 slammed into the *Rathaus'* upper floors, one after the other. Debris thundered down in front of the doorway through which they'd go. A great cloud of dust and grit rose. Arno coughed and rubbed at his eyes. He suddenly felt grateful to the SS man. He was pretty sure one of those rounds had burst on or in the room where he'd sheltered. If he hadn't vacated, he'd probably be chopped meat right now.

"Come on! Follow me!" Himmler's superman charged out through the dust. The others poured after him. No matter how solid the *Rathaus* was, it seemed more a trap than a shelter now.

Bullets sparked off paving stones and cracked by as the Germans on the other side spotted them on the move. One man from the strike force went down with a horrible screech. The rest kept running for the nearest pile of rubble behind which they could throw themselves.

Arno belly-flopped down in back of some bricks that had belonged to a chimney. The explosion that knocked them off their building hadn't blasted them all apart. They might even keep gunfire off of him . . . till he had to move again, anyhow.

He glanced over his shoulder. Yes, that was fresh smoke he smelled. The *Rathaus* was burning. Whatever happened to him out here, it wouldn't be so bad as roasting back there.

All the same, he felt as naked as a de-shelled snail in a Frenchman's garden. Out of the corner of his eye, he saw motion ahead. That had to be an enemy. He snapped off a couple of quick shots. The other guy went down, either hit or diving for cover.

Schmeissers and a couple of captured Russian PPDs chattered. While the men with them made the traitors keep their heads down, the others, Arno among them, scurried ahead. He'd just found new rubbish to shelter him when the 105 started smashing up some more of the *Rathaus*. Whichever side won this fight, Münster would have some rebuilding to do when it ended.

"Forward!" No one seemed to have issued the *Waffen*-SS man any doubts. Forward they went, and then forward again. Downtown Münster had plenty of ruins and wreckage to hide inside and behind. They lost a couple of men. They shot a few men fighting for the Salvation Committee.

That worried Arno. The guys on the other side had to know they were attacking. If those guys weren't dopes—and not all of them would be—they had to have a pretty fair notion of where the loyalists were heading. If they knew that, they could shift troops to stop them.

Baatz was about halfway to the 105 when he stopped caring. He couldn't have said why, but he did. He wanted to make it to the gun. He wanted to take out the crew. Whatever happened next . . . would happen. He might get back. He might not. Why borrow trouble?

He shot a traitor, then quickly ducked down behind some shattered stonework. The enemy soldier's buddy rattled the wreckage with a burst from his submachine gun, but he didn't hit Arno. The 105 boomed again. More of the *Rathaus* fell in on itself. More of it fell into the flames, too. Sure as hell, coming out here was better than staying back there would have been.

The attackers were taking flanking fire now. No other loyalist bands seemed to be in the neighborhood. They soaked up more losses, but they kept advancing. Arno had no idea whether the other side's medics patched up wounded loyalists or cut their throats.

Blam! Now Arno knew exactly where that goddamn 105 sat. When he slithered around the next corner, he was almost sure he could fire at the artillerymen who served it.

Before he could, a Panzer IV clanked around that corner, heading straight at him. "Fuck you!" he shouted—it wasn't fair that the stinking thing should be flying an Imperial German flag on its radio aerial.

Its cupola was open, the commander looking out. Arno fired at him. The panzer man tumbled inside, whether hit or not Arno didn't know. The SS sergeant flung a grenade, hoping it would follow the traitor in the black coveralls down through the cupola. But it bounced off the glacis plate and burst harmlessly on the paving. The bow machine gun sparked to life. Arno dove for cover.

"Come on, Adi! Step on it!" Hermann Witt shouted.

"I'm doing the best I can, Sergeant," Adi Stoss answered. "Some of these streets are narrower than the panzer, dammit."

From everything Theo could see, Adi was right. Like so many medieval towns, Münster hadn't been built with motor vehicles in mind. And it *really* hadn't been built with panzers in mind. Every time Adi had to make a tight turn, he bit out chunks of buildings that fronted the street too closely.

None of which cut any ice with the panzer commander. "Never mind the best you can. Just get there!" he said. "That's the best-sited gun we've got. It's knocking the shit out of them. We can't let the god-damn Nazis kill the crew or smash the breech block."

The same message dinned in Theo's earphones. He hoped it was genuine, and not leading them into a trap. Both men who backed the Salvation Committee and their foes used the same radio sets, the same frequencies, the same communications doctrine. Each side did its best to confuse the other, and each side's best seemed plenty good.

He'd used the panzer's bow gun more than he ever had in Russia. Fighting in a city turned out to be like that. He'd used the firing port in the side of the hull, too, keeping troublemakers at a distance with his Schmeisser.

He worried that somebody would toss a Molotov cocktail out a third-story window, say, and into the fighting compartment through the open hatch atop the cupola. That was one more thing you didn't need to fret about so much in Russia. Steppes and farm villages didn't grow three-story buildings.

One more corner. "There they are!" Witt yelled from the cupola. He yelled again a moment later, this time in pain. He fell back into the panzer like a red squirrel diving into a hole in a spruce. Then he gave another yell: "Canister! Blow the shitheads away!"

Theo was already working them over with the bow machine gun as the round slammed into the breech. He knocked down a rather plump fellow with a swastika armband just before the enemy soldier could jump behind a stone wall. Then he swept the machine gun to the left and hit the guy who'd thrown a grenade. That fellow was close enough for Theo to make out the SS runes on his collar patches. Theo's lips peeled back from his teeth in a savage smile. He'd always wanted the chance to shoot some SS men. Now he had it.

And then the canister round swept away everything in the first hundred meters of its path that might have been alive. He'd already seen the horrible things canister did to mere flesh and blood. That the flesh and blood out there wanted to kill him made him feel a little better about using it so, but only a little.

That some of the flesh and blood out there had hurt one of the rare men he counted a friend made him feel much better about using it so. He turned to look back over his shoulder and asked, "How the hell are you, Hermann?" Anxiety made his voice break like a fourteen-year-old's.

Witt gave back a grin almost as much a death's head as his panzer man's emblem. "My God! It talks!" he said, and Theo decided he wasn't going to parley with the Grim Reaper right this minute. But his left hand was clenched around his right upper arm, and bright red blood dribbled out between his fingers. "Flesh wound," he went on. "I'm pretty sure it missed the bone. I can wiggle my fingers and all." As if to prove it, he shaped a filthy gesture with his right hand.

Adi spoke in tones of professional interest: "Will they award you a wound badge for stopping one when you're fighting other Germans?"

"Now you can ask me if I give a fuck," Witt answered. "Lothar, help me get a wound bandage on this thing. Maybe you'd better stick me, too. It hurts pretty good. If the morphine leaves me too dopey to run the panzer, I figure you jerks can probably cope for a while. In the meantime, keep going till we can shoot at the *Rathaus*. We'll help that 105 blow up the rats in it."

"You probably aren't right at death's door," Adi said, which perfectly echoed Theo's thought. "And blowing up the *Rathaus* here will be a pleasure. Oh, you bet it will."

He'd grown up around Münster, or maybe in it. Theo knew that much about his tight-lipped crewmate. Adi'd had to do something, well, far out of the ordinary to need to make it into the *Wehrmacht*, too. After all this time together, Theo still wasn't sure what that might have been. Whatever it was, did records of it linger in the *Rathaus*?

If they did, no wonder Adi wanted to help knock the place flat. When the panzer edged up behind a heap of smashed junk that let its gun bear on the *Rathaus*, the driver whooped: "Hey-hey! It's already on fire!"

"We'll help it along," Witt said, and then, "Hurry up with that shot, Lothar. This business of stopping a bullet isn't a whole lot of fun."

Theo looked down at his left hand. He was missing a finger there. He had but didn't particularly rejoice in a wound badge. He'd caught a French bullet, not a German one. As far as what they did, the difference in nationality didn't seem to matter.

Lothar Eckhart got Witt bandaged and injected. Then the panzer's big gun started pouring HE shells into the *Rathaus*. Each burst turned more of the fine old building into fine modern junk. Several of the bursts started fresh fires, too. With hot metal fragments tearing through what probably amounted to cubic kilometers of paper, that was anything but surprising.

As the fires grew and spread, men in *Feldgrau* and others in black started scrambling out of the *Rathaus*. The panzer crew fired more HE rounds at the doorways: the range was too long for canister. Theo added bursts from the bow gun every now and again. Eckhardt chimed in with some from the coaxial machine gun in the turret, too. Neither one of them felt any great warmth for the diehard National Socialists.

Diehards they might be, but they did die. Some of them lay very still after they got shot. Others thrashed like a cat hit by a car. Theo concentrated on turning thrashers into still ones. He was putting them out of their misery—and he was making sure they wouldn't get up and start shooting at the panzer again.

Some of the Nazis made it to piles of brick and stone and God knew what in front of the *Rathaus* or off to the side. They did shoot back. Every once in a while, a rifle round would ring off the hardened steel of the Panzer IV's front plates. If no one was standing up in the cupola, though, you could fire rifles at a panzer from now till doomsday without doing worse than chipping the paint.

Theo glanced back at Hermann Witt again. "How are you, Sergeant?" he asked.

"Well, I've been better, but the morphine's working, so I've been worse, too—a few minutes ago, say." Witt's voice seemed to come from far away, but he didn't just close his eyes and go to sleep, the way a lot of people who got stuck did. He might not be thinking any too fast, but he was still thinking straight. After a longish pause to work things through, he went on, "I'll be laid up for a while. Till you clowns get a new commander, Adi, I'm putting you in charge."

"Me? That's got to be the dope talking, Sergeant." Adi sounded amazed and horrified at the same time.

Witt shook his head as if in slow motion or underwater. But he sounded very sure as he answered, "Nah. Theo doesn't want it"—which was an understatement, as he had to know—"and you're both senior to Lothar and Kurt. So tag—you're it."

"But—" Adi protested helplessly.

"I know what you mean. That won't matter, either, not under the Salvation Committee. Or it better not. So do what he tells you, you lugs," Witt said. Theo nodded. He didn't think the Salvation Committee would act stupid in the same ways the Nazis had. If it did, well, the country would need a revolution against the revolution.

When you were a civilian in a town where they were fighting a civil war, what could you do but hunker down and hope you didn't get killed? Sarah Bruck and her parents did exactly that. They got hungry. The power didn't always stay on. But they lived far enough away from the *Rathaus* and the cathedral that only a few stray artillery shells came down anywhere close by.

Sarah looked at the hole one of them made in the street with amazement. Her father eyed it with something more like amusement. "Believe me, dear, you put that next to the crater a five hundred-kilo bomb makes and you'd never even notice it," Samuel Goldman said.

"I believe you. I've seen those, too," Sarah answered. "But this isn't a little hole in the ground even if it doesn't have a bigger one next to it."

He considered that with professional deliberation before nodding. "Mm, you're not wrong," he said, as if giving her the accolade.

He went out later that afternoon. He wouldn't say where he was going. He came back carrying a cloth sack. When he opened it, he took out tinned meat, tinned cabbage, tinned potatoes, even tinned bread. "Where did you get this stuff?" Sarah gasped.

Father shrugged. "I have a few things saved for a rainy day. This looked rainy enough to use one or two."

"But—" Sarah said.

"But—" her mother echoed. Hanna Goldman found words to add

to that: "How could you have kept them, Samuel? How many times did the *Gestapo* search the house? Four or five, at least."

Samuel Goldman looked professorial again: professorially scornful. "What do blackshirts know about black-figure potsherds? Not much! Not even enough to steal them. But there are still a few people here in town who know a little more."

Sarah thought she remembered that black-figure pots were older than their red-figure counterparts. She wasn't even sure of that; it might have been the other away around. So she knew very little, if at all, more than the *Gestapo* men did. What looked like a broken chunk of a vase hadn't even seemed worth lifting to them. Evidently, that was their mistake.

"Did you get anything close to what they're really worth?" Mother asked.

He shrugged. "I got enough to keep us eating for a few days—maybe till the fighting dies down and we can spend money instead. The way things are right now, that's good value for what they're worth, especially when the other choices are nothing, nettle soup, and dandelion salad."

Hanna Goldman had no answer for that. Neither did Sarah. Her clothes hung looser on her every day. Her belly growled all the time. At bottom, you were an animal. When the animal started starving, it wanted to eat, and it didn't care how it got fed.

The animal inside Sarah was much happier after they opened some of those tins. Her father still seemed discontented. "I should have got some tobacco, too," he muttered. His pouch was empty, and he couldn't go hunting cigarette butts unless he wanted someone to shoot him.

Not long after dark came a sharp knock on the door. Sarah and her mother and father stared at one another in horror. *Not now!* she thought. *Not when they're throwing the Nazis out! It isn't fair!*

The knock came again, and a deep voice with it: "Open up! I know you're in there!"

What would he do if they didn't? Start shooting through the door? That seemed most likely to Sarah. It must have to her father, too, because he gestured helplessly toward the doorway. All at once, he seemed very old.

Legs numb with fear and despair, Sarah walked to the door and opened it. A tall man dressed all in black strode in. He carried a Schmeisser. A metal death's-head badge gleamed on his cap. He quickly closed the door behind him to keep light from leaking out.

He looked Sarah up and down. That arrogant stare made her want to hit him. So did the grin that stretched across his strong-cheekboned face. Then he said, "Hi, Sis. Haven't seen you in a hell of a long time."

Those numb legs didn't want to hold Sarah up. She had to lock her knees to keep from falling on the floor. More slowly than she might have, she realized he was wearing black coveralls, not a tunic and trousers. The glittering death's head was a panzer crewman's insigne, not the SS's.

"Saul?" she whispered.

"Guilty," he said. "Guilty of all kinds of things these past few years, I'm afraid." He nodded to Samuel Goldman. "Hey, Pop. Well, now I've been through the mill, too. Some fun, huh?" Only after that did he tack on, "Hi, Mom. Made it this far, anyhow."

Little by little, they all began to believe the prodigal son had returned. The story came from the wrong Testament, but none of them was inclined to be fussy. They crowded round Saul and hugged him and kissed him and pounded him on the back. The one thing they didn't do was make a whole lot of noise. They didn't want the neighbors to know they had anything to celebrate.

"What are you *doing* here?" Sarah asked after they dragged her older brother to the sofa.

"Well, we got pulled out of Russia to help sit on all the wicked rebels in Münster," he answered. "I thought that was pretty damn funny all by itself. Then when the generals staged the *Putsch* against the *Führer,* most of the crews in the regiment sided with the Salvation Committee." His face clouded. "I don't think my panzer gang killed anybody I was friends with. I don't think so, but I'm not sure."

Quietly, Samuel Goldman said, "I never had to wonder about that, thank God. The last time around, the civil war didn't start till after the regular fighting ended, and I managed to stay out of it."

"We got your letter," Sarah said. "We knew you got into the *Wehrmacht.* After that, all we could do was hope."

"And pray," her mother added. People were rarely as secular as they thought they were before hard times hit.

"You got it? That's good. I figured writing the Breisachs across the street was a better bet than sending it straight to you—as long as they didn't turn me in," Saul said. "And a lot of Aryans just went with the Jew-baiting because the Nazis told 'em to. They didn't all enjoy it."

"We've seen the same thing," Sarah agreed.

"How did you get to be Adalbert the panzer man?" Father asked. "How did you get papers that said you were?"

"I owe one of the guys I played football with for that—owe him more than I can ever pay back, I guess. He knew people who took care of it for me," Saul said. "These days, I think of myself as Adi more than I do by my real name. Unless you called me Moses, you couldn't have stuck me with a more Jewish handle."

"It wasn't a problem at the time," Father said stiffly.

"I suppose not," Saul allowed. "And it may not be a problem any more. The *Rathaus* and all the paperwork in it are up in smoke. I ought to know—my panzer helped blast it."

"My marriage certificate." Sarah sounded sadder than she'd dreamt she would.

Her brother stared at her. "Your what?" He shook his head. "I guess I'm not the only one who had a life while I was in the *Wehrmacht*. Who is he? Where is he? What's he do?"

"He's dead." Even now, Sarah started to puddle up when she said that. "He was Isidor Bruck, from the baking family."

"I know him. Uh, I knew him. I played football against him. Uh, I'm sorry," Saul said. "Too much, too quick. And now I've got to get out of here. I'm not supposed to be here at all, which is putting it mildly." He hugged and kissed Sarah and her mother and father once more in turn. Then he slipped out the door and vanished into blacked-out night. Sarah stared after him. Only the remembered feel of his arms around her made her doubt she'd dreamt the whole thing.

Chapter 23

Vaclav Jezek had fought in the slag piles of France's industrial north-east before. Crossing over the border into Belgium didn't change the way the landscape looked by one iota. But now the forces of the Czechoslovakian government-in-exile weren't fighting, even if they had come up to the front.

Not fighting ate at Vaclav. "What are we doing here?" he demanded of, inevitably, Benjamin Halévy.

"That's a big question, isn't it?" Halévy said. "Wouldn't you do better talking about it with a priest?"

"Oh, fuck yourself!" Vaclav exploded. "God damn it to hell, I want to kill Nazis. I feel like an atheist in a coffin, all dressed up with no place to go."

"Cute. Definitely cute." The Jew mimed applause. "They should put you on the radio. You'd have people in stitches."

"If you don't quit acting like a wise guy, you'll need stitches," Jezek said. "What are we supposed to do when they won't let us fire at the Germans? I can see the bastards over there, going about their business." He pointed to the Nazis' field fortifications. Sure as hell, the Germans in them didn't bother keeping their heads down. The ceasefire was holding as what they called the Salvation Committee slowly gained the upper hand on the loyalists or diehards or whatever name you wanted to stick on them.

"It was like this on the Western Front for a while right after the war started, too," Halévy said.

"When England and France stuck their thumbs up their asses while Hitler raped my country, you mean," Vaclav glossed bitterly.

"That's right." Benjamin Halévy admitted what no one could possibly deny. The Jew went on, "Next thing we knew, we were trying to keep the *Feldgrau* bastards from sticking a swastika flag on top of the Eiffel Tower."

"Served you right, too."

"I guess it did." Again, Halévy seemed to hope a soft answer would turn away wrath. "But I don't think that'll happen this time around. The Germans have seen they can't conquer the world. Now they're hoping like hell the world can't conquer them."

"Everybody's crazy to let 'em get away with a peace that doesn't knock the snot out of them," Vaclav said. "I mean, crazy. You think they won't try this shit again as soon as they patch things up at home? Third time lucky, some general will think, and maybe he'll be right."

"Maybe he will," Benjamin Halévy said with a somber nod. "It doesn't look like anyone's going to make Germany spit out Austria, does it? She's the biggest, richest country in Europe even without it. With it, she's the same thing only more so. But it seems as though most Austrians would just as soon be Germans, so there you are."

"Austria? Fuck Austria! Fuck Austria in the neck!" Vaclav said. "It looks like those shitheeled Slovak bumpkins will get to keep their own country, too, and the Fritzes will get to keep mine."

"If somebody called me a shitheeled bumpkin, I don't know that I'd want to stay in the same country with him," Halévy observed.

"Oh, for Christ's sake!" Like most other Czechs, Vaclav knew in his bones that his Slovak cousins damn well *were* hayseeds straight off the farm. Anyone who listened to their back-country accent for longer than five seconds would say the same thing. Anyone who knew how the Hungarians sat on them for generations and didn't let them even learn to count further than they could on their toes would, too. Benjamin Halévy didn't know any of that, as Vaclav pointed out: "You grew up in Paris."

"Why don't you say 'You damned Jew' and hand me my yellow star, too?" Halévy asked, a sardonic glint in his eye.

"That's not what I was talking about. I know what you're worth. I've seen it." Vaclav turned his head, hawked, and spat. "I know what Father Tiso's worth, too—not even that much."

"All right." Halévy stopped. He shook his head. "No. It's not all right. I'm sorry, Vaclav, but it's not. I know what you're worth, too. You're a hell of a good man. But when you start telling me that anybody—anybody at all—is this, that, or the other thing because he's a Slovak or a Jew or a German or a Chinaman or a Mexican or, or anything, you know what you're doing? You're doing Hitler's work for him, that's what."

Vaclav chewed on that for a few seconds. He found he didn't much care for the taste. He tried to spread it around by sharing it: "Tell me you never made fun of the Spaniards that way."

"Oh, I'm as bad as the next *con*," Halévy said. "We all are. People need other people to make fun of. I try not to be too much worse than the next *con*, though. I can shoot for that much."

Vaclav did some more chewing. Once he'd swallowed his next cud of thought, he said, "I guess it's like trying to live a Christian life but not trying to be just like Jesus. That's too much to ask of anybody."

"I expect it would be something like that." The Jew grinned crookedly. "Not that I'd know personally, you understand."

"Sure," Jezek said. They both chuckled. Vaclav lit a Gauloise. After a thoughtful puff, he went on, "You know what? Next to what they smoke in Spain, these fuckers are mild. Who would have imagined that?"

"Let me have one," Halévy said. After Vaclav did, he made his own comparison. "Damned if you're not right. I always used to think Gauloises were two parts phosgene and one part mustard gas. Now they don't seem so bad." He stuck out his tongue and tried to stare down at it. The effort made his eyes cross. "I must have had all my taste buds shot off."

"Wouldn't be surprised." But the jokes went only so far. After Vaclav had tossed away the butt, he said, "I'm still going to end up a man without a country. All of us here in the line are. You can see that coming, sure as shit. We've been fighting the goddamn Germans since 1938. Even if we promise to be nice boys, you think any German government'll let us back in?"

"Odds aren't good," Halévy admitted.

"Too fucking right, they're not," Vaclav said. "And I don't want to live in Böhmen und Mahren, anyway." He freighted the German names for Bohemia and Moravia with as much disgust as they would carry, and then some more besides. "I want Czechoslovakia back, dammit!"

"Complete with Slovaks? Complete with Sudeten Germans?"

"Rrr." Vaclav didn't like thinking that his former homeland made a proper country only if everyone who lived in it agreed that it should. The Germans mostly lived in the mountainous fringes of Bohemia and Moravia, the regions that made what had been Czechoslovakia defensible. The Slovaks filled most of the eastern third. And that didn't even worry about the Ruthenians or the Magyars or . . .

"I know it isn't right. I know it isn't fair." Now that Halévy had made his point, he did his best to sound sympathetic, even sorry. "But making peace now is like trying to unscramble eggs after you've dropped about two dozen of them into the pan over a hot fire."

"The Germans will pull out of Belgium and Holland. They'll pull out of Russia. They'll pull out of the countries up north. They won't pull out of Czechoslovakia. They'll just keep fucking us over and over. What am I supposed to do? Find a little war in South America or somewhere that needs a sniper with an antitank rifle? Killing people's almost the only thing I know how to do any more."

He wondered if he could get into Poland with his Spanish passport, with or without the antitank rifle. If he could, he might be able to sneak over the border into his native land. The Sudeten Germans hadn't wanted to be part of Czechoslovakia, and look how miserable they'd made life for the government. The Czechs wouldn't want to be part of Germany, so they'd probably try to make life miserable for their overlords, too.

He might be able to help. He might even have some fun helping. Soldiering taught you all kinds of evil tricks. Odds were the Germans would catch up with him sooner or later. He knew that, but he hardly cared. Why should he? He'd been living on borrowed time for years.

"Moscow speaking." The voice that came out of the radio sounded important and self-satisfied, as if the person doing the talking had just had a good dinner served to him by pretty girls not wearing much. It wasn't always the same newsreader, but it was always the same tone. Anastas Mouradian didn't care for it. He never had.

He'd never let on, either. Whom could you trust with an opinion like that? No one, not if you had any sense. The Mouradians had their flaws, but stupidity wasn't one of them.

"General Secretary Stalin has announced the incorporation of the Estonian Soviet Socialist Republic, the Latvian Soviet Socialist Republic, and the Lithuanian Soviet Socialist Republic into our glorious Union of Soviet Socialist Republics, bringing the number of constituent republics to fifteen," the announcer said. "The General Secretary has also announced that Polish Marshal Smigly-Ridz has agreed to cede the city of Vilno and the surrounding territory to the USSR. As Lithuanians are the largest element in the territory population, our magnificent General Secretary and the Politburo have determined that it should be added to the Lithuanian Soviet Socialist Republic."

The Politburo, Stas noted, wasn't magnificent. Well, how surprising was that? The Politburo might possibly have the authority to sneeze without Stalin's permission. It couldn't wipe the snot off its upper lip, though, unless the General Secretary countersigned the order.

"Thus the Soviet Union brings the war against reactionary imperialist and Fascist aggression to a triumphant conclusion," the newsreader declared. Stas wondered how many times he'd had to practice reading that so he could bring it out without bursting into wild giggles.

He glanced over at Isa Mogamedov, who also listened to the news in the officers' tent. Nothing on the Azeri's swarthy face showed he wasn't giving the report the grave attention it deserved. If he was sneering inside, he'd learned to do it so it didn't show.

Well, so have I, Stas thought. Not a raised eyebrow or a flared nostril betrayed what was going on inside his head. He didn't let out his own wild giggles and roll around on the bench clutching his sides, either. Sure enough, he was a disciplined fighting man.

He had to be. A triumphant conclusion? For the sake of a third-rate city that had been Polish, and for the sake of three new Soviet Republics whose people undoubtedly wanted nothing to do with the USSR, that nation had seen Byelorussia, much of the Ukraine, and the RSFSR almost to Smolensk devastated by years of attacks and counter-attacks. They would be more years getting back on their feet, if they ever did. Millions had died, probably as many as in the last war. Millions more were maimed. Millions more still had lost their homes, their livestock, their livelihoods . . .

The most you could say was that what they had was better than defeat, that Hitler's panzers might have rolled through Smolensk and even through Moscow, and that nothing would be left of the Soviet Union if that had happened. That was absolutely the most you could say, and if the newsreader had dared to say it the NKVD would have dragged him away—or perhaps shot him right on the air—before he could have finished getting the words out of his mouth.

As the newsreader had to do if he wanted to go back to his wife and children (and as his pompous voice suggested he wanted to do anyhow), he stuck to the script his minders had handed him: "Now that the war in the west has concluded, the workers and peasants of the Soviet Union can begin to reconsider some of the harsher and more unjust terms in the armistice imposed on us by the Empire of Japan."

That made heads come up all over the officers' tent. Everybody stared at the radio. So General Secretary Stalin wasn't going to let Japan get away with swiping Vladivostok, eh? That earlier war hadn't had anything like a triumphal conclusion.

Stas didn't know how smart Stalin really was; he'd never been in a position to find out. He did figure the Georgian was no dope. Stalin wouldn't have lived to rise to the top in the dog-eat-dog world of the Party after the Revolution had he been stupid.

Stalin also had sense enough not to choose more than one foreign foe at a time. He'd taken his lumps and liquidated his war with Japan when the fight against Germany heated up. Now that he wasn't battling the Fritzes for survival any more, he could start thinking about the Russian Far East again. Yes, he was shrewd.

He'd run things more shrewdly than Hitler had—no two ways about that. Go to war with France and England? Fine! Go to war with France and England and the USSR? Fine! Declare war on the USA while you were at war with France and England and the USSR? Fine!

Except it wasn't fine. Even Hitler's generals had finally figured that out . . . which was why the Salvation Committee ran Germany right now and the *Führer* lay unhappily in some nameless grave. If you took on the two biggest industrial powers in the world, the pair of them with four times your population, your story wouldn't have a happy ending even with England and France on your side. With them against you, too, you were . . .

Kaputt. A useful German word.

"The Union of Soviet Socialist Republics and the United States of America were allies at the end of the fight against Hitlerite Germany. In fact, that alliance is not the smallest reason the Germans overthrew their bloodthirsty tyrant," the newsreader said. Since Stas had just been thinking the same thing, he couldn't even disagree with the man. What was the world coming to? The broadcaster continued, "Now the USSR and the USA both find themselves with grievances against Japan. Working cooperatively, they will be able to stretch the Japanese to the breaking point—and beyond."

That might even be true, too. What was wrong with the newsreader, anyway? From what Stas was able to gather, the Americans' naval war against Japan in the Pacific hadn't always gone their way. Now, though, they'd taken back that island, Halfway or whatever it was called. They could build ships the way Russia built tanks.

And if they kept Japan busy at sea, and if China kept swarms of Japanese ground troops tied down, the Hammer and Sickle might yet fly over Vladivostok again. General Secretary Stalin might be able to have his newsreaders boast about bringing another war to a triumphal conclusion without blushing too much while they did it.

"I flew against the Japanese in the Far East for a while," Mouradian remarked to Isa Mogamedov.

The Azeri nodded. "Yes, you've said so before. What was it like?"

"Well, there was the time when I was walking over to see some planes and the officer who'd been in those parts longer warned me to keep an eye open for tigers," Stas said. That made Mogamedov sit up and take notice, all right. Stas went on, "And it was cold." He shivered, remembering. "Cold enough to make the worst winter day this side of the Urals seem like springtime." He did his best to impersonate a Russian: "Cold enough to freeze the Devil's asshole shut."

Mogamedov's off-key chuckle told him his best wasn't good enough. "Not eager to go back there, you're telling me?"

Stas shrugged. "I serve the Soviet Union! But if the Soviet Union wants me to serve it somewhere warmer, I won't apply for a transfer to Khabarovsk. Like I said, still tigers in the woods over there, too."

"And Japs," Mogamedov added.

"Yes. And Japs," Stas agreed. "But if the Japs kill me, they won't eat me—or I don't think they will." He knew a lot of what he thought he knew about Japan was Soviet propaganda. He wasn't so sure where, if anywhere, that stopped and something resembling truth started.

The newsreader began bragging about Stakhanovite shock workers shattering aluminum-production norms. A vodka bottle came by. Stas swigged from it. No, he didn't usually drink like a Russian, but when you listened to hot air like that, what else were you going to do?

Poker. Craps. Acey-deucy. Poker. Baseball. Craps. Poker. Chow. Sleep. Poker. Life on Midway.

Oh, and there was the radio. Some of the Marines there clung to it as a lifeline to the wider world they were no longer allowed to touch for themselves. Most of the time, Pete McGill steered clear of it. As far as he was concerned, it hurt more than it helped.

So he was one of the last to hear that the USA and Russia had agreed to an alliance against the Japs. When he did hear, he had trouble getting excited about it. "What good does that do us? We're still fucking stuck here on this shitty sandbox," he told the poker buddy who gave him the news. After a moment, he tossed a sawbuck into the pot. "Call."

The other Marine laid down three eights. Grinning, Pete showed him three tens. The other guy said something about his mother. At another time, in a different place, Pete would have tried to knock his block off, or maybe to murder him. On Midway, nobody had anything to spend money on, so it didn't seem to be worth much. Insults were devalued the same way. They'd used the ordinary ones so often, everybody ignored them. Ranking someone's mother over a medium-sized poker hand was like blowing a C-note on a cup of coffee. The Marines did it all the time, and didn't worry about it.

After collecting his money, Pete said, "I don't wanna end up here for the duration. I want to go out and kill Japs, goddammit."

"I want to go to Honolulu and screw me the first broad I run into, is what I want," the other Marine said. "Hell with the Japs. I have paid my dues with those fuckers, and somebody else can take my next turn. You'll find me singin' 'Roll Me Over in the Clover' with that Hotel Street chippy."

"Yeah, I want to get next to a woman, too," Pete said. "You bet I do. I've been here so long, some of you jerks don't look as ugly as usual."

A couple of the leathernecks in the poker game made as if to pull away from him. One fellow lisped, "I hope I'm not one of them, thweetheart."

Everybody laughed. "Mighty Joe Young's sister might go for you, Hank, but I don't," Pete said, and they all laughed some more. You could laugh when a guy played at being a queer, or you could punch him. Pete didn't know any middle ground there. Hank was a natural-born plug-ugly with shoulders as wide as a desk, so laughing seemed a better choice any way you looked at it.

"Do we really want to play kissy-face with the Reds?" asked the Marine who'd told Pete about the alliance. "Those guys are bad news, nothin' else but. You kiss them, it's like kissing a pig."

"I don't care," Pete said as he anted for the next hand. "As long as Japs end up dead on account of it, that's all that matters, far as I'm concerned. If I can't kill 'em myself, I'm happy when somebody else does it for me."

"Man," the other Marine said. "You've got it bad, don't you?"

"I guess maybe I do," answered Pete, who knew only too goddamn well he did. "They killed my sweetheart in Shanghai. They messed me up. I've been messing them up ever since."

They all knew his story. They'd been on Midway by themselves for so long, everybody knew everybody else's story. Everybody was sick to death of hearing everybody else's story, in fact. It was like going to a party where the phonograph played the same three records over and over till the neighbors started banging on the walls.

Pete tossed in his cards. It wasn't that he couldn't discard most of them and maybe draw something better. But the odds weren't great, and better probably wouldn't wind up good enough. Smarter to throw away and live to profit some other day.

When the sun sank into the Pacific, he unrolled his sleeping bag on the sand and went to bed there. They were putting the barracks back together. U.S. bombers had done a terrific job of smashing them up. But the weather was fine and mild. The dunes were just about as soft as the kind of mattress you'd get on a military-issue cot or bunk. Why bother, then?

Little by little, discipline on Midway was corroding. Pete could see it, but he couldn't see what to do about it. Nothing they did here now mattered, and they couldn't get off the island to go some place where what they did would count.

Stuck. Stuck, stuck, stuck.

The next morning, he ran into the quartermaster sergeant who'd issued him the new helmet he wouldn't get to use in action. Sure as hell, Vince Lindholm had pitched a hellacious tantrum when he realized he wasn't going to escape Midway, either. Since then, he'd settled down and turned into an ordinary Joe.

Pete waved to him. "How the fuck are ya?"

"I'm fucked, all right," Lindholm answered. "We all are. We didn't even get smooched."

"No. We all aren't fucked, and that's part of how come we're so fucked up." Pete realized he should probably have to pay a sin tax on his syntax, but that was how things had come out of his mouth. He went on, "How's about you requisition some broads for the island? If anybody can get us some pussy, I bet a quartermaster can."

"I wish!" By the way Lindholm said it, he really did wish. "The French would do it, or the Germans."

"Even the Japs," Pete said. "I don't think there were any of those waddayacallems—comfort women, that's the name they use—on Midway, but they set up whorehouses for their men all over the place."

"Any gals who did come here would be trapped on this lousy place as long as we are," Lindholm reminded him. "You wouldn't get a hell of a lot of volunteers for that."

"You might," Pete said. "Long as they didn't play cards or shoot dice, the girls who did come would be millionaires by the time they finally got to leave. And some of 'em might even figure it was their patriotic duty, like, to buck up our morale. I went round and round on this with a doc a while ago, but he was too high-toned, like, to want to try and do anything about it."

The quartermaster sergeant eyed him in amused admiration. "Beats me that you didn't talk him into it, 'cause you're good, you know? You're wasted as a Marine. You should be back in the States writing toothpaste commercials."

"If I could get back to the States, I wouldn't care what I was doing," Pete replied. "When I climbed onto Tern Island from the launch before I flew here, a guy in there with me kissed the pier because he'd been seasick. Put me back in America and I'd lay a big, wet smack on the first ground I touched, too. Bet your ass I would."

"So would I," Lindholm said. "So would everybody here."

"So send in whatever paperwork you need for some hookers," Pete said. "Maybe they'll send 'em. Even if they tell you no, how are you worse off?"

The quartermaster sergeant thought that over. Then he started to laugh. "I was going to say, because they'd call me Horny Vincent Lindholm or something like that—the nut who put in an order for dames.

But what the hell difference does it make, y'know? Long as I'm stuck on this goddamn island, who cares what they call me?"

He duly sent in the requisition, for ten blondes, ten brunettes, and ten redheads. It came back rejected in record time, with a stern warning against wasting any more of the War Department's precious time with facetious requisitions. He had to go all over Midway before he finally found a bookish Marine who knew what *facetious* meant.

"They thought I was kidding," he told Pete. "Kidding! Can you believe it?"

"Old fools," Pete said. "They haven't screwed in so long, they don't remember what the urge is like."

He did. Remember was all he could do, though. He had no idea when or if the old men who ran things would ever let him off Midway. In the meantime, there he stayed, on a sandy speck in the middle of the world's vastest sea. Forever or twenty minutes longer, whichever came first. That was sure how it looked.

Julius Lemp stared with something approaching religious adoration at the U-boat tied up alongside one of the piers in Kiel. "*Himmeldonner-wetter!*" he whispered. "If we'd had a few dozen of these when the war started, we would have swept the Royal Navy out of the North Sea and the Atlantic and starved England into surrendering in about three months."

Kapitän zur See Rochus Mauer looked pleased. He was a very senior engineering officer, a man who, in his own words, fought the war with a slashing slide rule. "Yes, the Type XXI is a whole different kind of boat," he said. "It takes performance to a new level."

"I'll bet it does!" Lemp exclaimed. "The jump between my Type VII and this is about like the one from a Panzer II to a Tiger, isn't it?"

"Well, something like that, perhaps." By the way Captain Mauer purred, Lemp would have bet he'd had a lot to do with the Type XXI's design.

If so, he had plenty to be proud of. The new boat's hull and conning tower were almost perfectly streamlined. The tower had a couple of

30mm gun turrets, one abaft the periscope and the other forward of it, so the boat could shoot at airplanes. Other than that, it was all metal with curves as sweet as a woman's. No projecting deck gun. No angles anywhere. It would slide through the water like a shark.

"Tell me again about the performance," Lemp said, as if he wanted to hear a particularly juicy dirty story once more.

"Speed on the surface is pretty much what you're used to—about sixteen knots," Mauer replied. "But that shape and the extra batteries we've loaded into the hull will gave you the same speed underwater. And if you stay below five knots, the enemy's listening devices won't be able to hear the engines."

"It's—gorgeous." Yes, Lemp might have been talking about a leggy chorus girl. He was head over heels, all right.

And he might get to have his way with a Type XXI, if not this boat then another one coming off the slips. The diesels that drove the U-boat on the surface and charged the batteries breathed through a *Schnorkel*. Not a single living skipper in the German Navy had more *Schnorkel* experience than one Julius Lemp. He'd fallen into a pile of shit when he sank the American *Athenia* by mistake, but now at last he'd grown out of it. And here he was, smelling like a rose.

"If only we could have had them even a couple of years ago," he said, longing in his voice.

"We—the development team—had worked out the proper hull form by then," Captain Mauer said. "But Dr. Walther had come up with a new hydrogen peroxide–powered engine that would have been wonderful . . . if only it worked better and didn't catch fire whenever you looked at it sideways."

"That doesn't sound so good," Lemp said.

"That wasn't so good. A U-boat with one of those engines in it was about as dangerous to itself as it was to the Royal Navy. The development team pointed this out to the powers that be. But Dr. Walther had political connections with people in the government. And so"—Mauer looked disgusted—"we wasted two years on boats with good hulls and death-trap propulsion systems."

"I hope we won't have to put up with that kind of nonsense any more," Lemp said. Despite the brave words, he couldn't help glancing up into the sky. The *Luftwaffe,* the most Nazified service in the *Wehrmacht,* kept fighting the Salvation Committee along with the SS and some diehard Army and Navy men. Bavaria was still a bloody mess, with Nuremberg and Munich remaining in Nazi hands.

"It would be nice if we didn't," Captain Mauer agreed. He'd worked for Hitler till the *Führer* got killed—maybe not always happily, but he had. So had an awful lot of other Germans. Lemp wanted to forget that he'd been one of them himself. He wanted to, but he hadn't managed it yet.

"I wonder what other little toys we might have had sooner if the Party hadn't kept pissing in the soup," he said.

Mauer started talking about airplane engines—talking with great enthusiasm and more technical knowledge than Lemp would have expected from somebody who specialized in designing U-boats. Lemp wasn't a bad technical man himself; a skipper had to know how his boat worked. He soon saw that he was outclassed, though. He did gather that the new engines could fly a plane without a propeller, and fly it faster than any prop could manage.

"A lovely application of engineering and physics—lovely!" Yes, Mauer was an enthusiast, all right. Of course, the other side had its own enthusiasts. Lemp remembered Admiral Dönitz's worries that sending Type VIIs out to sea was tantamount to murder because the limeys hunted them down so well.

He also wondered what would have happened had the Bolsheviks, not Germany's own generals, overthrown Hitler. He guessed Captain Mauer would have gone right on planning new and improved U-boats for the Reds . . . as long as they didn't shoot him for being a right-wing reactionary. He was one of those people who didn't care whom they worked for if they got to work at all.

And what about you? Lemp asked himself. Could he have taken a U-boat to sea flying the red flag of Communism? If the other choice was that firing squad, he suspected he could have. But he would have noticed more about his new masters than how they helped or hindered what he wanted to do anyhow.

He hoped he would have.

How could you know? Once you asked the question, the answer

seemed obvious. The only way you could know was by finding out. He hadn't just been willing to serve under the Nazis. He'd been eager. They promised glory. They promised promotions. They promised victory.

And if they'd delivered on everything they promised, chances were he'd still be eagerly serving under them to this day. Of course, if Stalin had delivered on everything the Russian Revolution promised, plenty of Soviet citizens wouldn't have greeted the oncoming Germans with bread and salt and welcomed them as liberators.

"You know something, sir?" he said to Rochus Mauer, not quite out of the blue.

"What's that?" the engineering officer asked.

"Politics is way too important to be left to politicians. All they ever do is make a hash of it."

Captain Mauer smiled. He had a rather foxy face, with bushy eyebrows, a russet mustache, and a pointed chin. "I won't try to tell you you're wrong, Commander. Politicians *do* make a hash of things. But do you know what else? Generals who end up running things make a hash of them, too. If you put engineers in charge, we'd only find some different way to foul them up."

"What's the answer, then?" Lemp asked.

"I haven't got one," Mauer said. "I wish I did, but I don't. We're people. Making messes is what we do. Love affairs should be great. And they are—till we see someone else we'd rather have. We spoil our children, or else we're so mean we make them hate us. We lie. We cheat. We steal. Is it any wonder our countries do the same?"

"When you put it like that, I guess not," Lemp replied.

Off in the distance, a machine gun rattled like one of those venomous American snakes. Lemp cocked his head toward the noise, gauging whether it was close enough to mean trouble. A couple of minutes later, a cannon answered. The machine gun fired another burst. The cannon spoke again, and then again. The machine gun stayed quiet after that. Lemp hoped the cannon belonged to the Salvation Committee.

"If all the men carried automatic rifles, machine guns wouldn't matter so much," Captain Mauer said.

"I understood that rifle rounds are so strong, it's hard to make an automatic rifle sturdy enough to stay reliable but light enough for a man to carry," Lemp said.

"From what I hear, they've developed a round halfway between the pistol cartridge a Schmeisser fires and a full-sized rifle round," Mauer answered. "It does the job. I haven't seen the weapon yet, but they're calling it a *Sturmgewehr*."

"An assault rifle?" Lemp echoed. "Well, isn't that interesting?"

Chapter 24

Aristide Demange sourly eyed the Germans going on about their business in southern Belgium. The truce between the new government in Germany and the Allies was holding. The business the *Boches* were going about was packing up and getting ready to go home. The matter-of-fact way they went at it suggested they'd been tourists here for the past few years, or possibly men who'd been assigned to work in a foreign land.

That might have been how they felt about it. Demange knew goddamn well how he felt about it. His trigger finger itched, that was how. There they were, figures in *Feldgrau*, some of them only a couple of hundred meters away. They weren't even trying to stay under cover. Of course he wanted to kill them!

Not all the French soldiers felt the same way, but some of them did. "Doesn't seem natural," one said, pointing toward the Germans. "Whenever I spot one of those *cons*, I know I'm supposed to shoot him. I know he'll shoot me if I don't, too."

"That's about the size of it." Demange nodded. "Only now we can't."

"Now we can't." The *poilu* nodded. "Seems a shame to let 'em go back to Bocheland without putting some holes in 'em, *n'est-ce pas*? In a few years, we'll have to kick 'em out of here again, chances are."

"I wouldn't be surprised," Demange said. "But knocking 'em flat so they'd know better than to try that kind of crap, the politicians have no stomach for it. It would cost a lot of lives, which they care about a little, and it would cost of lot of money, which they care about a lot. Keep taxes high and you might lose the next election, God forbid."

A truck rolled up, over on the other side of the wire. Some of the Germans piled into it. A couple of them kissed Belgian women good-bye before they did. One Fritz—an officer, by his cap—shook hands with a Belgian in a top hat. They exchanged bows. They didn't brush cheeks, but it was plainly a near-run thing. The officer got into the truck, too. Smoke belching from its exhaust, it headed off to the east.

Louis Mirouze came up in time to see the truck disappear behind a grove of beat-up apple trees. "Some more of them gone," the second lieutenant said.

"They aren't gone," Demange said. "If they were gone, they'd be under those fat black crosses they use on their military graveyards. They're just going back to get ready for the next round."

"It could be. I think it's all too likely, in fact," Mirouze said. "But I also think that won't happen tomorrow or next week or next year. What will you do in the meanwhile?"

"Whatever the fat *cochons* set over me tell me to do. What else?" Demange answered. "They'd have to cut me out of this goddamn uniform. I don't know how to take it off any more. How about you, kid?"

Mirouze's sallow cheeks turned pink. "You will laugh."

"Try me."

"At the university, I was a student of American literature. Well, no—of American writing. I am particularly interested in the popular magazines: the stories of the Old West, the crime stories, the love stories, the prize-fighting stories, the stories about rocket ships and Martians with eyes on stalks."

He was right—Demange did laugh. Then the older man asked, "Can you get a job teaching about that kind of stuff?"

"You are a practical type," Mirouze said with respect. "I read these things because I enjoy them. They fascinate me. America must be a very strange place. I have no idea whether I can get that kind of position. I won't starve if it turns out not to be possible. There is always work for someone who can translate between English and French."

"You aren't wrong about that," Demange agreed. "You would've come in handy if there were ever any limeys or Yanks within fifty kilometers of where we're at. How come you didn't say anything before about how you get a bulge in your trousers about this American *merde*?"

The younger man blushed once more. "I told you—you would have laughed. I found out very soon that you—please excuse me—did not always take me seriously."

If anything, that was an understatement. Demange had hardly ever taken Second Lieutenant Mirouze seriously. The rule, however, did have its exceptions. "I took you seriously whenever we messed with the *Boches*. You need a wheelbarrow to carry your balls, and that makes up for a lot of other crap."

"For which I thank you very much, sir," Mirouze said gravely. "If you could have seen how frightened I always was inside—"

"That doesn't mean anything. *Rien*, you hear?" Demange broke in. "The only people who aren't scared are the ones who're too dumb to know what can happen to 'em, and you aren't like that."

"There are some others," Mirouze said. "Hitler had many things wrong with him, but stupid he was not. He enjoyed the soldier's life in the last war, though, the fighting along with the rest."

"A few like that, yes," Demange allowed. "Not many. A lot of them get killed in a hurry. Some of the others grow up to be generals or politicians. They send out the next batch to get killed for them."

Louis Mirouze sent him a quizzical look. "If you feel that way about it, why do you stay a soldier?"

"Why? I'll tell you why. Because I'm fucking good at it, that's why. Our *con* of a colonel wanted to get me shot last Christmas, and he didn't give a shit if he threw away the whole company as long as I stopped one. But we took that village without losing a man, and we all slept warm in it, too."

"If you had a higher rank, you could accomplish more."

"If I had a higher rank, I'd be a *con* myself," Demange retorted. Something in Mirouze's face made him chuckle and shift his Gitane from one side of his mouth to the other. "All right, all right. If I had a higher rank, I'd be a bigger *con*. There. You happy now?"

"*Mais certainement,* Lieutenant." Mirouze sounded almost as dry as Demange could manage.

A couple of more German trucks rattled up to take away more troops. Each one also towed a 105mm howitzer. Demange knew he wouldn't be sorry to see those snub-nosed murderers disappear back into Germany. The trucks, though, sounded as arthritic as they looked. The Americans, now, the Americans by God knew how to build trucks. Demange knew little and cared less about American boxing stories. Trucks mattered, though.

American trucks, he thought, could even stand up to Russia's ruts and bogs. German models hadn't been able to; they started falling to pieces in short order. Demange couldn't get too scornfully amused about that—French trucks went to bits just about as fast.

More *Boches* climbed into the trucks. On Belgian roads, they'd do all right. Pretty soon, the *Wehrmacht* would leave the Low Countries. Everything would get back to normal. Or everything would except the endless kilometers of barbed wire, the minefields that would go on maiming people and farm animals for years to come, the trenches, the bomb craters, the reinforced-concrete fortifications that would take dynamite to remove . . .

Demange remarked on those. Mirouze looked back at him. "Well, sir, if you're going to worry about every little detail . . ."

"Ha!" Demange barked sour laughter. "You'd better watch yourself there, sonny. Bits of me are rubbing off on you. That's fine when you're in the trenches like this. Maybe not so good at the university, eh?"

"Maybe—but then you never know for sure," Mirouze answered. "If I booby-trap a professor's office, mm, that's one way to get ahead."

This time, Demange laughed for real. "There you go! And if the Germans get frisky again and the Army calls you back, you might get stuck with me again." He'd had plenty of worse men under him, but he was damned if he'd say so. If Mirouze couldn't figure it out, the hell with him. Demange grubbed in his pocket for his pack of cigarettes.

. . .

Chaim Weinberg stared at the Statue of Liberty and the skyscrapers stabbing the heavens as the *Ciudad de Santander* chugged into New York harbor. He'd grown up with all this stuff, but it still felt dreamlike to him. He hadn't set eyes on any of it since 1936.

Just about eight years, he thought in wonder. He'd been a kid when he set off to fight for the Spanish Republic. He wasn't a kid any more. A lot of things, yeah, but not a kid. He looked down at the wreckage of his left hand. He had the scars to prove he was no kid, all right. He had a son to prove he was no kid, too, a son he'd probably never set eyes on again.

Tugboats shoved the freighter against a pier. The *Santander* had only a few cabins. They said Chaim's was the best one. The good news was that he believed them. The bad news, unfortunately, was also that he believed them.

No—the good news was that he hadn't had to worry about U-boats on the Atlantic crossing. They'd all gone home to Germany. The coalition of generals and fat cats heading the new government didn't look to be any bargain. Compared to what the generals and fat cats had overthrown, though, they also didn't seem so bad.

The scene on the pier wasn't like the ones you saw in the movies when the big ocean liner came into port. No crowds in evening clothes out there, no band playing, no confetti. Next to no nothing. A short, broad-shouldered man in a dark brown fedora, a tweed jacket, and work pants stood there, along with a gray-haired woman wearing a flowered housedress.

Chaim waved. Moishe and Ruth Weinberg—his mother and father—waved back. "I gotta clear customs before I can see you," he shouted. A moment later, he yelled the same thing in Yiddish. His father waved to show he got that.

Sure enough, when the gangplank came down, it came down on the far side of a chicken-wire fence on wheels that they rolled out to keep people from just strolling on into New York City. Chaim shouldered his duffel bag and went into the customs shed. It wasn't as if he had a lot of treasures from Spain. A few old clothes, a big bottle of Spanish brandy for his folks, another one that he'd mostly emptied on the way over, some newspapers with photos of the Nationalist surrender—that was about it.

He pulled his passport out of his pocket to show it to the customs clerk. The green cover was bent and crinkled and stained with sweat and mud and blood. Some of the inside pages carried those stains, too.

As soon as the clerk opened the passport, he frowned. It wasn't because of the stains. As far as Chaim could tell, he didn't even notice those. He was looking for other things. "Don't you have any current identification?" he asked in annoyance. "This passport expired years ago."

"Well, I've got this." Chaim produced his discharge papers from the Army of the Spanish Republic. The document was full of seals and stamps and rococo typography.

But it cut no ice with the customs clerk. "Have anything in a language a man can read? English? French? German?"

"Nope. My mom and pop are waiting for me on the pier, though. They'll tell you I'm still the same *meshuggeneh* who got the passport."

"What have you been doing in Europe, in, ah, Spain"—the clerk went through the endorsements on the passport's back pages—"after this document became invalid?"

"Fighting Fascism," Chaim answered proudly. "I can show you my picture in the paper when the Nationalists finally gave up. It's pretty little, but you can still spot my smiling *punim*."

He started to pull the newspaper out of the duffel. The clerk waved for him to stop. "Mr. Simmons!" the fellow called. "We have a difficult case here, I'm afraid."

Chaim's heart sank when he saw Mr. Simmons. From pale, bald head to gold-rimmed round glasses to respectable suit, the man was the spitting image of mid-level bureaucrats all over the world. What would he make of a rough-talking Marxist-Leninist Jew with out-of-date travel documents?

"What's going on?" he asked, and his voice was as gray as his jacket.

The younger clerk and Chaim took turns explaining. Each talked over the other. Pretty soon, each was making a point of talking over the other. Mr. Simmons listened. He asked a few questions. He looked at Chaim's passport, and at his smashed left hand, and at his discharge papers. Then he asked, "When you were in Spain, Mr. Weinberg, did you know an Abraham Lincoln named Wilmer Christiansen?"

"A long time ago," Chaim answered. "Redhead, wasn't he? Poor guy got killed on the Ebro in '38, if I remember straight. He was all right, Will was. How come?"

"He was my nephew," Simmons said. "Now let's get this straightened out, shall we?"

And they did. With a few thumps from a rubber stamp, the irregularities in Chaim's paperwork disappeared. The clerk who'd called Simmons over looked discontented, but he kept his mouth shut. When you called your superior over and he did something you didn't expect, you were stuck with it.

Duffel bag over his shoulder again, Chaim walked out of the customs shed. He put the duffel down to thump his father on the back and hug his mother. "Your poor hand! *Vey iz mir!*" Ruth Weinberg exclaimed.

"It's okay," Chaim said. English felt funny in his mouth. He'd used it less and less as time in Spain went by. Americans in the Abe Lincolns kept getting hurt or killed, and Spaniards took their places. German-speaking Internationals could handle his Yiddish. He'd spoken Spanish whenever he went behind the lines, too, except when he was talking with Dr. Alvarez.

"You want I should carry the sack?" his father asked when they headed for the closest subway stop.

"Thanks, Pop. I can do it," Chaim said. His head might have been on a swivel. None of the buildings here had been hit by bombs or artillery. Out of all the windows he saw, only one or two were boarded up. No bullet holes scarred concrete or pocked wooden doors. Cars and trucks and buses all seemed new and freshly painted. People didn't have the pale, scrawny, wary look that went with hunger and fear. To someone newly come from Spain, everybody looked rich.

His mother saw the amazement on his face, but didn't understand why it was there. "It's the war," she said apologetically. "Nothing's been the way it ought to be since those filthy Japs jumped us."

Chaim wondered if she'd ever seen a Japanese man in her life.

There were some in New York City, but not many. But that wasn't why he dropped the duffel on the sidewalk (butts everywhere—not many folks here needed to scrounge them) and laughed till he had to hold his sides. It was either laugh or cry. Laughing felt better.

It did to him, anyhow. Ruth Weinberg looked mad. "I said maybe something funny?" she asked, her voice sharp.

"Yeah, you did, Ma. Sorry, but you did," Chaim answered. "If this looks bad to you . . . This is so much better than anything I saw in Spain, I don't know how to tell you. Now I believe all the stories you guys tell about the shtetls, on account of I've seen that kind of stuff myself."

"So why did you go over there, then?" his mother said.

"Because the Republic was fighting the kind of *mamzrim* who start pogroms, that's why," Chaim said. "Because now Spain is free." That was the simplest way to put it. He didn't talk about reeducation camps, or about his suspicion that he would have wound up in one if he'd stayed in the Republic much longer.

"What will you do now that you're back?" his father asked as they went down the steps to the trains.

"I dunno. Whatever I can find." Chaim worried about it not in the least. In a land like this, dripping with milk and money, he was sure he'd manage something.

When word of the peace with Germany reached the Ukraine, Ivan Kuchkov figured they would do one of two things with him. Either they'd toss him him out of the Red Army and ship him back to his collective farm or they'd put him on the Trans-Siberian Railway and turn him loose against the Japanese. Now that the Fritzes were old news, the fight against the little yellow monkeys was warming up again.

But no. They had something else in mind. His regiment had gone east, all right, but not very far east. They were still this side of Kiev, combing the countryside for Ukrainian nationalist bandits. The Ukrainian rats had jumped straight into bed with the Nazis, hoping to use them to pay back the Soviet government for starving their country into collectivization.

Now the Nazis were gone. Even the stupid Germans couldn't stomach them any more. But the bandits, or some of them, kept fighting. They had their reasons for hating the Red Army. And they knew they'd get forever in the gulag or a bullet in the back of the neck if they gave up, so what did they have to lose by going down rifle in hand?

"Fuck me if I wouldn't sooner take on those Hitlerite pricks," Kuchkov complained after a nasty skirmish with the Banderists. "When they got in trouble, they retreated. These pussies, you've got to kill 'em."

"And they're trying to kill you till you do," Sasha Davidov agreed mournfully. He had a bandage on his right forearm. It was only a graze, but you didn't want to make even a nodding acquaintance with somebody else's bullet.

"Too goddamn right, they are." Ivan muttered more obscenities under his breath. He had the bad feeling he knew why his regiment had drawn this stinking, dangerous duty. Someone who could give orders that moved units around was still working on paying them back for plugging that political officer.

He glanced over at Davidov. The little Jew looked back. His shoulders went up and down in a small shrug, as if to say *What can you do?* Ivan already knew what he could do: not a goddamn thing. He couldn't even complain to Lieutenant Obolensky. If he did, the company commander would tell him *They're screwing me the same way they're screwing you.* And he'd be right.

Go over the lieutenant's head? What a joke! Anyone with fancier shoulder boards would tell him *Shut up and soldier, soldier!* That had only one answer: *I serve the Soviet Union!*

If *I serve the Soviet Union!* was all you could say, no point to complaining in the first place. Besides, if he talked to anybody of higher rank than Obolensky, the Chekists would hear about it. Yes, this was a nasty duty. Yes, no one in the blue that was the NKVD's arm-of-service color would shed a tear if a bandit put one through his brisket.

But they could find worse things to do with him—and to him—if he kicked up a fuss. Right now, they figured he wasn't worth the trouble. If he made them change their minds . . . He didn't want to find out what would happen then.

And so, the next morning, his section combed through the riverside woods again, flushing out Banderists. The bandits were in the woods, all right, in them and well dug in there. Had they been Germans, the Red Army would have pasted the woods with a few dozen Katyushas and then sent in troops to scrape up the stunned survivors.

They were only Banderists, though. Nobody who could order up the rockets wanted to waste them on worthless Ukrainians. The regiment got to clean them out the hard way, the old-fashioned way, then. If some soldiers got killed taking care of it, well, you could always find more soldiers.

The bandits fought with a motley mix of Nazi and Soviet weapons. They had an MG-34, but fired it only in short bursts. Ivan guessed they were low on 7.92mm cartridges. They wouldn't get any more from the Fritzes. Once what they had was gone, it was gone for good.

They had to know they were licked. Without the Nazis to help them out and to distract the Red Army, they hadn't a prayer of winning. They stayed in their foxholes and fought it out anyway. Some of them stayed quiet till the Red Army men went past them, then shot their enemies in the back. The Russians had used that trick against the Hitlerites whenever they could. Seeing it turned against them wasn't so much fun.

"Give it up, you fools!" Sasha Davidov shouted to the Ukrainians. "All you'll do is die here."

"Suck my dick, you Communist whore!" a Banderist yelled back. Yes, they knew what they were doing. They knew why they were doing it. They were bound to know it was hopeless, too. They went ahead and did it anyhow. That made them very brave or very stupid, depending on how you looked at things.

The Red Army men took only a couple of prisoners. One of the Banderists actually gave up—he decided he would rather die slowly than all at once. Kuchkov's men found the other guy behind a tree with a wound in the shoulder and another in the side.

"If you feel like doing me a favor, you'll finish me off and not let the Chekists get their claws in me," the Ukrainian said in his accented Russian.

"I will if you want," Kuchkov said—he had no more use for the

NKVD than he did for the Banderists. "Fuck your mother, are you sure?"

"Fuck you in the mouth, I sure am, Red," the injured man replied. "I hurt like a son of a bitch. Might as well get it over with."

A short burst from the PPD gave him what he wanted. One of the men in Ivan's section must have said something about it to Lieutenant Obolensky, because the company commander took Ivan aside and said, "Are you sure you should have killed that bandit?"

"You mean the wounded prick? Fuck yes, Comrade Lieutenant! He was shot a couple of times. I hope some whore would do that for me if I asked him to. Even the Hitlerites'd put a sorry bastard out of his misery sometimes."

Speaking carefully, Obolensky replied, "I hope it doesn't get back to State Security that you killed the Banderist to keep him from telling them whatever he knew."

"Oh." Ivan considered that, but not for long. Then he laughed. "Fuck 'em all, you know? They can already drop on me because of Vitya and the *politruk*. If the cunts do, they do. *Nichevo,* right?"

"*Nichevo*—right," Obolensky said. "But there's a difference between not being able to do anything about it and swimming around in gravy before you jump into the wolf's mouth."

"I guess so, Comrade Lieutenant. You're a goddamn good guy, you know?"

"*Spasibo,*" Obolensky said gravely.

"You're a goddamn good guy," Ivan repeated, "but fuck 'em all anyway. I've been doing this shit too cocksucking long. I'm not scared any more. I don't want 'em to jug me, but I'm fucking sick of worrying about it. They shoot me? So, fine—they shoot me. They send me to Kolyma? Kolyma can't be too much worse than some of the fuckstorms I've already been through."

"I believe you," Obolensky said slowly. "The NKVD would have a much harder time keeping the country in line if everybody felt that way."

Ivan only shrugged. What he really wanted to do was ask the lieutenant who'd blabbed about him. He didn't waste his time, though. Obolensky wouldn't tell him. He knew as much without asking. In the lieutenant's footwraps, he wouldn't have answered a question like that, either. Obolensky needed people to tell him things. And if Ivan found out who the rat was, that bitch would be a fatal accident that hadn't happened yet.

So Kuchkov shrugged one more time. He might be able to find out without asking anybody, at least in so many words. He might not read or write, but he sure as hell could add two and two.

Then he could fix things so the Banderists did his dirty work for him. Or if not them, the Japs. Sooner or later, the regiment *would* head for the Far East. The Japs were supposed to be just as much fun as the Germans, only in a different way. Yeah, they'd give plenty of chances for payback. You bet they would!

The big, snorting American lorry rolled away from the front. "And so we bid farewell to beautiful, romantic Belgium," Alistair Walsh said grandly as he sat in the back with a squad's worth of men. "We say good-bye to the exotic natives and their quaint and curious customs, and to our fellow holidaymakers from the strange and distant land of Deutsch."

"Blimey," Jack Scholes said. "Staff's gone clean barmy, 'e 'as." By the way the rest of the Tommies nodded and rolled their eyes, they sided with the gritty little private. No, Scholes had a new lance-corporal's single chevron on his left sleeve: a parting gift, as it were. Well, it wasn't as if he hadn't earned the stripe the hard way.

"Not me," Walsh said. "You blokes have no poetry in your souls— that's what the trouble is."

"Or m'ybe you've got rocks in your 'ead," Scholes said. Again, by all the signs a vote would have gone his way.

Walsh pulled a new packet of Navy Cuts out of his breast pocket. After lighting his own, he passed the cigarettes around. "He may be balmy, but he's not a bad old bugger," one of the soldiers said, as if he weren't there. Most of the others nodded one more time. They were, after all, enjoying his bounty. He was about as much a politician as any other staff sergeant, and not shy about buying popularity.

The canvas top was spread over its steel hoops to keep sun and rain off the passengers in the truck. Walsh could see out the back, but that wasn't much of a view: the road the truck had just traveled over, and a little off to one side of it. The farther from the front they got, the fewer the smashed trees and flattened houses he spotted.

"Bloody fucking hell," said Gordon McAllister, who sat next to him. The big Scot's burr only added to the sincerity of the sentiment. "We lived through it." He didn't talk much. When he did, it was to the point.

Unless we run over a mine or something ran through Walsh's head. He left it there. You didn't want to say some things, for fear of making them come true. Any educated toff would tell you such magical thinking was superstitious nonsense. Walsh didn't care. *Not* mentioning such things couldn't make matters worse.

On they went. They met no mines, for which the staff sergeant was duly grateful. They did have to get off the road once, to jounce along on a corduroyed track through a field. When they came back to the paving, Walsh saw why they'd left: a repair crew was filling in an enormous crater.

"Fritzes must've dropped that one about an hour before the shooting stopped," Scholes said.

"Why'd they send us down this stinking road, then?" somebody else asked. "Couldn't they find one without a big fucking hole in it?"

That was one of those questions without any answer, of course. Maybe the fellow who'd planned the withdrawal had no idea about the bomb crater. Maybe he'd figured the corduroyed stretch would handle the traffic. Maybe he hadn't given a damn one way or the other. Maybe the driver was lost.

Or maybe, and perhaps more likely, nobody'd given a damn one way or the other. The British Expeditionary Force was leaving Belgium. By lorry, by train, by bus, and, for all Walsh knew, by stagecoach, the Tommies were pulling out and heading for Calais and the other Channel Ports. Pretty soon, they'll all be off the Continent and back in Blighty again.

Most of their German counterparts were already out of Belgium and Holland and even Luxembourg and back in the *Vaterland*. Walsh wondered what the Salvation Committee would do with all the young men they'd have to demobilize, and how unhappy those young men would prove when they had trouble finding work.

For that matter, he wondered how his own country would cope with swarms of demobilized soldiers looking for jobs. That hadn't been easy the last time around. This go looked no easier.

It wasn't his problem, though. The people who would have to worry about it were the bright young men in the government: the bright young men who were his friends and acquaintances, thanks to an accident of fate.

If Rudolf Hess had chosen to parachute into some other field . . . Walsh shook his head. In that case, someone else would have fetched the deputy *Führer* to the authorities, and one Alistair Walsh never would have found his affairs commingled with those of the great, the famous, and the powerful. But Hess had come down in that field outside of Dundee, and Walsh had taken him back into the town, and nothing was the same as it would have been otherwise. Better? Worse? How could he know? But surely different.

He wondered what had happened to Hess since Hitler's untimely demise. He didn't recall hearing anything about Hess since then, not that the man with the bushy eyebrows died a brave Nazi death, not that he was still alive and fighting, not that he'd been captured, not . . . anything.

His high-placed friends would know. Once he got back to England, he could find out. If he remembered. If he didn't, that wasn't the biggest thing in the world, either.

After a while, the lorry pulled off onto the shoulder. "Break time," the driver announced. "Grab some grub, brew some char, go off into the bushes and set your minds at ease."

"I don't keep my mind there," Walsh said.

"You've got to remember, Staff—you're gettin' old," Jack Scholes said. The other Tommies in the back of the truck chuckled. The driver whooped—Walsh couldn't give him trouble once this ride ended.

They washed down whatever they happened to have on them with tea brewed over smokeless cookers. Then they climbed back into the lorry. Before long, they crossed from Belgium into France. Walsh never would have known it, except that they passed two flagpoles, one flying a tricolor of black, yellow, and red, the other a red, white, and blue three-striper.

As night was falling, the lorry pulled into a tent city on the outskirts of Calais. "This is where I came in," Walsh said. "Where I came in three different times, as a matter of fact."

"Next time you get over 'ere, you can pay your own way," Scholes said with a sly grin.

"I've seen all kinds of funny places on His Majesty's shilling," Walsh said in musing tones. "France and Belgium and Norway and Egypt . . . I never would have set eyes on the Pyramids and the Sphinx if I hadn't gone there on duty. That's something I'll remember the rest of my days. Christ, chances are I'd never even have seen Scotland if I'd stayed a miner."

"No loss." Private McAllister was as glad to be away from his homeland as Walsh was to have escaped Wales.

"'E's right, Oi reckon," Scholes said, grinning still. "'Ow much would you 'ave missed it?"

"Not bloody much—for all kinds of reasons." Again, Walsh saw Hess' parachute coming down in that field. That had turned his life inside out and upside down, sure as hell. He went on, "I got shot in France, and I got shot in Africa, too. Wherever you do it, it's not something I recommend. I didn't get shot in Norway, but God only knows why. The Fritzes up there gave it their best try, no doubt about that."

"An' now they're leaving, an' that Quisling sod 'oo 'elped run the place for 'em, 'e's got to find 'imself somewhere to 'ide," Scholes said.

"Him and Mussert the Dutchman and Degrelle the Belgian and more besides," Walsh agreed. "They're all homegrown Nazis, so I don't know if the Salvation Committee will even let them hole up in Germany. If their own people catch 'em, they'll win a noose or a bullet."

"Tell me they don't deserve it, Staff," the younger man said.

Walsh shook his head. "I can't. I think they do. Then maybe we'll have a little peace and quiet—till the next crop of gangsters and traitors gets taller and starts to need cutting down, anyhow."

Chapter 25

Peggy Druce scooped bacon out of the frying pan with a slotted spatula and set the rashers on paper napkins that would soak up the
grease. After cracking eggs into a bowl that already held some heavy
cream and stirring the mix, she started scrambling them in the pan.

Watching from the kitchen table, Dave Hartman blew a stream of
cigarette smoke up toward the ceiling. "You're so smooth when you do
that," he said admiringly.

"Practice," Peggy answered. "Not like it's the first time I ever fixed
bacon and eggs." At her age, there weren't many things left to do for
the first time. Too many of the ones that were left had to do with getting old and getting feeble and dying. The longer she didn't find out
about those, the happier she would stay.

But Dave took her words in a different sense. "That's it!" he said,
and nodded in complete concord. "That's just it! You remind me of a
guy who's been working a drill press so long, he knows in his sleep all
the things it can do and all the things he can do with it. When I mess
around in the kitchen, I'm more like somebody who's maybe heard of
a drill press but hasn't hardly seen one."

"I'll bet you do fine." Peggy had trouble imagining Dave as less than competent at anything to which he set his hand. She served up breakfast. "Do you want another cup of coffee with this?"

"Sure. Thanks, sweetie."

After she poured for him and for her, she put the frying pan in the sink and filled it with soapy water. That would save on elbow grease when she did the dishes. Things wouldn't dry out and stick to the inside of the pan like cement. "Why can't they make a frying pan where it's enamel or something else smooth in there, so you could wash it easier?" she said.

"You could . . ." Dave stretched out the word, and the silence after it, while he thought things over. Then he went on, "I bet it'd be swell to begin with. After a while, though, you'd bang on the enamel with your spatula and your big fork and your serving spoon, and the surface would get as scratched up as steel does, or maybe worse. Same with the grit from cleanser, and you couldn't use steel wool. If you had nothing but wooden kitchen tools and you washed your frying pan with a sponge and soap all the time, it might stay okay long enough to be worthwhile."

"I guess." Peggy was glad he didn't make her sound like a jerk even while he picked to pieces what she'd thought was her good idea. She continued, "There ought to be something like enamel that food wouldn't stick to but that you wouldn't need to baby."

"Yeah, there ought to. Only trouble is, I have no idea what that'd be," Dave said. "I wish I did—I bet I could get rich off it." He shrugged. "I'm not a metallurgist, or a chemist, either. Working with metal and stuff, you pick up bits and pieces, but bits and pieces are all I'll ever have. For a guy who quit school halfway through the tenth grade, I've done okay for myself."

"You sure have. Your hands know just what they're doing." Peggy winked at him. "They probably do when you're at work, too."

He blushed like a kid still wet behind the ears, though her language hadn't been even slightly blue. He was more straitlaced about those things than Herb. Talking dirty had made Herb laugh and got him excited. It shocked Dave, all the more so since he thought of her as a high-class lady. That didn't stop him from enjoying her company when they were together in bed, or why would she have just cooked him breakfast? It did mean she behaved differently with him from the way she would have with her ex-husband.

Herb hadn't been Peggy's first man, though she didn't know if he knew that. He had been the first whose likes and dislikes she'd paid close attention to. Now she was learning somebody else.

And somebody else was learning her, too. They'd fumbled some to begin with, each finding out what worked with the other and what didn't work so well. That seemed strange and interesting. She and Herb had known the right answers without thinking, which might have been part of the problem. The other part was that, after she got back from Europe, they'd known without caring.

Care Dave did. If he was as precise with his lathes and presses and punches as he was with her, he had to be the best machinist in Pennsylvania, if not in the whole country. And he still seemed surprised she wanted to fool around with him. She found that flattering and funny at the same time.

He glanced over at the clock above the stove. Her eyes followed his. It was a few minutes before eight. "Want I should turn on the radio, see what's gone wrong since last night?" he said.

"Sure. Just because it's Sunday, that doesn't mean everything's perfect," Peggy said.

She'd never had trouble living without much in the way of religion. Neither had Herb, who was too cynical to believe in things he couldn't see for himself. Dave wasn't somebody who sang hymns in church, but he took for granted the beliefs he'd soaked up as a kid. Peggy hadn't exactly shocked him, but she had made him blink a few times.

He clicked the knob on the little kitchen set. When the sound came up, a smooth-voiced announcer was flogging Bon Ami cleanser. He claimed it didn't scratch. Dave's raised eyebrow called him a liar.

"This is Lowell Thomas with the news," came next. "The Soviet Union has declared martial law in newly annexed Lithuania after two assassins, one armed with a bomb, the other with a submachine gun, murdered Field Marshal Ivan Koniev, Stalin's military governor, as he traveled by car from his residence to his office in Kaunas. Kaunas is currently the capital of Lithuania, though the recently incorporated Vilno may take the other city's place.

"Speaking from Finland, Lithuanian exile groups call Koniev's assassination a powerful blow for liberty. Russian reprisals in occupied Lithuania are said to be very harsh, although not much news has come out of the USSR following the announcement of the killing."

"God help the Lithuanians," Peggy said. "Stalin will jump on them with both feet, and he'll put on hobnailed boots before he does it, too. He's not quite Hitler, but the choice between them was always the choice between worster and worstest."

Dave hoisted an eyebrow again. "You talk funny sometimes, know that?"

"No comment has come from the White House yet," Lowell Thomas went on. "The United States has not officially recognized the Russian occupation of Lithuania, Latvia, and Estonia, any more than we have officially recognized the German occupation of Czechoslovakia."

"But we ain't gonna fight about any of them," Dave put in. Peggy nodded; it looked the same way to her.

"American freighters continue to carry trucks, tanks, planes, and other military supplies to Murmansk and Archangel," the radio said. "No one expects anything the USSR does in Lithuania to hurt the Russian-American alliance against Tojo's Japan."

Peggy nodded again. Sure as hell, that sounded like the way the world worked. The little peoples, the Estonians and Latvians and Lithuanians and Czechs, got the shitty end of the stick while the big countries did as they pleased. The Iroquois and Cherokees and Apaches might sympathize with the minnows on the other side of the Atlantic. They sat on reservations; their European counterparts were under martial law. And the sympathy wouldn't do anybody any good.

"American bombers pounded Wake Island again," Lowell Thomas said. "And fast American patrol and torpedo boats—PT boats, the Navy calls them—have raided the fringes of the Japanese Empire and inflicted damage all out of proportion to their size. Our submarine war against Japanese shipping also is producing important results."

He could say it. People here would mostly believe it. Why not?

They couldn't very well hop aboard one of those PT boats to check for themselves. German and Russian propaganda worked the same way. Did truth lie behind the words?

When she put that question to Dave Hartman, he just said, "We'll all find out, won't we?" And that was about the size of that.

Kurt Poske nudged Saul Goldman. "How'd it feel to see your folks at last, Adi?" the loader asked.

"Weird. That's the only word I can think of," Saul answered. "I mean, I'm glad they made it through the bombings. I'm glad they're safe. But I don't belong there any more."

"Huh," Poske said, chewing on that.

Saul wished he were talking to Theo instead. Theo would understand what he was talking about: Theo didn't fit in anywhere, either. No wonder he played goalkeeper. Kurt was too sane, too normal, to get it.

Or Saul thought so, till Poske said, "You've been at the front too long, is what it is."

"That sure may be some of it," Saul said. "Although my old man was in the trenches the last round, so he knows about that. Now he knows I know about it, too. But the big thing is, I like being a panzer man better than I liked anything I was doing when I used to live here. Even if I weren't, ah, what I am"—even now, he had trouble saying he was a Jew—"I wouldn't have anything going for me except this."

"You're not the only guy I know who talks that way," Poske said. "Me, I want to get home. My old man's a cabinetmaker. Well, he's in an aircraft plant now, but that's what he does. It's a good trade. I did some before I got called up. I'll be able to handle more now, maybe take over the business when my dad decides to pack it in."

"I don't have anything like that to go back to," Saul said. And wasn't that the truth! No matter how much his father wished he would, he cared nothing for ancient history. He'd learned some in spite of himself, but it didn't do anything for him.

"You could play football," Kurt said. "You're good enough. You might make some real money doing that, not *Wehrmacht* pigeon feed."

"For a little while, I might. Not for long. I'm already twenty-seven, so I've got maybe six years, tops," Saul said. "If I tear up a knee or break an ankle, it's all over right there. I love to play—you know that. But I can't count on football."

Poske's gray eyes met Saul's brown ones. You always thought of the loader as the dummy in a panzer crew because he had the simplest job. But Kurt, Saul realized, wasn't such a dope after all. He said, "Can you count on the *Wehrmacht*? Do you still want to be a *Stabsobergefreiter* when you're forty-five? Will the big shots want you in that slot then?"

"*Scheisse*," Saul muttered—that was much too good a question. The *Wehrmacht* didn't officially know he was a Jew, of course. But what it officially knew and what it knew were two different things. No *Mischling* or Jew could become even an *Unteroffizier*. They all topped out at the highest grade of senior private. Or they did now. Saul said, "I hope the rules will change now that the Nazis aren't making them any more."

"Well, there is that," Kurt allowed. "They went overboard, no two ways about it. What could you do, though, when they'd kill you or toss you into Dachau if you complained?"

If everybody had complained, right from the start . . . If everyone's clothes had sported yellow stars when Jews were ordered to wear them . . . But how often did human nature work that way? Most of the time, people were just glad to watch somebody else get it in the neck. That meant *they* weren't. You thought of yourself first, then of your kin, and then of other folks like yourself.

You had to have an elastic soul to stretch it wider than that and think of people not much like you as your fellow human beings. Most folks' tolerance didn't go so wide. The Nazis weren't dopes. They'd understood that, all right.

So Kurt wasn't a hero and he wasn't a martyr. Hardly anybody was. You admired those few brave people, but who wanted to imitate them? "You couldn't do anything," Saul said. "You always played square with me, and that was plenty."

"Thanks, Adi." Kurt Poske eyed him again. "That's not even your real name, is it?"

"No, but so what?" Saul said. "By now I'm more used to it than the one I was born with." He meant that. He'd been Adi Stoss all through the war. Trying to go back would just confuse him. Like the rest of the world, he already felt confused enough.

If they changed the rules, if they turned Jews into citizens again, they might let him become a noncom. He thought he would make a pretty fair sergeant and panzer commander one of these days. Nobody would try to push him around, that was for sure. And when he wondered what he needed to do and how to go about doing it, he could model himself on Hermann Witt.

That was funny, wasn't it? The son of a professor of classics and ancient history hoping to become a *Feldwebel* and go on telling a panzer crew what to do? It would have been hysterical, not just funny, if he hadn't thought his father would be proud of him rather than horrified.

You wanted to defend your country if it needed you. Of course, you also wanted your country to defend you if you needed it. Hitler's *Reich* hadn't done so well on that score, not if you were a Jew. The Salvation Committee was bound to do better there. It couldn't very well do worse.

If they ever figured out that Adalbert Stoss and Saul Goldman were the same person, more than his religion might stand between him and sergeant's rank. There was the small matter of a murder charge. Or there might be. His panzer had helped smash the *Rathaus* in Münster to charred rubble. If his file there hadn't gone up in smoke, water from fire hoses might have turned it to unreadable pulp. He could hope so.

Here came a kid in black coveralls with a Schmeisser in his hands and a worried look on his face. Seeing Saul and Kurt sitting on the grass by their Panzer IV, he said, "Excuse me, but is this the machine that needs a new driver?"

"That's right," Saul answered. "It was my slot till our commander got shot. I didn't know if they'd send us another sergeant or a new driver."

"Looks like they're gonna put you in the turret to stay, Adi," Kurt said. "Congratulations, man."

"Thanks," Saul said. He turned back to the kid. "If you're going to drive, I guess I am in charge of this traveling madhouse for a while. I'm

Adi Stoss, and this other lazy bum here is Kurt Poske. Who the hell are you?"

"I'm Claus Valentiner." The new man presented his *Soldbuch*. The pay book showed that he was indeed a trained panzer driver, that he'd seen a little action with a unit in Belgium, that he'd come back to the *Vaterland* to recover from a leg wound, and such less relevant details as his gas-mask size (1—small) and blood group (B).

"Welcome to the zoo, Claus." Adi wasn't sure how welcome Valentiner would be. One more new guy to find out about him. He reminded himself that Judaism probably wasn't a capital crime any more. He reminded himself, yes, but he still had a hard time believing it.

"Doesn't seem like there's a whole lot of fighting left," Poske said. "If they were going to send us down to help take Munich, they would have done it by now."

"Too bad. I'd like to go after the blackshirts," the kid said. "My uncle went into Mauthausen. He died in there. Heart failure, the telegram said. Right! You kill somebody, sure his heart stops."

He'd back the Salvation Committee, then. He would if he was telling the truth, anyhow. Having told a pile of his own lies, Saul always wondered about that. Well, nobody would say anything important in front of this new guy till he showed what he was. Theo wouldn't say anything in front of him any which way.

Saul waved at the panzer. "Want to take a look at your new home? If I'm really going to command a full crew, I'll clear my junk away from the driver's seat."

"Sure. Thanks," Valentiner said. They walked around to the left front of the machine. Saul opened the hatch. The kid climbed inside.

London. But it was a London Alistair Walsh barely remembered, a London that might as well have been at peace with the whole world. London wasn't quite. The UK remained at war with Japan. But Japanese planes weren't going to drop bombs on London Bridge and the British Museum. The blackout was over. Rationing remained, but if you had money to spend you could have yourself a hell of a spree.

On a staff sergeant's pay, Walsh couldn't buy himself that kind of spree here, the way he might have in India or Alexandria. In India or Alexandria, though, he would have celebrated along with other long-serving noncoms. When you were part of the Army's backbone, naturally you made friends with your fellow vertebrae.

In London, to his lasting wonderment, he had Friends in High Places. That came from his unplanned meeting with Rudolf Hess, too. Winston Churchill did his best to keep Chamberlain's appeasement-minded government from throwing in with the Fritzes. Winnie was glad to discover Walsh felt the same way. Walsh still marveled that a great man should have wanted to know what he thought, much less cared.

Then a drunk in a Bentley ran Churchill down. They said he was a drunk, at any rate. Walsh never believed it. It was too convenient. The Nazis and the Reds arranged "accidents" like that. They weren't supposed to happen in civilized countries like England.

Only this one had. Because it had, younger MPs who couldn't stand the German alliance, men like Ronald Cartland and Bobbity Cranford, noticed Alistair Walsh. He'd resigned from the Army in disgust, but he still had military connections that they used to help overthrow Chamberlain's successor, the even more pro-German Lord Halifax. *Coups d'état* weren't supposed to happen in civilized countries like England, either. So much for that.

And now Walsh sat in the warm, smoky comfort of the Lion and Gryphon, the pub near the Houses of Parliament where big chunks of the coup had been plotted. With him sat Cranford, Cartland, and several of the others who'd helped hatch the plot. Walsh had a pint of best bitter in front of him. Most of the rest preferred whiskey, but they made sure his mug stayed full.

Once in a while, they even let him buy a round—they knew he didn't care to be carried all the time. Never mind that they could have bought and sold him as they pleased. *A man's a man for a' that*, he thought—a Scot's sentiment, but one a Welshman understood, too.

He went off to the jakes. When he came back, he found his pint magically refilled. "Obliged, gentlemen," he said.

"My pleasure." Ronald Cartland had fought in France, too, as a captain. That made Walsh take him even more seriously than the others. They spoke the same language, as it were. Cartland went on, "It's good to see you back, and back in one piece."

"Thank you, sir," Walsh said. "Have we got a peace here, or is this just a rest before we all start thrashing about on the floor again?"

The Tories looked at one another. "A peace or not a peace—that is the question," Bobbity Cranford misquoted. Walsh had no idea where his nickname came from, but everybody used it. He clowned more than the others, perhaps to live down to his silly handle.

"If 1919 taught us anything, it taught us not to hope for too much," Cartland said. "The War to End War . . . didn't. Chances are this one won't, either. When we go back—ay, there's the rub."

"Not until the Yanks and the Russians finish with the Japanese. That gives poor, battered Europe a little breathing spell, anyhow," Cranford said. The other Tories nodded.

So did Walsh: it made sense to him. But he asked, "What about us and the Japanese?"

"With Singapore and Malaya and Burma gone, I fear we're riding the Yanks' coattails in that war," Ronald Cartland said. "The logistics are impossibly bad for us to go it alone that far away. We may get back what we've lost—I don't see how Japan can hope to stand up against enemies like that. How long we can keep it once we do get it back is another question, though."

"How do you mean?" Walsh asked. England had ruled the lands that made up her empire longer than he'd been alive. As far as he was concerned, that meant she could and would keep on ruling them throughout his lifetime and beyond. That came as close to forever as made no difference.

Not to his way of thinking, at any rate. But Bobbity Cranford replied in mournful tones: "With Japan spurring them on, the Burmese have declared their independence."

"The same way Slovakia did when Hitler told it to." Walsh's lip curled. That cut no ice with him.

"It looks as though Slovakian independence will stand," Cranford said. "If enough of the people in those parts don't fancy being ruled from Prague, trying to drag them back into the fold would start a new little war. And if enough of the Burmese can't stomach rule from London, the same applies there." He picked up his whiskey glass, tossed back what was left in it, and waved for reinforcements. Then, his tone more mournful yet, he went on, "The same applies to India, of course."

"India!" Walsh exclaimed. India was far and away the most important part of the empire on which the sun never set. Without it . . . Without India, it would feel as if the sun were setting on the British Isles.

But all the young Tories gave back somber nods. "Gandhi and Nehru and the Hindus want us gone. So do Muhammad Ali Jinna and the Muslims. Heaven only knows what they'll do to one another if we should leave, but they all want us to pack up and go."

"They'll likely slaughter one another by the carload lot," Bobbity Cranford said. "They want us to pack up and go all the same. You rule an empire because the people you're ruling don't think they've got any better choices of their own, and so they let you choose for them. It's not like that any more. We've spread nationalism across the whole world, and now—"

"It's coming home to roost," Walsh finished for him.

"That's about the size of it," Cranford said.

The barmaid came by to fill up the politicos' whiskey glasses and Walsh's pint mug. She was a cute young thing. Walsh wouldn't have minded a go with her, but she had eyes only for Ronald Cartland. He'd always been like catnip for those of the female persuasion.

After a pull at his fresh pint, Walsh said, "That's about the size of it unless you're a Czech or a Lithuanian or some poor bugger like that."

"I can tell you the difference," Cartland said—he didn't seem interested in the barmaid, even if she was interested in him. "The difference is, the Germans and the Russians don't care how many people they kill to keep the rest quiet. We haven't the stomach for a policy like that these days."

"Is that our blessing or our curse?" Walsh asked.

"Probably." Bobbity Cranford could sound cheerful and foolish about anything. Walsh had taken a while to realize that just because he sounded that way didn't mean that was how he felt.

"We went to war to keep Hitler from killing swarms of Czechs and other folks he didn't care for," Walsh said. "So much for that."

"So much for that," Ronald Cartland agreed. "But then again, Hitler went to war to conquer all of Europe—the whole world, for all I know. So much for that, too. And so much for Hitler with it. When you try to put the pieces back together again, you shouldn't be amazed if no one comes away with everything he might have wanted."

"Mm." Walsh stared down into his mug of bitter. He hadn't looked at things from that angle. "You've got a point, sir. But it seems like a devil of a cost to leave everybody unhappy walking out of the play."

"You're right. It does," Cartland said. "Of course, I've also heard diplomacy called the art of leaving everyone dissatisfied." Walsh hadn't heard that. He wasn't sure he liked it, either. Like it or not, though, it seemed to be what the world had.

These days, Sarah Bruck was never sure what she'd get when she turned on the radio. The Salvation Committee didn't run things nearly so smoothly as Dr. Goebbels had. Goebbels, these days, was holed up in the Italian embassy in Berlin. Sarah wondered how long that would last. Mussolini was having trouble of his own hanging on to the reins. If he got shot down like Hitler or had to run for his life, the new government might well throw Goebbels to the wolves.

News certainly sounded different now. Broadcasters quoted foreign reports, sometimes even when they said unkind things about Germany. There were also stories about the crimes and cruelty of the SS and the SD. Of course, it was in the Salvation Committee's interest to let people know how foully the Nazis had behaved while they held power. Then the people would be less likely to want the bastards back.

The civil war was almost over. A day or two could go by without Sarah's hearing gunfire. Diehards still held out in the Bavarian mountains and in a few places in Austria, but even they were starting to see it was a losing fight.

Bit by bit, the country was starting to seem as if it might remember what peace was like. They'd started printing new banknotes and postage stamps without the swastika on them. Old ones still circulated—

there were too many to get rid of them all. But one of these days the hooked cross might go back to being just a decoration.

The Salvation Committee quietly went about dismantling other Nazi excesses, too. Toward the end of a newscast, an announcer said, "It has been decided that the *Reich* Citizenship Law of September 15, 1935, is no longer in effect. Persons whose status changed from citizen to resident under the provisions of that law are restored to full citizenship so long as, in the interim, they have not been convicted of a crime that would entail the loss of that right. All marks of distinction formerly required of such persons, whether on their identity documents or on their daily attire, are abolished from this time forward."

He went on to talk about something else. Sarah stared at the radio. If she hadn't been paying attention, she would have had no idea what he'd meant. That might have been part of the idea. He'd gabbled on like a bureaucrat. He hadn't mentioned Jews once, not in so many words. Plenty of listeners might not have noticed what he said. The *Reich* Citizenship Law of 1935 didn't matter to them.

It did to Sarah. She ran into the kitchen, where her mother was peeling potatoes. "They've canceled the law!" she exclaimed. "We can be people again!"

Hanna Goldman needed a moment to understand what that meant, but only a moment: certainly less time than anyone not a Jew would have. "That's so good!" she said. "Does that mean we can take the stars off our clothes?"

"It sure does," Sarah answered. "I want to do it right now and burn them."

"*I* want to take them off and save them," her mother said. "If you ever meet someone new and have children of your own, they should see what happened to us."

Sarah frowned, then nodded. "Well, you're right. Father would say you have a better sense of history than I do."

"Father . . . Did the radio say whether the Jews whose jobs the Nazis stole would get them back again?"

"It didn't say one way or the other," Sarah replied. Samuel Goldman wasn't the only one of those, of course. They ran into the tens of thousands. Professors, lawyers, doctors, dentists, civil servants . . . .

Sarah wondered how many of them were even still alive. Because he was a wounded veteran of the last war, Father'd had it easier than most, and so had his family. Not easy, never easy, but easier.

Mother's mouth turned down at the corners. "Chances are that means no. Well, what can you do? We're all still here, thank God. Even Saul's here! I wish he'd come back again."

"He's not the same as he was—or else he's more the way he was than ever," Sarah said. "He doesn't fit in with us very well any more . . . except with Father. Father may not get along with him, but he understands him."

"They've both been through the war," Mother said. "Father used to wake up screaming in the middle of the night once or twice a month. He hardly ever does any more, but he used to. Do you remember?"

"Not really. I never thought about it," Sarah said.

"You were little. It was just something that happened, and it didn't worry you. It worried me—I'll tell you that!" Hanna Goldman said.

"Do you suppose Saul wakes up like that these days?" Sarah asked, adding, "I hope he doesn't."

"I hope he doesn't, too, but I wouldn't be surprised if he did," Mother said. "Do you want to grate some horseradish for me?"

"Sure." Sarah scraped the long, pale root over the grater. Mother didn't want to talk any more about people she loved waking up screaming, and who could blame her for that? Sarah didn't even want to think about it. The more she tried not to, though, the more she did.

When Father came home, he was practically hopping up and down, he was so excited. "They've decided we're Germans after all!" he said, and then, "Well, they've decided that, since the Nazis said we weren't and the Nazis were wrong about everything, we have to be. That's almost as good. It's good enough! I'm going to burn my yellow stars."

"I said the same thing," Sarah told him. "Mother said we should save them so we can show them to the ones who come after us."

"Did she?" Samuel Goldman's eyes swung toward his wife. "Did you? That's a good notion, dear. The things we most want to forget are the ones we most need to remember. Sometimes, anyhow."

Was that why he'd woken up screaming? Because he couldn't forget? It looked that way to Sarah. She didn't ask him. She didn't want to make him remember anew. Instead, she said, "You should go over to the university and pay people a call."

He laughed. "That would scare them, wouldn't it?" But then his gaze sharpened in a different way. "You know, I just might visit them. I'd like to find out if Friedrich came through in one piece."

Friedrich Lauterbach had studied under Father. After he got his own academic position, and after Hitler made it impossible for Jews to teach any more, Lauterbach had bought articles from Father and published them under his own name. It was as much as anyone could safely do for a Jew, and far more than most would have done. But then he'd gone into the *Wehrmacht,* so that had dried up.

Of itself, Sarah's hand fluffed at her hair. Friedrich Lauterbach was reasonably young and reasonably personable. Before he put on *Feldgrau,* he'd as much as said he might have been interested in her if she weren't a Jewess. She didn't know that she would have been interested in him that way, but she didn't know that she wouldn't have, either. Once upon a time, Germans and Jews had often intermarried, and no one except the Nazis and a few extremely Orthodox Jews got upset about it.

Now? Now Sarah supposed it was legal again. She had no idea what that meant to Friedrich Lauterbach. She also had no idea what it meant to her. Even if he still liked her, even if something sparked inside her when she saw him, would she want to have anything to do with someone who hadn't gone through the troubles she and her people had known?

By the way Father watched her from under his eyebrows, he was thinking along with her. She had no idea whether any of it meant anything. Lauterbach might lie in a poorly marked grave in Belgium or Russia. Even if he'd come back, he might have found an Aryan sweetheart. And even if he hadn't, he might not care for her any more. Or she might decide she didn't care for him.

But she answered, "Yes, that would be good to know." And so it would. Because if the war had taught her anything, it taught her that you never could tell.

Chapter 26

The regiment rode to Kiev in American trucks. Lieutenant Obolen-sky made a point of telling the men in his company that the trucks were American. Ivan Kuchkov hadn't known before, but the news didn't astonish him. These big, blocky, powerful machines sure as hell hadn't come out of any Soviet factory. They were nothing like the flimsy junk the Nazis used, either. So their being American made good sense.

Of course, had Obolensky told him they came from the men in the moon, that also wouldn't have astonished him. The way they domi-nated these rotten Ukrainian roads showed him they were from no-where close.

Only a couple of men gushed about how wonderful the trucks were. Ivan's eyes met Sasha Davidov's for a split second. The guys who were going on about it had never been the sharpest tools in the shed. The lieutenant had tried to warn people, but they didn't catch on. If you got all excited about how great something foreign was, somebody would be listening. Somebody was always listening. Somebody was always remembering, too.

Banderist bandits fired at the trucks a few times. The drivers fired back. One truck in three sported a pintle-mounted machine gun in the cabin. They wouldn't be accurate shooting on the move, but they could make a Ukrainian nationalist lie low instead of blasting away with his own weapon.

Kiev swarmed with Red Army soldiers. Some, like Ivan's regiment, were there to board trains that would eventually link up with the Trans-Siberian Railway and the war at the far end of it, the war against the little yellow monkeys. Others, along with slightly smaller swarms of NKVD men, did their best to keep the bandits from shooting up taverns with PPDs or tossing grenades into movie houses or planting bombs along the train tracks.

In a low voice, Ivan told Davidov, "For once in my life, I hope those Chekist cunts know what the fuck they're doing."

"That'd be nice," the Jew agreed, also in tones that no one else was likely to overhear.

Naturally, there weren't enough railroad cars. Delaying the buildup of the attack against Japan was unthinkable, unimaginable. The USSR hadn't fought Japan for several years? What did that have to do with the price of vodka? The authorities made do with their too-small number of cars by cramming more soldiers into each one. If that caused problems for the troops, again, so what? Soviet soldiers were fungible. They always had been. They always would be.

"If they're going to stuff us together this tight, the least they could do is smear us with oil, the way they do with those little canned fish," Davidov grumbled.

Ivan leered at him. "How about with fucking bacon grease?" he said.

He didn't faze Sasha. "If you want to fuck with bacon grease, Comrade Sergeant, that's your business," Davidov answered. "Me, I'd sooner get the girl so wet I don't need any."

As the soldiers laughed at him, Kuchkov said, "*Yob tvoyu mat'*— with bacon grease, the dry-pussy whore." But he was laughing, too. Sure as hell, Sasha had scored.

The rich, rolling plains of the Ukraine went drier and browner as the train chugged east. The overcrowded cars started stinking like the inside of a submarine. The toilet gave up on the second day. After that, it was honey buckets. The men covered them when they could and dumped them when they got the chance. The damn things still reeked. Everybody smoked all the time. The food was worse than at the front, and there was less of it. The vodka ration was smaller, too, because they weren't in action. That gave everybody something else to complain about.

They clanked past what looked to Ivan like a big granite prick. It had writing on the west side, and also on the east. That didn't help him, of course. He dug an elbow into Sasha Davidov's ribs. "What's it say?" he demanded.

"We've just passed from Europe into Asia."

"Does that mean we're almost there?"

"Fuck, no!" Sasha said, startled into *mat*. "Not even close."

"Too goddamn bad. This is a big cocksucking country, y'know? No wonder all the cunts on the borders want to bite chunks off of it."

"No wonder at all, Comrade Sergeant."

As usual, the little Jew knew what he was talking about. Pine forests replaced the near-desert outside the windows, and seemed about as endless. When they stopped on a siding at night, Ivan heard wolves howling. He and the men in his section were all scrunched up against one another, trying to find positions comfortable enough for sleep.

After what seemed like forever and was about a week (time blurred in that crush of a car), they came to Irkutsk. Ivan gaped at the vast expanse of water east of the town. "Fuck me in the mouth! Is that the ocean?"

"That's Lake Baikal, Comrade Sergeant," Sasha Davidov said.

"Well, shit, how did I know? I've never seen the fucking ocean." Kuchkov chuckled harshly. "Guess I still haven't."

Lieutenant Obolensky had been one car farther forward. He stuck his head into the one that tried to house Ivan's section and said, "Come with me, you guys. This company is getting reassigned to a Guards regiment. That means we did a hell of a good job fighting the Fascists and the bandits."

Guards regiments, Guards brigades, Guards divisions, were the Red Army's elite, the upper class in the classless society. They got better weapons, better uniforms, even better tobacco. Units earned the title with their combat performance. As Obolensky said, winning it was an honor.

Later, Ivan realized he should have heard alarm bells inside his head. But that was later. At the moment, he was as pleased and proud as his company commander. "You heard the lieutenant, you whores!" he shouted. "Stick your dicks back inside your pants, grab your crap, and get moving!"

His legs complained as he stumbled off the train. Fresh air felt like a kiss from a pretty girl. Then, out of nowhere, what seemed like a front's worth of NKVD men with PPDs surrounded the scratching, yawning, smoking soldiers.

"Hands up!" the Chekists screamed in ragged unison. "You are all under arrest! You are traitors of the *Rodina*!"

They always said that. They meant traitors to the motherland, but it never came out of their mouths that way. Ivan had heard as much from zeks who'd got out of their clutches. Now he heard it for himself. It sounded stupid, all right. No matter how stupid it sounded, though, the bastards finally had him.

He thought about dying bravely, but where was the percentage in that? He put down his PPD and raised his hands. So did the rest of the soldiers. Vitya Ryakhovsky started blubbering. He knew too well what this was about. Ivan did, too. Yes, the NKVD had a long memory. You couldn't get away with shooting a political officer, even by mistake. If the Nazis and the Ukrainians hadn't disposed of these men, the Chekists would take care of it themselves.

They really wanted Vitya, Ivan, and the lieutenant. They probably wanted Sasha Davidov, too, because he was a smart kike, and smart kikes caused trouble. The rest of the guys in the company? Would the Chekists turn them loose? Not likely! Maybe the population in some camp had dropped below the prescribed norm. Maybe the NKVD didn't want witnesses. Who could guess? Who cared? What difference did it make?

The NKVD men separated them from one another and searched them. They stole whatever they pleased. That was part of the fun of being a Chekist. They beat them up, too. That was also part of the fun.

Ivan rolled into a ball and tried not to let them kick anything vital. He'd been beaten before; he knew what to expect. He yelled his head off so they'd think they were hurting him worse than they were. The stupid pricks hadn't even found one of his little holdout knives.

When they got done knocking him around, they tore off his shoulder boards. "You're a traitor, not a soldier!" an NKVD lieutenant screamed in his face. Ivan did his best to look miserable. Sooner or later, he would catch a break. Maybe he could get away. Or maybe—more likely—he could make a place for himself in the gulag the way he had in the Red Army.

A column of new zeks, hands tied and joined to one another by ropes, stumbled north out of Irkutsk a few days later. A handful of Chekists with machine pistols herded them along. "Kolyma, you sorry bastards!" they jeered. "That's where you're headed! North of the Arctic fucking Circle! You'll freeze your nuts off! It's summer, but you'll freeze 'em off anyway!" They laughed and laughed. Ivan kept his mouth shut and his eyes open. Sooner or later, he'd find a chance for . . . something. He hoped he would, anyhow.

Saul Goldman waved his arms like a sardonic tour guide. "Welcome to beautiful, romantic, historic Münster," he said. "I can tell you where a lot of interesting things used to be, but most of 'em aren't here any more, so why should I bother? We liberated this place clear to hell and gone, didn't we?"

Theo Hossbach nodded. Theo made the perfect victim for someone playing tour guide: he hated talking more than he liked complaining. But Saul didn't exaggerate much. What the RAF hadn't managed to smash in years of intermittent bombing, the fight between the Salvation Committee and the Nazi diehards had. Most of the center of town was a rubble field the likes of which Saul hadn't seen this side of the Soviet Union, and only seldom there.

German flags—old Imperial German flags, now reborn under the Salvation Committee—flew from the buildings and chimneys that still stood. Here and there, hardheaded National Socialists had sneaked out at night to chalk swastikas on walls and paint them on sidewalks and the fronts of houses.

Prisoners cleaned up the Nazi propaganda. Most of them wore shabby *Feldgrau* with all emblems removed; a few were in shabby black that had been treated the same way. Soldiers in full uniform with tricolor armbands kept the prisoners working.

"C'mon. Let's go over to the zoo," Saul said. "That hasn't taken such a beating." Theo nodded again and stuck up his thumb. Most Germans adored zoos. This one, and the park surrounding it, lay west of Münster's city center. Both sides here had done their best not to fight in it. Only a few new shell holes cratered the fancy gardens.

Several people strolling through the gardens waved to the two panzer crewmen. "About time you fellows ran out those fools!" a man called. Had the Nazis won their war, he probably would have called them geniuses. Well, had the Nazis won their war, the generals never would have risen against them. Saul understood that, however little he cared for it.

To his surprise and relief, no one in town had recognized him yet. Maybe he wasn't so well-remembered from the football pitch as he thought. Or maybe people noticed the the black panzer coveralls and the black service cap with the death's head and the pink piping and paid no attention to the face between the one and the other.

In the zoo, a bear ate oatmeal with chunks of flesh in it. "Looks like it came straight from one of our field kitchens," Saul said. Theo chuckled. It was funny, but it was funny because it was true.

A few cages farther down, a leopard tore at a big hunk of meat. It was probably horsemeat, but all the same . . . Saul hadn't got letters from home, but his crewmates and the other men in his unit had. Lots of letters complained about how miserable civilian rations were. Meat or fish or fowl of any kind was hard to come by. You had to know somebody, and even that didn't always help.

Saul supposed it spoke well for the German people, or at least for the clout of German zookeepers, that the animals got what they needed even when people went hungry. What the beasts ate wouldn't have fed that many more human mouths.

An elephant pulled hay out of a manger with its trunk. That might mean some horses somewhere weren't getting full rations, but it didn't have anything to do with people. When people got hungry enough, they ate all kinds of strange things, but nobody ate hay.

A pretty girl was watching the elephant eat lunch, too. She smiled at Saul and at Theo. Theo had always been shy around women. Saul hadn't, but he wondered what this one would say if she found out he was circumcised. She wasn't so very pretty that his trouser snake thought he had to find out.

Around the corner from the elephant, some chamois nimbly jumped here and there in a rocky enclosure. They paused every so often to eat hay, too. Next to them were some kangaroos. A couple of the females had joeys' heads sticking out of their pouches. When you could get your animals to breed in a zoo, you knew you'd made them feel at home.

Another pretty girl was standing in front of the kangaroos and watching them hop about. That was Saul's first thought. Then he did a double take. The girl did one at the same time as she recognized him, too. "Well, hello!" she said. "I didn't know whether I'd ever see you again or not."

"Hello, Sarah." Saul hadn't known whether he'd see her again or not, either. He turned to Theo. "Theo, this is my sister, Sarah. Sarah, Theo Hossbach is the radioman in my panzer."

"Hello," Theo said, and sketched a salute.

"Hi," Sarah answered. She looked a question at Saul.

He knew which question it was, too. "Theo's all right," he said quickly. "He's better than all right, in fact. He knows. He's known for a long time. He's never said boo."

"Boo," Theo said.

They all laughed. Sarah said "Hello" again, this time in a different tone of voice, as if Theo was someone she might like. Then she said, "It's good to be able to come to the zoo. We couldn't even do that for a long time." A few bits of thread were sticking up from the left breast of her blouse. She must have missed them when she removed the yellow star.

"Well, come on, then," Saul said. "Do you think a couple of panzer men can keep you safe from the animals in the cages—and from the animals outside of them?"

"I've never worried about the ones in there." Sarah pointed to the kangaroos.

"Those aren't dangerous. All they do is hop," Theo said. "Did you see the leopard back there? He's eating about half a horse."

"No, I was coming from the other direction," Sarah answered. "Anyway, the really dangerous animals aren't the ones that live in the cages. Like Saul said, they're the ones that build the cages."

"You've got that right," Theo said. He looked over at Saul. "Saul?"

Saul looked back at him. "Saul." He nodded. That wasn't the only reason he eyed his crewmate, though. He hadn't heard Theo talk so much in quite a while.

Sarah, meanwhile, glanced from one of them to the other. "Oops," she said. "I should have said *Adalbert*."

"Don't worry about it," Saul told her. "Theo doesn't say anything to anybody. Most of the time he doesn't, anyway."

"Who, me?" Theo said. "Let him who is without sin cast the first aspersion."

"Ouch!" Saul said. He turned to his sister and spread his hands in apology. "I didn't know he had that in him."

"Maybe he can get it removed," Sarah said. "But I don't mind silly talk. It feels good. If somebody talks silly talk at you, he thinks you're a human being. Nobody seemed to think we were for a long time."

"You've got that right," Saul said. She'd gone through more anti-Semitism than he had. What they did to civilian Jews got worse after he escaped into the *Wehrmacht*. He didn't want to think about that, so he didn't. He pointed to the aviary. "Let's go see the birds."

They saw the birds, or some of them. Bomb fragments had torn open the wire mesh more than once during the war. There'd been some escapes. Saul wondered if hornbills or cocks of the rock were trying to make a living in bushes around the town.

A snack-seller had a tray of pretzels. Saul got some. "You people saved Germany!" said the old man with the tray. He wouldn't take Saul's money.

"Thank you very much," Saul said.

After the old man was out of earshot, Theo said, "These taste like salt and sawdust. Who knows what was in the dough?"

"Who cares?" Sarah said. Theo shook his head to show he didn't. They ambled through the zoo, chatting and laughing.

"Pass me the centimeter wrench, would you?" Adi Stoss was messing around inside the Panzer IV's engine compartment.

Saul. His name is Saul, Theo Hossbach reminded himself as he handed him the wrench. But when you'd been thinking of somebody by one name for several years, adjusting to another wasn't easy. It especially wasn't easy when the other fellow plainly wanted to hang on to the name he'd been using, the name the *Wehrmacht* knew him by.

Theo looked around. Nobody else was close to them. He wouldn't have worried about Lothar or Kurt—not very much, anyway. Claus Valentiner was another story. Theo hadn't known him long enough to be easy around him. With Theo, *long enough* was usually a long time.

Usually. Not always. Since the coast was clear, he said, "Your sister's nice."

That got Adi out of the panzer's engine. He had a grease smear under one eye. He looked more like a Saul than an Adalbert, grease smear or no grease smear. "Is she?" he said. "I haven't seen enough of her lately to know. Hell, till I went back at the house I had no idea she'd been married and widowed since I, ah, left."

"She had?" Theo said. Sarah hadn't mentioned that at all at the zoo. "What happened?"

"British bombing raid. Got her husband and his folks. Would have got her, too, only she wasn't home for some reason."

"Oh," Theo said. "Too bad." He was spending more words than he did most of the time. But he couldn't remember when he'd talked as much as he had at the zoo.

He could hardly remember the last time he'd spent so long in a pretty girl's company, either, even if her brother was along, too. He'd had a few leaves in Breslau, but he hadn't taken advantage of them that way. He wondered why not—it wasn't as if he didn't get the itch like any other young man. Getting it and scratching it, though, were two different things. To scratch it, he'd have to talk to a girl first, to show her what a good fellow he was. To him, that seemed somehow more intimate than lying down with her in bed.

Or it did most of the time, anyhow. "Sarah's easy to talk to, too," he said.

"I don't hardly know about that, either. You were banging your gums pretty good there, though." Adi looked at him sidewise. "So am I going to have a Hossbach in the family? My old man would like it— I'll tell you that."

"He would? Why? I'm a gentile." Theo was surprised into more words yet.

"He wouldn't care. You're named Theodosios. Pop would care about that. You bet he would."

He'd said that his father was a professor of ancient history. Theo hadn't kept that in the top drawer of his mind—it had been a while ago now. But he remembered when something jogged him, sure enough. "He really wouldn't care?" Theo asked.

"No, I don't think so," Adi said. "Although he may feel more *Volkisch* now, on account of everything that's happened lately." He used the word so beloved of the Nazis with a sardonic twist all his own.

Theo thought that over. If people despised you because of what you believed, what would that make you do? It might make you drop your beliefs and try to seem as much like everybody else as you could. Or it might make you cling to them all the tighter. He could see going either way. If your ancestors had hung on to their beliefs in a line stretching back three thousand years, wouldn't you be more inclined to cling tighter? Theo thought so.

"I wouldn't blame him if he did," Theo said. "Or Sarah." She hadn't acted as if she wanted to spit in his eye because he wasn't Jewish. She might just have been polite with her brother's *Kamerad,* though. How could you tell with women? Theo had enough trouble telling with men.

"Big of you," Adi said, which made Theo's ears heat. Adi went on, "Stick your head in here with me, will you? Something's still screwed up with this fan linkage, but I can't see what."

Before long, Theo found the trouble. Machinery gave him much less trouble than people did. Machines were more predictable and less complicated. They did the same things again and again unless they broke. Then you fixed them, and they did those things some more.

People . . . Who could tell what people would do next? Half the time, they didn't know themselves till they did it. A lot of the time, they didn't know what they'd done or why, even afterwards. That was how things looked to Theo, anyway.

"Good job. Thanks," Adi told him once he'd got the linkage back in order. "Two heads were better than one. Or yours was better than mine."

Still uncommonly talkative, Theo said, "You're making a good panzer commander."

"Am I? I'm glad you think so. How come?"

"You give other people credit. Hermann did that, too."

"He sure did. I'm trying to act like him. Not so easy—he had more patience than I do. But I am trying, and I'm trying not to be too trying, too." Adi loosened the props and let the armored, louvered decking slam down over the engine compartment. "I'll tell you something else, since I know damn well you don't flap your gums too much. If I never take a panzer into combat again for the rest of my life, I'll be the happiest guy in the world. What do you think of that?"

"Sounds good." Theo held up his left hand to show off the finger that wasn't there. He mimed getting shot. "Once is plenty."

"Once is twice too often," Adi said. Theo nodded. Adi went on, "Bad enough when we were fighting foreigners. Our own people . . . ?" He scowled and muttered under his breath. "Yes, I know they were Nazis. Yes, I know they would have done horrible things to me if they got the chance. But they were Germans, dammit, and this isn't exactly a Russian uniform I'm wearing."

"Nope." Theo couldn't argue with that.

Adi's chuckle would have curdled milk. "Funny, isn't it? My father and I don't see eye-to-eye about all kinds of things. He thinks I'm a jerk because I don't care about the old-time stuff he's interested in. And he couldn't care less about football or anything like that. But we've both always wanted to be Germans, and to hell with the Germans who didn't want to let us."

"You can be now." Theo paused and decided he needed to revise that: "Maybe you can."

"Maybe. Uh-huh. That's about it." Adi didn't sound gloomy, though. "I'll tell you something, man. It's a hell of a lot better deal than all the shit Hitler dumped on us."

Theo didn't know what to say: again, he couldn't very well disagree. So he did what he usually did when he didn't know what to say about something—he didn't say anything about it. He had something else on his mind, anyway. "Adi? . . . Um, Saul?"

"Adi, please. We're both more used to it. What's up?"

"Where do you live, Adi?" Theo blurted. Open mouth, insert foot—the Hossbach way of doing things.

Except Adi didn't start laughing at him. Adi didn't even smile, or not very much. He didn't go *So you want to pay a call on my sister, do you?* He just told Theo where the family house was and gave detailed directions for how to get there.

"Thank you," Theo said when he finished, as much for what he hadn't said as for what he had.

"No worries, Theo. You're aces in my book," Adi said. "And that and half a Reichsmark will buy you a seidel of beer."

"Heh." Theo acknowledged the attempt at a joke.

"Is that any way to talk to your panzer commander?"

"Heh, *Herr* Panzer Commander!" Theo sprang to attention as he might have on the parade ground and saluted as if Adi were a field marshal. They both laughed for real then. Why not? It didn't look as if they'd have to go to war again for a while, anyhow, against their own folk or anyone else.

Peggy Druce had just hauled the vacuum cleaner out of the closet when somebody knocked on the front door. It wasn't even ten o'clock yet on a Saturday morning: early for a traveling salesman. Whatever the guy was flogging, he was damn lucky she hadn't plugged the Hoover in yet. While it was running, she never would have heard that shy little knock.

Any excuse not to vacuum for a while seemed like a good one. She hardly ever spent money with drummers, but listening to the fellow's spiel might be entertaining. If it wasn't, she could tell him to take a hike. She hurried to the door and threw it open.

Albert Einstein stood on her front porch.

No, she wasn't dreaming. The mournful face, the bushy gray mustache, the flyaway hair . . . He was as recognizable as Charlie Chaplin or Harpo Marx. "I am looking for Mr. Herbert Druce," he said, his voice quiet and accented. "You would perhaps be Mrs. Druce?"

"That's right," she said, which might or might not have been technically true—but how often did Einstein land on your porch? She stepped aside. "Please—won't you come in?"

"Thank you so much," he said, and he did. A taxi sat out by the curb. The driver was reading some kind of pulp. As Peggy shut the door, Einstein went on, "Is Mr. Herbert Druce at home?"

"No, he's not here right now," Peggy answered, which was certainly true and just as certainly misleading. "This has to be about the big, fancy bomb, doesn't it?"

Einstein looked at her in a new way. "You know about this? He spoke to you of this?" He took on the expression of an unhappy bloodhound.

"Not any of the technical stuff," Peggy said. That, for once, was the truth, the whole truth, and nothing but the truth. "But that nobody was sure you could make it work at all, and that even if you could it would take years and years and wouldn't be worth the money and work you'd have to sink into it."

"It is this last part that I would like with him to discuss," Einstein said.

"Don't stand there in the front hall," Peggy told him. "Come on into the living room, for heaven's sake. Can I get you some coffee? What do you take in it?"

"Cream and sugar, please. Again, I thank you so much." He let her lead him in there and sit him down in the comfy chair that had been Herb's. Seeing cigarette butts in the ashtrays, he got out his pipe and lit it.

She quickly heated up the coffee that was sitting on the stove.

When she brought him a cup, she asked, "Why do you need to talk with Herb about that? Why didn't you do it a while ago now?"

"I needed some work to learn who had recommended to kill the project," Einstein answered. "For clear—for obvious—reasons, this is not made known. Also, and more important, the political situation has changed."

"How do you mean?" Peggy said.

"In Germany, they have no longer the Nazis running things," Einstein said, sending unreadable smoke signals up from the pipe. "The Nazis, the Nazis were most of them very ignorant people. With the men now in charge there, this is not so. Many physicists had to leave Germany—"

"Because they were Jewish," Peggy broke in.

That big, shaggy head bobbed up and down in a nod. "You are right. But not all German physicists Jews are. Some able men, some fine men, stayed there. If they build this bomb, if their government helps them this bomb to build, it is bad for every country that is not Germany."

He sounded a hundred percent sure. He made sense, too. If there was or could be one of these super-duper bombs, the country that had it would be like a brigade of Tommy gunners squaring off against a Roman legion. It would be a fight, but not a fair fight.

"I say this to you. I will to your husband say it," Einstein cautioned. "It is not a public thing, you understand."

"Of course," Peggy said quickly. "But what do you want Herb to do about it?"

"If I can make him see this is *wichtig,* ah, important—"

"*Ich verstehe,*" she put in.

Even his smile seemed sad. "Ah, so you do! That is good. Where was I? *Ja* . . . If I can make him see how important this is, I can perhaps persuade him to reconsider his report and to change it. This may return to the project the money and the momentum it needs."

If anyone in the world could make Herb change his mind once he'd made it up, Albert Einstein might well be the man. But whether anyone could was a whole different question. Having known Herb her whole adult life, Peggy was inclined to doubt it.

Still, Einstein deserved the chance. "Let me tell you where to find him," Peggy said. "In fact, here—I'll write it down for you." She scribbled his new address and his telephone number on a sheet from a scratch pad. "You can use the phone here to make sure he's home if you want to."

"Home?" Einstein asked.

"Uh-huh," Peggy said unhappily. "We . . . got divorced not too long ago."

"I did this also. It is something that happens. A pity, but it does." Einstein stuck Herb's address and number into a jacket pocket. "I think I will not telephone. A phone call is easy not to believe. If he is out . . ." The physicist shrugged. "I will another time come back. I am in Princeton, in New Jersey. It is not a long trip to make."

"No, it isn't," Peggy agreed. Princeton wasn't more than forty miles northeast of Philadelphia. An hour by train, more or less, plus whatever time you needed to travel in town.

Einstein stood up. "I am pleased to meet you, Mrs. Druce, and I thank you for the good coffee." Something glinted in his eyes. Amusement? Chances were he wouldn't have said so much to her had he known she and Herb weren't married any more. She'd tricked it out of him just by holding her cards close to her chest. Coughing, he added, "Please do not spread word of our little talk here."

"I already told you I wouldn't," Peggy said. "You can ask Herb if you don't trust me. We may be divorced, but he'll still tell you I don't gossip about anything important."

"There is no need. I believe you," he said. She knew she would go on feeling good about that for days.

She walked out to the front door with him. If any of the neighbors saw him and asked her questions about it . . . She didn't know exactly what she'd say, but she did know it wouldn't be anything that involved super-duper bombs.

Einstein went down the walk to the cab. The driver saw him coming and tossed his magazine aside. Einstein got in. Peggy wondered if he would make like an absent-minded professor and forget which pocket he'd used to stash Herb's address. He didn't, though; he found it right away. The cabbie started up the engine and drove off.

"Wow! I mean, wow!" Yes, Peggy was talking to herself more now that she lived alone. But if a surprise visit from the greatest physicist in the world didn't rate a few words, what the dickens would?

She wanted to call Dave and tell him who'd knocked on her door. But he'd be at work—and telling him would count as gossip. Einstein had been smart to warn her. She wanted to tell everybody she knew.

Einstein had been smart? Peggy laughed at herself. Einstein *was* smart. Being smart was what made him Einstein—well, being smart and that silly hair. He might not have lost Herb's address, but he sure hadn't found a comb any time lately.

How many smart Jews had Hitler chased out of Germany? Peggy didn't know, but she was sure it wasn't a small number. Countries needed people like that. Now America had them and Germany, even this maybe-new Germany under the Salvation Committee, damn well didn't. Served the Germans right.

"Ha!" Peggy said. She knew the person she could call. She hustled back to the phone and dialed. If he didn't answer, no harm done. But he did. "Herb?" she said, "Listen, you'll never guess who I just sent over to your place . . ."

Read on for an excerpt from the first novel in
Harry Turtledove's thrilling new series.

THE HOT WAR
Bomb's Away

PUBLISHED BY DEL REY BOOKS

Not quite so smoothly as Harry Truman might have liked, the *Independence* touched down at Hickam Field west of Honolulu and taxied to a stop. The DC-6's four big props windmilled down to motionlessness. Truman had traded in FDR's executive airplane, the *Sacred Cow,* for this more modern one in 1947. He'd named it for his own home town. The bald eagle on the nose warned the world of America's strength.

Warm, moist, sweet-smelling air came in when they opened the door. Truman grumbled under his breath just the same. In spite of that fierce-beaked eagle, America wasn't looking any too strong right this minute. The Red Chinese had cut off something like three divisions' worth of troops between the Chosin Reservoir and Hungnam. In spite of air raids and naval gunfire and godawful casualties of their own, the Reds were chewing them up and spitting out the bloody bones.

People were calling it the worst American defeat since the Battling Bastards of Bataan went under in the dark, early days of World War II. It was a hell of a way to go into Christmas, only a week away now. And it was why Truman had come to Hawaii to confer with Douglas MacArthur. In October, MacArthur had flown to Wake Island to assure Truman Red China wouldn't interfere in the Korean War. Which would have been nice if only it had turned out to be true.

And MacArthur had also been the architect of defeat in the Philippines. Yes, he'd had help, but he'd held command there. Truman hadn't been able to stand him since well before that. MacArthur had led the troops that broke up the Bonus Army's Hooverville in Washington when the Depression was at its worst. Didn't a man have to be what they called a good German to go and do something like that?

Truman didn't care for looking up at MacArthur, either. Not looking up to, because he didn't. But looking up at. Truman was an ordinary, stocky five-nine. MacArthur stood at least six even. He seemed taller than that because of his lean build, his ramrod posture, and his high-crowned general's cap. It wasn't quite so raked as the ones the Nazi marshals had worn, but it came close.

Looking out a window in the airliner, Truman watched a Cadillac approach the *Independence*. "Your car is here, sir," an aide said.

"I never would have guessed," the President answered. The aide looked wounded. Somebody—George Kaufman?—had said satire was what closed on Saturday night. Well, sarcasm was what got a politician thrown out on his ear. Truman walked to the doorway, saying, "Sorry, Fred. I've come a long way, and I'm tired. The weather will be nicer outside. Maybe I will, too."

By the look on Fred's face, he didn't believe it. Since Truman didn't, either, he couldn't get on his flunky. The weather *was* nicer. Washington didn't have horrible winters. Honolulu didn't have winter at all. It was in the upper seventies. It never got much hotter. It never got much colder. If this wasn't paradise on earth, what would be?

The limousine took the President to Fort Kamehameha, just south and west of Hickam Field. The fort had guarded the channel that lead in to Pearl Harbor. It was obsolete now, of course; the Japs had proved as much at the end of 1941. Being obsolete didn't mean it had got torn down. The military didn't work that way. No, it had gone from fort to office complex.

A spruce young first lieutenant led Truman to the meeting room where MacArthur waited. The five-star general stood and saluted. "Mr. President," he rasped. The air smelled of pipe tobacco.

"At ease," Truman told him. He knew the military ropes. He'd been an artillery captain himself in the First World War. Knowing the ropes didn't mean he felt any great affection for them. "Let's do this without ceremony, as much as we can."

"However you please, sir," MacArthur said.

They did have a big map of Korea, Japan, and Manchuria taped to the conference table. That would help. Truman stabbed a finger at the terrain between the reservoir and the port, the terrain where the American troops were in the meat grinder. "What the devil went wrong here?"

"We got caught by surprise, sir," Douglas MacArthur said. "No one expected the Chinese to swarm into North Korean in such numbers."

"There were intelligence warnings," Truman said. And there had been. MacArthur just chose not to believe them, and made Truman not believe them, either. The general was finishing up his own triumphal campaign. He'd defended the Pusan perimeter, at the southern end of the Korean peninsula. He'd landed at Inchon and got behind the North Koreans. He'd rolled them up from south to north, and he'd been on the verge of rolling them up for good . . . till the Chinese decided they didn't want the USA or an American puppet on their border. MacArthur'd guessed they would sit still for it. Not for the first time, he'd found himself mistaken.

"Intelligence warns of everything under the sun," he said now, with a not so faint sneer. "Most of what it comes up with is moonshine, not worth worrying about."

"This wasn't," Truman said brusquely. MacArthur's craggy features congealed into a scowl. The President went on, "The question now is, what can we do about it?"

"Under the current rules of engagement, sir, we can't do anything about it till too late," MacArthur said. "As long as American bombers aren't allowed to strike on the other side of the Yalu, the Chinese will be able to assemble as they please and bring fresh troops into the fight in North Korea without our disrupting their preparations in any way."

"How much good will bombing north of the river do, though?"

Truman asked, holding on to his temper. North of the Yalu sat enormous, hostile Red China. Bomb Red China, and who knew what kind of excuse you were handing Joe Stalin? "Won't they hit our B-29s hard? The Superforts were world-beaters in 1945, but they haven't done so well against North Korean air defenses. The Chinese should be better yet on that score, don't you think?"

"If we use ordinary munitions, we will slow them down to some degree but we won't stop them. You're absolutely right about that, sir." MacArthur sounded amazed the President could be right about anything. That might have been Truman's imagination, but he didn't think so. His Far East commander went on, "But if we drop a few atomic bombs on cities in Manchuria, not only do we destroy their men and rail lines, we also send the message that we are sick and tired of playing around."

"The trouble with that is, if we drop A-bombs on Stalin's friends, what's to keep him from dropping them on ours?" Truman returned.

"My considered opinion, your Excellency, is that he wouldn't have the nerve," Douglas MacArthur said. "He doesn't have that many bombs. He can't—he just dropped his first last year. And he must see we can hurt him far worse than he can hurt us."

"Once the pipeline gets moving, they come pretty fast, though. And he has a hell of a lot of men and tanks in Eastern Europe, too," the President said. "They could head west on very short notice."

MacArthur shrugged. "We can destroy swarms of them before they get into West Germany. And how sad do you think the French and British will be if we have to use a few bombs on West German territory?"

Harry Truman's chuckle was dry as a martini in the desert. "I'm sure they would wring their hands in dismay." He scratched the side of his jaw, considering. "If we'd been able to get our forces out through Hungnam, I wouldn't think of this for a minute. The atom is a dangerous genie to let out of the lamp—deadly dangerous. But now the Chinese are bragging that they really can do what Kim Il-sung had in mind—they want to drive us into the sea and turn all of Korea into a satellite."

"Yes, sir. That's exactly what they want to do," MacArthur agreed.

"We'd betray our loyal allies in the south if we let them get away with it, too. The enemy has the advantage in numbers—China always will. He has the advantage in logistics, too. He's right across the river from the fighting, and we're six thousand miles away. If we insist on fighting a war with our hands tied behind our backs, what can we possibly do but lose?"

"You've got something there." Now it was Truman's turn to sound surprised. He hadn't expected arrogant MacArthur to make such good sense. In other words, he hadn't looked for the general's thoughts to march with his own so well. He'd already ordered the bomb used once, and ended a war with it. How could ordering it into action again be anything but easier?

PHOTO © M. C. VALADA

HARRY TURTLEDOVE is the award-winning author of the alternate-history works *The Man with the Iron Heart; Guns of the South; How Few Remain* (winner of the Sidewise Award for Best Novel); the Worldwar saga: *In the Balance, Tilting the Balance, Upsetting the Balance,* and *Striking the Balance;* the Colonization books: *Second Contact, Down to Earth,* and *Aftershocks;* the Great War epics: *American Front, Walk in Hell,* and *Breakthroughs;* the American Empire novels: *Blood & Iron, The Center Cannot Hold,* and *Victorious Opposition;* and the Settling Accounts series: *Return Engagement, Drive to the East, The Grapple,* and *In at the Death.* Turtledove is married to fellow novelist Laura Frankos. They have three daughters: Alison, Rachel, and Rebecca.